A COLD
WIND FROM
MOSCOW

Rory Clements was born on the edge of England in Dover. After a career in national newspapers, he now writes full time in a quiet corner of Norfolk, where he lives with his wife, the artist Naomi Clements Wright. He won the CWA Ellis Peters Historical Award in 2010 for his second novel, *Revenger*, and the CWA Historical Dagger in 2018 for *Nucleus*. Three of his other novels – *Martyr*, *Prince* and *The Heretics* – have been shortlisted for awards.

To receive exclusive news about Rory's writing, join his Readers' Club at www.bit.ly/RoryClementsClub and to find out more, go to www.roryclements.co.uk.

Also by Rory Clements

Martyr
Revenger
Prince
Traitor
The Heretics
The Queen's Man
Holy Spy
The Man in the Snow (ebook novella)
Corpus
Nucleus
Nemesis
Hitler's Secret
A Prince and a Spy
The Man in the Bunker
The English Führer
Munich Wolf

A COLD WIND FROM MOSCOW

RORY CLEMENTS

ZAFFRE

First published in the UK in 2025 by
ZAFFRE
An imprint of Zaffre Publishing Group
A Bonnier Books UK Company
4th Floor, Victoria House, Bloomsbury Square, London, WC1B 4DA
Owned by Bonnier Books
Sveavägen 56, Stockholm, Sweden

A CIP catalogue record for this book is
available from the British Library.

Hardback ISBN: 978-1-80418-508-7
Trade paperback ISBN: 978-1-80418-610-7

Also available as an ebook and an audiobook

1 3 5 7 9 10 8 6 4 2

Typeset by IDSUK (Data Connection) Ltd
Printed and bound in Great Britain by Clays Ltd, Elcograf S.p.A.

Zaffre is an imprint of Zaffre Publishing Group
A Bonnier Books UK company
www.bonnierbooks.co.uk

For Phoebe

With love

CHAPTER 1

February 1947

The laughter and the horror began in the dead of winter in the centre of Moscow.

It would have been a short, pleasant walk from the Lubyanka to the Kremlin, but Leonid Eitingon and Lavrentiy Beria went by chauffeured black car which pulled to a halt off Ivanovskaya Square.

They had had a strenuous morning witnessing the execution of a former Politburo member in a cold cellar. It had not gone as planned.

Now, after a brief lunch, they were on their way to meet Stalin. Stepping from the car, they walked along the snow-cleared path. Finally out of the driver's earshot, Eitingon said in a low voice, 'What does he want?'

Beria shrugged. 'Perhaps to cut out your eyes and make you eat them. Or if he's in a bad mood, well, who knows?'

'Your sense of humour will be the death of you one day, Comrade Beria.'

'And will you fire the bullet?'

'Of course.'

'And I would do the same favour for you.'

Both men smiled. Both knew they would happily kill the other.

Their papers were checked at the security desk and they were waved through. They climbed the stairs together to the second floor. Striding down a seemingly endless empty corridor, their feet were silent on the spotless carpet, until they came to the great man's office where two guards snapped to attention.

'Good day, Comrade Beria,' the senior of the two said. 'Good day, Comrade Eitingon.' He gave a brisk bow of the head to each of them in turn, then pushed open the tall, heavy door.

Eitingon feared no man. And yet he was always tense and nervous when approaching Stalin. Because Stalin was more than a mere man. Wasn't he?

The doorway led into Stalin's outer office where three secretaries sat at three desks. They were all men, one military, the other two clad in civilian tunics. Eitingon had never learnt their names and doubted he ever would.

One of the three stepped from his writing table and led the way into Comrade Stalin's office, then departed without a word.

Stalin was facing the other way, gazing at a large canvas screen where a black and white movie was playing. He clapped his hands in delight, then turned and nodded to the newcomers.

'Come in, comrades, come in.' He gestured to the projectionist and his interpreter. 'Stop the film and leave us. I'll call you back shortly.'

The projectionist fumbled with the machine and the screen went blank, then he and the female interpreter hurried away like frightened mice.

'It is called *Great Expectations*, a British film. Crazy bourgeois bitches, Lavrentiy, crazy. I will send it to you. You must watch it.'

If Eitingon or Beria had bothered to look around they would have seen three portraits glaring down at them from the walls – Marx, Engels and Lenin – but their eyes were fixed on the man they had come to see: Josef Stalin. He rose from his chair and welcomed his two visitors with warm handshakes. His pipe was in his mouth, belching out fragrant smoke.

At the general secretary's bidding they sat with him at the long conference table which dominated one half of the room. He asked them if they would like refreshments, some beer perhaps, but they both declined.

Stalin placed his pipe in a large ashtray, then leant forwards. 'Thank you for coming here today, comrades. Lavrentiy, how are you proceeding with Problem Number One?'

'The project proceeds at pace, Comrade General Secretary. We have been producing plutonium for seven weeks now.'

'But that is not a weapon. When will we see the weapon?'

'Soon, I trust.'

'Soon?'

'Within two years.'

'Let's make it one year, at the most.'

Eitingon watched Beria's bespectacled face, saw the stiffening of the neck as though a blade hovered, ready to slice through flesh and bone, saw the bead of sweat on his brow.

'It is not easy,' Beria said. 'Great precision is needed. Flerov and Kurchatov assure me that certain things simply cannot be rushed. We must listen to the scientists.'

'Must? Must? Do you say *must* to me, Lavrentiy? Shoot one or two. That will focus minds.'

'They are not easily replaced.'

'Find someone of no consequence to eliminate and suddenly the big men will become a great deal more productive. And this morning's work? How did Koloskov meet his end?'

Beria grinned, baring his white teeth. 'It was like a comedy, Comrade General Secretary. Boris Koloskov was on the floor, on all fours like a dog, crawling around, begging for mercy, weeping uncontrollably, crying out "*Long live the revolution, long live Comrade Stalin*" as though that would save him. I have rarely laughed so much.'

Stalin roared with laughter until he began to choke. Then he wiped his eyes with his sleeve. 'Like a dog, Lavrentiy? I should have seen it.'

'This went on for a minute, maybe two. Blokhin tried to grab him, but Koloskov slid away. In the end Blokhin just let off shots at random. One in the foot, another in the arm, his stomach, his balls maybe, face, brain. All over his body. I lost count. You know, we try to make it easy for these people. A tidy neck shot, but then one like Koloskov makes it difficult for themselves.'

'He always did lack dignity.' Stalin made a swatting motion with the back of his hand. He would give Koloskov no more thought. 'So back to Problem Number One. While the Americans obliterate a stretch of sand and palm trees in the Pacific with their atomic tests, they remind us that we are at their mercy and we know they will not hesitate to use these things against us.'

Beria and Eitingon said nothing. It was wise to know when not to interrupt the boss.

Stalin's voice was gruff and smokey, his accent still that of a peasant from Georgia, commanding but not overly aggressive. He turned his attention away from his smooth secret police chief and addressed his other visitor directly. 'Comrade Eitingon, I have told you before but I tell you again, you did fine work for the Party and for the future of mankind in Mexico.'

There was a pause. Eitingon nodded his thanks for the compliment. *Mexico.* The assassination of Leon Trotsky.

'Which is why I have chosen you for another special task,' Stalin continued. Sometimes the smallpox marks on his face seemed angry; today they were calm, soft, like his mood. 'We here in this place know our enemies. They do not know theirs, but they are learning and they *will* soon understand, which means our advantage will not last. So we strike first and secretly.'

Eitingon understood that he was talking about the West. Many over there were so naive and foolish that they still thought of the Red Army as a friend.

'You will go to England, Comrade Eitingon.' Stalin picked up his pipe, realised it was dead, tapped out the ash and began tamping in some more tobacco, then lit up. He disappeared momentarily behind a cloud of smoke, then reappeared. 'Your special task is to protect a very special man and ensure the success of Problem Number One. I am told the information he provides is invaluable – but now he is in danger.'

Eitingon nodded.

'But that is not all. You will also spread a little chaos. England is a ruin, the proletariat and their masters are weary, broken and despairing. They are vulnerable. You will add to their troubles with some black work. And you will awaken the sleepers, the useful idiots. In this way you will camouflage your true purpose.

'Be as precise and ruthless as you were in Mexico,' Stalin continued, 'and the battle will be won before they even know that the war has begun. The English have a nice saying – one I learnt from Cripps – *We will catch them with their pants down.*'

He spoke the words in strangulated English, but both Beria and Eitingon understood them well enough.

Stalin's impressive moustache twitched and his mouth broke into an impish smile. His guests instantly took the cue and all three men laughed out loud.

'With their pants down! You will create chaos while they are taking a shit!'

The horror had begun. The laughter had finished.

CHAPTER 2

Cambridge, England

It was a brutal, blood-drenched day. The news report said icebergs had been seen off the coast of Norfolk and that starved songbirds had fallen from trees, their tiny bodies frozen solid. But for Tom Wilde the most remarkable thing was the peach.

Solitary and magnificent, it sat there in the iced-up shop window. Where had it come from, this splendid piece of fruit, in the middle of the most bitter winter? A winter where basic food was in desperately short supply.

A perfect dusky pink peach, the first one Wilde had seen since before the war. A burst of colour in a monochrome world.

In front of it, handwritten in pencil on a piece of card, was the price: seven shillings and sixpence. Half a day's wages for a working man, but Wilde knew as soon as he saw it that he had to have it. For his son. Johnny had never tasted peach and he was six years old.

Perhaps Wilde might cut a sliver for himself, just to remind his tastebuds of the flavour. And of course he'd have to give a piece to the new housekeeper, Janet Spring. The thought that his wife Lydia wouldn't be there for the little feast was hard to take. She was away at college in London, taking a medical degree, and he missed her.

For a few moments, he simply stood and looked at the fruit. Around him, the town of Cambridge had a strange spectral beauty, clad in white like a bride. Not fully white, if truth be told, but then how many brides were pure and untouched? King's College Chapel, crowned in white, had never looked more glorious.

The snow was swirling and gusting. Huddled into his overcoat, his face numb with cold, he opened the door and entered the shop accompanied by a white flurry and the tinkling of the bell. He stamped his snow-clogged boots on the mat and looked around. The shelves were almost bare. A few potatoes, bruised and sad, a couple of cabbages and some sprouts. Not much else.

'Morning, Professor Wilde, how can I help you today?' The grocer, in his threadbare brown coat, tried to smile and sound welcoming, but he looked as grim and downtrodden as the few vegetables that adorned his shop. He wore a scarf round his neck and thick woollen gloves. There was no warmth in here and his breath blew freezing vapour into the air.

'The peach.'

'Ah yes, the peach. A real treat for someone, that is.'

'Where did you get it?'

He touched the side of his nose with his gloved forefinger. 'Best not to ask. That way you'll hear no lies. No fruit rationing, though, sir, so it's all perfectly legal and above board.'

'It's February, you don't even have carrots or parsnips and yet somehow you have a peach in the window. Are there others?'

'No others, that's the only one. As rare and prized as the Koh-i-Noor. Do you want it?'

'Of course I do . . . but the price.'

'Come on, prof, a crown and a half's nothing to a man like you.'

'I could go to the pub and buy everyone beer for the same amount.'

'Indeed you could, sir.'

'Damn it, I'll have it.'

'You won't regret it.'

Having handed over the money, a ten bob note with half a crown change, Wilde asked the shopkeeper to look after the precious fruit so that he could collect it on the way home; for the moment he had to go to college to meet someone and he didn't want to risk damaging the peach by carrying it with him.

Beneath his heavy overcoat he wore a jacket, pullover, shirt and vest. On his hands he had thick woollen gloves and still he was freezing, his eyes watering from a gust of wind, but for a minute or two he forgot the cold. And then the moment passed.

Trudging on, the dampness penetrated his boots and damp-ened his spirit. The council had been working hard to keep Trumpington Street clear, but it was a hopeless task, for there had been fresh snow every day for over two weeks. Now it was banked up against the ancient walls, pristine from the new fall but grubby and oily beneath.

No cars were in evidence, nor buses. It was impossible to ride a motorbike in this so he had left the Rudge at home, not that he had any fuel for it – or for the Riley for that matter.

It was almost dark by the time he reached college and, of course, there were no lights. Electricity came on and went off like the tides. Symptoms of a deep malaise that sometimes made him despair of his adopted country.

He would relocate to his American homeland in a heartbeat. England was reduced to dire poverty while everyone in America seemed to eat steak, drive a large automobile, own a fridge and a TV set. In Britain, you had to queue for potatoes and bread, Scotch whisky was unobtainable, television broadcasts had been halted and most roads were impassable even if you were one of the very few who owned a car and could get petrol.

And if you could afford ninepence for a seat at the cinema you had the wealth of America rammed down your throat week after week just to remind you how poor you were, all courtesy of Hollywood.

Of course, he knew that things weren't that simple, that America had shortages, too, but the truth was that they had a great deal more than Britain, which seemed to have suffered catastrophe after disaster after calamity in the eighteen months since the war's end.

A summer of drenching rain and now this. Yes, he'd go to the States. Sunny Florida or Southern California would have to be an improvement. It would be good for Johnny, get some fresh, nutritious food inside him. Florida oranges, that was the thing. Good for all of them, come to that, not just the boy. New clothes would be a fine thing, too; the jacket beneath his overcoat was entering extreme old age, its threadbare elbows having been patched not once but twice.

But go to America? Lydia wouldn't hear of it. She was just over a year into her five-and-a-half-year medical course at St Ursula's and a ten-ton pantechnicon wouldn't move her.

And so they were stuck here in the hungry gloom. Waiting for the broad, sunlit uplands promised by Churchill.

As he entered the ancient gateway to his college, he poked his head into the porter's lodge.

'Your visitor, Mr Glasspool, is in your rooms, professor,' Scobie the head porter said. 'Been there half an hour. No fire in the hearth, though, I'm afraid, so the poor chap'll be shivering. Coal's down to two days a week for dons and undergraduates alike.'

'We should have installed gas fires.'

'Not going to happen this winter, is it? I invited your visitor to wait here with us in the lodge for a bit of warmth, but he said he would prefer to go on through to your set.'

So Everett Glasspool had managed to get here. He must have had one hell of a journey up from London.

'Couldn't get us a small scuttle of coal, could you, Scobie?'

'I'll see what I can do, sir.'

'Thank you. And what about the post – has that got through?'

'Miraculously, it has, sir. But not milk. None for three days. I've heard tell of livestock freezing to death in the fields.'

'I've heard that, too.'

'Water pipes are iced up all round college. The baths are out of order, not that there's any soap anyway. This is worse than the war, much worse. I've taken to wearing a woolly hat and gloves to bed. It's all so damned shabby. England's dying, professor.'

Wilde smiled bleakly. The euphoria of May 1945 really had given way to general despondency. But things would get better, wouldn't they? 'We'll get through it, Scobie. Springtime will come, as always. But tell me, what's the word on Bobby?'

'Still poorly. Not expecting him back this week.'

Bobby – Wilde's 'gyp' or college servant – had already been laid up for two weeks. It was thought he had a bronchial infection, for he had a persistent cough, but he had been ailing since Christmas and had finally retreated to his bed at the end of January. Now the doctor wanted to do some more tests. The dreaded word *cancer* hadn't come up officially, but on hearing the symptoms, Lydia had suggested it quietly to Wilde when they spoke on the phone, and it was beginning to seem horribly likely. 'Persistent coughs are not good, Tom,' she had said.

Wilde's eyes met Scobie's and they both knew what the other was thinking.

'But he's being looked after?' Wilde asked. 'He's being fed properly and kept as warm as possible?'

'Oh yes, he's got friends and neighbours looking out for him. And he's tough as old boots, our Bobby. Take more than a winter chill to do for him.'

Wilde nodded and made a mental note to pay him another visit.

'When's it going to end, professor, this damned weather?'

'I wish I knew, Scobie. Still, look on the bright side – good ice skating on the Fens.'

'Not so good for one undergraduate. He lost two toes to frostbite out there.'

'Dear God.'

'He'd got hold of a flask of rum and things went from bad to worse after he downed a few too many nips. Actually, he's lucky to be alive because he took off one of his skating boots for some reason known only to himself, then settled down for a snooze in a snowdrift. Fortunately his chums found him and carried him back here.'

'Not one of my history students, was it?'

'No, sir. Natural sciences, I believe.' He handed Wilde a candle and a box of matches. 'I think you'll need this, professor. Electricity will be off for at least another hour.'

Paths had been cleared through the quads but the snow was falling heavily again, undoing all the good work. It occurred to Wilde, not for the first time, that it would be far better if the undergraduates all went home for the duration of the bad weather, for the food and heating were both inadequate in college.

But sending them home was easier said than done, for transport veered between difficult and impossible, and many students' families were stationed abroad. So the young men, the greater portion of whom were demobbed members of the armed forces whose education had been interrupted, were left to shiver in their rooms and burn whatever scraps of wood and coal they could find for a little warmth. They probably wished they were back in a fox-hole on the front line; couldn't be any colder.

Last summer they had all gone wild, as they had before the war. Too much drink had been taken, practical jokes and dangerous escapades had been undertaken with joy and laughter. Love affairs had flourished and rules had been broken without heed to the consequences. That was the way university life should be, but now it was all silent and humourless. Fun had left the world.

As he opened the door to his rooms, he was thinking of the peach. In his mind he could almost smell it and taste its lush juice. He hoped to God it was as good as it looked.

He flicked the light switch from force of habit, but nothing happened because it was the afternoon power cut, and so he struck a match and lit the candle. The first thing he noticed on entering was the silence then, through the flickering gloom, the ice on the window and, finally, the dark, huddled shape on the floor in front of the hearth.

A corpse. With an ice-axe protruding from the side of its head.

In an instant, the peach seemed of no consequence.

CHAPTER 3

He recalled meeting Everett Glasspool only once before, four years ago. It was during the war while he was serving in London with the OSS – the Office of Strategic Services. January 1943, that was it. Glasspool was an agent with MI5 and they had encountered each other at a joint training session when the British security men were passing on their expertise to the new American spy agency. He hadn't made much of an impression on Wilde, which was a good attribute in an intelligence officer. Perhaps he had always passed through life unnoticed.

But the name was interesting, because Wilde wondered how it had come about and what the word Glasspool meant. As a historian, how could he not be intrigued by such things?

He had intended to ask him the provenance of the name today, but that wouldn't happen now. Wilde did not need a doctor's opinion to know that the man was dead but he put the back of his hand to his throat anyway. There was no pulse, but despite the cold of the room and the death-bleached pallor of the face, the body was still warm. Glasspool had not been dead long. Probably not more than twenty minutes or so. He must have been killed soon after he entered Wilde's rooms.

The sharp end of the ice-axe was embedded in the side of his skull and there was a bloody gash higher up on the head where a first blow – probably with the adze surface – had struck home. The blood was thick but not yet totally coagulated in the hair and streaking down his neck onto his white shirt, his grey suit jacket and dark blue overcoat.

The eyes were open, cloudy but blue. He recalled those eyes. Glassy blue, he had thought them. The only distinguishing feature other than his name.

Wilde put a call through to the porters and asked Scobie to summon the police and an ambulance. Something had happened to his visitor.

'I was about to get a scuttle full of coal over to your rooms, sir. Shall I get the nurse over as well?'

'No point in either, I'm afraid, Scobie.'

'Ah. Message received and understood, sir.'

It occurred to Wilde that an officer as senior as Chief Inspector Reginald Carter would not normally have deigned to take an active role in a criminal investigation. Perhaps it was the manner of the death and the location – in one of Cambridge's oldest colleges – that had stirred him from his offices in St Andrew's Street and brought him to Wilde's rooms in the company of a constable.

'Well, I think you're probably right, Professor Wilde. It looks very much as if he has been killed with an ice-axe.'

Good guess, thought Wilde, given the fact that the corpse lay in front of the officer, the sharp point of the ice-axe still deep inside his temple.

'And I think we can probably rule out suicide from the nature of the two wounds,' Carter continued. 'The first blow would almost certainly have knocked him unconscious and so he would have been unable to inflict the second.'

Another good guess. Did police qualifications these days include an ability to note and state the blindingly obvious? Both strikes had clearly been made with immense force.

'Still, the police doctor will have to confirm cause of death for the coroner. I believe he'll be along soon. And then, the railways allowing, I am told that a ministry man is coming up from London to assist with our investigations. Though Lord knows, I think we could manage this ourselves.'

A ministry man. He meant, of course, a man from MI5, but Carter didn't know the exact details; all he knew was that military intelligence was taking an interest in the case.

'In fact, professor, I believe it was you who placed a call to London before I arrived. Rather presumptuous of you, don't you think?'

It wasn't a question, but a statement of opinion. Carter's tone was accusatory, resentful at being bypassed perhaps.

Wilde addressed the criticism. 'As I mentioned to you on the phone, the deceased is Lieutenant Everett Glasspool, chief inspector. He was a member of the security services and I had met him once before. Clearly it was important that his senior officer be informed without delay.'

'And that would be Mr Bentall?'

'*Miss* Bentall.'

'Really? A woman in military intelligence?'

'Really.'

Carter snorted. 'What, I wonder, is the world coming to when a man's superior officer is a female. My good lady wife would be appalled if she heard such a thing. Remarkable days, Professor Wilde, remarkable days. All rather disturbing, if you ask me. How things have changed in my forty years of life. The unfortunate effect of two world wars, one must suppose.'

Wilde didn't bother to reply this time. How would this strange officer cope with the information that Wilde's own wife was presently training to be a physician?

'The question we must ask ourselves, chief inspector, is who had access to my rooms? Unless the killer scaled the roofs and outside walls, the only ways in are through the front gate – which you used – or the rear gate. When unlocked, both are manned.'

'Which means?'

'Which means the assailant most likely works here in a serving capacity or as student or teacher. Or is an acknowledged visitor who must have signed in.'

'I'll need a list of names.'

'The porters' lodge will provide that for you. Everyone is checked in and checked out.'

There was a knock at the door. Wilde turned and was relieved to see his old friend Rupert Weir, the police doctor. In summer or winter, he wore a tweed suit, his ample belly pushing out against his waistcoat. But on this occasion, his suit was encased in a heavy overcoat, which spoke volumes about the weather they were enduring.

Weir took a deep breath and glanced around the room. 'Well, well, Tom, what do we have here? Someone defiling your inner sanctum?' He was holding a torch, which he shone around the room, his gaze shifting from Wilde to the chief inspector and his constable, who were giving him stern looks.

'Don't touch anything until the fingerprint men have been along, Dr Weir,' Carter said.

Weir gave the officer a disdainful look, one suggestive of mothers being taught to suck eggs. 'Of course. But I imagine the killer wore gloves, particularly in this Arctic weather.' The doctor asked Wilde to hold the torch, then moved closer to the corpse and made a cursory initial examination, checking the warmth of the dead flesh with the back of his hand, then turned to Carter. 'Get this body along to the mortuary as soon as you have finished dusting for prints. There's really nothing more for me to see here in the meantime. Certainly not in this light. Do you have a name for the deceased?'

'Everett Glasspool,' Wilde said. 'Freya Bentall sent him up here to talk to me. Another member of her team is on his way.'

'Ah, well this is one for the funny boys. They'll want their own autopsy.'

'Without doubt,' Wilde said.

The chief inspector did not look happy. He was being excluded from the conversation and clearly feared his authority was being undermined in front of the watchful eyes of his constable. 'I'll need you to come down to St Andrew's Street to make a statement, Professor Wilde.'

'Of course. Tomorrow morning, perhaps. Or right now if you prefer.'

'Tomorrow it is. But first, what can you tell me about the deceased?'

'Apart from his name and line of work, very little.' Glasspool had seemed like a middle-class Englishman who had somehow found his way from frontline military into the security service, like many others during the war. They hadn't exchanged many words at that meeting in 1943, but he recalled an accent that placed the young man firmly among the well-to-do. Public school and, very likely, Oxford. He was well-built, rather athletic, the sort who might have put up a decent fight if he saw the attack coming, but he hadn't.

Beyond that, nothing. Freya Bentall might fill in a few gaps when they spoke.

CHAPTER 4

There were obvious questions. Was Glasspool the intended victim? A case of mistaken identity was perfectly feasible. Was the killer after Wilde himself? If so, why? It was also possible – but unlikely – that the killer had got the wrong set of rooms.

The probable answer was that Everett Glasspool *was* the target. In which case what was the motive? How did the killer know that he was coming to Wilde's rooms in Cambridge on that specific day?

All this raised other questions: was it really possible that the killer wasn't a visitor, but one of the students, dons or college servants?

He left the police to their work, asking them not to disturb his papers. On the way down from his rooms, he noted the snow that had carried indoors onto the staircase was now turned to dirty slush by a succession of feet. No clues to be found there.

There must have been footprints in the snow, leading away from the scene of the crime, but the snow was consistent and heavy and there was no trace of them. Footprints were being obliterated within minutes.

He walked across the courts to the porters' lodge where Scobie produced the entry/exit book for the past two days. There were few visitors and most of the undergraduates and dons seemed to have been sitting tight in their rooms. The chances were that many of them had not even risen from the warmth of their beds.

'My figures suggest we have just eighty-eight undergraduates in residence at the moment,' Scobie said. 'And fifteen dons, not including you – because although you have rooms here, you're not really in residence.'

'Kitchen staff, porters, gyps, bedders?'

'About forty. Of course, they all come and go on a daily basis. Their faces are all familiar to us – no one new in recent weeks. I'll get their names to you, professor.'

'And give them to the chief inspector.'

'Indeed.'

What they needed, of course, was a witness. Someone who had seen a man – most likely a man given the physical savagery of the attack – entering his staircase or hanging around Old Court. Surely someone must have noticed something, even if they were just looking out from their window. But that had to be a matter for the police and the intelligence officer, when he arrived.

For himself, Wilde wanted to get to London in a hurry, to talk to Freya Bentall for he still had no idea why Glasspool had been sent to Cambridge to meet him. Naturally, the thought also occurred to him that he would be able to spend some time with Lydia during the trip. He looked at his watch and wondered whether any trains would run this evening. It was just possible.

'Could you put a call through to the railway station, Scobie – see when the next London train is scheduled.'

'Information I already have, sir. It's six-thirty or thereabouts. The only one this evening.'

'Then I'll be on it. If anyone wants me, I'll be calling through to pick up messages.'

On the way home to pack an overnight bag, Wilde trudged past the greengrocer lost in thought. The snow had stopped falling momentarily, but it would come again as it did every day. The weather was remorseless and unprecedented in its severity. A few steps on he remembered the peach and turned back.

It had already been removed from the window, which was now entirely bare. The shopkeeper greeted him with a smile and delved down beneath the counter, then held up a brown paper bag. 'Here we are, sir, still in perfect condition. I confess I had one myself earlier today and I can promise you it is sweet, ripe and full of glorious juice. You'll believe you're out in the tropics when you bite into that.'

'It's mostly for my boy. His first taste.'

'And it will do him the world of good. He's a lucky lad.'

Wilde accepted the bag and took his leave of the shopkeeper. Suddenly it all seemed pointless. Where was the joy in a piece of fruit while a young man's corpse lay cooling in his college rooms? The poor bastard. His thoughts turned to Glasspool's family;

hadn't enough mothers and fathers received the heartbreaking news of the death of a beloved son these past few years?

Johnny was playing outside in the snow with the new housekeeper-nanny, Miss Janet Spring. She had arrived at the beginning of January. Lydia had found her through an old friend who had taught her at Girton before the war. She was twenty-eight and had apparently worked in the War Office as a secretary, but was no longer needed in peacetime.

'Janet comes from a big family so I'm sure she'll be just fine with your boy,' the friend had told Lydia. 'She just needs somewhere to stay and a chance to earn a little money while she works out her future.'

Wilde wasn't certain. 'She has no references as a nanny or housekeeper,' he said to Lydia when they were alone together.

'So what? We'll interview her together and if we both like her, we'll give her a month's trial. Anyway, you'll be here to keep an eye on her.'

'Fair enough.'

When she turned up she seemed much younger than they expected. Many women of her age were already married with children of their own, but Janet Spring seemed nowhere near that sort of maturity. She was cheerful, though, and full of life and Johnny took to her straightaway, more playmate or elder sibling to the boy than his guardian.

Wilde stopped at the front gate and watched them playing for a minute. The electricity had come on and they were lit by the yellow glow from the sitting room window as they constructed some sort of snow monster with horns made of sticks and eyes made of pebbles.

Johnny was laughing and the sight gave Wilde confidence that perhaps this young woman was indeed the right person to look after him while Lydia was away doing her medical degree.

Janet turned and saw him, her eyes bright behind her spectacles. She picked up a handful of snow, scrunched it into a ball and launched it at him. Wilde laughed as it hit his shoulder.

'Is that really the best you can do, Janet?' he said, quickly fashioning a snowball of his own.

'Come on, Johnny, let's get Daddy!'

Wilde held up his hand. 'Wait, wait. I've got something special. It could get damaged in a snow fight. Let's go inside and I'll show you.'

In the kitchen, beneath the dim gleam of the electric light, Wilde held up the brown paper bag. 'Who can guess what this is?'

'Sweets!' Johnny shouted. 'Sweets.'

'Even better than that.' Carefully he pulled open the bag and took out the peach, holding it up like a jewel to be gazed upon and appreciated with awe.

'What is it, Daddy? Is it an apple?' The boy's face had fallen.

'No, it's a peach – and it should be even sweeter and juicier than an apple. Do you want a bite – or shall I cut it into pieces?'

'Is it all for me?'

'I thought Janet might like a bite. Me too – but you can have most of it.'

'What about Mummy?'

'Well, I don't think we'll be able to keep it fresh for her. Come on.' He opened the drawer and took out a sharp knife then cut it into pieces, slice by slice. They all tried it, savouring each mouthful, swirling the juice and allowing it slowly to slide down their throats only when all the flavour had been experienced. It was every bit as good as the greengrocer had promised.

'Daddy, this is so good! And the skin's all furry.'

'It's wonderful, Professor Wilde. Where on earth did you get it?'

Janet Spring's eyes were bright. There really was something childlike about her, but that didn't mean she wasn't capable and trustworthy. Well, they'd have to trust her, for what was the option?

'The greengrocer. Where he got it from is another matter. I won't tell you what it cost.'

'I can't remember when I last had one. I haven't even had a banana since before the war. No, I tell a lie – I had one in 1940 just after I left Girton.'

The peach was a brief respite for there were more pressing matters to deal with. 'I'm only here to pack a small bag, Janet. I'm going to London this evening, so this will be the first night with just you and Johnny in the house. Is that all right with you?'

'Of course, that's why you're paying me. We'll be fine.'

The train to London should have taken an hour, but it kept stopping. Railwaymen, aided by other local people and prisoners of war from nearby camps, worked tirelessly through the darkness to clear drifts from the line. At nine-fifteen in the evening, Wilde made it to Burton's Hotel around the corner from MI5 headquarters in Curzon Street. As soon as he had deposited his bag in his room he went back down to reception and put a call through to St Ursula's Hospital Medical School and asked for a message to be passed on to Miss Lydia Morris in the student hostel. Tell her that her cousin Tom was calling. He gave the number of the hotel and asked to be called back.

It was code, of course. The school did not accept married women, so Lydia was there under false pretences, using her maiden name and pretending she was a single woman and not a mother.

Ten minutes later, she called him.

'Tom, you're in London. This is a Mayfair number.'

'I'm at the Burton, meeting Freya Bentall in the morning. It's all very last minute – can't really explain on the phone.'

'Can I see you?'

'That's my plan.'

'The Old Bell in twenty minutes.'

The pub was warm, smokey and rowdy. A young man was tapping out a popular tune on the stand-up piano and there was much laughter. Snow might be banked up outside, and the windows frosted, but inside, there was nothing but cheer.

Wilde and Lydia embraced and held each other in a long hug. They hadn't seen each other in three weeks and there was much to catch up on, but first he had to tell her about the events of the day and his reason for being here in London.

'A body in your rooms, Tom?' She looked aghast. 'That's horrible.'

He gave a sombre nod of the head. What more could he say?

'You attract trouble like pollen attracts bees. You are a very dangerous man to know, Mr Wilde.'

'But you understood that before you married me.'

'Anyway, what does she want from you?'

'Who, Freya Bentall?'

'Of course Freya bloody Bentall. Has it not sunk into her addled brain that you are retired from secret work and the sodding war is over anyway?'

Her language broke the funereal darkness of the moment and he laughed. 'You've become coarser since you embarked on this medical course.'

'No place for the prudish in medicine, Mr Wilde. Bodily functions are at the heart of everything we do. Anyway, what does the bloody woman want?'

'I don't know what she wants, but it's polite to let her have her say, especially since it now involves a murder.'

'I've really lost count of the . . . oh, what the hell, where's that drink you promised me? I need brandy.'

Wilde went to the bar and ordered a large brandy and asked them whether, by any chance, they might have some Scotch. No chance, just an unnamed brandy.

They settled down at a cosy corner table and sipped their drinks. The brandy wasn't too bad, probably Spanish or Portuguese, but that was very acceptable given the state of the world.

'What is your hotel like, Mr Wilde?'

'Oh, Burton's is very pleasant, Miss Morris. A bit shabby around the edges, like everything else in this benighted country. But, miracle of miracles, I managed to wangle a double bed and the radiators are working. Perhaps you'd like to come and examine the bed and later you can sample their breakfast.'

'I have a lecture first thing in the morning. Diabetes.'

'I'll stand you a cab.'

'Come on then, drink up.'

CHAPTER 5

Wilde was depressed by the state of London. It was still full of holes. Gaps in streets where houses once stood, where bombs had fallen. Cambridge had suffered, of course, but it had begun to recover whereas the London bomb sites remained rubble – presently adorned with a ghostly carpet of ice and snow – and seemed unlikely to be turned back into buildings for the foreseeable future. If there was a plan to clear the sites and re-build, it wasn't obvious to the casual observer. The reason was simple, of course: Britain was broke.

In the morning, after a night of passion and an all-too-brief breakfast, Wilde kissed Lydia and ushered her towards the taxi. He closed the vehicle's door after her, then waved to her as she set off back to St Ursula's. Neither of them had had much sleep, but they were content and warm. As she disappeared from view, he turned and went back into the hotel for a couple more coffees and toast and to read a copy of *The Times*, which was much diminished in size because of the paper shortage. There was no good news anywhere; unrest in Palestine, food shortages everywhere, the Nuremberg trials, harsh criticism of Manny Shinwell, the minister of fuel and power.

No mention of murder in a Cambridge college.

At nine-fifteen, he paid his bill, checked out and walked the short distance to Leconfield House, the home of MI5, the security service, in Curzon Street, just to the east of Hyde Park.

Wilde was expected. He signed in and was shown up to Freya Bentall's dull and rather utilitarian office. She was sitting behind a remarkably tidy desk but stood up when he arrived and welcomed him with a formal handshake and invited him to take a seat.

'I can offer you coffee but it's not wonderful.'

'I've already had three cups, so I'll decline, Miss Bentall.'

At their first meeting, in the autumn of 1942, she had been dismissive of him, describing him to a colleague as 'some bloody history professor who wants to be a spy'. It had been said deliberately loud enough for Wilde to hear, but things had improved between them since then and a mutual respect – and even some warmth – had developed.

Her background was law, and she was known as a formidable advocate. But her work for the security service had proved to be her true strength and purpose in life. Other senior officers spoke of her interrogation prowess in awed tones. It was not just that her questions probed, but that they took you by surprise and delved into the subconscious places where secrets nestled.

She must have been about fifty now – maybe a year or two older – and was beginning to look her age. The cares of the job, Wilde supposed. He was rather surprised that she hadn't got around to retiring or, at least, returning to the law, where the pay would be a good deal better. Perhaps she came from wealth and didn't need the money.

'Won't you call me Freya?' she said. 'I loathe the whole spinsterish Miss Bentall thing.'

Wilde was surprised. He had never expected this, but he smiled and said he would be honoured and suggested that she, too, might use his first name.

'We've been through a bit together, haven't we, Tom?'

'Well, yes.'

'And yesterday, darling Everett Glasspool meeting such a horrible end – and poor you for finding him.'

'It was pretty damned awful.'

She smiled with an uncharacteristic tenderness and he knew he was being worked over, softened up for something.

'He was the one man I was sure of, Tom. I'm surrounded by good people, of course, but Everett was the one I trusted above all others, the one man I never had cause to doubt. I know his family, you see, and I was responsible for bringing him into the service. Yesterday I had to make the phone call. They live down Dorset way, so in these conditions it was too far to go in person.'

'I'm sorry.'

'Trust is everything to me. Which is why, of all people, I sent him up to see you.'

'That sounds ominous.'

'I know it makes it seem as though everyone else is untrustworthy, which is not the case at all. I could happily trust everyone, but ... look, forgive me, I'm having trouble explaining myself clearly. The thing is there's a threat and it comes from within the organisation, so I have no option but to put a question mark over everyone's head.'

'An enemy within? Guilty until proven innocent? Are you sure about this?'

Her eyes drifted to the door as though making sure it was closed tight. 'I'm afraid the murder of Everett Glasspool confirms in the most barbarous manner that my information is sound.'

'Do you want to tell me?' He knew instantly that it was a question he shouldn't have asked because it suggested he might be interested in the answer. And he wasn't. He wasn't at all interested in Freya Bentall's dark world of secrets. He was interested in being a professor of history and a father and a husband.

But the question was out there now and Freya Bentall wasted no time in taking advantage of it.

'Have you heard of Reinhard Gehlen? I wondered if perhaps you had dealings with him before the OSS was shut down.'

Wilde searched his memory bank. 'The name means something, I think. Clearly from the war. Remind me.'

'General Reinhard Gehlen. *Generalleutnant* Gehlen to Adolf and his chums. Your Counter-Intelligence Corps certainly knows all about him. He was Hitler's chief of military intelligence in the eastern sphere until they fell out in the last weeks of the war. You could be forgiven for thinking that a man in such a position must have been privy to Nazi atrocities and might now be on trial at Nuremberg.'

'That sounds a reasonable assumption.'

'So why should anyone have dealings with such a man?'

'A fair question.'

'Well, your compatriots *are* dealing with him – and so am I. Last summer he set up a security operation in the American sector of Germany with the wholehearted approval of the US Army. He had brought home his archives from the east and so was able to offer in-depth knowledge of the political and espionage operations of the Soviet Union. That was something that both the Americans and the British lacked. Your guys grabbed it with both hands.'

'Sounds like we're supping with the devil.'

'Needs must. The Americans have allowed him to set up an anti-Soviet network, feeding intelligence to the US military, but his methods are questionable, because he is making use of former SS and Gestapo men.'

'Not good.'

'It's realpolitik. We have no option because we need him. Apart from his archives, he also retained contacts and inform-ants behind the Soviet lines – something that no one else in the West possesses.'

Wilde knew it to be true from his own time in the OSS. Neither British nor American intelligence had a single source of informa-tion in Moscow outside the walls of their embassies.

'So, this Nazi general, Freya, why are you mentioning him now? And should you even be telling me all this now I'm a civilian?'

'Probably not. But let me explain. I've met Gehlen a couple of times. He's charming, urbane, patriotic. He has the decency to confess that he bought into Nazism wholeheartedly but says he now concedes he was wrong. I know, I know – he would say that, wouldn't he. The important thing is, we got on. Above all, he is a committed anti-communist which, in the new world, is an important consideration.'

She paused, her teeth biting her lower lip, and suddenly Wilde realised that this was hard for her, whatever it was. It was personal and emotional and she was uncomfortable.

'Go on.'

'Last week he called me on a secure line. He said he had a warn-ing for me. He had heard that an operation was being mounted in Britain. What the NKVD calls a Special Task, which is usually a euphemism for murder on foreign soil.'

Wilde frowned. 'Go on.'

'Gehlen believes we're the target.'

'We?'

'Military intelligence. MI5, SIS.'

'Actually, I think I'll have that coffee. Or perhaps tea?'

Freya Bentall pressed a button on her phone. 'Pot of tea, please, Marcia.' She turned back to Wilde. 'Gehlen says it is a classic communist tactic as devised by Beria and Stalin: first undermine the security services, then the way is open to infiltrate the political establishment.'

'Nothing new there. That's always a threat.'

'Gehlen believes we've already been penetrated. He claims we are riddled with moles, both in MI5 and the wider community. The Soviets have been laughing at us for years.'

'Then you have a big problem.'

'He mentioned one traitor in particular. Codenamed *Virgin*, which doesn't help much. I find myself looking at everyone, even the secretaries, and asking myself: whose side are you on?'

The tea arrived and Bentall went silent for a minute while her secretary put down the tray and left the room, closing the door firmly behind her.

'Why are you telling me all this, Freya?'

'I need your help. If there are traitors within the organisation, then I need someone from outside whom I can trust. I wanted you to work with Everett Glasspool. The two men I trust above all others.'

'I'm a history professor now, nothing more.'

'Look, Tom, you must realise it can't go on like this. Harry Truman made a bad mistake when he disbanded the OSS. In the new world of East versus West, America will need to re-enter the war of secrets. So the OSS will be back soon in some form. It will *have* to be. And it will need good agents – people like you – to knock the new men and women into shape. Makes sense to keep yourself in trim awaiting the day, doesn't it?'

'That is the most ridiculous sales pitch I have ever heard.'

The MI5 officer laughed at last. 'You drive a hard bargain, Tom.'

'I'm not bargaining, I'm just giving you the facts. We're halfway through the Lent term, I have lectures to deliver and supervisions to conduct. Believe it or not, I'm not sitting by the window gazing out at the snow all day.'

'But you're already involved. They know about you. The fact that Glasspool was found in your rooms proves that. The fact of his murder proves that Gehlen was right – and that a Soviet action is under way. They either followed him there to Cambridge or they were waiting for him – in which case there's already a leak from this office. For how else would they have known that I had sent him up to see you.'

'Why *did* you send him up, by the way?'

'To have the conversation we're having now. To try to get your assistance. To drag you down here and get you to work together. I thought I'd already said that.'

'I could ask you how you might think I could help, but I won't – because it isn't going to happen.'

Bentall picked up the milk jug. 'Milk? Sugar?'

'No sugar, thank you.'

As she poured a little milk into the two cups, she sighed. 'Very well, Tom, we'll put your part in this to one side for a moment. But let me ask you a simple question. When you saw the ice-axe in the side of Everett Glasspool's head, what came to mind?'

'To check whether there was any sign of life, of course.'

'But beyond that, once you knew he was dead.'

'Well, Trotsky. That's how he was killed in Mexico.'

'My immediate reaction, too.'

'Is this all supposed to be scaring me, Freya?'

'The ice-axe wasn't coincidence. They are trying to unnerve us. It's a deliberate tactic to sow dissension and distrust so that we turn on each other. We both know that there are MPs, trade union leaders and others whose loyalties lie with the soviet system. But not within the service – until now.'

CHAPTER 6

'So what exactly would you expect me to do?' Wilde said. 'Hypo-thetically.'

'Join MI5 on attachment.'

'Are you serious?'

'Perfectly. I wanted you to work with Everett, but now we have to try something different.'

'I hesitate to suggest you're losing your mind, Freya, but the idea of me joining MI5 is laughable.'

'I'm serious.'

'How would that work? Would the service even accept an American?'

'You're married to an Englishwoman and you have an English son, which makes you British enough in my book.'

'Oh, come on. I'd stick out like a blazing beacon. Your enemies would see me a mile off. Anyway, they must already know of my link to you – because your man was murdered in *my* rooms.'

'I'm not saying there's no danger, but it is perfectly rational that you should be here. As I said, the OSS or something similar will have to be re-formed sooner rather than later. We both know it was a suicidal act by Truman to close the agency. Even he must be seeing that now. So taking you in for a bit of catch-up training will be us doing our bit to help our Yankee allies.'

'You mentioned danger. That's an understatement.'

'You may be American but you have a stake in helping Britain. This is your country now.'

'What exactly would you want me to do? No one is going to confide in me.'

'Identify the threat and neutralise it.'

'That simple, eh?'

'I didn't say it was simple.'

'Where would I even start?'

'I have suspects. Perhaps not suspects, but men of interest. Three of them. That doesn't mean any of them are guilty, but they're a starting point. They were all here during the war so they're well embedded. No one has been watching them because if any of them *are* communists, they were on our side from Barbarossa onwards. Now the fault line has changed. We are enemies. Unlike some others, I always knew that.'

Some others. Was she, perhaps, talking about Churchill and Roosevelt who met Stalin at Yalta and unforgivably gave him a free hand to swallow up Eastern Europe?

Wilde was silent for a few moments. Freya Bentall had a point. This *was* his country now.

At last he met her eyes. 'I'm going back to Cambridge this afternoon because I have a lecture to deliver first thing in the morning and then a meeting at Magdalene, but I promise I will think about your request. I'll talk about it with Lydia. I also have a responsibility to my undergraduates and my son, you understand.'

'Yes, of course, I understand.'

'One question before I go. We have to work out who might have access to my rooms. Do any of your three *men of interest* happen to be Cambridge alumni?'

'I'm ahead of you, Tom. All three studied there. None of them from your college, though they might have known it. There's something else: when I pressed Reinhard Gehlen he mentioned a possible Cambridge link. He said that the university has long been important to Soviet intelligence, that it has been infiltrated since the late twenties or early thirties. This isn't new information to him, just something he learnt out east during the war. At the time, he wasn't interested in Britain, let alone Cambridge, but he stored it away in his brain. Beyond that, he was pretty vague.'

Well, Wilde certainly knew of one recruiter for the communist cause at Cambridge: Horace Dill, history professor, now deceased. They had been friends and Horace had made little secret of his politics. His work to bring undergraduates into the communist fold was widely suspected. Many found it rather amusing, as though it were some sort of game. Wilde had never found it particularly funny.

'These three men – do you want to tell me a bit about them? Names, for instance.'

'Gus Baxter, Shadox Stone, Cecil Eagles. Do you know any of them?'

'I don't.'

'Well, Baxter is a snob with a taste for the low life. Stone is a northerner with a chip on both shoulders and takes himself altogether too seriously. Eagles would look down his nose at the King but is quite amusing company. They are all effective and valuable agents in their own way. My greatest wish is that none of them is a traitor.'

He rose to go.

'I need you, Tom,' she said.

'But how could it possibly work? How would I get close to your men?'

'You will be one of us – fully accredited. You will be assigned to each of those three in turn. They will be told to bring you up to date on tradecraft. They won't like it, but they'll do it because they have to accept orders.'

'Your optimism knows no bounds, Freya.'

'Except I don't feel at all optimistic, Tom. I'm worried sick – and I'm heartbroken by Everett's death. He was like family to me.'

He saw the pain in her eyes and he nodded. 'Let me sleep on it.'

It was dark when Wilde arrived home and he was tired after a night with little sleep, but it was only five o'clock. The snow had stopped falling, the streets of Cambridge were unlit and deserted and there was a ghostly air, his footsteps silent in the soft snow.

He was about to put the key in the lock, but Johnny and the new nanny beat him to it by opening the door for him. The electricity was on, which was a mercy. Wilde put down his bag and scooped up the boy.

'I saw Mummy – and she sends you hugs and kisses.'

'When is she coming home, Daddy?'

'As soon as she gets a chance. She's very busy.'

'And have you got another peach, Daddy?'

'Sadly not, but maybe there will be some sweets in the shops soon.'

'I liked the peach. You could stroke it like a cat. But I wouldn't want to eat a cat.'

The new housekeeper asked if she could get him something to eat or drink, though there wasn't much in the house. 'Tea and toast, perhaps?'

'Not at the moment, thanks. First I have to go out for an hour or two and then we can all have supper together.'

'You know, Mr Wilde, I heard something awful. There has been a murder at your college. A man stabbed to death, they say.'

'Yes, Janet, I heard something about it. Dreadful thing.'

Wilde had only come home to drop off his overnight bag. He wanted to call in at the police station to give the required statement and talk to the porters at college, but first he had a rather more important task.

Bobby did not look well, but he was fully dressed and managed to answer the door. The hallway of the tiny house was desperately cold.

'Shouldn't you be in bed?' Wilde asked with a concerned smile.

'Can't lounge about, professor. Not in my nature.' He had barely got the words out before he descended into a coughing fit, turning his head to one side and putting a handkerchief to his mouth. Wilde couldn't help noticing the blood-flecked sputum that emerged.

He put his arm around Bobby's shoulder. His college servant was at least a head shorter than him and his already thin frame was almost skeletal now. 'Come on, Bobby, let's get you sitting down.'

'Sorry, professor,' he gasped through hacking coughs, 'this isn't much of a welcome.'

Wilde held out a bottle of gin which he had discovered at the back of the larder. God knew how long it had been there. Neither he nor Lydia drank the stuff; he preferred Scotch, she liked a glass of wine. 'A little something for you, Bobby. Wish I could have brought more – grapes, for instance.'

'Oh, gin'll give me more of a lift than grapes. More valuable than gold these days. Thank you, Mr Wilde, you're a gentleman.'

They went through to the little kitchen, which at least had a wood stove throwing out some heat, and sat opposite each other across a two-person table. Everything was cramped in this desolate little dwelling, with almost nothing in the way of luxury. The only picture in evidence was a framed photograph of a racehorse and rider. Wilde had seen it before and knew that it was Bobby as a young man aboard one of the horses he rode professionally before the terrible fall that left him with a limp and a crushed jaw and ruined his dreams of being a jockey.

The tiny house told a rather sad tale, Wilde knew, for it was the physical manifestation of Bobby's poor lot in life: cheated of the career he desired, he never found married bliss. And yet despite everything, Wilde would say that Bobby was a happy man. He loved the college and was always welcoming and helpful, well beyond the call of duty. On occasion he had even risked his safety on Wilde's behalf.

'So what's all this I hear about a corpse in your rooms, professor?' Bobby poured shots of gin into two ancient and cracked glasses.

'You heard then? Why am I not surprised?'

'Word gets about in this town, Mr Wilde, and I've got friends.'

'Let me guess, Scobie's been to see you. Actually, Bobby, I was hoping I might pick your brain on the subject. My initial thought is that the killer must be someone who lives or works in college. No one else could slip in, could they?'

Bobby took a slug of gin and began coughing again. 'Ah, that's better,' he said as the coughing subsided. 'Best medicine in the world. Soothes the old throat a treat. Anyway, this murder, you don't think—'

'That I was the real target? I suppose it's a possibility, but probably not.'

'Well, you must have racked up a fair few enemies over the years, what with your extra-curricular activities, professor.'

Extra-curricular activities. They were long words for Bobby. Wilde grinned. 'Indeed, Bobby, a fair few.'

'So you want to know how someone could have slipped in? Well, cash talks.' Bobby rubbed his fingers together, the global indicator of money.

'A bribe?'

'Possibly. Food shortages and the black market have turned a lot of people into criminals. People will go to great lengths to get a chicken in the pot these days. Don't tell me you haven't bought yourself a little something on the side these past couple of years. And you never asked me too many questions when a bottle of Scotch miraculously appeared in my cupboard, as I recall. Well, you've got to make life worth living, haven't you?'

Wilde nodded, his thoughts turning to the peach. Where *had* that come from if not the black market? 'You're not suggesting someone who works at the college murdered a man for money?'

'No, but he might have found him a way into the grounds for a quid or two. Helping him pose as a delivery driver bringing coal or potatoes, perhaps? Who knows?'

Of course, a delivery man. The porters should have details of deliveries. Would there have been any yesterday in the atrocious weather, though? Surely there must have been, because an institution the size of the college could not function without frequent food deliveries, however basic the fare available.

'So someone on the inside – from the kitchens perhaps?'

'Well, they're not all saints in there, but I don't want to go around accusing anyone of anything. If someone was helping, I doubt they realised they were assisting a murderer. No one's going to risk the long drop for a pound or two.' The coughing began again.

Wilde reached over and patted Bobby on the shoulder. He could see that the man was losing energy fast and did not want to push him further. 'I'll leave you now, Bobby. I think you really do need a little lie-down.'

'Oh, it's nothing, just this bronchitis seems to hang on. I'll be right as rain in a few days.'

'Wrap up warm and look after yourself. Who's feeding you?'

'The widow Ambrose, my neighbour. She comes over with my lunch and supper. A saint she is, that woman.'

'That's good to hear. Anyway, perhaps you'd get a message to me if you have any thoughts – or if you hear anything from your mates.'

'Don't need to ask. Of course I'll do that, Professor Wilde, don't you worry.'

'Look after yourself, Bobby. The college isn't the same without you.'

'Kind of you to say, sir.' Bobby smiled, but his face had a wraithlike sheen, the skin tight on his cheekbones.

Wilde feared the worst.

There *had* been a delivery the previous day. A box of books from W. Heffer & Sons. 'Who brought it, Scobie?'

'Said his name was Miskin, new man at Heffers. J. Miskin, that's all I got. Said the books were for the library, so I let him through without question.'

'And he didn't sign in?'

'Well, I scribbled his name, but we don't usually bother too much with the delivery men, I'm afraid. But I seem to recall he was a good-looking young man, well spoken. Sort of fellow you'd expect in a bookshop, I suppose, so no great surprise. Oh my God, do you think . . .'

Wilde did think. This was the killer. 'What was he wearing?'

'He was all wrapped up, heavy greatcoat, scarf, hat, boots. Difficult to know whether he was thin or fat under that lot. He had a bit of class about him. Could have been one of your undergraduates, professor, but he wasn't because I'd have recognised him. Spectacles. Tortoiseshell, I think, but I could be wrong about that. About five eight or nine. Sort of average.'

'Voice – English or foreign?'

'Oh, very English. Crikey, Professor Wilde, I've messed up good and proper, haven't I?'

'I'm going to go and talk to the library just to be sure.'

'I'm afraid none of them turned up today.'

'Well, check with them when you can, Scobie, but I doubt whether any books were ordered or received. In the meantime, write down everything you recall about this delivery man. And don't blame yourself. The killer was a professional – he'd have got to Lieutenant Glasspool one way or another.'

Wilde took his leave of Scobie, trudged through the snow to St Andrew's Street, where he wrote a brief statement of fact for Chief Inspector Carter, then made his way home.

He shared a frugal supper with Janet and Johnny and sat down to read for an hour before putting his son to bed with a story. Downstairs, he joined Janet in the sitting room and for a while they sat in companionable silence.

'Tell me a bit about yourself,' Wilde said at last. 'Which part of the country are you from?'

The last of the coal was glowing in the hearth, but not really giving out enough warmth to combat the cold draughts that seeped through the windows and beneath the door. Wilde and Janet both wore thick pullovers and scarves and gloves, which gave them an almost comical air. She was sitting beside him on the sofa and he was aware that she was a little too close to him, but it was innocent enough.

'I was born in New Zealand but we came to England when I was nine. I'm the youngest of five, the baby of the family. After New Zealand we lived in Somerset, so I suppose that's where I really grew up.'

'What did your parents do?'

'Daddy tried his hand at sheep farming, but he decided it wasn't for him. In fact, he hated it. Couldn't bear sending them off for slaughter. He really wanted to be a painter – an artist. Mummy doesn't really do much to be honest, except fight with Daddy. Much of my childhood was spent shut away in my room covering my ears. Home was a constant battleground between my parents and my siblings. But I was studious and in time I managed to secure a place at Girton.'

'You were there a few years after my wife, I believe.'

She pushed her glasses up her nose, as though the word *studious* had reminded her of them. 'Yes,' she said. 'I studied English literature. I had dreams of writing novels, but then along came

Hitler and I decided to do my bit for the war effort and took a ministry job. Secretarial, of course. They weren't going to give anything difficult like real war work to a soppy girl, were they?'

Wilde nodded. There were openings – Freya Bentall's place in MI5 proved that – but he knew that such opportunities were few and far between for women. 'And now?'

'And now I'm a housekeeper and a nanny to a lovely little six-year-old called Johnny.'

'But that's not what you want to do in the long term, is it? Girton qualifies you for a great deal more.'

'Long term, I just want to get through this ghastly winter, Mr Wilde.'

'Don't we all, Janet, don't we all.'

'I'll see if I can get a job as a librarian. If not, I'll try my hand at teaching.' She left it there. Silence descended again, but just for a few moments. Wilde leant forwards and poked the embers to encourage a little more heat to emerge.

'I'm not sure how much I'd enjoy teaching, mind,' she said. 'I have this feeling there's something more for me. If Jane Austen and Charlotte Brontë could write novels, why not Janet Spring?'

'Why not, indeed.'

'But I haven't found a story yet. One day, perhaps. And if that doesn't work, I don't know what I'll do.'

Marriage, he supposed. Children of her own? She was good with Johnny – more like a playmate at times than a nanny – and she was a fine-looking young woman behind those glasses, so men would certainly be interested. But he said nothing on the subject for he knew how demeaning Lydia would find such a suggestion. Why should she measure herself on whether or not she had a man, Lydia would demand? Had we learnt nothing from Emmeline Pankhurst and her sisters in the fight for the universal franchise?

'I suppose you're wondering why I am not married,' Janet said, as if reading his thoughts. 'I had a boyfriend, a Canadian bomber pilot. He was killed at the end of '44. I thought we would probably get married.'

'I'm sorry.'

'Yes, me too.' She gave a sad shrug, then laughed rather oddly. 'God, I don't know why I said that. It's a stupid lie, something I tell people. He wasn't killed. The swine ran off with another woman just before Christmas, but that doesn't sound as good as dying heroically in the service of Britain, does it?'

Wilde nodded. Was he supposed to laugh along with her? He wasn't at all sure.

'You know, professor, the truth is I admire Mrs Wilde for what she's doing. I'd love to be a doctor, but I was never very good at the science subjects, biology and chemistry, so medicine seems to be out of the question. Perhaps I should become a dancing girl! Go to Paris and join the Folies Bergère? What do you think?'

They both laughed at that, then Wilde looked at his watch. 'Bedtime, I think. I'm off back to London after my lecture and meeting tomorrow, but you'll be all right, won't you?'

'Of course.'

'And there's enough food?'

'We'll survive.'

'Perhaps I might be able to pick up something more interesting in town. You never know.'

'Oh, I do hope so.'

He went to Johnny's room to check up on him. The boy was snuggled beneath a mass of blankets and looked at peace with the world. He blew him a silent kiss, then pulled the door to and there was a slight creaking, but Wilde was sure he hadn't disturbed him.

His own bedroom was unheated and, without the warm presence of Lydia, unwelcoming. He shivered as he stripped off and put on his pyjamas. Standing barefoot in the bathroom, he brushed his teeth and washed his hands and face in the icy water.

Climbing into bed, he didn't even try to read because he would have had to keep his hands outside the bedclothes to hold the book. So he just switched off the light, and wrapped the sheet and blankets and eiderdown tightly about him. He wasn't going to be warm tonight, but it was just about bearable.

As he lay there, waiting for sleep, his thoughts turned to the question of Freya Bentall. He hadn't quite decided what to do about her request, but he knew himself well enough; the chances are he would offer some assistance. The only real question was, how much – and how exactly would it work? He couldn't afford to stay in London full time, he had undergraduates to teach and supervise, so it would be a matter of commuting on the train once or twice a week.

And then there were the other questions: how much could he actually do to help her? Her idea of recruiting him as an MI5 officer and assigning him to the care of three other officers with question marks hanging over them seemed unwieldy. Clearly born of desperation.

The thoughts subsided. Sleep was almost on him when he heard the soft whisper of a door being opened somewhere in the house. The creak of a floorboard. Or was it his imagination, the settling of wooden beams as the temperature dropped? Surely not, because he also sensed the padding of silent feet. He must have inadvertently woken Johnny because this always happened when he was disturbed or had a bad dream in the night. He would want to crawl into bed with Mummy or Daddy or both of them.

Wilde climbed out from under the sheets and blankets and opened the door. It wasn't Johnny, but Janet. She was standing there in her thin nightie, shivering, her arms crossed.

'Janet?'

'My bed's so cold, Mr Wilde.'

CHAPTER 7

The conversation with Janet Spring was difficult. Wilde was pretty certain she already had three or four blankets. 'There must be some more bedding in the linen cupboard.'

'But I can't sleep.'

'You can borrow one of my pullovers. And do you have any socks?'

She shook her head.

'I'll find you a pair of mine. Come on, Janet, get yourself back to bed. Just wrap yourself up in any old clothes.' He smiled encouragingly. 'It's the same for all of us.'

She didn't move. Was it his imagination or did she want him to put his arms around her?

'Off you go, Janet. We don't want to wake Johnny.' As gently as he could, he insisted that she return to her bed.

She was attractive, her figure not dissimilar to Lydia's. What puzzled him most was her intention: if she was so cold, why was she wandering around without her dressing gown?

This was an educated young woman in her late twenties, not a girl. Huddling into her nightie, blinking behind her glasses as though she were fighting back tears, she turned away and shuffled across the landing towards her room.

'Good night again, Janet.'

'Good night, Mr Wilde.'

When she was gone he was almost tempted to lock the bedroom door but decided that would be a bit excessive.

Over breakfast the next morning, she apologised, after a fashion.

'I suppose I should have wrapped up better, Mr Wilde.'

'I'll see if I can find another couple of blankets. I'm sure I could borrow some from the college stores. How about that? I'll even see if they have an eiderdown. More than half of the undergraduates are away so there must be some spare bedclothes.'

'Thank you.'

He wasn't convinced that that was all she wanted from him, but it was a problem he had not encountered before. Nor did he want to discuss it with Lydia and add to her worries.

If Janet Spring was embarrassed, she didn't show it as they ate their meagre breakfast. As always, she made Johnny laugh and kept him happy before the snowy trek to school. Wilde took his leave of them and said he would call, because he wasn't yet sure when he would be back.

At the door, her eyes met his then looked away.

His first stop was the lecture theatre, where his subject was *A Winter's Tale*, not *The Winter's Tale*. He immediately confessed that the title was a poor joke, and that his talk would have nothing to do with the similarly-named Shakespeare play and everything to do with everyday life in Elizabethan times and how the ordinary people coped with the changing of the seasons.

The hall was less than half-full, which didn't surprise him, but at least those hardy few who had managed to crawl out of bed seemed to enjoy his attempt at humour on a cold morning. Hopefully they understood that he was using winter as a means to an end, simply to move away from politics, royal courtiers, war and the arts.

He wanted to describe the truth about the lives of the great majority of English people – the groundlings who would have paid a halfpenny out of their paltry wages to watch *The Winter's Tale*.

Afterwards, he had a meeting with Scobie in the porters' lodge. Scobie told him that the cardboard box and books the delivery man brought had been found abandoned at the back of the chapel. There were only three books – almost certainly they had been covering the ice-axe.

'Well, let Chief Inspector Carter know. I haven't got time to deal with the man.'

'Not very impressive, is he, professor?'

'That's the understatement of the decade, Scobie. By the way, has a ministry officer been here yet?'

The porter nodded. 'Yes, sir. Captain Greenway. He's been talking to everyone around the college. In fact, he's here now. Do you want me to find him?'

'No, he doesn't need me. He'll talk to Miss Bentall or the police if he finds anything. Oh, and could you ask someone to deliver two or three blankets to my house, if there are any available? I'll bring them back when the weather warms up. An eiderdown or two would be welcome as well.'

'Leave it with me, sir. Must be plenty of bedding spare.'

His next stop was Magdalene College on the west bank of the Cam, to meet some bloody Soviet education delegation. How had he let himself be sucked into such a tedious waste of time?

He found them in the Combination Room in front of a roaring log fire. Clad in dark panelling, it was not a large room, making it one of the snugger and more welcoming retreats frequented by the fellows of the various colleges. A servant was adding an ash log to the hearth and there was a hubbub of conversation from the other dozen or so men present, each holding a glass of sherry.

They turned at his entrance and he made eye contact with the Magdalene master, Allen Ramsay, who nodded in recognition, then turned back to his conversation with two other grey-heads.

Wilde wasn't at all sure what he was doing here and wished he hadn't come. It had seemed like a good idea last week when he had agreed to represent the college. It now felt little short of preposterous.

'Bit of unpleasantness in your rooms, I hear, Tom.'

He swivelled at the sudden voice in his left ear and realised that Philip Eaton was at his shoulder. Wilde didn't smile; he wasn't pleased to see the former MI6 man.

'I thought you had taken your pension, Eaton.'

'Returned to my alma mater and was accepted as a fellow in thanks for my service to King and country. Couldn't think what else to do with myself after retiring from the SIS.'

Now Wilde smiled. *Retiring from the SIS.* The treacherous bastard hadn't retired from the Secret Intelligence Service, he'd been thrown out – and Freya Bentall had played no small part in his defenestration.

'Trinity, of course,' Eaton continued. 'Spend my days reading Pliny and Tacitus and sipping sherry, and I've made it clear that I am always very happy to help with supervisions or even the occasional lecture if so required. And that's not all. Last summer I rediscovered a love of cricket – as a spectator, of course, my playing days being long gone, what with my injuries. And so I enjoy a very amenable life. A man could almost forget his wounds. Actually, I have been meaning to call on you for a few months now, Tom, but never quite got around to it. Not very mobile these days.'

Wilde was astonished. Eaton was never the most garrulous companion and yet here he was giving his life story.

'But that said, I'm not ready for the bath chair and ear trumpet yet.'

Wilde glanced down. Eaton had his cane as always, having badly damaged his left leg in a road incident which had also claimed his left arm. Despite his enthusiasm for his new life, he seemed much diminished, as though he had shrunk by a couple of inches. But that might just have been imagination, for his devious eyes were bright enough. And he was still standing.

'So tell me, what's all this dreadful stuff about a corpse in your rooms?'

'You mean you don't know, Eaton? I'd have thought your old contacts in the service would have kept you informed.'

'Oh, no one talks to me anymore. I'm yesterday's man. Anyway, old boy, I can tell you're keeping mum and you're not going to answer my questions. Taught you the secrets game too well, didn't I? So come on, let me introduce you to our friends from Moscow.'

The Russian was bulky and broad-chested with fraught, serious eyes and a mouth that affected a respectable imitation of a smile. He wore a surprisingly good suit: more Jermyn Street than Moscow clothes queue.

'Comrade Lukin, please let me introduce you to Professor Thomas Wilde, whose subject is history. Tudor history to be more precise. Tom, this is Commissar Lazar Lukin of the People's Commissariat of Education.'

Lukin shook his head and waved his hand dismissively. 'No, no, Mr Eaton. It is now known as the Ministry of Education. You must move with the times. The Soviet Union is a modern evolving society and government departments are changing.'

'Forgive me, comrade.'

'It's nothing.' He smiled with his mouth then nodded to Wilde and they shook hands. 'So your game is history, Professor Wilde.'

'Very little in the way of Russian history, I'm afraid.' Wilde was trying to get the measure of Lazar Lukin. His English was first class with a mixture of accents – Russian and American. It was a fair assumption that he would be reporting back to the Kremlin on everyone and everything he encountered. Even before the war ended it had started to become clear that that was the way the Soviet Union's representatives abroad operated.

'Well, it is a pleasure to meet you, Mr Wilde.'

'The pleasure's all mine. And I can assure you that no one is more interested than me in expanding the horizons of our young people – the students of both Cambridge and of Moscow. They must travel to each other's countries so that harmful preconceptions can be done away with. That is the path to peace.'

'Of course. Our sentiments entirely.'

'Have you been in America, Comrade Lukin?'

'Why do you ask?'

'You speak very good English – but your accent . . .'

'Yes, I spent the war years there as part of the Soviet Purchasing Commission. Sixteenth Street, Washington DC. I was in the Metals Division, so this is a big change for me – and a welcome one.'

'You mean education – or England?'

'Both. Influencing young minds and then there is the matter of your weather.'

'Ah yes, not much we can do about that, I'm afraid.'

'Don't apologise, professor. This is paradise for anyone who has endured the winters of northern Byelorussia.'

'I'm not sure a lot of people would call it paradise right now. Anyway, I'm glad to hear you're thinking of opening up your borders to student exchanges.'

'You mention my accent, Mr Wilde. I have an ear for such things myself – do I detect a little American in your own voice?'

'Very astute, Mr Lukin.' Wilde realised that Philip Eaton was still at his side, not contributing to the conversation. 'You're suddenly very quiet, Philip.'

'Oh, I concur with everything you both say. Nothing to add, I'm afraid. Just enjoying the sherry and the heat from the fire.'

Wilde had thought – hoped – that he'd seen the last of Eaton in 1945. But here he was, as though no unpleasantness had ever occurred between them. He was standing a little away from the Russian, leaning to one side on his stick, his back to the fire. Did they already know each other before this event? To hell with surmise, pose the question.

'Are you two old friends by any chance?' He looked first at Eaton, then at Lukin.

'No, no,' Eaton said, his face stiffening slightly. 'Why do you ask?'

'Just wondered.'

A chilly gust entered the room and three more dons entered. The Magdalene master waited a few moments while they took glasses from a silver tray proferred by a serving man, then clinked his fountain pen against his own glass. 'Shall we get down to business, gentlemen? Comrade Lukin has some ideas to propose and I hope you will find them eminently satisfactory.'

The meeting dragged on for an hour. Wilde knew a couple of the other dons and exchanged a few pleasantries with them, then moved on to another member of the Soviet delegation before deciding there really was nothing more to be learnt here. All well and good if the Soviets were serious about a series of student exchanges. Anything to take the tension out of relations between East and West. He took his leave of the master and nodded to Eaton and Lukin, who had not moved on from each other's company.

The Russian reached out and touched his arm. 'We did not get much of a chance to discuss our ideas, Professor Wilde. I would like to hear your thoughts in detail. Perhaps I might call on you before I return to Moscow.'

'Please do, but you might not find me here. London calls.'

'And I am moving on to the dreaming spires of Oxford. But I'm sure I'll find you.'

The train was slow again, the weather bitingly cold. Nothing would ever improve in this forsaken sub-arctic nation. Icebergs off Norfolk? Had that happened or was it some fisherman's tale? Wilde wasn't renowned for being credulous, yet it had the ring of truth.

Before leaving, he had called Freya Bentall and they had arranged to meet at his hotel. She wasn't there when he arrived, but a porter took his case to his room and he stayed in the lobby with a good cup of coffee, wondering how these expensive hotels had access to luxuries that were denied to the ordinary people of Britain. He knew the answer, of course: the hotels brought in much-needed foreign currency from international dealers who might be willing to pay hard cash for British goods and services.

She looked furtive as she came through the front door of the hotel into the reception area. He had never expected to see her like that. Freya Bentall, in his experience, was not a woman given to anxiety. But her eyes were everywhere, as though expecting an assassin to emerge at any moment.

Their eyes met and she flashed him an uneasy smile.

'You made it, Tom. Is there a quiet room where we can talk undisturbed?'

'I'm sure there must be.'

He asked at the desk and they were shown through to a comfortable little side room. When the door had been closed, Freya Bentall stood at the head of the rectangular table, her knuckles white as she clutched the top of the chair.

'What is it, Freya?'

'Gehlen's man – the contact who informed him of the Soviet plans – is dead. No trial, no appeal. Bullet in the back of the head in a dark cellar in Moscow. The body hauled away, the concrete floor hosed down. I'm told that's the usual way, justice Stalin-style.'

'And Gehlen thinks there's a link to events here, I take it?'

'Oh yes. In his mind, this new killing along with the murder of Everett Glasspool confirms everything he's told me.'

Wilde's first reaction was to conclude, not for the first time, that he was being played by Freya Bentall. She was a skilled manipulator, the best, so she would use every trick to get him on board. And if that meant making out the world was about to end, then she'd do it.

'Did you give your lecture, sort out all your loose ends?'

'Mostly. And I went to a meeting at Magdalene which might interest you. A Soviet education delegation was there to discuss the possibility of opening up student exchanges. I was college representative.'

She nodded. 'I heard about that. We checked them out and it all seems above board. They'll be going to Oxford, Birmingham, Edinburgh and Manchester as well, I believe.'

'What you might not have known was that our dear friend Philip Eaton was there with the Cambridge reception party.'

She looked genuinely shocked. 'Eaton? Good God, what was *he* doing?'

'He's back at Trinity, but surely you knew that?'

'No, I didn't – and please don't refer to him as *our friend*. In my mind, he's fortunate not to have been strung up for high treason.'

'Well, you had no evidence against him. Suspicions, yes – and some circumstantial stuff – but nothing you would have wanted to air in open court with the press present.'

'Perhaps the Soviet justice system has its advantages. A cold, windowless cellar. Bang, you're dead.'

'You don't believe that, Freya.'

'Don't I, Tom? Are you sure?'

He was sure, but then again he wasn't. He had witnessed her ordering violence to obtain information when she feared many might die if there was delay. But there was something else here.

'You want vengeance for Everett Glasspool, don't you?'

Her shoulders stiffened. 'I want justice. Retribution, perhaps. Vengeance is too harsh a word.'

However she phrased it, whatever words she used, she wanted the killer to be identified and dealt with. But Gestapo-style torture and NKVD-style assassination? No, he couldn't see her authorising those. 'Well, let's put it this way, Freya. I couldn't work with you if you believed in execution without trial.'

She gave him a confidential smile. 'You know me too well. Of course I don't believe in the methods employed by Stalin and Hitler. Perhaps a slap around the head, but nothing more. There *are* frustrations though. Anyway, tell me more. Who else was there?'

'If you must know it amounted to sod all. The only Russian I spoke to went by the name of Lazar Lukin. Intelligent, bilingual, spent time in America, almost certainly a spy.'

'They all are, Tom. We've just been too slow on the uptake since the 1920s. Lazar Lukin, yes, I heard his name. He's fully accredited – arrived bearing diplomatic papers a few days ago. Our files have no record of him before that, so perhaps you'd give me a full written description of your impressions. We'll have to see what else we can discover. His real name would be a good start.'

'He said he'd like to meet me again to discuss student exchanges in more detail.'

'Was there anything about him that might make such a meeting useful?'

'He told me that during the war he was with the Soviet Purchasing Commission in New York. It would be interesting to know if anyone in MI6 or the Foreign Office recalls someone of that name.'

'I can look into it. Anything else?'

'He wasn't a big man but I got the impression he had immense strength. And without wishing to be over-dramatic, there were his eyes. They were cold. Killer's eyes.'

'Then take him up on his offer to meet. Which brings me back to the other matter. Will you join MI5?'

He shrugged, beaten into submission. 'I'll give you a week of my time, and that's it.'

'Thank you. And tomorrow you will meet Gus Baxter, our cleverest and most debauched officer.'

CHAPTER 8

The introductions were made in Freya's office and then the two men were sent on their way. What now, Wilde wondered?

Gus Baxter supplied the answer. 'I think we should start with a drink, don't you? Fancy slumming it?'

'Is that your idea of teaching me tradecraft, Baxter?'

'Absolutely. No better way.'

'You lead, I'll follow.'

Gus Baxter put his arm around Wilde's shoulder as though he had known him all his life and brought his mouth uncomfortably close to his ear. 'Whisper it, Wilde, but we're going *south* of the river to the sort of place no one in the service knows exists. They'd look at you with blank eyes if you ever suggested it to them. "*South of the river, old man? Do you mean France?*"' Baxter chuckled.

Wilde heard the words and recoiled from the gust of alcohol that infused the man's breath. Fifty per cent proof at the very least.

They were standing on the icy pavement outside Leconfield House. Baxter raised his right arm and a black cab skidded to a halt beside them.

'Walworth Road, my man.'

'I'm not going over there, mate. The bridges are all skating rinks and my tyres are slick.'

Baxter pulled a pound note from his pocket and waved it in front of the cabbie's eyes. 'This change your mind, will it? Come on, driver, where's the Dunkirk spirit? If the little boats could make it across the Channel, you can get over the bloody Thames.'

'Make it a guinea and I'll give it a go. It's at your own risk though – don't blame me if we end up in the river.'

Freya Bentall had used all her charm on Baxter. 'Take him under your wing, Gus, refresh him. He was one of us in the war – OSS – and he needs to get back in the game. A little bird tells me Harry Truman will be bringing the service back in some form or other.'

'My pleasure, ma'am.'

Baxter was a man of a class that Wilde knew well from his own experiences of English public school life. Arrogant, educated in the classics, careless or even contemptuous of the feelings of others. He wore an expensive suit, sea island cotton shirt with a scuffed collar and a silk tie that was clearly never cleaned or brushed down – and shoes that, by contrast, were polished to a mirror shine. Wilde realised that Baxter didn't care what anyone thought of him. His own pleasure was all.

They settled down in the back of the cab. 'Of course I know what this is all about,' Baxter said.

'You do?'

'Oh yes. Mother Bentall has a case of raging paranoia. Thinks we're all up to no good so she wants you to spy on the spies. Nothing at all to do with helping US intelligence get up and running again. Surely the FBI could do that for you. No, she thinks we're all fiddling our expenses and bunking off on unnecessary jaunts. But how the hell would she know? She's office-bound, shackled to her damned desk. She has no concept of life in the field.'

Wilde smiled and nodded. He was pretty sure that Freya had a perfectly accurate image of Baxter's working practices. If Baxter was smart, Bentall was smarter.

'So *are* you spying on me, Wilde?'

'If I said no, would you believe me?'

'No, of course not.'

Baxter and Wilde had been told that they would be working together for two days. Baxter's mission was simply to show Wilde around, explain his intelligence-gathering methods, but without revealing any operational secrets.

There was a respite in the snowfall and the road south and east via Trafalgar Square and Westminster Bridge had recently been cleared, so the journey wasn't too bad until they came to the Elephant and Castle, where a bus had slewed into a lorry, blocking the road.

'I think this is about as far as I can take you, gentlemen,' the driver said.

'Bugger. Oh well, nice day for a walk.'

They climbed out and Baxter handed the cabbie five shillings. 'Oy, what's this? I said a guinea.'

'And I said Walworth Road, so go and fuck yourself up the arse with a broomstick.' Baxter put two fingers in the air and strolled off without a backward glance.

It was mid-afternoon, the sky was already darkening and Wilde wondered what he was doing in this forlorn, bombed-out, iced-over wasteland, a part of London which had probably looked no more inviting before Goering sent over his bombers.

More to the point, why was he here with a louche MI5 agent who, if he *was* a traitor, was hardly about to give himself away. This whole idea was an act of desperation on Freya's part and, for some inexplicable reason, Wilde was going along with it.

Deep within himself he knew why he had agreed to help. It was because someone had had the temerity to commit murder in his rooms, his place of quiet, his home from home. How dare anyone invade his space in such a cruel and brutal manner?

The agreement with Freya was that he would work for a week, no more. If nothing came of his time with the three men who headed Freya's list of potential suspects, then they'd call it quits. Wilde had gone so far as to sign on so that he was officially on a short-term engagement with the service, but he refused to take any pay. 'Give it to the Royal British Legion,' he had said.

Together, he and Baxter trudged along Walworth Road through the oily slush, past hard-pressed mothers dragging their children home from school or queueing outside shops for bread and pota-toes, past workmen shovelling snow from the paths. This was a poor part of London. People struggled to stay alive and the chil-dren looked underfed. No one had an ounce of fat on their bony frames and it occurred to Wilde that there might be cases of rick-ets in these back streets, a grim reminder of the days of Dickens a hundred years earlier. Hard times.

Halfway down the long thoroughfare, Baxter stopped outside a broad-fronted pub isolated between two bomb sites. 'And here we are, Wilde, not far from East Street, home of the famous mar-ket and birthplace of Charlie Chaplin. But most importantly, it's the location of a delightful boozer named The Green Bear. We're about to enter Hades so keep your wallet safe about your person.'

'The Green Bear? Why here?'

'South London's finest drinking club – and a place of pick-ups. Generally just called the Bear.'

'Pick-ups?'

'Oh, you know. Girls, boys, black-market hooch, scandal, secrets . . . you'll learn more from the spivs here than from the snoots in the clubs of Pall Mall. But mostly, there's the hooch. Come in and meet the crowd.'

The place was heaving and it was still the working day. Wilde's initial thought was, *This is a bloody knocking shop.* The drinkers were divided sharply between those he decided were paying for services – and those being paid. There were good-looking young women with too much makeup and plenty of promise, thuggish men with too much swagger and an air of danger, thin underfed men with sharp faces, bow legs and quick fingers that might slip into your pocket.

And then there were the other ones, the incongruous ones who stood out. A bit older, thirties, forties or even grey-haired fifties. The customers, probably. The men who brought the money here – always men – and paid for services rendered.

'Get all sorts, barristers, MPs, stockbrokers. They can get their heart's desire here, things denied them at home,' Baxter said.

One man in particular caught Wilde's eye. He looked out of place, standing alone at the bar, wearing a decent but inexpensive grey suit and a plain red knitted tie with a gold tiepin. He had the appearance of a man whose working life was spent a fair distance from Walworth.

'What's your poison, Wilde?' Baxter asked.

'Scotch,' he said, more in hope than expectation.

'Well, your luck might just be in.'

Baxter pushed his way through to the bar with Wilde in his wake. Within a few moments two large whiskies arrived and they toasted each other and downed them.

Wilde looked along the bar at the solitary man in the grey suit. He cut a sad figure.

'You know who that is, don't you, Wilde?'

'I get the feeling he should be familiar.'

'That's Len Goodrick, Ministry of Supply. Junior minister or something.'

'So what's he doing here?'

'A very good question – and I think we should find out. Let's just watch him for the moment.'

Wilde didn't delve deeper. He was here to observe Baxter and those he met, to watch and learn.

Two more whiskies were ordered and this time they sipped them more slowly. Baxter had his back to the bar, scanning the room. 'Goes back bloody miles this place, Wilde. Well, not miles maybe, but a long way. Snooker room at the back, various little rooms for cards and you know what.'

Wilde could imagine.

'See that fellow over there.' Baxter jabbed him in the arm to get his attention. 'The bald one with the brightly-coloured shirt and the Churchill cigar and the acolytes all round him. No, don't stare, just glance at him. That's Terry Adnams.'

'Means nothing to me.'

'Not heard of Terry Adnams? Which stone have you been hiding under? Top gangster, London's Al Capone. Known far and wide as Axeman Adnams. He owns this joint. Notorious bastard. Kill you if you cross him. Come on, I'll introduce you. Just show him a little respect, all right, and you'll be safe enough. He'll love your accent.'

'I'm in your hands, Baxter. I suppose you know what you're doing.'

'Oh, believe me, I do. You'd be surprised how often the worlds of crime, politics and espionage collide and fuse together. You're here to learn, aren't you, Wilde? Well, let me educate you.'

Adnams threw wide his arms. 'Gus Baxter, my man! Come here, you dirty old sodomite.' A cloud of cigar smoke emerged from his mouth and Baxter recoiled.

'Hey, who are you calling old?'

'You're a bad boy, Baxter. A very bad boy.' His eyes strayed to the new customer. 'And what's this you've brought me?'

'This is my American friend Tom Wilde. He's very impressed that he can get a glass of Scotch whisky here.'

'He can get whatever he wants if he has the silver. An elephant if he so desires, though I usually like to sell them in pairs. What do you want, Tom?'

'The whisky is just fine.'

'A Cuban cigar, perhaps. Rolled on the thighs of virgins.'

Wilde shook his head. 'Not a smoker, but thanks for the offer.'

'You don't smoke! Everyone smokes, Tom.'

Wilde was standing face to face with Adnams. They were about the same height, but Adnams was bulkier and barrel-chested. He stood like a fighter. 'If you don't mind my saying so, you have the look of a boxer, Mr Adnams.'

'Terry to you, Tom. And yes, you're right, I like a bit of pugilism.' He eyed Wilde up and down. 'You know what, Tom, you look like one, too.'

Wilde smiled. 'Middleweight, but no more than a little sparring in my local gym these days. What about you, light-heavy?'

'No, no. Middle like you – just bulked out a bit in recent years.'

Adnams punched air. His fists came in a lightning-fast one-two feint, stopping just short of Wilde's face. Wilde didn't flinch.

'Didn't move an inch. What are you, brave or slow?'

'Slow, I suppose, these days.'

'But you never completely lose it, do you, Tom? Still going to the gym, are you? Which do you use? Ain't seen you down the Walworth club.'

'I come from Cambridge and I use Joe Spinks's place.'

Adnams's brow knitted as though he hadn't quite heard right. 'Did you say Joe Spinks?'

'I did.'

'Well, bugger me sideways, Joe bloody Spinks! Featherweight Joe. How is the little fucker?'

'Not what he was, but he'll never throw in the towel.'

'Cambridge, eh? Wish I'd known he was there. Done a bit of business up there recently. Could have paid the old feller a visit, gassed about old times.'

'I'll pass on your best wishes if you like.'

'Do that. Say hello from Terry Adnams, yes? Featherweight Joe, eh? He was an animal, that man, a fucking animal. He'll remember me because we were on the same bill once and we both won our divisions. I was young, starting out. He was at his peak. That was a party and a half that night.' He shook his head and grinned. 'Poor Joe should have won the British title a few months later but got sick, had to pull out and never got another chance. Bloody tragedy.'

'He still feels it.'

Suddenly Adnams took Wilde in his arms and squeezed, then kissed him on both cheeks.

'Any friend of Joe Spinks and Gus Baxter is a friend of mine. Your money's no good here – drinks are all on me tonight, Tom. And anything else you might require. All night long. Drink us dry and fuck yourself to a standstill.' He ran his finger in an arc, pointing in turn at the various girls. 'Take your pick if you're that way inclined. If not, we cater to all sorts here. Just ask Baxter.'

'I'm a married man.' Wilde was trying to catch his breath, the air crushed from his lungs and now being filled with acrid smoke. He was aware of Baxter at his side, listening, saying nothing, tipping the ash from his cigarette and sipping Scotch. Watching. Like a cat crouched beside a hedge where sparrows nested.

'Then you'll be wanting a bit on the side, won't you,' Adnams said. He threw up his left arm and waved across the room. 'Oy, Dolly, get your tits over here, darling. Someone I want you to meet.' He turned back to Wilde. 'So you're a Yank, are you? But your accent – sounds just as much English as Yank.'

'Yes, I'm American, but I've spent a lot of my life in England.' He didn't mention that he was half Irish. He loved his Irish blood – inherited from his mother – but there was too much intolerance about these days and it wasn't worth going into at this time and in this place.

'I like a Yank myself. Done us proud in the war with nylons, Hershey's and open wallets for the girls. Some of my best customers and some of my best suppliers.'

Wilde took it to mean the black market.

Dolly was snaking her way through the crowd. The way she moved, the languid carriage of her perfect body, the soft curl of her long blonde hair, was sex itself. The other women in the room had the marks of their profession; too much makeup, too obvious cleavage, too much leg, haunted eyes above feigned smiles.

But this one – Dolly – had class. No, Wilde thought, *class* was the wrong word. There was nothing royal or aristocratic about her. Nor did she have the symmetry of a model. She was earthier than that.

What made her stand out was the promise of bliss in bed and intelligent eyes that foretold great conversation and laughter in the morning over breakfast.

Why was he even thinking like this? It must be the whisky. Why couldn't he take his eyes off this gangster's whore?

He looked to his side at Baxter and noticed that his eyes were elsewhere, on a pretty young man at the bar. The junior minister, Goodrick, was talking to him. Wilde wasn't surprised.

'Play the gee-gees, do you, Tom?' It was Adnams talking.

'Not as a rule. Maybe the Grand National and Derby, but that's all.'

'Well, if you ever want a bet, come to me. No one will give you better odds. Ah, and now here she is. Cleopatra in all her bloody glory. Take your time, won't you, Doll?'

'Got to show off my assets, Terry.'

Her voice wasn't quite as sweet as her appearance. Cockney perhaps.

'Well, I'm sure Tom here appreciates your lovely assets. Tom, this is Dolly, prettiest girl in Walworth.'

'Hey, you told me I was the prettiest girl in London.'

'Did I, Doll? Well, I'm sure you are, but I ain't seen all the girls in London, so it's difficult to compare. Anyway, say hello to Tom. He's my guest tonight and I want him treated well.'

She turned her smile on Wilde and held out her small hand. 'Hello, Tom. What are you, an MP or something?'

'No, he's a boxer from Cambridge town and he's an American and he's a pal of Gus. That's all you need to know.'

Wilde could not avoid taking her hand. It was limp and soft. Their eyes met. His first impression was that she was biddable and vulnerable, but her eyes told a different story. He saw strength and independence. She'd be pliant enough when it suited her, but that wasn't the only game she played. She wouldn't be pushed in a direction she didn't want to go.

'My pleasure,' he said.

'And are you going to buy a girl a drinkie?'

'What would you like?'

'Port and lemon.'

Adnams summoned over one of his men. 'Fetch a port and lemon for Dolly, and put it on the house.'

'Yes, chief.'

'And whatever my friends here are drinking.'

'Of course, chief.'

Adnams slipped the man a coin, then turned back to Wilde and Baxter. 'If you'll excuse me, gentlemen, I've got a bit of business to see to out the back. Might catch up with you later. Pleasure to meet you, Tom.'

'Likewise, Terry.'

'Good man. Look after them, Doll.' And with that he was gone, his boxer's strut enough to make the drinkers part and leave a clear path through to a door somewhere at the back of the bar.

Dolly moved closer to Wilde and he could smell her expensive French perfume. 'So if you're not a politician, what are you?' she said. 'You might have been tough enough in your day, but you're not a bloody pro boxer, that's for sure.'

'I'm a history professor.'

'What? Having a laugh, aren't you? That'd be a first for me.'

'What about you? Is Dolly your real name?'

'What do you think, prof?'

'I think it's your working name.'

'Smart guy, aren't you.'

'Well?'

'All right, I'm Amelia. My family call me Amy. But you can call me Dolly.'

'As you like,' he said, laughing.

And then the lights went out.

CHAPTER 9

The room was pitch dark. There was cheering and jeering because the regulars were used to it; blackouts happened every day.

Wilde felt a hand on his hip. *Her* hand. It couldn't be anyone else's and it wasn't there by mistake. It was moving, along his thigh, then between his legs. He backed away, but the hand followed. Someone struck a match and then a couple of candles on the bar threw an eerie light into the darkness.

He took hold of her hand and moved it away.

'Don't you like that, Tom?'

'Not what I'm looking for just at the moment, Dolly.'

'You sure? I'm good, you know.'

'I'm sure you are and I'm equally sure it's not for me.'

'Suit yourself, sweetie, but it's on the house. Terry's put me at your disposal. If you prefer someone else, of course . . .'

It was then that he noticed Baxter was no longer at his side. In fact, he was nowhere to be seen. The candlelight was flickering and faces were indistinct, but he felt certain he should be able to see the man.

Dolly followed his eyes. 'What is it, Tom? You looking for something?'

'My companion, Gus Baxter. He was here a minute ago before the lights went out. Now he's vanished.'

'Don't worry about Gussie. He'll be in a back room with one of the boys. Or two maybe. Who knows, eh? Each to their taste, that's what Terry always says. Anyway, if I can't offer you anything spicier, how about another drinkie?'

He noticed that his glass was empty again. God, he was drinking the stuff fast; that's what came of abstaining for so long. When a dry spell ends, well, it fair pelts down. 'Go on then.'

She took his glass and headed for the bar. Wilde noticed that the man in the grey suit – Len Goodrick – was still there, but alone again. On a whim, Wilde went over to him and leant on the bar at his side.

'Goodrick, isn't it? Len Goodrick?'

The man turned as though he'd been hit. His face clenched. 'Do I know you?'

'No, no. But I thought I recognised you. I must have seen your picture in the papers. Ministry of Supply, isn't it?'

'Who are you?'

Wilde produced his best smile and put out his hand. 'Wilde, Tom Wilde. I'm a history professor at Cambridge.'

Goodrick did not accept the handshake. 'Really? You're straying a long way from home, aren't you. What exactly is your business in Walworth?' His accent was from the North or Midlands.

'Probably the same as you – I wanted a drink. A friend brought me, told me I could get whisky here, and so it has proved.'

'You're one of Beaverbrook's filthy newshounds.'

'No, what makes you think that?'

'You use every trick in the book. You'd pretend you were my long-lost brother if you thought I'd wear it.'

Wilde was puzzled. 'Am I missing something?'

'I beg your pardon?'

'I was just wondering why you might suspect I was a journalist. Do you have something to hide?' Wilde was astonished at himself. Why would he ask such an unpleasant question of a man he'd just met, and a minister of the Crown at that? Perhaps it was the whisky.

'You're a disgrace. You and your rag. So, bollocks to you, Mr Wilde or whatever your name is. I suggest you go and fuck yourself and leave me to drink in peace.'

Wilde shrugged and turned away. Dolly was holding two drinks, one of them a very large Scotch which she handed to him, the other a port and lemon.

'Don't mind him, Tom, naughty Len's just here for the boys. Likes a bit of rough.'

Where the hell was Gus Baxter? How could a professional intelligence officer entrusted with his care simply up and leave him in the lurch? Damn it, his mission was to watch Baxter, catalogue his movements, make a note of the people he met. Now he was stuck in a bar with a working girl and a glass of black-market Scotch. 'Can we go through to the back, Dolly?'

'You want a game of snooker – or something else?'

'I want to find Baxter.'

'He'll be with Julian. He won't thank you for disturbing him.'

'Julian?'

'The pretty boy.'

'Well, let's go and find out.'

The main back room had two men on the door. They were heavies, fighting men with muscles rippling beneath rolled-sleeve shirts. Wilde looked at them in disbelief. It wasn't that warm in here. What sort of idiot wore shirt-sleeves in this weather when sane people didn't remove their jackets and certainly wore a thick pullover? The lengths to which some people would go to look hard and threatening.

Dolly spoke to the men and they let them both through. Even in the flickering light of a dozen candles, he could see that the room was larger and smokier than the taproom at the front of The Green Bear. This was boss Adnams's inner sanctum, an illicit gambling hall, the place where he ran his business and where he made the big money.

There was, indeed, a snooker table, but there were roulette and poker tables too. The far wall of the hall was dominated by a blackboard displaying odds on certain events: the 2000 Guineas, various motor and dog races, the Grand National, of course – if the snow cleared in time for any of them to be run.

Wilde scanned the room. It was even busier in here and the candlelight gave it a strange, eerie feel of an underworld. What was it Baxter had said? *Welcome to Hades* or something. There was still no sign of him. Had he planned his disappearance all along, a neat way of losing his shadow?

'Damn it, where is he? If he's with this Julian, where would they be?'

'Sometimes he takes him off to a room for the night, but they could be in the bogs for a quickie.'

Wilde downed the whisky. It was a reaction to his irritation. He could usually hold his drink, but he knew he was imbibing too much tonight and he didn't care. He was angry with Freya Bentall for putting him in this position, and he had a strong desire to pummel this bloody effete Englishman Gus Baxter to the ground, if only he could find him.

He held out the glass to Dolly. 'Fill me up . . . please.'

She took the glass and laughed. 'You got a thirst on you tonight, Professor Tom.'

While Dolly went off in search of more whisky, he stood looking about him, hoping to catch a glimpse of Baxter. The atmosphere was raucous; some laughter, some angry voices raised, odds being shouted. This was unfamiliar to him, a continent away from the solitude and blessed quiet of a Cambridge college and home.

To the far side of the hall, not far from the blackboard, voices were raised even more. There was shouting and swearing and his focus was drawn through the glimmer of candlelight to the scene. Someone threw a punch. There was a yell of rage and pain, a flurry of punches from both sides. Two men were squaring up to each other. One of them was tall and broad, the other no bigger than a jockey. The smaller one launched an upper cut and the big man staggered and stumbled.

Other men were gathered around the edges, making space for the fighters, urging them on, eager to witness a dust-up. A couple on the sidelines began to barge each other. More fists flew, the shine of a blade. It was looking bad. Baxter or no Baxter, this was not a good place to be.

Then it really kicked off. Punches came fast and furious, more knives, a spurt of red, a brawl with no obvious cause and no clearcut divide between the fighters. Everyone seemed to be hitting out at everyone. Hitting or stabbing. Snooker cues became weapons, so did glasses. Candles were knocked over, cigarettes were stubbed into arms and faces.

Dolly was back at his side, whisky in hand.

'Here you are, prof.'

He accepted the glass and took a deep swig. 'Time to go, I think, Dolly.'

'What, you worried about the fight? Don't pay no attention to them. It's just a dispute about a bet or arm-wrestling or something. Happens all the time in the Bear.'

'It's looking nasty.'

'Silly. Only a bit of blood. The fun's just beginning.'

But it wasn't. As suddenly as the fight began, it stopped. Terry Adnams had appeared from nowhere. He was up on the platform in front of the blackboard glaring down on the crowd with malicious, fearless eyes.

The brawlers looked up at him and backed away. Some wiped blood from their mouths, others quietly put down their weapons or slid them into pockets. No one said a word.

'Anyone want some?' Adnams said, his voice quiet but laden with menace.

In his right hand, he swung an ice-axe. He smacked the flat of the blade into his left palm. Then his eyes met Wilde's across the room and he winked.

CHAPTER 10

Had Adnams really winked? Had he really been swinging an ice-axe? Wilde needed a clear head, but he didn't have it. He had to get out of here. He handed the empty glass back to Dolly. 'I'm off,' he said. 'If you see Baxter, tell him I'll meet up with him tomorrow. He'll know where.'

'But I was enjoying your company, prof. You seem like one of the good guys. And the boss likes you.'

'And I enjoyed your company, Dolly, but I'm a married man and I intend to stay that way.'

She smiled at him. 'You really are one of the good ones, aren't you? Not many like you about, Mr Wilde.' She kissed his cheek and then headed off. Another group of men caught his eye. They were sitting at a card table with a female dealer, all oblivious to the fighting. But they were very visible because of their expensive clothes and Silvikrin hair. Men from north of the river. Civil servants, perhaps, lawyers, stockbrokers, all feeding a deep need.

Wilde let Dolly go and made his way out into the darkness of the Walworth Road. The street lamps were all off and there were no electric lights from the windows of shops or houses. Only the occasional glow of a cigarette.

He very much wished he had a torch because it was snowing again and he didn't know this part of London. There was no traffic and he doubted any buses would be running in these conditions. There would certainly be no taxis.

Huddling into his coat, gloved hands deep in his pockets, he began to retrace his steps back to the Elephant and Castle, very aware that he had downed more than half a bottle of Scotch and his acuity wasn't what it might have been. In a word, he was drunk, which was an unusual state in recent years.

The strange thing was, his inebriation was rather pleasant, the snow seemed to be warm on his face and collar and a song kept running through his head: 'Red Sails in the Sunset'. Why that, of all things?

He began to whistle. A woman, head down, appeared from nowhere and brushed past him, dragging a reluctant child by the arm, and then was gone. He knew that other people were out because he could occasionally hear voices or see the flare of a match, but the snow was so heavy that they were no more than ghostly figures in the curious dark white light.

The blow to the head came without warning. It didn't render him unconscious, but his knees buckled and he tried to make sense of it. Had he walked into something – a signpost or a telegraph pole? Then came the second blow and his legs gave way completely and he fell forwards into the snow.

He hadn't been knocked out, but he was dazed and in pain, his gloved hands scrabbling in the soft, silent snow. He was being attacked and he tried to turn to see the assailant, but his face was pushed down and held there.

Hands were all over him, rifling through his pockets, searching for something. His wallet, he supposed, his money.

And then the kicking started and he knew that there were at least two of them – because he was being booted in the ribs from both sides. He held his hands protectively around his head, unable to fight back.

'Keep your fucking face down or you're a fucking dead man.'

It was an unfamiliar voice, but the accent was local and male, that's all he could tell. He felt a heavier blow to the back of the skull. The last thing he heard was the voice again, which seemed to say, 'Fuck off back to ponceland,' but he couldn't be sure. In the moments before darkness fell, he had a curious sensation of being lifted, and then nothing.

When he came to, he had no idea how long he had been unconscious. Seconds? Minutes? An hour? The warm sensation of inebriation was long gone. His torso was in pain, so was his head. The sharp throb pummelling him from within like a steam hammer. He felt sticky blood and sharp ice clawing at his face and his mouth was full of his own gore.

As he tried to push himself up, he realised he was no longer on the pavement. Beneath his weirdly-angled body, he was clawing at snow-coated rocks and bricks and icy lumps of wood. He had been slung on a bomb site like a sack of coal.

He didn't really want to move because every slight motion sent shockwaves of pain through his body. Better to stay here and sleep it off. Sleep or die, it hardly mattered which. Anything was better than movement.

But he *had* to move. Some spark in the fog of his brain told him he couldn't stay here, couldn't die. He had a family to look after, students who needed him, a mother in America.

Inch by inch, slowly, he turned and twisted and managed to get to his knees, squatting with his hands on unstable rubble, the ice now seeping through his gloves into his frozen fingers.

Realisation dawned that he probably had no broken bones, but where was the blood coming from? His mouth certainly, probably his head or face, too.

Then again, maybe he did have broken bones – his ribs. Only one way to find out; he had to get to hospital. There was just enough cognisance in his throbbing brain to realise that hypothermia was a real possibility. Lydia had been talking about it only recently because they had seen a patient at St Ursula's who nearly died from exposure to the cold.

One handhold at a time, he dragged himself across the icy bricks and stones in the direction he hoped was the road. At last he made it, and collapsed again on the pavement.

And then he heard the sweetest voice.

'One too many lemonades, sir? Come along now, let's get you home.'

He managed to pull up his head and found himself gazing into the face of a tall police officer.

He woke in hospital without any idea of the time, the day – or even where he was.

A nurse saw him struggling to raise himself on the pillows and came over.

She smiled at him. 'Take it easy, sir. You've had a nasty accident. How are you feeling this morning?'

'I've felt better. Where am I?'

'Guy's Hospital. I'm afraid we don't know your name. You had no papers or wallet on you.'

They had all been stolen, of course. 'My name's Wilde,' he said. 'Thomas Wilde. Can I get a message to someone?'

'Of course, Mr Wilde. You know we couldn't really work out what happened. It seemed you had a few drinks and you've got three nasty bruises on your head and plenty more on your body. The police think you might have been attacked and robbed.'

'I was attacked. And yes, I confess, I had had a couple of drinks.'

'Well, the police will be wanting to talk to you in due course. But for myself, I would say you should perhaps try to be a bit more abstemious in future. I notice you already had a scar on the side of your head.'

'That's an old wound.' A bullet had scraped his temple several years earlier.

'Well, be more careful. You'd be surprised how many incidents we see involve alcohol in one way or another.'

'Thank you for your very sound advice, nurse. And now that message if you would – to Miss Freya Bentall. Curse it, I can't remember the phone number . . .'

Finally, he got a message through to her and two hours later she turned up at his bedside. A nurse brought them both cups of tea.

'You've been in the wars, Tom.' She was trying to sound comforting, but her tone did not disguise her true feelings. This was serious and she was unhappy.

'Yes, I have.'

'What happened? And where was Baxter while this was going on?'

He told her all about the events at The Green Bear and the disappearance of Baxter, then the attack outside. Finally, he recalled his last sighting of Terry Adnams, swinging an ice-axe.

'Are you sure?'

'I'm not sure of anything, Freya. I also recall he mentioned doing some business in Cambridge recently.'

'And so you put two and two together.'

'I'm afraid I was barely capable of adding one and one by that stage. I just wanted to get out of there before I got caught up in something unpleasant.'

'Was this a warning, an attempt on your life or a simple robbery?'

'Probably the latter, but who knows?'

'Were you followed from The Green Bear?'

'It's possible. Perhaps probable. The place seemed full of villains.'

'Should we raid them, bring in Adnams for questioning?'

'That's a decision for you. Talk to Baxter. He knows Adnams.'

'I have a slight confession to make, Tom. I knew about Adnams and I asked Baxter to take you to the dives he frequents. The Special Branch have been taking an interest in the Adnams gang for some time. Apparently they are known for attacking people with ice-axes. It's their weapon of choice. You didn't imagine it.'

'Well, that's pretty damned relevant.'

'All the mobs have their preferred weapon. The docklands men use stevedore hooks, the Camden thugs like to swing a bottle of stout in a sock and the travellers from out Essex way will wrap a tailboard chain around your head. It's their trademark. I'm told the chains are particularly nasty. And we both know what damage can be done with an ice-axe.'

Wilde sipped his tea. 'Well, that's all very interesting, Freya, but why would the death of Everett Glasspool be the work of a villain from South London?'

'Perhaps they were hired by someone else.'

'Does that happen outside Chicago?'

'It wouldn't be the first time the Soviets have sub-contracted what Stalin calls black work. Trotsky's killer wasn't a member of the NKVD and he wasn't even Russian, but those who sent him in to do the deed were.'

'Baxter mentioned something about the worlds of crime and espionage colliding.'

'It's not so rare. The Bolsheviks in Moscow robbed banks to fund their revolution. The ends justify the means, so they say.

Adnams has form so we'll check whether he matches any finger-prints found in your rooms.'

'The ice-axe had no prints. Everyone's wearing gloves.'

'Well, I'll get a police photograph of him up to your college, see if anyone recalls seeing him. In fact, I think I'll get the Special Branch boys to pay him a visit, check his movements over the past few days and see what he has to say for himself. Meanwhile, tell me your impressions of Gus Baxter.'

'He's a piece of work, but you already knew that – which is why you use him. He consorts with people that others would shun.'

'Exactly, men who use ice-axes and tail chains.'

'He was very skilful in losing me and leaving me stranded. Good tradecraft, he'd call it. I call it damned rude and unprofessional. Deduce what you will from all that. Could be a prima facie case against him, I suppose.'

'Of what? I need more.'

'Well, don't look at me. I'm going back to Cambridge to nurse my head, look after my son and supervise my undergraduates. By the way, there were a few men who looked rather out of place at The Green Bear. One in particular caught my attention – a junior minister in the Ministry of Supply. Name of Goodrick. Len Goodrick.'

'God's teeth, what was Goodrick doing there? He works closely with Lord Portal and Michael Perrin.'

'Who?'

'Portal, controller of atomic energy production at the Ministry of Supply, and his deputy Perrin, the man who does most of the work. He would be the one to brief Goodrick.'

'I had no idea. Is this relevant?'

'We'd better find out. Anyway, what was Goodrick up to?'

'Looking for pretty young men apparently. Baxter put it succinctly when he said they're all there to buy something they can't get at home. I tried talking to Goodrick but he told me to get lost. He thought I was a reporter.'

'You said there were others. Who were they?'

'I don't know. Dressed well, sleek hair, silk ties. Playing cards for money.'

'Military men?'

'Not quite robust enough for that, but who knows. Baxter said it wasn't unusual for city types and lawyers to make their way there. Anyway, I didn't get any names, I'm afraid. Only Goodrick.'

'No matter. Can you leave hospital today?'

'I hope so.'

'You can stay at my flat in Mayfair. I have a spare room.'

'I told you, I'm going back to Cambridge.'

'One night. Please, Tom. You did promise me a week after all. I'll cook supper and we can talk things over. The gas is just about working, so it'll be warm enough, I hope. We'll look after you while you recuperate.'

'We?'

'My housekeeper, Ethel, and me. And perhaps we can get Lydia over from St Ursula's.'

It made sense. He didn't want to arrive home looking a wreck. And there was something else, wasn't there? Something in the way Freya was pleading for him to stay.

She wanted his company.

CHAPTER 11

Freya Bentall came back to the hospital after lunch and eased Wilde into a ministry car. He was sore and stiff but mobile.

On the way to her home, Wilde asked about Gus Baxter. 'Has he turned up yet and explained himself?'

'Oh yes, he's turned up. He's rather angry with you. Wants to know where you got to and why you just wandered off without him?'

'Is that his idea of a joke?'

'Don't worry, I gave him a piece of my mind. I also asked him about Len Goodrick and the other men you mentioned. He didn't add much, but he admitted he'd known about Goodrick's interest in young men but didn't think he was a security risk. I need to have more words with him about that.'

Freya had been lucky. Two houses in her street had been bombed into oblivion during the Blitz, but the building containing her first-floor apartment had survived with only the loss of its windows, which had now been replaced.

Freya showed Wilde into a large bedchamber. 'This will be yours, Tom,' she said. The room was chilly, but it had a double bed with plenty of bedclothes, a broad window onto the street and heavy drapes. 'I trust Lydia will be able to spend the night with you.'

He had already called her before leaving the hospital. She hadn't answered because she was in a lecture, but he had left a message asking her to come over. Now he asked Freya if he could use her telephone, and placed a call to home.

The new housekeeper-cum-nanny picked up.

'Janet, it's Professor Wilde. Is everything all right?'

'Yes, professor, we're fine. The college brought blankets and eiderdowns, which are very welcome. Would you like to talk to Johnny?'

'I would.'

A few moments later, a small voice came on the line. 'Hello, Daddy?'

'Hello, Johnny. I won't be back tonight, I'm afraid. Are you all right with Janet?'

'Yes, she's nice. She's taught me a card game called gin rummy. Where are you, Daddy?'

'London. I've been working here.'

'Is Mummy there?'

'No, but she will be later. I'll get her to call you. Be good, Johnny.'

'I will, Daddy.'

Janet came back on the line and Wilde explained that he had a few more things to do in London but intended to be home before the weekend. He then put down the phone and hobbled into his bedroom. He had been lucky; no bones were broken, but he was covered in bruises and lesions and he wanted nothing more than to climb into bed with two aspirins and sleep for a few more hours.

Freya followed him. 'Can I get you anything, Tom? Tea, perhaps?'

'All I want is sleep. What time is it?'

'Two forty-five.'

'Wake me about five-thirty if you would so I can freshen up before Lydia arrives.'

'Of course. I've got to go back to the office, but Ethel will be here. If you need anything, just call out to her. She's a dear.'

Ethel, her cleaning lady whose nodding acquaintance he had made ten minutes ago.

'She's managed to get some mince and is making us shepherd's pie for supper. All I've got to do is pop it in the oven when I get home and, hey presto, a feast. Gas pressure permitting.'

'I'll look forward to it. Should have my appetite back by then.'

'Good man. I'll leave you to your siesta.'

With her gone, he stripped down to his underwear and shivered as he glanced at his various injuries, then he climbed into bed, pulled half a dozen blankets around him like a chrysalis in its cocoon and was asleep within moments.

'You look a state, Tom,' Lydia said when she saw him.

'Is that your professional diagnosis, Dr Morris, or do I need a second opinion?'

'I think you can take it from me.'

They were in Freya Bentall's sitting room, the only warm part of the flat. It was comfortable, very English, with a fine Axminster carpet, slightly frayed armchairs, a large leather Chesterfield, a couple of paintings on the wall, including a rather good seascape. The wireless was tuned to the Third Programme, an orchestra playing some unidentified classical music.

'A glass of wine, perhaps?' Freya asked her guests. 'I still have a few bottles of pre-war Gevrey-Chambertin which should be very drinkable. Yes?'

'It might be wasted on me,' Wilde said.

'Oh, give it a go. Hair of the dog.'

'Thank you.'

Wilde and his wife were sitting on the sofa. A sticking plaster covered a cut above his left eye. She pushed a stray hair back into place, then leant against him and clutched his hand. 'Are you going to tell me what's going on, Tom? What happened to you?' Her voice was soft, concerned. Her tender anxiety was very welcome.

'I got beaten up and robbed on the Walworth Road in South London.'

'And I'm sure you're going to explain to me exactly why you were there.'

'I'm not sure I can.' He looked across to Freya, who could hear the conversation as she stood at the sideboard uncorking the wine.

'It's all right, Tom. She has to know the truth.'

'I suppose it has something to do with the murder in your rooms.'

He told her everything from start to finish. 'But it's over now. I'm clearly the wrong person. If there are traitors planning murder and mayhem, they'll see me coming a mile off.'

Lydia accepted a glass of red wine from Freya. 'Thank you.'

'My pleasure. And he's wrong, of course. You can see that, can't you, Lydia?'

'Convince me.'

'I need someone from outside the service, someone I can trust. Otherwise, with Everett Glasspool dead, I'm rather isolated.'

'What about your senior officers?'

'Percy Sillitoe, the director general? He's not really one of us. A copper through and through. Doesn't understand the subtleties of counter-espionage. As for Guy Liddell his deputy, I *think* I trust him, but there are nagging doubts. Everyone thought he'd get the top job because he did terrific work against the Nazis, but does he have the same commitment to holding the line against the Bolsheviks?'

'So why didn't he get the top job?'

'Why indeed? Maybe there are doubts in government. Why else would Herbert Morrison have passed him over for a time-serving plod?' She held up her glass. 'Anyway, bottoms up.'

They all drank. Wilde nodded. 'That's very fine.'

'And I'm sure you both understand that what I have been telling you is not to be repeated outside these four walls.'

'You can trust us,' Lydia said. 'And yes, of course, Tom will help you, won't you, Tom?'

Was she serious? He creased his brow and his head throbbed. 'Are you sure, Lydia?'

'You've come this far. If Freya needs you, you've got to help.'

'What about Johnny?'

'He'll be fine with Miss Spring. She comes highly recommended and she's a sweetie. Johnny already tells me he loves her.'

'Are you sure?'

'Of course I am. Why?'

'Well, what do we really know about her? She's hardly been with us any time at all.'

'Has something happened between you? You haven't picked a fight with her, have you?'

'No, of course not.'

'Well, that's settled.' She smiled at Freya. 'Everything's sorted out then.'

'And perhaps you might like to stay here, Tom. Our budget for expenses won't stretch to the kind of hotels you tend to favour.'

Wilde shrugged. 'I'm not sure I have any say but, yes, of course this would be a very convenient base for me.'

'Perfect. All we need now is for the oven to generate enough heat to cook supper. I thought we could eat on our laps with forks as it's shepherd's pie. A bit more relaxing for you, Tom.'

He poured the rest of the wine down his throat. His future had been decided for him by these two women. One day he's beaten to a pulp by strangers, the next day he's thrust into the line of fire by his wife. Hardly worth holding back on the wine.

Lydia got up and followed their hostess. 'Do let me help you, Freya.'

'Oh you've already helped me more than you can imagine, Lydia. But yes, you could do the honours with the wine. I think your man needs another glass.'

Lydia was at the sideboard with glass and bottle. A black and white photograph in a silver frame had caught her eye. It showed Freya and a younger woman in a delightful country garden.

'Who's this, Freya?'

'That's my niece, Emily. Isn't she lovely? I brought her up and she's the love of my life.'

CHAPTER 12

After supper, Lydia told Tom he would get a better night's sleep without her and, anyway, she had work to do first thing. She held him gently, kissed him goodnight and spoke softly in his ear. 'I hope you don't mind me taking Freya's part, but she needs your help, Tom, she really does. That murder in your rooms has shaken her.'

Which accorded with his own sentiments. And yet the very thought that Freya could be scared was preposterous. But then again Lydia was rarely wrong about such things and he had noted himself how keen Freya was that he should stay with her.

More than anything, he trusted Lydia's instinct and judgement and he managed a smile. 'I take your advice as always, darling.'

'And Johnny will be fine. He's in good hands. I call him every day and I would be able to tell immediately if something was wrong.'

He slept well and woke refreshed. Sitting on the edge of the bed, wrapped in blankets against the bitter cold – he gazed at the fingers of ice which had crept up the inside of the windowpanes.

Stretching his legs, rotating his arms, moving his head from side to side, he decided the aches were easing. He checked that he could walk without a limp. He was OK, a bit stiff in the joints, but that was to be expected. After dressing, he went to the kitchen, where he found Freya and Ethel.

'Ah, Tom, you're up,' Freya said. 'Another day or two in bed should see you right.'

'No, I'll have a shave and come with you to Leconfield House.'

'Are you sure? You'll need some strong coffee then.'

'No chance of a razor about the house, I suppose?'

'I'm afraid not.'

She poured him a cup, which he sipped with pleasure. 'That's better. But where in God's name do you find it?'

'Ah, that would be telling. The privileges of power, Tom.'

An hour later they arrived at Leconfield House. Gus Baxter was skulking outside Freya Bentall's office.

He glared at Wilde and shook his head. 'What happened to you? The lights go out and suddenly you're not there. Didn't wander off with young Dolly, did you?'

This was too *Alice in Wonderland* to bother replying.

'And then you get yourself beaten up by a footpad! That's what comes of slinking through South London after dark with a wallet full of cash in your pocket. The spivs and dippers would have seen you coming a mile off.'

'Get into my office, both of you,' Freya said. The switch in tone was remarkable, thought Wilde. The warm, genteel hostess of the previous evening was suddenly the no-nonsense senior MI5 officer.

She made them both sit side by side facing her across the desk.

'Now then, Baxter, I want everything you've got on Goodrick.'

'Well, what do you want me to say? I told you, everyone knows Len Goodrick plays for the other side. He doesn't shout about it, but he's never made much of a secret of it.'

'Well, I didn't know. He's blackmail material, Baxter. He's a junior in the bloody Ministry of Supply for God's sake. How could you not have known he was a security risk?'

'I was watching him. I wanted a fuller picture before bothering you with it.'

'It's your job to bother me.'

Baxter sighed and his gaze shifted to the window. He was biting his nails and Wilde couldn't help noticing how filthy they were. 'I was trying to work out whether he had any dodgy contacts. Not much point in going off half-cock with these things.'

'You tell me everything and you let me decide what's important. I want your report on Goodrick by lunchtime.'

'Your wish is my command, Mother.'

'It's not a wish, it's a bloody order. And if you ever call me that again, you'll be cashiered before day's end. Without a pension. Now get out.'

Baxter shrugged and rose. Wilde was about to follow him.

'Not you, Wilde,' Freya said, reverting to his surname. 'You stay here. I have another task for you.'

With the door closed, she afforded him a smile. 'I'm sorry about that, but it was necessary. Baxter is a law unto himself. I'd get rid of him in a heartbeat but actually he has his uses. Gets to the places no one else can.'

'So what do you have planned for me? A second day with Baxter?'

'No, I want you to meet Cecil Eagles.'

'Now I think of it, I believe I have heard his name at Cambridge. Was he one of Horace Dill's young men?'

'Indeed, he was. Also an old friend of Philip Eaton. They matriculated together. He inhabits a very different world to Baxter, but no less important for that. He's not happy about being landed with you, so you will have to engage all your charm, Tom.'

'Is he here?'

'No, he should be at home in Soho. He likes to sleep late. I'll tell him to expect you at noon. If he's in a reasonable mood, you'll probably find him quite congenial company, if a little eccentric.'

She smiled at him and suddenly he saw the truth. He wasn't here as an investigator trying to discover the name of a traitor; he was here as bait.

Cause panic in the enemy ranks and flush them out.

Bait. He was a worm wriggling on a hook. The problem with bait was, it tended to be chewed up in the initial contact.

CHAPTER 13

Cecil Eagles was still in his silk Chinese dressing gown when he opened the door to his apartment. He was a little taller than Wilde, but slightly hunched. His face was long with the mournful eyes of a bloodhound, yet it somehow contrived to be regal and haughty.

'Wilde, I presume.'

'Pleased to meet you, Eagles.'

His eyes strayed to Wilde's bruised cheek and the sticking plaster on his brow. 'I heard you'd bashed yourself. Come in, won't you. I'll only be a few minutes.'

From what Wilde had been told, he knew that Eagles must be in his late thirties and yet he could easily pass for sixty. His face and whole demeanour were lived in and somewhat world weary.

As Wilde stepped into the sitting room, he was astonished by the wealth of artworks that seemed to adorn every surface inch of Eagles's living space. A young man in shirt sleeves and bare feet ran past him, clutching shoes and various other items of clothing.

Wilde threw Eagles a questioning look.

Eagles dismissed the look with a flap of his hand. 'Oh, don't worry about Willie. She's the chambermaid. Aren't you, dear?'

'If you say so, Cecil,' Willie replied and disappeared into a corridor.

Eagles raised his limpid eyes to the heavens and let out an exaggerated sigh. 'Can't get the staff, Wilde. Or may I call you Tom? Anyway, what shall we do with you today? Mother has granted us an exeat.'

'Tom will be fine, and you just go about your business. Think of me as a ghost at your shoulder.'

'No, you will be my very special friend and to start with, we shall enjoy some art. There's a gallery opening I must attend, just off Piccadilly. How about that? For the moment, sit yourself down, enjoy my pictures and I'll be back in two shakes of a lamb's prick.'

Wilde sank into the sofa and took a closer look at Eagles's works. Was that a Renoir? His gaze drifted to the wall on the right opposite the window and alighted on a field of lavender: a Monet, perhaps? On a stand near the door, he spotted a little statue of a ballet dancer. Wilde was no expert but they all looked extremely fine and probably rather expensive.

Freya's flat was also comfortable and very English, but this place was at another level of sumptuousness. It was, indeed, a little gallery in its own right – and a very good one at that. Cecil Eagles was clearly in no need of the money he received from the ministry for his work as an MI5 agent.

Ten minutes later, he arrived back, dressed in a fine suit with a cravat tumbling foppishly at his neck rather than a tie. 'All set, Tom?'

The new Chalke Gallery was in Albemarle Street, occupying a prime space not far from Brown's Hotel. Despite the bitter weather outside, it was full and noisy with a large band of art lovers enjoying the free white wine and the company of friends without bothering too much with the paintings on the walls.

Wilde looked about him appreciatively.

'This place is a marvel, Tom,' Eagles said. 'At last it feels as if London is coming alive again. One little private gallery and saleroom might not seem much to the layman, but it means there's something to live for – some hope for the future after the last seven years. Some beauty in a broken world.'

'You'll have to talk me through it.'

'Don't you have any art?'

'A few paintings, but only one with a name you might recognise – a Winslow Homer I inherited from my father.'

'Well, that's certainly not to be sneezed at. I'd love to see it one day.' Eagles lifted his magisterial nose towards the far side of the room. 'You see that little fellow over there, the one with the ridiculous spectacles and the vast overcoat?'

'Yes, I see him.'

'That's Stanley Spencer the pornographer.'

'I've seen his work, he's not a pornographer.'

'No, of course he's not, but that's what Alfie Munnings has been calling him. Apparently a scrapbook with some private pictures he made, nudes of his wives, has found its way into Munnings's grubby mitts and he's not happy. Haven't seen them myself but I'm sure they're perfectly respectable – nothing an art student wouldn't do in life class. But the upshot is that Munnings and Spencer are not the best of chums. Frightful prude and pompous bore, Munnings, but he's not here today, thank the heavens.'

'I take it you're not an admirer.'

'Well, that's the strange thing, Tom, I confess I actually rather like Alfred's paintings.'

'May I ask you something, Cecil – why exactly are we here? What does a little art gallery in Albemarle Street have to do with your work for the service?'

'Perhaps nothing, perhaps everything. My job is to protect the country – and you can find enemies of the state in the most unusual places. They are like bedbugs, inhabiting all sorts of nooks and crannies. You'll find them in the finest furnishings and they're the devil's own job to get rid of. Anyway, just follow me around, Tom, and you might learn something.'

Or not, thought Wilde.

A waiter with a tray of drinks passed into view. Eagles took a glass, Wilde declined.

'On the wagon, Tom?'

'A bit early in the day.'

Cecil's hangdog eyes widened. 'Well, look who it is, the lady of the hour herself. Do you see that gorgeous creature over there, Tom? Do you know Lady Chalke?'

'I've heard of her.'

'Then you must meet her. Vivienne's a darling and she knows everyone who's anyone in this town and this is her gallery. Some of the better paintings are from her collection. Well, her ghastly husband's, anyway. He just acquires as an investment, but she tells him what to buy. Come on, let's say hello.'

Vivienne Chalke oozed Bloomsbury. She had that elite, entitled look of Woolf, Bell, Strachey and Grant. It occurred to Wilde that she not only *thought* herself above the rest of humanity, she knew it. Her hair was untamed, her gown flowed from another, pre-austerity age and smoke wafted from a ridiculously long cigarette holder.

She held out a limp hand. 'And you are?'

'Tom Wilde.'

'Well, I'm very pleased to meet you, Mr Wilde. Can I ask what your interest is? Are you a dealer or a collector?'

'I'm a friend of Cecil Eagles.'

She turned and smiled at Eagles. 'He's a bit older than your usual boys, Cecil.' She turned back to Wilde. 'And what do you do, apart from following this reprobate around?'

'I teach history at Cambridge.'

'How simply wonderful for you.' She didn't sound remotely interested, let alone impressed.

'Yes,' he said, 'yes, it is. And what do you do, Lady Chalke?'

'Well, clearly I'm a gallerist now. I also daub a bit, though I wouldn't dare show any of my work to the picky Cecil Eagles. He's insufferably rude.'

Eagles feigned an expression of wonder and joy. 'Darling, I didn't know you painted. You must show me some samples one day. Expose yourself to me. I'm sure you are an undiscovered genius – and I want to be the one who reveals you to the world.'

'What utter tosh, Cecil. You're not going near my paintings because you'd flatter me to my face and then go behind my back and tell everyone else how hideous it all was. I know you too well. Anyway, I want you to bring this fabulous handsome man to our little celebration cocktail party this evening. You will come, won't you, Mr Wilde? Just an informal gathering. Drinkypoos. No need to dress.'

Wilde turned to Eagles. 'Well, Cecil?'

'Of course you must come, dear man.'

Was he being honest or was he horrified? No matter, Wilde was going. 'Then thank you, Lady Chalke. I should be delighted.'

She smiled at him and touched his hand with her long elegant fingers. 'My pleasure, Tom. And by evening's end we shall have turned you from a dusty don into a connoisseur of all things artistic. Now if you'll excuse me, I must circulate.'

With that, she wafted off, her hair and multi-layered gown seeming to float behind her. Wilde's eyes couldn't help but follow the woman, until he caught sight of someone else: a man with a rather remarkable suntan. A man he was sure he knew from somewhere.

Cecil Eagles inclined his head towards Wilde's ear with a whisper. 'Don't tell a soul, Tom, but the fabulously wealthy and snobbish Vivienne Chalke is a rabid commie.'

Wilde's eyes were elsewhere. The suntanned man seemed awfully familiar, from a few years back. 'Do you know that fellow, Cecil?'

'Should I?'

The memory came flooding back. 'He was at the Cavendish before the war. I had a friend who worked there and I remember being introduced to him. What was his bloody name? Something German. Now I remember – Rheinhaus. Basil Rheinhaus. He's a scientist. Excuse me while I go and say hello.'

'Why on earth would you want to talk to a dreary scientist? Endless streams of equations and calculus. Utterly tedious.'

'We have a mutual friend.'

Eagles pulled back his shoulders and met Wilde's eyes. 'Professor Wilde, you have accompanied me to a gorgeous gallery at Mother's request. It is full of beautiful people. Ignore the dullard. Leave the scientist to his test tube and microscope.'

'I can't help wondering what he's doing here.'

Eagles swept a hand through his overlong hair. 'I imagine Vivienne invited him because he has money and likes to buy paintings as an investment. Certainly not for his witty repartee and charming company. If he's a scientist he's probably made a fortune inventing and patenting some dreary machine. A new sort of rivet, perhaps. By the look of the fellow I'd guess he's been spending his ill-gotten loot sunning himself in Tahiti. He's here because art dealers have to suck up to people like that – wealthy men with more cash than taste.'

Wilde couldn't work out why the presence of Rheinhaus was so unsettling. Perhaps it was just the healthy tan he sported at a time when everyone else was as pallid as death. 'Well, I'm going to find out.'

'Suit yourself. Mother told me to hold your hand, but you're an adult so I can't really stop you.'

'Mr Rheinhaus?'

The man turned sharply, surprised at the voice coming from behind his left ear. 'Yes?'

'My name's Thomas Wilde, we met a few years ago. The Cavendish.'

'Really? I don't recall.' The English was good with an American accent, but the hint of German was still discernible.

'You worked with my friend Geoff Lancing.'

'What of it?'

'I just wanted to say hello.'

'Well, hello . . . and goodbye.' Rheinhaus turned away without a word.

Wilde reached out and pulled his sleeve. 'Don't turn your back on me.'

Rheinhaus swung around, his eyes on fire. 'Really? Who the hell are you?'

'I told you.'

'Do you have a name?'

'I told you that, too. Wilde. Tom Wilde.' Wilde was angry now.

The man with the tan pushed out his chest. 'I've had enough of this.'

There was nothing more to be said. The man had no wish to know him. The encounter had left him with an uneasy sensation. Why had Basil Rheinhaus been so unhappy about being recognised?

He momentarily lost sight of Cecil Eagles, then spotted him across the room in conversation with the artist Stanley Spencer.

Wilde took a moment to look at the pictures, then Eagles was back at his side. 'I got the feeling your conversation with your old scientist chum didn't go too well.'

'Very observant of you, Cecil. No, we didn't get on like a house on fire. There's something about the man. Do *you* know anything about him?'

'Never seen him or heard of him. I was more of a classics man myself. Left science to the bores, the ones without any conversation.'

'But why is he here? Why is he so bloody suntanned?'

'I'm really not sure I care. Come on, enough of this, let's go and find some lunch? The Ritz, I think – and you can pay.'

CHAPTER 14

Over coffee and brandy at the end of a meal full of inconsequential tittle-tattle, roast beef and red wine Cecil Eagles finally got to the point. 'So tell me, Tom, what's this all about? Why am I supposed to nursemaid you?'

'Didn't Bentall tell you? The word is out that Truman realises he messed up and he'll be bringing back some version of the OSS. Bentall's trying to mend a few broken fences between London and Washington by giving me a little re-training.'

Eagles snorted. 'Utter tosh. I don't believe a word of it. Mother is up to something – and so are you, Tom.'

'What can I say? If she's up to something then she hasn't told me.'

Eagles looked up at the wall clock and rose from the table. 'I've got to go. I'll leave you with the bill and see you in Kensington this evening. Thank you for a delightful luncheon, Tom.'

Freya Bentall slapped the first edition of the *Evening News* on her desk. 'Page two, column five.'

Wilde picked up the newspaper and turned the page. GOODRICK RESIGNS the headline said. It was a short piece, only three paragraphs long. The story was that Mr Leonard Goodrick, MP, had regrettably left his post at the Ministry of Supply because of a family situation. He thanked Mr Attlee for the faith he had placed in him and assured the country that the Labour government retained his wholehearted support.

'What's this about?'

'The *Herald* and the *Express* have both put together a story about his homosexual adventures, but they won't run it because Attlee has slapped a D-notice on them. National security.'

'Just as you were saying to Baxter.'

'Goodrick is deeply involved with the work presently going on at Harwell, the atomic energy research establishment. They're building an experimental nuclear pile there. You don't need to be Einstein to suspect what the ultimate aim might be.'

'A British A-bomb.'

'Quite. But I didn't say that and nor will you.'

'So that's why he was so concerned that I might be a newspaperman.'

'I want you to go and talk to him today. He's at home in Fulham. We need to know who tipped off the *Express* and *Herald*. Is this just an everyday newspaper sting or has he been set up by an enemy? In particular, was there an attempt at blackmail before the papers got the story?'

'Why don't you send one of your regular officers?'

'Because I want to know whether Baxter had any part in Goodrick's downfall. Why did they just happen to be at The Green Bear at the same time?'

'Is Goodrick married?'

'Separated, lives alone.'

'Give me his address, I'll go now. But first, there's another thing I want to mention. Cecil took me to Lady Chalke's gallery opening and I chanced upon a man I met before the war, a scientist called Basil Rheinhaus.'

'Really, that's rather interesting. I heard he was back.'

'Do you know the name?'

'Of course. He's a highly respected nuclear bod. He went to America with Tube Alloys and was at Los Alamos. Did you talk to him at the gallery?'

'I tried to, but our conversation didn't go well. He seemed uncomfortable at being recognised and he got my back up.'

'I suppose you originally met him at the Cavendish in Cambridge?'

'Yes, through a mutual friend, Geoff Lancing.'

'You might also know that Rheinhaus is originally Swiss German but is now a naturalised American. He's been with the US team in the Pacific Ocean – in the vicinity of Bikini Atoll.'

'Which explains the suntan.'

'Rather better weather. Sunshine and big bangs. Rather odd that you should come across two men with an interest in atomic science in a short space of time. See if Goodrick knows Rheinhaus.'

'If he'll talk to me, of course.'

'Oh, you'll find a way to charm him.'

'By the way, apropos of nothing, Cecil told me that Vivienne Chalke is a communist.'

Freya laughed. 'That's hardly a secret, Tom. They all flirt with it, all her set. First they were Fabians, then Bolsheviks, although some went the other way in the thirties and got into bed with Adolf. Right or left, a fellow traveller is a fellow traveller, nothing more, and is easily discountable. Anyway, it's Eagles I'm interested in, not her.'

The house was small in a side street which had managed to avoid the bombing but still looked down at heel. No one had bothered to shovel the snow from the road or pavements in recent days and it was trodden and slushy and dirty.

Wilde checked he had the right address and walked up the short path to the front door. He had already noted that the curtains were all closed, both ground and first floor.

There was no bell, so he knocked at the front door. There was no reply, so he knocked again. And again.

Finally, he heard the soft pad of footsteps. He bent down and pulled back the letterbox. 'Mr Goodrick,' he called. 'I need to speak to you.'

'Go away, damn you.'

'Please, I'm not a reporter.'

'There's something in your voice. Where have I heard it?'

'The Green Bear in Walworth. You thought I was a reporter, but I'm not. I repeat, I'm *not* press. I'm with the security service. I understand you're under immense pressure, but if you'd just give me a couple of minutes of your time.'

'Go to hell. Attlee's got my resignation letter, which is all he needs. I shall give up my seat in due course and disappear into blessed obscurity. Is that enough for you?'

'I beg you, Mr Goodrick, let's keep this part unofficial. If we can talk, I won't take notes and there will be no recording. I know you're separated, but you surely have a family. Perhaps your parents are still with us. They will be confused at the moment, and they will want to know that you are leaving politics for the best of motives. If you assist me, it can only help you – and, perhaps, the country and your family.'

There was silence on the other side of the door for half a minute, then Wilde sensed a shuffling and heard the key in the lock.

He was in his pyjamas, dressing gown, thick socks, woollen gloves and slippers. He was unshaven and his hair was unkempt. He had a half-smoked cigarette between his lips. Taking a step back, he gestured with his open palm to Wilde to enter the hallway.

'I can't remember, did you tell me your name?'

'I'm Tom Wilde.'

'And you're what? MI5, Special Branch?'

'Something like that.'

'Who do you report to?'

'I'm not at liberty to say.'

'Sillitoe ultimately, I suppose. Oh God, not Freya bloody Bentall?'

'Why would you mention her?'

'I don't know. Intuition, perhaps. The sense that there's some Soviet element to this and she's the expert on Moscow. Someone was certainly out to get me. Anyway, come in. I have nothing to offer you, I'm afraid, and no source of heat.'

They settled into the sitting room, which was dark from the closed curtains and barely warmer than outside.

'You mentioned a Soviet element, Mr Goodrick.'

He shrugged. 'Pretty obvious, isn't it? Who else wants our atomic secrets? My responsibility involves auditing and approving money and equipment for Harwell and the other nuclear installations. Two days ago it was suggested to me that I might like to share certain information in return for my private life being kept private. I had no hesitation in telling the wretched swine to go to hell, but I knew I was done for. Defiance was never going to save me. Next thing I know, I've had a call from the *Daily Express*. Then Number Ten said I had to resign but that they could kill the newspaper story with a D-notice. So now here I am – an example to anyone else who might try to defy Comrade Stalin and his chums.'

'But what did you have to offer them? You're a politician not a scientist.'

'You know, I'm not at all sure what they wanted. Supply details, I suppose. Just to have their claws deep in me in case they ever needed anything. Keep me on side, a way into Harwell. But they might have been better off with a civil servant than me.'

Perhaps they already had a civil servant, thought Wilde. 'Casting their net as wide as possible.'

'I'm sure you're right. We've been too forgiving with the Reds. Filthy bastards.' He drew deep on his cigarette. It was almost down to the last half-inch. He blew out smoke then immediately took another drag and threw the burning remains of the item into the cold, dead fireplace.

'Anyway, you did what you had to do. I'm only sorry that it has been at the expense of your career.'

'My own bloody fault. Anyway, what were you doing at the Bear, Tom? Spying on me, I suppose.'

'No, I had no idea who you were at first. I was interested because you seemed out of place among that crew.'

'Why were you there then?'

'I was there with a friend. He thought I'd find the place interesting.'

'And did you? Also, what's happened to your head? Walk into a door, perhaps?'

'I was beaten and robbed after leaving the Bear.'

Goodrick laughed. 'They would have spotted you as a mark straightaway. Just like someone did with me.'

'Perhaps we could get down to business now. Who tried to recruit you to the Soviet cause? Someone from the embassy, perhaps?'

'Oh, a Russian certainly.'

'Did he have a name? I take it we're talking about a man.'

'Yes, it was a man. He said I could call him Ivan. Very funny.'

'Why didn't you report his approach immediately?'

He laughed again. 'Guess.'

'Because you couldn't afford to have your sexuality revealed.'

'Very clever, Tom Wilde.'

'But now you can give us his details. Full description, where you met him. Testify against him if we can find him.'

'I suppose I can. But do I want to? Do I want my private life paraded any more than it is being already? I'd probably end up with a longer time in jail anyway. These judges, they can just about put up with treason – but moral turpitude? Oh no, send the depraved bugger down and throw away the key. No, that's not the way forward for me. You do what you like with the information, but count me out.'

'At least describe the man. Where did you meet him?'

'He came to me here. Very smiley chap, very friendly, you might almost call him charming. Like you, he asked if I could spare him two minutes of my time. Well, as an MP, I'm pretty used to people coming up to me with questions, proposals and problems and I always try to listen. That's the job.'

'Describe him.'

'Muscular fellow, about your age, full head of hair. I did notice that he had a remarkably western taste in fine tailoring. Oh, and he came bearing gifts.' He indicated a sideboard near the cold hearth where an empty bottle stood. 'Vodka, a gift from the people of the Soviet Union. And then he gave me his second gift – a foolscap envelope with photographs in it.'

'Ah.'

'Graphic, horribly compromising photographs. Ivan said they had plenty of copies and would be sending them to Downing Street and the newspapers. I can never show my face in public again.'

'One day it will be forgotten.'

'Will it?'

Wilde managed a grim smile. He felt for this man. It would be difficult to convince him that all would be well at some time in the distant future. He changed the subject. 'Do you know my colleague Gus Baxter?'

'Baxter? Yes, I know of him and we say hello in passing. We frequent the same dives and I've seen him around, but he isn't really my type. Was he the friend who took you to the Bear?'

'He was. Merely a casual acquaintance, you say – but how did you first meet? Did he introduce himself?'

'As I recall he offered to buy me a drink in some Soho joint, or maybe it was the other way round. Anyway, it was never going to go beyond that. His filthy fingernails, for heaven's sake. And he smells unwashed.'

'There was another man I wanted to ask you about. Basil Rheinhaus, the atomic scientist. Name mean anything to you?'

Goodrick shrugged, then rose from his armchair, clutching his dressing gown around him. 'Excuse me a moment, I'm dying for a pee.'

Without another word, he was gone from the room. Wilde stayed where he was, frozen to the spot. He heard soft but hurried footsteps on the stairs. Floorboards creaked. A door slammed shut.

Moments later, there was a single gunshot. Then silence.

CHAPTER 15

The body was sprawled on the bed. Len Goodrick had put the muzzle of the pistol in his mouth, pointing upwards into the brain. There was a great deal of blood and other matter on the pillow and bedhead and wall.

Photographs were scattered around. Happy photographs of his family which he must have been looking at in his despair before the knock at the door temporarily halted his suicide plans.

Wilde felt sick to his stomach. Was there anything he might have done, anything he might have said to save Goodrick's life? Perhaps not, but he should have guessed what was in the poor man's head and he should have made more of an effort to help.

On the floor, torn in half, was another picture, with Goodrick clearly visible and identifiable, naked, mounting another man from behind. Wilde recognised him as the young man from The Green Bear. The one that Dolly had called Julian. Julian the pretty boy.

A lover not just of Len Goodrick but Gus Baxter too if what Dolly said was true.

Wilde stood looking at the corpse for a whole minute. The massive damage to the head told him that there was nothing to be gained in searching for a pulse or calling an ambulance. Finally, he went back down to the hall where he had noticed a telephone. First he called Freya at Leconfield House, then he called the police, gave them a brief rundown of events, hung up, and quietly left the house.

At Freya's insistence he went to her office, bringing the torn photograph with him, and gave her a fuller version of his meeting with Len Goodrick and his final moments.

Freya Bentall shook her head. 'Number Ten is furious, Tom. "That's all we bloody need" was the quote that was passed on to me by my secretary after she informed them of Goodrick's suicide.'

Wilde was aghast. 'A man is dead, Freya, his family will be heartbroken – and the government is worried about *itself*? Good God, what is the world coming to?'

'Shocking, I agree – it just goes to show how bad things are becoming. The centre cannot hold.'

'Well, I'm certainly falling apart.'

'One more thing. Did you get a chance to ask Goodrick about Rheinhaus?'

'I asked, but he didn't reply. I thought he was about to tell me, but instead he wandered off and put a bullet in his head. I think you need to talk to Rheinhaus himself urgently. For myself, I've had enough for a bloody lifetime today. I'm going to curl up with something strong and make an early night of it.'

'You can't. You're going with Cecil Eagles to Vivienne Chalke's little event. I want to know who's there, who he talks to, the whole shebang.'

'No, that's asking too much.' Apart from anything else, it sounded deadly. But he knew he would go.

Wilde made it to Kensington at eight. On the way there, his mind kept drifting to Harwell, the atomic energy research establishment near Oxford. Clearly, the Soviets had been trying to find a route into that top secret institution. And they thought they had found a way, through Len Goodrick. That was what this was all about; Moscow wanted its own A-bomb and they were looking for secrets.

Goodrick's flat refusal to betray his country had brought terrible vengeance down on his head.

Yes, this was all about the atomic bomb.

Which made him wonder what he was doing following Cecil Eagles to a meaningless cocktail party. Unless, perhaps, Rheinhaus was there.

The Chalkes' house was a large white-painted building to the south of Kensington High Street. Beautifully presented, almost a mansion, reeking of great wealth.

Cecil Eagles had arrived already and the place was heaving. The crush of bodies gave the main room a warmth it might not otherwise have had.

With nothing else on offer, Wilde grabbed a glass of champagne from the tray of a passing waiter and edged his way into the throng. Eagles saw him and hailed him.

'Tom Wilde, you made it. I wasn't sure you wanted to come.'

'Wouldn't have missed it for the world, Cecil.'

'See that fellow over there, the rather dour one. That's Harry Pollitt, general secretary of the British Communist Party. HMV, I call him. His Master's Voice. Ties himself in knots trying to obey the conflicting diktats of Stalin and the Comintern. One moment he was for the war against Hitler, the next he was against, and then he was for again. And here he is, hobnobbing with London's arty-farties. The grim little bugger has no shame. No bloody shame whatsoever. Do you want to meet him?'

'Not particularly.'

'This place is riddled with them, fashionable commies who keep the working classes at arm's length, which is why I come here and inhabit this world, to keep an eye on them.'

'Shouldn't you keep your voice down a bit?'

'Oh, they know who I am. Do you think they haven't got moles inside MI5?'

'Really? And who might they be?'

Eagles shook his head. 'Well, if I knew that, old chap, I'd put the finger on them like a shot. By the way, did you hear the frightful news about that junior minister, Goodrick? Blighter's only gone and topped himself. Apparently there were some saucy snaps of him doing the rounds.'

'Not sure I've heard of the man,' Wilde lied.

Eagles met his eyes and affected a knowing smile. 'Is that the best you can do? I thought you were an old hand at this game.'

'I have no idea what you're talking about, Cecil.'

'And I'm the King of Prussia. Anyway, let's hunt down some proper drinks and see if we can't find dear Vivienne. I rather got the idea she took a bit of a fancy to you.'

They found some brandy, but there was no immediate sign of Vivienne Chalke. Wilde drank slowly; he didn't want a repeat of the night at The Green Bear. He was in two minds. One part told

him this was a waste of his time, the other part made him wonder whether this might just be the perfect place to be. He sensed
conspiracy and intrigue behind the benign masks of these fellow-
travelling actors and artists.

At first he tried to stay with Cecil Eagles, but inevitably
they parted and joined other conversations. It was the nature of
the event.

Finally, he bumped into Vivienne Chalke, who was standing
in the centre of the room regaling a group of acquaintances with
reminiscences of Pablo Picasso. 'My dears, such a small man, but
such an enormous ... brush.' They laughed loud and long and
Wilde suspected they had all heard the joke before.

She turned and came face to face with Wilde. 'Well, it's my new
friend. Tom something.'

'Wilde.'

'And are you?'

'Only when my students make me very angry.'

'I suppose you've heard that one a few times before.'

'I've lose count.'

'Have you met my husband yet?'

'I'm afraid not.'

'Lucky you. Avoid the ghastly man at all costs. He's simply hideous. An absolute banker. I only married him for his filthy lucre.
I think he was here somewhere but he's probably upstairs fucking some of the waitresses. When the revolution comes I shall
demand he's the first capitalist in front of the firing squad and I
shall insist on giving him the coup de grâce.'

'So a loving marriage then. How does he feel about you?'

'Who cares, so long as he keeps signing the cheques. God, it's
cold in this house. My husband might be one of the richest men
in the country but he seems unable to get coal delivered and the
gas is reduced to a trickle. What's the point in it all, Tom Wilde?
Wouldn't you like to see a revolution? Surely life in Moscow is
better than this.'

'I wouldn't bet the house on that.'

'Remind me, what is it you do?'

Wilde laughed. 'You weren't very impressed when I told you, so maybe I'll say something else. How about secret agent? Professional assassin?'

'Oh yes, you were a history professor. But if I'm honest, I rather prefer your second and third choice career options. Much more thrilling. Anyway, that's not the reason I invited you here. The thing is, I like your face. I very much want to paint you, Tom Wilde. Can I? Not this evening of course, but soon. Do say yes.'

'Can I think about it?'

'Thank you, thank you. Together we'll make wonderful art.' She leant forwards and swathed her exotic body around him. He was engulfed by a cloud of Coty powder and French scent.

And then she was gone.

Now where was Cecil Eagles? His eyes scanned the packed room, finally coming to rest near the far door. He was talking to a man and suddenly they were both looking his way. Wilde put up a hand to say 'here I am', then began to ease his way through the melee. As he did so, Eagles's companion vanished through the doorway, but Wilde had already recognised him.

It was a face he had seen before. Just the once. In the steamy warmth of Magdalene College's combination room in Cambridge.

A Russian who called himself Lazar Lukin, a member of a delegation from the Soviet Ministry of Education. A Russian with a taste for expensive English tailoring. A man, perhaps, with a side interest in blackmail and espionage.

All circumstantial evidence, perhaps, but it didn't seem impossible that Lazar Lukin was 'Ivan', the Russian who tried to turn Len Goodrick into a traitor and drove him to suicide.

'Who was that, Cecil?'

'God, I'm not sure I can stand this place a moment longer. The unspeakable types Vivienne Chalke surrounds herself with.'

'He looked familiar.'

'What? Who are you talking about, Tom?'

'The man you were chatting with less than two minutes ago. He just skedaddled through the door when he saw me. I'm sure

I've seen him before in Cambridge as part of a Soviet education delegation. I recall his name began with L. Lazar something.'

'I didn't catch his name. Fellow just came up to me and asked where he should go for a piss. He sounded East European – most probably Russian. I really don't know where Vivienne finds half the people she invites to these events. You say you know him? Well, be careful, Tom. These Soviet delegations are little more than covers for spying. I'd better keep an eye on him. Honestly, the people Vivienne knows!'

'Actually, I think I'll go and look for him. I know he wants to have a chat with me about student exchanges, so why not now?'

Eagles shook his head. 'Damn it, Tom, you're a law unto yourself.'

Wilde found Lazar Lukin in the corridor outside the main hall where the party was held.

'Isn't it . . . yes, it's you, Professor Wilde.'

'Good evening, Mr Lukin.'

'Well, of all the gin joints in all the world.'

'You said you'd find me.'

'I did say that, didn't I? Well, well, this is a pleasant surprise.'

'I take it you are an acquaintance of the Chalkes.'

'Am I?'

'This is their house, full of fellow travellers. Must almost feel like home to you.'

'I'm afraid you've lost me, Mr Wilde. I am here with Ambassador Zarubin before heading off to Oxford.'

'No matter. I saw you with Cecil Eagles and thought you might like to discuss student exchanges. I'm sure my college would be delighted to have a few Soviet visitors for a term or two and also send some back to Moscow in exchange. Modern language students, historians, natural science bods, that sort of thing. Good for world peace and understanding among nations, yes?'

'Of course. That is precisely the sort of thing I am looking for. You're obviously the right man, comrade professor. Shall we arrange a meeting? A place of your choosing to work out some firm proposals? Your London home or a hotel, perhaps, when I return. What are you doing next week?'

'Oh, lecturing undergraduates. That's what I do for a living. Give me a number where I can reach you and I'll let you know a good time.'

'You can leave a message for me at the Soviet Embassy.'

'And your first name – Ivan, wasn't it?'

'No, why would you think that, Professor Wilde? My first name is Lazar. Lazar Lukin.'

'Oh, I thought that was what your old friend Cecil Eagles called you.'

'Really? I hardly think so.'

CHAPTER 16

It was late when he got back to Freya Bentall's flat and he was hungry and chilled to the bone. She offered him leftovers from the previous evening's meal – no more than scraps. It didn't look appetising. 'I'm afraid my privilege only runs so far,' she said. 'I have a tin of corned beef and a couple of turnips, but it's Ethel's day off and I'm not a very inventive cook. Your choice, Tom.'

'The remains of the shepherd's pie will be just fine.'

'Good man. Do you know what I long for above all else in these days of rationing, Tom, even above decent food?'

'Go on.'

'Soap. I just wish the common man and woman in the street and on the train could be given the wherewithal to wash again. I never quite get used to the overpowering stench of sweaty human bodies.'

'Worse in summer, surely. Less sweating at this time of year.'

'You'd be surprised. But enough of my complaints. Tomorrow I want you to go in a completely different direction from Cecil and his louche contacts. Now it will all be about trade unionists and communists, who are often one and the same person nowadays.'

'I'm pretty sure they were all at Kensington this evening.'

'Vivienne Chalke's friends? They're all dinner party revolutionaries. They love talking the talk about equality and fraternity and they're more than happy to express solidarity with the working man, but they'd be horrified if their cosy world was ever disturbed by a real blood-red insurrection. Because, of course, they would be first against the wall.'

'Harry Pollitt was there.'

'The exception proves the rule. Anyway, what did you discover?'

'I discovered Cecil Eagles lying to me. I've told you about Lazar Lukin from the educational delegation. Well, he was there, talking with Cecil.'

'And Cecil lied to you how?'

'He told me he didn't know Lukin, that the Russian was simply asking him the way to the lavatory. A little while later I spoke to

Lukin and he almost seemed to confirm that he and Cecil know each other. Now how could that be?'

'I'll talk to Cecil.'

'There was something else. Len Goodrick described the man who tried to blackmail him with the obscene photos as a Russian with a taste for expensive English tailoring. Well, that describes Lukin.'

'Well, that *is* interesting. I'll see if we can have him watched.'

'Lukin still wants to talk to me. I can arrange a meeting.'

'That would help. We can follow him from there. But first, I'm assigning you to Shadox Stone tomorrow. He knows the working-class world inside out and produces useful information . . .'

'But?'

'But, yes, I harbour doubts about him. See what you can find out. I am already indebted to you for your assessments of Baxter and Eagles.'

'I'm not sure how much I've helped. I can't have put your mind at ease about either of them.'

'You'd be surprised. Anyway, that's enough for this evening. Just time for a little drink – and then we both need a good night's sleep, because we'll be rising at four.'

'Oh, and Vivienne Chalke asked me to sit for her. She wants to paint my portrait.'

Freya Bentall raised a sceptical eyebrow. 'Lucky you, Tom. What she really means is that she wants to get you into bed.'

'You're a cynic, Freya.'

'I'm a realist. I know a bit about Lady Chalke. Tell you what, why don't you take her up on it? Perhaps you'll learn a thing or two.'

'I'll tell Lydia what you said.'

'I mean the portrait stuff. Not get into bed with her. I'd rather like to know more about her, particularly her link to Lukin.'

'One more thing, Freya: what's really going on? Is this about moles in MI5 – or is it about the atom bomb? What exactly are we fighting?'

'For our lives, Tom. For our very existence.'

'Then come clean with me. This is about the Harwell atomic establishment, isn't it? Moscow is trying to infiltrate the project?'

'Of course.'

'Then why am I in London?'

'Because it starts here, with Westminster and Whitehall – with us. Harwell is well-protected physically. The police detachment at the site are always on full alert and word has been sent to them to double their security checks.'

'I'd like to go to Harwell. Is that possible?'

'It might be possible if I considered it either relevant or helpful, but I don't. I need to know who in MI5 is working for Moscow. And if the path leads on to Harwell, then we'll see.'

Her reply did nothing to ease his concerns. He had made a promise so he would stay and do her bidding. More than that, he now understood the critical importance of his mission. 'Where's that drink you offered?'

'Here.' She held up a bottle of Scotch. 'I called in a favour to get this. It's all for you – but take it easy. We've got a very early start.'

Shadox Stone was lounging back with his feet on Freya's desk when she arrived with Wilde at the office just before dawn. He didn't bother to shift himself, but took a deep drag of a thin roll-up and kept his eyes closed.

'Morning, Mother,' he said without shifting or even looking at her.

She pushed his feet off the desk, snatched the cigarette from between his fingers and stubbed it out in her ashtray.

'Get up, Stone.'

'And there was me thinking you loved me like a long-lost son.'

Slowly, he got to his feet. He was wearing a raincoat and a flat cap, both of which must have seen better days. He was thin, his face pinched and he could have passed for a bookie's runner, but Wilde already knew that there was a great deal more to Shadox Stone than met the eye; his father might have been a humble factory worker who died in the First World War, but Shadox had secured a scholarship to Cambridge and emerged with a first-class degree.

He nodded to Wilde, 'Morning, your worship.'

'The name's Tom Wilde.'

'I know. Mother told me. It seems I'm to hold your hand today and show you what's what among the lower orders. Maybe we'll get you a whippet as cover, shall we?'

'Go on, both of you. Get out. You know very well what's wanted of you, Stone.'

'Well, the thanks I get.'

A car was waiting for them on Curzon Street. 'Smithfield,' Stone ordered the driver, then turned to Wilde. 'Get a nice bacon sandwich there to start the day right. Meet some real working men.'

'And then what?'

'Communist Party headquarters if you like? See if they'll talk to us. Or there's a big union meeting out in Docklands. There'll be calls for a strike. Be interesting to see who the troublemakers are. That suit you?'

'Is there any point to all this?'

'You tell me, sunshine, you're the one who wants to be shown the ropes. Leastwise, that's the way I heard it. We're doing you a favour, yes?'

The bacon roll was good. It came from a window on the far side of the great meat market. A woman in a greasy apron was frying thick rashers on a hot plate in a space no bigger than a cupboard and serving them up – complete with HP sauce and a cup of sweet tea – to an endless stream of market porters and meat cutters finishing the night shift.

'Ah, that's better,' Shadox Stone said as he swallowed the last of his breakfast. 'Best start to the day.' He lit a roll-up, took a deep drag and then asked Wilde if he wanted one.

Wilde declined the offer. 'Seems you've got London sorted out, Mr Stone.'

'I can show you the best late-night drinking holes and the lowest dives. But bacon baps? This is the place to come. Well, if you can't get bacon at Smithfield, where can you, Mr Wilde?'

They stood side by side, sipping their steaming cups of tea.

'Maybe docklands,' Wilde suggested.

'Yes, you can probably get one there too.'

'No, I meant, take me to the docks. Show me how the unions work and what you're looking for.'

He shook his head. 'No, I don't think so. Let's just call it quits. You asked what this was all for and, on reflection, there doesn't seem to be a good answer to that. So you go your way and I'll go mine. We both know this is a bloody waste of time.'

'Miss Bentall insists I accompany you.'

'I won't tell her if you don't. The thing is, you see, I have real work to do. People I need to talk to – on my own.'

'You mean I'll get in the way?'

'To be brutally frank, sunshine, that's exactly what I mean. So just finish off your cuppa and then the day's yours. Go off and catch a matinee at the flicks. Whatever you want – make a snowman if you're that way inclined. I'm sure you've got better things to do than hang on my coat-tails.'

Wilde was pretty sure he had, but he didn't like being given the brush-off. That was what Gus Baxter had done to him in The Green Bear, wasn't it? Obviously word had found its way around Leconfield House that there was a nosy, irritating Yank in the office and no one wanted to know.

'All right, I'll just find my way back to Curzon Street and repeat this conversation to Miss Bentall. See what she has to say.'

Stone was silent for a few moments, then suddenly he took his cigarette out of his mouth and stubbed it out on Wilde's coat, twisting it until the sparks died and the ash fell, leaving a burn mark on his collar. 'Going to tell tales to teacher, are you? You fucking do that, sunshine. You do that.'

Wilde was much stronger. He could have floored him with one punch, but he merely gripped Stone's wrist and pushed him away. 'Be careful, Stone. I like this coat.'

'Piss off back to fucking America.'

'For what it's worth, I live and work in Cambridge and I have a British wife and son. I love this country.'

'Oh yes, I forgot. Harrow boy, weren't you. Little Lord Snooty. Don't worry, I know all about you, Professor Wilde.'

'Don't come the inverted snob with me. You're Cambridge. Trinity, wasn't it?'

'That really doesn't make me your friend, sunshine.'

Stone thrust two fingers at him, then turned and strode away into the pre-dawn gloom.

Wilde watched him go then placed his empty cup on the counter. He smiled at the serving woman who was clearly bewildered by the confrontation she had just witnessed, and considered his next move.

In a way, he was rather pleased. He wasn't the slightest bit interested in either Shadox Stone or the dockers and union men. Their politics were an open book and just because men like Harry Pollitt and the other communists called for change that didn't make them terrorists.

As for Stone, if Freya had doubts about him she could find some other way to have the man investigated. Wilde could help her, but not like this.

Increasingly, a bug in his brain kept telling him that the threat wasn't here. It was at a village in the English countryside near Oxford. That was the place that held the secrets Stalin wanted. You didn't need to be Machiavelli to know that the Soviets were desperate to build their own plutonium bomb. And the quickest way to do that was to steal secrets from those who had already done it.

Yes, whatever Freya Bentall said, it was clear that Harwell was the place. The atomic energy research establishment. This was all about the bomb. The brutal attempt to corrupt Len Goodrick told him that, as did the curious arrival of a scientist from Bikini Atoll, scene of America's latest A-bomb tests.

Stalin either wanted Harwell's secrets – or he wanted to destroy the place.

Wilde brushed the remains of the ash from his coat and took his leave of the woman in the bacon stall.

Huddling against the pre-dawn cold, he traipsed slowly across the icy flagstones of the echoing market, thinking hard.

If Freya wouldn't help him into Harwell, he'd do it his own way.

CHAPTER 17

Wilde hadn't seen Freya this angry.

'He just walked off and abandoned you? God in heaven, first Baxter, now Stone. Who do these people think they are? I'm going to kill Shadox Stone.'

'Can we just put that all to one side for a moment. I've been thinking. To hell with Shadox Stone, I need to find Lazar Lukin and I need to go to Harwell.'

'I've told you my thoughts on that.'

'Please, just trust me on this.'

'It may not be possible.'

'If anyone can fix it, you can. In the meantime, I'm going to pay another visit to Vivienne Chalke.'

'Why is none of this putting me at ease, Tom?'

A maid answered the door of Lady Chalke's house in Kensington. Wilde asked to speak to her mistress and was ushered into a chilly side room to wait.

Ten minutes later, Vivienne floated in, swathed in bright Asian fabrics. 'Tom Wilde, you came to me. I'm so thrilled.'

She extended her hand, palm down, and he registered that he was supposed to kiss it, so he bent down and did so.

'Now then,' she continued. 'When can we get started on you? Not today obviously, I've far too much on. How about the day after tomorrow?'

'I'll have to check my diary and get back to you on that.'

'Well, it would be simply perfect for me. And I will of course lay on a splendid lunch. Do you like lobster?'

'Haven't had it for a while, but yes, I do like it. Actually I was rather hoping you might be able to help me in the meantime. I met a fascinating character at your gallery opening and I would very much like to get in touch with him. I run a little society for my undergraduates where we gather in the junior combination room and have a stimulating talk from someone with a good story to tell, followed by questions. Your friend would be perfect but I have no contact details for him.'

'I have many fascinating friends in all the arts and sciences, so you'll have to be a bit more specific, Tom. A name would be most helpful.'

'Basil Rheinhaus. I understand that he's a physicist of some note.'

'Well, yes, he is most certainly brilliant, but hardly your sort of subject matter. You're history, aren't you?'

'Oh, we cover all manner of things in the society. Broadens the mind.'

'Very well, I'll give him a call now if you like.'

'I don't want to bother you. If you'd just let me know where I might find him . . .'

'No, no, let's go and telephone him right now. Strike while the iron's hot.'

Wilde had no way out. He didn't want this call to go through; he wanted to turn up uninvited on Basil Rheinhaus's doorstep.

Vivienne Chalke consulted her address book and dialled the number.

'Basil, is that you? Vivienne here . . . thank you, yes, I was very pleased with the opening and our sales went very well . . . yes, we must get together again . . . actually, I have a friend who very much wants to talk to you . . . hold on, I'll just hand him over.'

Wilde took the telephone from her hand. 'Mr Rheinhaus, forgive me for intruding on your peace again. I rather think we got off on the wrong foot. My fault, I'm sure . . . yes, this is Professor Wilde. Tom Wilde. I'd very much like to meet up with you and put a proposal to you . . . hello . . . hello . . .'

The line was dead. For a few moments Wilde held the phone to his ear hoping that it was merely a momentary blip. But no, Rheinhaus had hung up on him.

He replaced the receiver.

'Did something go wrong, Tom? We usually have quite a good line here.'

'He doesn't want to talk to me.'

'Oh dear, that doesn't sound like Basil.'

'Can I ask how long you've known him, Vivienne?'

'Since before the war. What I first adored about him was his love of art, particularly the Vienna Secession painters. But I do know that he can be a bit dour and unforthcoming with new people.'

'If I could just meet him in person, perhaps I could get through to him.'

'Leave it with me. I'll call him this evening and put in a word for you.'

'Thank you.'

She shivered and clutched her flowing gowns to her slender bosom. 'Tell me, when are we going to be warm again? This is so demoralising. I just want to go to Florida or Kenya.'

'Can't be long, surely.'

'Look, I'd love to offer you coffee, Tom, but I really am rushing around like a mad thing this morning. But do check your diary about the day after tomorrow. I just know you'll make a marvellous sitter.'

Wilde had tried to see Rheinhaus's number in Vivienne Chalke's address book, but she had covered it with her hand.

From a nearby kiosk he made a phone call to the Soviet Embassy asking to be put in touch with Comrade Lazar Lukin of the special education ministry delegation. He was told that Comrade Lukin was not presently there but perhaps Mr Wilde would like to call back later.

This was going nowhere fast.

Then he had another idea. Geoff Lancing might just be able to point him in the right direction, if only he could find him.

The thing about Geoff – born Augustin G. Lancing – was that he, too, was a nuclear scientist of some note at Cambridge's Cavendish Laboratory. At least he had been before the war came and he decided to put his flying skills to use in the service of the nation as a fighter pilot. What was he doing now? Was he back in the lab?

They hadn't fallen out but they had gone their separate ways since 1939. Surely the Cavendish would know where to find him.

And he, possibly, might know the whereabouts of his old colleague, Basil Rheinhaus.

'Of course we remember you, Professor Wilde. How could we ever forget?' The secretary to Professor Sir Lawrence Bragg, director of Cambridge's Cavendish Laboratory, sounded delighted to hear Wilde's voice on the phone. 'How can I help you today, sir? I'm afraid Professor Bragg isn't here at the moment.'

'Actually, I'm trying to make contact with Dr Lancing – Geoff Lancing.'

'Ah, I'm afraid he's not here anymore. He quit physics for the RAF and, I believe, was something of a hero.'

'But he survived, didn't he? Has he not returned to science?'

'I'm not sure, sir. Look, can you just hold for a minute? If he's been in touch with Professor Bragg in the last few years, he'll be in our address book.'

Wilde waited, listening to footsteps and the rustle of paper. Finally, the secretary came back on. 'Professor Wilde?'

'Still here.'

'Dr Lancing's Cambridge address and telephone numbers and a couple of other addresses have all been struck through. I'm afraid we don't have a new telephone number, but there is an address dated late last year.'

'Go on.'

'It's a place called Marbourne in Berkshire, sir. Actually I know it quite well because I used to live in Didcot and we'd cycle out there. I recall it was a very pretty little village with thatched Tudor cottages and a lovely tea shop. They had the very best fruit scones. Only thruppence.'

CHAPTER 18

Wilde made his way back to Freya's apartment. Ethel welcomed him with the offer of vegetable soup and a slice of bread for lunch, which he accepted gratefully.

'I'm just going to make a couple of telephone calls, Ethel. I'm pretty sure Miss Bentall won't mind and I'll leave the money.'

'Of course, sir.'

His first task was to call the Soviet Embassy again, but there was still no sign of Comrade Lukin. 'It is likely that he is at Oxford University. Is there a number on which you can be contacted, Mr Wilde?'

'I'm afraid not. This phone is borrowed and I'm around and about.'

'Well then, you will just have to keep trying. We will tell Comrade Lukin that you called.'

He hung up and rang his college. Scobie the head porter took the call. 'Good day, professor, I was hoping you'd get in touch.'

'It's not Bobby, is it? Not bad news?'

'No, sir. No change. I visited him this morning on the way in. Still coughing a lot, but not complaining. But then he wouldn't, not in his nature.'

'Was there something else then?'

'A rather curious message, sir, which I struggled to make head or tail of. A lady named Amelia Coster called, asking to be put in touch with you.'

'I'm not sure I know an Amelia Coster. Did she give you any more information or a contact number?'

'No number, sir, but she said you might remember her better as Dolly and that you would know where to find her. She seemed to think it was all rather urgent, but wouldn't say what it was. She had an interesting accent, certainly not Cambridge.'

'You're a sucker for punishment, ain't you, prof?'

'If you say so, Dolly.'

'Heard you got a right going over on the Walworth Road after you left here last time.'

'Who told you that?'

'Word gets around. Anyway, you seem to be healing all right. So what you doing back here among the low life? Looking for another beating – or do you want to get your own back, you being a boxer and all?'

'I was told you were trying to contact me.'

It was mid-afternoon and The Green Bear was just gearing up for another night of hard drinking, gambling, smoking and other vices. Wilde had trudged here from Mayfair, across Westminster Bridge in an hour and a half. He had tried to hail a cab, but without joy.

'Now why would I want to contact you, prof?'

'You tell me. I was also given the idea it was a bit urgent.'

She was smiling, sidling up to him, flirting, but he realised it was just a game. She couldn't be seen imparting information to a newcomer, not in this neck of the woods where grasses ended up with broken skulls.

'Look like you're interested, professor. Bit handsy, bit of a drool over my assets.' She was stroking his arm, nestling into his neck, talking in whispers.

'Is there somewhere else?'

'Place across the road where we entertain our gentlemen. Sutherland Walk. Just shake your head and step away like you're not interested then meet me there in ten minutes.'

Her meeting place was merely an upstairs room with a wooden chair, a double bed, stained sheets and pillows. The room smelt of sex, sweat and despair. There was no lock on the door, so Wilde let himself in and waited. He simply stood there because he could not bear to sit on the chair or the bed.

'Disgusting, isn't it,' Dolly said when she arrived. 'The punters don't care but it makes me want to throw up every time I come here. It's not mine, though, so I can't do anything about it.'

'You don't actually live here?'

'No, Kennington me. Above the tobacconist near the Tube. Very convenient.'

'I'm sorry you have to do your work in a place like this.'

'It's a living, prof. Everyone's got to earn a crust.'

'I wish there was some way out for you, Amelia.'

'There will be – one day. I've got big plans. Anyway, we can talk about that later. First, though, can you tell me again exactly what you are, prof? Because you sure as hell ain't just a bloody history teacher.'

'But that's exactly what I am.'

'And Gus Baxter's a bus driver, I suppose. Come on, prof, you're talking bollocks. You came to the Bear with Gus and everyone knows he's some sort of secret spy or something.'

'Think what you like, Amelia or Dolly. Sounds like there's a secret side to everyone at The Green Bear. Perhaps you'd like me to change my name, too.'

She was carrying a large handbag and suddenly began rifling through the contents, bringing out a half bottle of something unlabelled and two small tumblers. 'Drink, prof?'

'What is it?'

'Scotch, just how you like it.'

'Go on then.'

She poured two glasses, large for Wilde, small for herself. 'Thing is, you see, I know something that the secret cops might pay good money for.' She lowered her voice. 'I know that Terry Adnams hired out or sold one of his ice-axes and I'm pretty sure it was used in a murder.'

Wilde was already cold, but it felt as though a sliver of freezing water was trickling down his spine. 'Tell me more.'

'Well, I don't like murder and I've never been mixed up in such a thing, so this knowledge scares me. It makes me an accomplice – an accessory after the fact – and it's burning a bloody hole in my brain.'

'Who told you about it?'

'Terry did. There was three or four of us and he was laughing about it. Said the axe had done for some poor bastard up in

Cambridge – and I know that's where you come from. Terry and the others were laughing themselves silly and I had to pretend to think it was funny too. But inside, I was as scared as a bloody baby.'

'Why would he have said that in front of you?'

'Are you having a laugh?'

'What do you mean?'

'I mean that's what Terry does. That's how he keeps everyone terrified and under his control. Lets us know he's a killer and makes it clear he'll kill us if we step out of line. He's a braggart. Acts big and ruthless to scare the life out of everyone around him. And it works – no one dares cross him.'

Wilde understood. That was how such men maintained power. 'Who bought the ice-axe?'

'I thought you might ask that.'

'And?'

'Well, information like that has got to be worth something, hasn't it? Got to be worth the kind of money that gets me out of this shithole of a life and gives me a chance to make something of myself.'

'How much are you looking for?'

'How much you willing to pay, prof? You dress well, look as though you earn a tidy sum. And your secret spy bosses can chip in a barrel-load, I'd guess.'

'I haven't said I'm willing to pay anything. If you have information about a murder it's your duty to go to the police. Otherwise, you're right – you're an accessory after the fact and you could go down for a very long time.'

She finished off her drink, put the glass on the mantelpiece over the cold hearth and hugged her arms tight around her slender body. 'You think that's my big worry, a spell in Holloway? My big worry is an ice-axe in *my* head and a shiv across my throat, prof. That's what scares me – that's why I need the moolah to get out of this place.'

'Why are you telling *me* all this, Dolly?'

'I dunno. You look decent, I suppose. You've got a trustworthy face. You're clearly a somebody – and that's what I need. Someone who can help me.'

'What about Gus Baxter? Surely you know him better.'

'Trust Gus? You got to be bleeding joking.'

'I might be able to get you twenty pounds.'

'Twenty bloody knicker? I need a monkey, nothing less.'

'A monkey? That's five hundred, yes?'

'Of course it is.'

'I have to tell you that that is completely unrealistic. No chance. No chance at all.' Wilde shrugged. 'I'm sorry.'

'Sorry won't cut it. Five hundred will buy me a nice new-build house out in Surrey with a little left over for furnishings. It'll buy me a new life, away from all this.'

As though shot, her body went stiff.

They had both heard footsteps on the stairs. Without a moment's hesitation, Dolly began to roll down one of her nylon stockings. 'We've just had a shag, right?'

The door opened and Terry Adnams filled the space with his bulk. As he stepped in, Dolly was rolling the stocking up again. 'You can leave the money on the mantelpiece, prof,' she said, her voice now harsher. Businesslike. Like a tart who's just done the deed with a punter.

Adnams grinned and put up his fists for a bit of fake sparring. 'I heard you'd come back and found our Dolly. Good for you, Tom. A marital bed can be a bloody lonely place, can't it, eh? Sort you out nice, did she?'

Wilde nodded. He had got the gist of her camouflage manoeuvre with her nylons and he was busy removing a couple of ten shilling notes from his wallet.

'No, Tom, I told you, your money's no good here. Any pal of Joe Spinks is a friend of mind, so Dolly's on the house. Anyway, come and have a little drink with me back at the Bear.'

He pushed the notes back into the wallet. 'That's a fine offer, Terry, but the wife will be looking for me, so I really can't hang about.'

'Course you can. One for the road.'

He couldn't get out of the drink and followed Adnams back to The Green Bear. They left Dolly behind and went to the back area where the men played snooker, shouted the odds and gambled away their earnings.

From there, Adnams took Wilde through to his own office, a surprisingly plush and warm space with a large sofa, a desk, even a television set – blank, of course.

'This is the cockpit, Tom. This is where I control my empire.'

'You've got an empire, Terry?'

'Perhaps not as big as the British or Roman empires yet. But who knows? Lad's got to have dreams.' He went to a sideboard with a dozen bottles of fine whisky, brandy and wine. 'What's your poison today?'

'A very small Scotch would see me right.'

Adnams poured a couple of huge measures and handed one to his guest. 'Bottoms up, mate.'

'Cheers.'

They clinked glasses.

'So you've had your evil way with the lovely Dolly, Tom. She's a bit of all right, isn't she? Cream of my crop.'

'She's very beautiful.'

'More than that, she's a saucy minx. So what else can I do for you? Also, what can *you* do for me? I'm sure there are many mutually profitable possibilities for us to work on.'

'I can't see how I could offer you much, Terry. I'm only a humble university professor. Unless you want to learn a bit about Tudor history, of course. Perhaps you'd like a copy of one of my books.'

'I would like that very much – a signed copy if you will. Now that would be something to show the world I've arrived. That'll make my day. I guess you must have lots of contacts, a man of your standing in the world. Your old students are probably presidents and prime ministers by now.'

'One or two are doing quite well for themselves.'

'Well there you are, see. You're just the sort of man I need.'

Wilde had caught sight of an ice-axe on the top of Adnams's expansive desk.

'Do you like that, Tom? It's an ice-axe.'

'It looks pretty deadly.'

'It's just a little toy of mine. As used by mountaineers the world over. Lovely thing, eh? Scares the living daylights out of my enemies.'

'You could inflict a nasty injury with that, Terry.'

'Indeed I could. I could also inflict a nasty injury with my bare fists, as has been demonstrated on more than one occasion. But there's none of that between you and me, Tom. I was impressed by you the moment I saw you. I said to myself, there's a man I can do business with.'

'Not sure what sort of business you mean.'

'You'll be surprised. Take Gus Baxter, for instance. He's an important man. He does me favours, I do him favours. You're probably thinking I'm an ignorant git, Tom, and you could be right because I left school when I was ten and roamed the streets. So I'm uneducated but I taught myself to read and write and I ain't stupid.'

'You seem to get some interesting people here. I noticed that government minister the other day – Len Goodrick. I heard he quit his post and later was found dead.'

'Yes, Tom, I heard that, too. Shocking news, shocking. A deeply tragic turn of events.'

'Did you know him?'

'Just to say hello to. He came here quite often. Had his needs. Well, we all do, don't we?'

Wilde threw back the rest of his Scotch. He really didn't want to drink so much but he wanted to get away from this place. 'That was excellent whisky, Terry – and now I really must take my leave.'

'Of course. And come back soon. Try another of the girls. They may not all be as pretty as Dolly, but they're all ten out of ten in the sack.'

CHAPTER 19

Wilde returned to Curzon Street, where he sat down with Freya Bentall. 'It's been quite an interesting day.'

'I can't wait to hear.'

He went through the events since their last meeting. She was still fuming about the behaviour of Stone in abandoning him at Smithfield Market and kept asking about it, but her mind became more focused and calm when he mentioned the meeting with Dolly, otherwise known as Amelia Coster.

'If she knows who killed Everett, then we should get the Special Branch to bring her in.'

'She won't say a word unless we give her money. She's demanding five hundred pounds.'

'That's ridiculous. We might pay a few shillings to informers but we don't have sums like that to throw around.'

'If you just pick her up, I fear her life could be in danger.'

'Let me take advice from on high. Why do you think Adnams is so brazen? It's as if he's inviting suspicion to fall on him.'

'I asked Dolly the same thing. She said he likes to scare people and thinks he's untouchable.'

'He clearly doesn't believe you're just a history professor.'

'You're right. They all seem to regard Gus Baxter as a spy, too. It's a bit of a standing joke to them.'

'This really does have to be a case for the Special Branch. Everett's murder is primarily a police matter. So what now, Tom? Do you have a plan?'

'Well, there's the pressing matter of Harwell. And I want to find Basil Rheinhaus.'

Bentall looked uneasy. 'You can't just make the security of Britain's atomic research facility your concern, Tom. You're an American citizen – and your country's McMahon Act specifically separates your atomic programme from ours, to His Majesty's Government's intense annoyance, I might add.'

'I'm not going to shout about it in the US Embassy.'

'You don't understand quite how sensitive this is. We initiated much of the research that led to the manufacture of the bomb and now we're being excluded. You have to tread very carefully.'

Wilde smiled and nodded. 'We're not going to agree on this, Freya.'

'Just concentrate on the matter in hand. Focus on your mission for me. Find out whether there's a rat in the house.'

He said nothing.

'Tom? What don't you understand, for pity's sake?'

'I thought we'd been over this. Yes, your German friend Herr Gehlen says there are moles in the security service. But there's more than that. This isn't just about MI5. Two men of interest have crossed my path – Len Goodrick and Basil Rheinhaus. Both have been engaged in one way or another in the nuclear pro-gramme. And then there's the Russian, Lukin – almost certainly the blackmailer who drove Goodrick to his death. If you want my assistance, how do I ignore all that? You're asking me to fight with one arm tied behind my back.'

He paused, waiting for a response.

'Go on, Tom, you haven't finished your diatribe.'

'There's nothing more to say. I need to find Rheinhaus and I need to get into Harwell. You can help me.'

She shook her head grimly. 'If I could, I would, but I don't think I can.'

CHAPTER 20

This was just like home. Lazar Lukin stopped at the crest of a rise and breathed in the cold air. Just like the bitter winters of Byelorussia. This was his favourite time of year. Skiing in silence through the forest, rifle on his back, hunting.

If the revolution had never come, he might have settled in the far-off northern wilds of his homeland and made a living as a hunter, for it was one of the skills at which he excelled. His speciality was tracking. Wildfowl, elk, reindeer, wolf, man. The last of those was the best: manhunting. That was the one that took the brains and the nerve. He didn't always kill the wildfowl, the elk, the reindeer, the wolf. Sometimes he just stopped and watched them and allowed them to move on unmolested. Just seeing them, knowing they were at his mercy, gave him pleasure enough.

Man was another matter. It was the kill, the fear in the eyes, the admission of defeat that satisfied. He had always understood that life was not just a matter of survival, it was a competitive sport. The winner lives, the loser dies.

His skill in the game and the absence of pity was the reason he had been chosen for this mission as well as all the other black work around Europe, the Middle East, the Americas. He was highly thought of by Stalin and Beria, and he intended to keep it that way.

Now and then his work made the news, when the name was big enough. The Trotsky kill in Mexico back in 1940, that was big. That made him extremely popular with the general secretary.

Lukin's name at birth was Nahum Eitingon and he came from Shklov on the banks of the Dnieper in Byelorussia, but in his adult years he had had many names and had learnt many languages. He changed his first name to Leonid at a time when it was not wise to be identified as Jewish and later he adopted names to suit the situation. Jack, Pierre, Ahmed and more. Now he was Lazar Lukin, special delegate from the Soviet Ministry of Education.

His eyes were the thing; men had likened them to scalpels cutting into the soul. Many who had seen those eyes close up were not alive to describe them. Many had died in extreme pain and degradation, begging for mercy, begging for release. His mouth smiled easily, his eyes never.

Today, out here in snow-crusted England, his brown hair and ears were concealed beneath a thick woollen cap, his feet were enclosed in boots strapped into skis.

The Englishman arrived moments later. 'I prefer skiing downhill,' he said, panting from the exertion.

'Not many mountains in this part of the world, comrade. But cross-country skiing is a bit faster than motor car in these conditions. Where are all the roads? No one told me England had winters like this.'

'We don't. This was imported from the East, especially for you, Lazar.'

'Hah! So how far now?'

The Englishman consulted his compass and looked at the map. 'A mile at the most.'

Who was it who had said that to conquer a country, one must first conquer their secret service? Lavrentiy Beria, of course. In his time as chief of the Soviet secret service in Georgia, he had worked to destroy the intelligence operations of their close Caucasus neighbours Persia and Turkey, assassinating their top agents one by one, leaving the Soviet Union free to infiltrate their spy agencies and governments with Soviet-approved men. It was a simple idea, and effective.

'We can do this on a bigger scale,' Beria had told him at the final briefing after their meeting with Stalin at the Kremlin. 'Your main task is to protect our source, but there are other possibilities.'

Lukin understood. Britain was impoverished, sickly and on the verge of economic collapse. The British Empire was crumbling, their soldiers were dying in Palestine, India would have its independence soon enough. Even the Americans had turned against their British friends, cutting them adrift from their nuclear programme.

'They are no longer a great power,' Beria had continued. 'This is the perfect moment for the little chaos the comrade General Secretary suggested.'

Lukin had nodded. Comrade Beria was simply repeating much of what Stalin had said, but it was wise not to point that out. When Lavrentiy Beria outlined a plan or instructed you to carry out a special task, the reply was 'Of course, comrade. You are correct, as always.' You did not argue with Beria if you liked being alive.

'Our people will identify your targets,' Beria had continued. 'It will be as easy as a bear-shoot in Moscow Zoo. But it must be subtle, not slaughter. They must know it is us so that they fear us, but you must not be caught. So be elegant, Leonid, as only you can.'

It was all a sideshow, of course. He was here to carry out his special task and that was what concentrated his mind. It involved his favourite sport: manhunting. He had to find Rheinhaus. Nothing else really mattered.

He thought he had come close in London. The Englishman had been convinced Rheinhaus would be at the home of a fellow traveller, one of the useful idiots. But he hadn't been.

Basil Rheinhaus had vanished.

Now, in England, somewhere south of Oxford, Lukin and the Englishman carried on skiing through the deep virgin snow and came to another low rise and looked down on a former army camp.

'And so we are home.'

Home for the moment was a semi-cylindrical hut made of corrugated iron in an abandoned barracks. It was a place without comforts of any kind, but it was safe, a place in the heart of southern England, not too far from London and within striking distance of the Harwell atomic research establishment. They had spent the previous night here and now they would bed down again.

It was safe because these old army camps were now occupied by the dispossessed – former servicemen who had been demobilised only to discover that they had no homes to go to. The police didn't bother them, for this squatting was a reasonable solution to a seemingly insoluble problem, one that Attlee's Labour government was struggling in vain to deal with.

'Let's eat and prepare for tomorrow,' Lukin said.

'Do you think he will come to Harwell?'

'It's our best chance.'

'And when he does?'

'We'll be waiting and watching.'

They had put up camp beds and had concealed food stores in one of the Nissen huts. They had one person for company, an army squaddie, still in his uniform, which suggested he might have deserted rather than been demobbed. The Englishman had paid the soldier to keep an eye out for their property, telling the man that they were going off in search of supplies and work.

The soldier appeared at the doorway to the hut.

'Everything all right, soldier?' the Englishman said.

'Yes, sir. Your things are all safe, sir.' He said *sir* because the man was obviously of the officer class.

'Good man.'

'Any joy in your search of supplies, sir?'

'I'm afraid not, but we've probably got a spare can of beans you could have.'

'That's very decent of you. Shouldn't have left the service, should I? Always got a good feed in the army. Never realised I'd miss the NAAFI so much. Also, I'm wishing I could have learnt to ski, like you two gentlemen.'

'Even better going downhill in the Alps in proper waxed skis. These are a little old-fashioned, but easier than walking.'

The soldier disappeared. Still wrapped in their heavy greatcoats, scarves and gloves, Lukin and the Englishman cooked their own baked beans on a primus stove and slathered the result on slices of five-day-old bread.

'I keep wondering if the ice-axe was wise,' the Englishman said.

Lukin shrugged. 'It was perfect. Sow confusion and they will come to believe there is an enemy within, destroying them one by one. They won't know who it is, and so they will turn on each other and devour each other, eat each other alive like ravening beasts. This is how it works. Believe me, I know these things.' He had seen it before, in Persia, in Turkey.

There was a knock at the door to their hut.

'Yes?' the Englishman said.

'It's me again, Private Godwin, sir.'

'Well, come in, soldier.'

The door opened. Private Hubert Godwin stood to attention.

Lukin smiled. 'Yes, you want some more beans, perhaps?'

'No, it's just that I meant to tell you something, Mr Lukin. We've got some welcome company. One of your countrymen has arrived and is staying in Hut Twelve along the way. I took the liberty of mentioning you to him and he said he would be pleased to make your acquaintance. I hope that is all right?'

'My countryman? You mean Polish, of course?' This was not good. Lukin had a smattering of the Polish language and it was a useful guise, but he would never pass muster to an actual Pole.

'Yes. He was a pilot like you. Hurricanes, he said. Speaks pretty good English but I'm sure you would both enjoy a conversation in your own tongue.'

'Well, thank you, soldier. I shall look forward to meeting him when I have had my meagre meal.'

The soldier smiled broadly. 'Well, he's here now, gentlemen, at my very shoulder. Allow me to introduce you both to Pilot Officer Teodor Sapkowski. I think that's how he pronounces it.'

Lukin acted without hesitation. His mouth smiling, he stepped forwards to greet the new arrival with his right arm extended. 'Comrade Sapkowski, it is my pleasure,' he said in broken Polish.

The Polish pilot looked puzzled but he reached out his own hand to be shaken, just as Lukin removed the pistol from his pocket with his left hand, brought it up to the side of the man's head and pulled the trigger.

Still smiling, Lukin turned to the soldier and shrugged helplessly as he pushed the muzzle into his face. 'I'm sorry, soldier, but I really have no choice.' He pulled the trigger for the second time.

The Englishman looked on, no emotion visible. He removed a handkerchief from his trouser pocket and began to wipe the blood splatter from his face.

'Wrap them up in tarps,' Lukin said, 'and deposit them behind old furniture or stores so they are not immediately visible, then let's eat.'

The train to Didcot wasn't too bad. The snowfall overnight had been light and this morning it had stopped. Wilde found himself gazing out across the whiteness of England with pleasure. Yes, the lights failed all the time, there was little heating and a shortage of food, but this really was quite special.

He was in a carriage with a young curate and they got to talking about the state of the country. The clergyman was bursting with optimism. 'God will provide, just as He did in the war. Only a few weeks to go and we'll have the most wonderful spring imaginable.'

'What happens when all this snow and ice thaws? Aren't you worried about the prospect of floods?'

'We must look to the Lord and pray.'

Wilde let the man carry on in the same vein until Didcot without bothering to dispute points of faith or theology. His mind was elsewhere. Before catching the train at Paddington he had called Cambridge to check up on Janet Spring and Johnny. Doris, their cleaner, answered the phone.

'She's just walking Johnny to school and trying to get some bread, professor.'

'Is everything all right there, Doris?'

'Yes she seems to be coping very well and your son seems happy. Nothing to concern you, sir.'

'Well, if you're sure, give her my very best regards and tell her I have to stay down here for three or four more days and then I'll be home.'

'Of course, sir. And Miss Spring seems a great deal better in herself now.'

'Better than what?'

'Well, she was a bit poorly for a day or two but not so much that she couldn't carry on with her work, so there really is nothing for you to worry about.'

'Tell her I'll try to call her later today.'

CHAPTER 21

Getting from the station at Didcot to the nearby village of Marbourne was easier said than done. In the end it took him longer than the train journey from London because there were no taxis at the station and the bus service was intermittent at best. Finally he walked, hitched a lift with a postal van part of the route, then walked again the rest of the way.

The village, which stood in gently rolling farmland, would have been picturesque at any time of year, but it was exceptionally so with the coating of snow. It had everything you could want in an English community – two pubs, a church, a small shop, an elementary school and a village hall. And at least half the houses were thatched and half-timbered.

He found the address he had been given by the Cavendish secretary easily. There were only two streets in the village and the house he was looking for, the unimaginatively named Rose Cottage, stood alone, with a paddock on either side, not far from one of the pubs – The Woodsman's Arms, which faced the green.

He walked up a short gravel drive, its coating of snow having been shovelled to the side. There was no bell so he used the knocker. No answer. He waited, then rapped again. This time he heard footsteps and a young woman with a baby on her hip answered the door.

'I'm sorry. I was in the middle of changing her. How can I help you?'

'I'm looking for Dr Lancing, Geoff Lancing.'

'Oh, he's at the atomic village. Usually gets home about five-thirty. Do you want to leave a message for him?'

The atomic village. Harwell, of course. Wilde looked at his watch. It was only ten-thirty, which meant he had seven hours to kill.

'What time does the pub open?'

'The Woodsman's? That's eleven. He's been doing a roaring trade in this weather because it always has a log fire and it's the warmest place in Marbourne.'

'Thank you.'

She looked him up and down, assessing him, then smiled. 'Geoff's my husband. Is there any way *I* can help?'

'I'm an old friend.'

'Really? Tell me more.'

'From Cambridge. My name's Tom Wilde.'

She broke into a smile. 'Well, pleased to meet you, Mr Wilde. Come indoors, I can put down the baby and we can introduce ourselves properly. How about a cuppa?'

'Thank you, that's very kind.'

'Truth is, it's nice to have grown-up company. Babies are lovely, but I've found that their conversation is a tad limited.'

They went through to her kitchen, which was remarkably modern and well appointed, with a comforting Aga range. 'We just keep this room warm and live in here,' the woman said, putting the baby in a cot and filling a kettle. 'Tom Wilde, eh? Now that sounds familiar. I think I might have heard of you from Geoff. Cambridge, you say?'

'Yes.'

'Well, I'm Cathy and my little one is Peggy,' she said.

'She's gorgeous.'

'She is, isn't she. Good as gold too. So did you work with Geoff at the Cavendish?'

'No, I'm a history don. But we're very old friends. We used to live in each other's pockets, to be honest. He had the run of my rooms and we'd meet up for a drink and a chat most days. But I haven't seen him since before the war. I know he quit the Cavendish and joined the RAF, but we lost track of each other like so many people. Scattered by the war.'

'Well, he's back on the science beat now, working at the atomic village, chatting endlessly about neutrons and isotopes and heavy water. I'm sure he's mentioned a historian friend. Tudors, was it, by any chance?'

'Late Tudor – Elizabethan. Geoff did try to teach me the rudiments of nuclear fission and the splitting of the atom but it was rather a lost cause. I nod and say yes and pretend to understand.'

'Actually, I *do* understand what he's saying because I'm a physicist too. I worked with Otto Frisch and Rudolf Peierls in Birmingham. That's where I met Geoff. I don't know if you heard but he was shot out of the sky in 1942 and his injuries meant he couldn't fly again, so he went back to science at a time when particle physicists were much in demand.'

'His injuries?'

'Actually, he healed pretty well in the end. You won't notice a thing.'

'And you're a physicist too?'

'I *was*. Little Peggy put an end to all that, didn't you, Peggy darling?'

The baby gurgled. Cathy put the kettle on the hob and fished out two cups and a teapot from a cupboard, then hunted around for the tea caddy. 'Chaos in here,' she said.

'Looks pretty organised to me.'

'Really? Well, I don't know what you have gathered about the atomic village, but they're throwing up huge numbers of prefab bungalows for us. I want to stay here but Geoff thinks we might be required to move. Apparently it's a security thing as much as anything else. They want to keep everyone on site – they're very strict on such matters and I suppose I can see their point of view.'

'So I wouldn't be able to just walk up to the entrance and ask to see Geoff?'

'No, I'm almost certain you'd be turned away without ceremony.' She spooned tea into the pot and left it to brew.

'The word is they're building an atomic pile.'

'Well, you obviously know a bit about the place. I hope you're not a spy. You don't look anything like one. And yes, you're right, it's the delightfully named Gleep – graphite low energy experimental pile – what the Americans are now calling a reactor. One day we won't need coal or gas or oil – everything will be powered by nuclear. By the way, am I right in thinking you're American, Tom?'

'Half American, half Irish, British wife and son. My wife Lydia used to publish poetry, now she has unleashed the scientific side of her nature and is training to be a doctor.'

'Good for her. I might do something similar one day. By the time Peggy is old enough for school, the world of atomic science will probably have left me a long way behind.' She poured the tea and passed Wilde a cup. 'Sugar?'

'No, thank you.'

'Good, because I haven't got any.'

They sat down at the table with the steaming cups in front of them. Cathy was homely, clever and sweet-natured and Wilde was delighted that Geoff had found happiness after the traumas of 1939 when he had lost his beloved and very glamorous sister Clarissa. Those days had been very bleak in Cambridge with war looming and Hitler taking a malign interest in the work of the Cavendish laboratory.

'You know, Tom, we don't have a telephone but I could try calling Geoff from the box on the green and see if he could get home early.'

'Are you sure?'

'Why not? He's owed some time off. I'll just drink my tea first. In the meantime I'd rather like to keep you prisoner here so I can pick your brain. I don't know what he was like in the old days, but my husband can be a bit taciturn so he hasn't actually told me a great deal about his life before we met.'

'Not sure I can help you much.'

'He says he hasn't got family. But surely everyone has some sort of family somewhere, however distant.'

Wilde hesitated. Was it his place to reveal details of Geoff's life to his wife? Why not? 'Well, of course there was his sister.'

'A sister? I had no idea he had any siblings.'

'She's dead now. Died in a flying accident in 1939. Her name was Clarissa and she was quite a famous actress.'

Cathy looked astonished. 'Clarissa Lancing was his sister? He never told me. I never made the connection. Good Lord, how remarkable.'

'He was devoted to her and deeply traumatised by her death. Perhaps he can't bring himself to talk about her.'

'He doesn't even have a picture of her. I'm shocked, Tom, really shocked. I've seen all her films and I never knew. I don't know what to say.'

'Perhaps I've spoken out of turn.'

'No, he should have told me, I have a right to know such things. But is she really dead? I know she's presumed dead – it was all over the papers – but no one knows what happened to her, do they?'

'I'm certain she's dead. And Geoff's sure too.'

She put down her empty cup. 'Would you look after Peggy for a minute or two, I'm going to try and call him.'

Geoff Lancing arrived home at half past one, having walked two miles through the snow from the Harwell atomic site. All he had been told was that they had a visitor he might wish to see. When he pressed her for a name, she simply said, 'It's a surprise, Geoff. A rather nice surprise. Come on, you deserve an afternoon off.'

Wilde opened the door to him.

For a few moments, Lancing didn't seem to recognise the face in front of him. Then he laughed out loud. 'Tom Wilde, my God!' He thrust out his hand.

'I know you're English and reserved but we can do better than that, Geoff,' Wilde said, and then the two men clapped their arms around each other and hugged.

They stood back and gazed at each other with warmth and delight.

'What is it, Tom, seven years? Eight?'

'About seven and a half by my reckoning.'

'God, those were ghastly days.'

Indeed they had been, thought Wilde. Days of love and death in the summer of 1939, just a few weeks before the war tore everyone's life asunder. A time when he proposed marriage to Lydia, when Geoff fell in and out of love, and when good people were killed by bad people.

'I think this calls for a beer or something. What in heaven's name are you doing in this neck of the woods, Tom?'

'I discovered you were here and I came looking for you. The Cavendish had your address. Your delightful wife let me in and has shown great forbearance in showering this total stranger with kindness and cups of tea.'

'I'm amazed you got here given the state of the roads and railways. Have you ever seen anything like it?'

'In Chicago and Massachusetts but not here.'

Lancing suddenly seemed to realise that they weren't alone and looked over his old friend's shoulder at his wife. 'Darling, I've told you about Tom, haven't I? Claims to be a history professor but spends most of his time saving civilisation from the forces of evil.'

They all settled in the kitchen, warmed by the Aga and the primal, irresistible, scent of newborn baby. In these surroundings it occurred to Wilde that Geoff Lancing really had found the happiness he deserved.

'Tom's been telling me all your secrets, Geoff,' Cathy said.

'I very much hope not.' His eyes were fixed on Wilde's. 'That aside, I imagine you have some ulterior motive for being here. I think I know you well enough to realise that.'

'Actually, I confess I do. You're my go-to nuclear physicist.'

'Carry on, I'm all ears.'

'You once introduced me to a chap called Basil Rheinhaus at the Cavendish. I'm trying to find him.'

'Basil Rheinhaus, eh? Not the very best at theory, but good in the lab, as I recall. I believe he went to Los Alamos in summer '45 a couple of months before they exploded the gadget. Perhaps he's still over there. I seem to recall he has American nationality. Why, what's this about?'

'I wish I could tell you, but I'm not quite sure myself. He's not in America, though. He was with the US team at Bikini Atoll but he's in Britain now.'

'Well, I haven't seen him nor heard a dicky bird from him.'

'What about Klaus, Geoff?' Cathy suggested. 'He was at Los Alamos so he must know Rheinhaus pretty well. Perhaps they're still in touch.'

'Klaus?' Wilde asked.

'Klaus Fuchs, a German refugee from Hitler. Took a bit of a beating from the Gestapo before deciding he would be safer in

England. Now head of the Theoretical Division at Harwell – my immediate superior, in fact.'

'And he knows Rheinhaus? Perhaps I could talk to him.'

'It's possible, I suppose. Fascinating chap, the very best theoretical brain there is. Dead cert for a Nobel gong sooner rather than later. Not sure the Yanks could have built the bomb without him and he might well perform the same trick for us . . .' He stopped as though thinking he might have gone too far even making such a suggestion. 'Were we to ever want one of course. But that's way beyond my pay grade.'

Wilde understood. Such matters were not to be discussed outside the confines of the Atomic Energy Research Establishment or the highest reaches of government.

Lancing turned to his wife. 'You know, you're probably right, Cath. There's every possibility Klaus knows what Basil's up to.'

'Is there any way of talking to this Klaus Fuchs?'

'Well, he lodges at Abingdon but he's at work at the moment. If you want to meet him, I could give him a call and see if he'd like to come over for an early supper with us. He's a very sociable fellow – and he fancies Cathy rotten so he'll probably jump at the chance.'

'You do talk nonsense, Geoff.'

'I've seen the way he looks at you.'

'Even when I was pregnant? Even with a babe in arms? You do come up with the most utter rot. Very flattering though. Anyway, Tom, what's the answer – would you like to meet this supposed Lothario?'

'I rather think I would.'

'And you're going to stay the night here, aren't you?' Lancing added. 'You can't come all this way in such foul weather and then just disappear for another seven years.'

'I'd be delighted to stay if it's not too much trouble for you and Cathy.'

'Of course not. And talking of foul arctic weather, guess what I saw on my walk home – a pair of skiers crossing a field near the old army camp. Now that's the way to get about.'

CHAPTER 22

'Are you sure that was him?'

Lukin snorted with scorn. 'I have the eyes of a Siberian goshawk. If I say I saw Wilde, then I saw Wilde. I have met him twice and I would be able to pick him out in a football crowd. He walked into the village then disappeared into a house. Why? What is he doing here?'

'Perhaps he is visiting friends. Just a coincidence.'

'You believe in coincidence and you are still alive?'

'So what do we do?'

'What do you think we do? We have played with them enough. Their time is up.'

Lancing was how old now? About thirty-seven by Wilde's reckoning, probably half a dozen years older than his wife. He was small in stature, as slender as ever but showing his age a little with the hint of grey about the edges. Wilde wondered what injuries he had suffered to cut short his RAF career, but nothing was obvious. He held himself upright, there was no limp.

They talked endlessly during the afternoon. But there were subjects that were off limits. One of those was Clarissa, his beloved elder sister. Cathy tried to get him to talk about her but Lancing shut her down. 'Another day maybe. There's too much pain there.'

They talked about Lydia and Lancing was delighted to hear she and Wilde had married and had a son.

Eventually, Wilde tried to bring the conversation around to Harwell but met a brick wall.

'I'm not supposed to say a word about our work, I'm afraid,' Lancing said. 'I'm a bit of a stickler for that, which might seem a bit ridiculous to you given that Hiroshima and Nagasaki rather blew the lid off things. But I can tell you that our work at Harwell is one hundred per cent peaceful – power generation rather than explosive devices.'

Wilde accepted the reassurance with a smile but he was well aware that the peaceful and militaristic elements of the atom were intrinsically linked. What was done in the name of power generation at Harwell could be turned to weapons, just as ploughshares had been melted down and forged into swords and spears in earlier generations.

It was clear to him, too, that Harwell must hold many secrets that a belligerent enemy would very much like to get its hands on.

'I don't want to know about the science. It's the people there and the security. Are they safe?'

'What do you mean?'

'I mean trustworthy.'

'I think so, yes. We're not at war for heaven's sake.'

The conversation went on all afternoon, with much laughter and many reminiscences of Cambridge days. Lancing wanted to know all about Lydia and Johnny and insisted that when the weather improved they must all come down to Marbourne as a family. Somehow they would all be squeezed in.

Cathy merely listened most of the time. It was clear to Wilde that she was delighted to be learning something of her husband's past which had previously been denied her. Only the problematic matter of his sister was out of bounds.

And then, at six o'clock, Klaus Fuchs screeched to a halt outside the house in a little sports car, jumping out with a bottle of Riesling wine. He was tall, fresh-faced with round spectacles, a receding hairline and a rather superior curl to the mouth that might be mistaken for a perpetual smile. Or sneer. He was probably in his mid-thirties given his history but he could have passed for mid-twenties.

Wilde had been warned by Lancing that Fuchs was not just a very dangerous driver but could be difficult to understand. His English was good enough, but he still had a strong German accent made more obscure by having to wear a plate in his mouth, the result of a Gestapo officer's punch to his jaw.

He was charming and softly-spoken, but he annoyed Cathy with his non-stop smoking.

'I wish you wouldn't light up all the time with Peggy in the room,' she said.

'Forgive me, dear Cathy, I shall go into another room for my cigarettes.' He looked to Wilde and Lancing. 'Would you care to join me, gentlemen?'

'Too bloody cold in the other rooms,' Lancing said. 'Let's just have supper, then you can go and smoke on your own somewhere. In the meantime, Tom has a question to ask you.'

'Really? Fire away, Tom.'

'Well, I'm trying to contact a scientist named Basil Rheinhaus. Geoff thought you must know him from your time in America.'

'Rheinhaus? Of course I know him. He is a good friend of mine. We worked closely together in Los Alamos and we drank together too. A fine fellow. I think he is probably in the Marshall Islands now, helping to blow up dilapidated ships and tropical beaches.'

'No, he's left Bikini Atoll. He's definitely in England,' Wilde said. 'Would you expect him to make contact with you?'

'Well, yes, I most certainly would. And if he doesn't want to work in America, I would hope that he might find a role here in Harwell or at Springfields.'

'What's Springfields?'

'Oh, Springfields is near Preston. It's the new plant for refining uranium. But if he's there – or indeed anywhere in the country – I really would have expected him to come and say hello and have a drink with me.'

'Perhaps he will. If he does, I'd very much like to hear from you.'

'But Geoff tells me you are a history professor from Cambridge. What makes you want to find Basil Rheinhaus?'

It was a question Wilde had been expecting and he was aware that no answer was going to be entirely satisfactory, so he went with the simple option. 'I'm afraid that's a private matter, Mr Fuchs.'

'How very mysterious.'

Supper was produced, just as the lights went out and so they ate by candlelight. Meagre portions of fried liver – meant for two adults but stretched to four – with mashed potato and tinned peas and onion gravy, followed by apple pie.

Apropos of nothing, Wilde noticed that Fuchs was left-handed. He held his glass in his left hand and reached for the salt and pepper with his left hand. Wilde approved. He disliked the English habit of beating left-handedness out of children.

Fuchs and Lancing gossiped about the people they worked with until Cathy told them to please remember that they had a guest who did not work at Harwell, and then the subject turned inevitably to the bitter weather.

After supper, Fuchs was allowed one cigarette at the table, then he looked at his watch and said, 'I must be getting home. The road to Abingdon is clear but who knows how long that will last.' He shook hands with the two men and lingered a little too long in holding Cathy's hand and kissing her cheeks. Her husband raised his eyes to the heavens and shook his head.

When he had gone, Wilde insisted on helping with the dishes while Cathy made up a bed for him in the spare room. It occurred to him that while this trip had turned into a wonderful reunion with an old friend, it had all been rather a waste of time and effort as far as the task at hand was concerned.

Except it hadn't been, had it? For Wilde had observed Fuchs's face closely when the name Basil Rheinhaus was first mentioned. For a brief moment he had looked extremely uncomfortable and blinked rapidly behind his round spectacles before quickly regaining his composure.

Now why should that be? What was it about Rheinhaus that made his old friend Klaus Fuchs so ill at ease?

They all retired to their cold chambers at ten o'clock just as the lights came back on. Wilde had been given a single bed with four blankets and was lent a pair of his host's pyjamas and soon managed to get to sleep, buried beneath the bedding.

The next thing he knew was an urgent whispered voice in his ear. 'Get up, Tom. Here, take this.'

Take this? Take what? He was bleary-eyed, his mind was a blur, the room was in darkness, but he woke in an instant when he realised that Geoff Lancing was putting the butt of a pistol into his hand.

'What is it?'

'We've got company at the back door. Cathy woke to feed the baby and heard sounds, voices.'

'Is this thing loaded?'

'Full clip. Mine, too. Safety's on. Come on, let's go and make our presence felt.'

'We can't shoot burglars.'

'They're not burglars. Come on. Quietly.'

Lukin and the Englishman had watched the house for hours. They had seen the second visitor arrive and had looked at each other in amazement. 'Well, well,' the Englishman said. 'I think that's confirmation.'

'Just trust me, comrade. Always trust me,' Lukin said.

The visitor had been there for two hours and had then departed by motor car. Later, the candlelight in the house was replaced briefly by electric lights until they, too, were extinguished and silence reigned.

There had been no snowfall during the evening and though the cloud was thick and low and the air was still, the likelihood of more snow imminently seemed improbable.

They were at the back door, wearing woollen balaclavas, preparing for their entry when the light went on. Through the kitchen window they saw the woman of the house with her baby and they shrank back into the darkness of the garden until she left and switched off the light again.

'This is fucking cold, Lazar, I'm not sure how much longer I can wait around. Can we do it now?'

'Lucky you had us to win the war for you, eh, Englishman?'

Wilde and Lancing crept down the narrow uneven staircase to the kitchen. They carried no light, no candle but they each had a pistol held out in front of them.

Above them, shut away in the main bedroom, Cathy lay in bed with the baby at her breast, stroking the child's brow with the soft palm of her hand. The mother was calm and steady, for courage was in her nature.

At the entrance to the kitchen, which was at the rear of the house, giving way to the white expanse of their unfenced garden and the open countryside, Wilde and Lancing stopped. They heard sounds and then saw the faint yellow glimmer of an electric torch outside the half-windowed door. There was muted shattering as a hammer broke through the glass and a hand reached in.

Lancing didn't hesitate. He pointed the pistol at the top of the back door, just above head height, and pulled the trigger. The crack of the gunshot broke the silence of the night.

Wilde was horrified. 'Damn it, Geoff, what have you done?'

'They're not burglars. We both know that. They don't want to steal anything – they're here because you are.' He moved steadily towards the door. Waited a few seconds with the gun held in his right hand trained into the dark jagged space above painted wood then, with his left hand, pulled the bolt back and threw open the door.

No one was there.

CHAPTER 23

Their first instinct was to go out into the night to follow the trail, but then Wilde stopped. 'I think you have to stay here to protect Cathy.'

'They're after you, not her.'

'You might be right, but we can't take the risk. They could come back expecting me here. You stay, I'll go after them. Have you got a torch?'

'Tom, if you follow them carrying a lit torch you'll be the easiest target in the world. We have to assume they are armed and have murder in mind. We'll go at dawn.'

No more discussion was needed. They realised that they were both right, and so they would wait until morning. In the meantime, Lancing tried to comfort his wife but she didn't need comforting.

'One little gunshot in the night to scare off a burglar is not going to make me a nervous wreck, Geoff. You did what had to be done. I have lived through bombing – we all have. Friends died in North Africa and on the beaches of Normandy. My own husband – you – shot down planes and was himself shot down. By the way, did your gunshot hit anyone?'

'There was no cry, no blood in the snow.'

'I suppose we'll have to call the police though.'

'We'll talk about that later.'

No one slept well except the baby.

At first light, with the last of the tea inside them, Wilde and Lancing set out. They were wrapped up as warm as possible and had the pistols in their coat pockets. Their plan was to follow the tracks they found – two sets of skis – returning in the direction whence they came.

Wilde had asked about the guns. 'Why do you have two pistols in the house, Geoff?'

'War souvenirs. Doesn't everyone have them?'

Wilde supposed that many people probably did, as well as a great deal of other booty – Iron Crosses, Nazi daggers, swastika flags, German helmets.

The tracks were simple to follow because it had not snowed in the night and the morning was grey, overcast and cold. They crossed the fields and the low hill that backed on to the Rose Cottage garden, and zig-zagged out into the surrounding farmland in the direction of the old decommissioned army base, all the while moving closer to the atomic energy establishment at Harwell, which Lancing pointed out: a fenced-in area with two aircraft hangars, and a mass of new and older buildings.

'That's what, two miles away?' Wilde asked.

'Something like that.'

They stopped a hundred yards from the camp with its Nissen hut barracks and more permanent brick and concrete offices stark against the skyline and considered their next move.

'That's clearly where they came from and where they returned,' Lancing said.

'Rather close to the atomic village.'

'Let's go and give them a piece of our mind. They came to kill you, Tom, you do know that? So don't hesitate to shoot.'

Geoff Lancing had changed from the self-effacing, almost timid friend of the 1930s. His time as a fighter pilot had hardened him. Or perhaps it was the events leading up to his sister's death that had shattered his innocence. Those days in the last peacetime summer had been brutal, occasioned by a Nazi attempt to destroy the Cavendish laboratory and set back Britain's nuclear project. Wilde, Lancing and his sister Clarissa had all been deeply involved in one way or another.

And now here they were again, minus Clarissa, and once again it seemed likely – perhaps certain – that atomic science was at the heart of a series of deadly incidents. But this wasn't the Nazis, was it? They were a spent force. This was the agents of another tyranny that had taken its place.

Lancing's new toughness was understandable but it was also alarming. War was over, they were on the side of civilisation.

Only murderers went around Britain with a gun ready to shoot someone without warning.

Side by side, guns in their gloved right hands, they trudged stealthily through the snow to the barracks. At first it seemed deserted, completely empty. They followed the ski trails to one hut, but there was no one there, then the next and the next.

In the fifth hut, they hunted for clues and found two bodies.

It was clear that the corpses were not those of the men who had appeared at the door of Rose Cottage. For one thing, they had been shot in the head and face and there was no gun nearby. Secondly, the corpses had been hidden. Thirdly, there were no skis to be found in the camp – but there were fresh ski tracks leading away from the barracks in the vague direction of the town of Didcot.

One of the bodies was clad in military khaki, the other in an air force flying jacket. They were stiff, from rigor mortis and the deathly cold.

Wilde knelt at their side and searched their pockets and quickly found their wallets and ID cards. The soldier's name was Hubert Godwin, the RAF man was a Pole named Sapkowski.

'We have to contact the police, Geoff. I mean this has to be dealt with now – so our pursuit of the ski trail ends here. The cops will have to break out the armaments chest.'

'The killers will be long gone.'

To Oxford, perhaps, thought Wilde. That wasn't so far – maybe fifteen miles at the most – and he knew someone who had been heading in that direction recently. Comrade Lukin.

'God knows what you've got yourself into, Tom, but I really wish you hadn't brought it to my door.'

'I'm sorry. I've no idea how they found me here. I'm really not sure how anyone could have followed me from London.' What, he wondered, had really brought these killers here? Had they already been in the vicinity, perhaps at this camp? Their motive was obvious: a malign interest in the nearby atomic research establishment.

Wilde and Lancing returned across country to Rose Cottage and called the Harwell special police from the telephone kiosk on the green.

'I'm going to leave this in your hands and make my way back to London, Geoff,' Wilde said. 'It's up to you whether you mention me or not. You've probably already deduced that I'm working with the security service.' He handed him a scrap of paper with the number at Leconfield House. 'If I'm not there and you need to contact me, talk to my immediate chief, Miss Freya Bentall.'

'Of course. Pointless us both being here telling the same story. I'm disinclined to mention my own pistols or the gunshot in the kitchen.'

'I'm with you on that. No need to complicate matters. Just say you went for a walk and stumbled across the crime scene. I assume Cathy will go along with the story.'

'Oh yes. Dr Cathy Lancing is utterly reliable.'

'Let me know if you discover any more about the dead men, why they were there and why they were killed. I'm inclined to think they were innocent bystanders killed in the crossfire, poor bastards. Wrong place, wrong time.'

'I'll call you. And don't forget, you're to come back with Lydia and your boy as soon as the days get a little longer.'

'A wonderful prospect for the not-too-distant future. One thing before I go, does the name Len Goodrick mean anything to you?'

'I've got a feeling it does, but why?'

'He was junior minister in the Ministry of Supply, which of course has responsibility for Harwell. He killed himself after being blackmailed by a Soviet agent. There were compromising photographs of him and another man.'

'Oh God, yes, I saw a couple of paragraphs saying he had resigned. Then he killed himself? How bloody awful.'

'But you didn't know him?'

'We in the Theoretical Division don't have much to do with the Ministry of Supply. John Cockcroft might point you in the right direction. He's our chief man, director of Harwell.'

'Will he talk to me?'

'I honestly don't know, Tom. An inquiry might be better coming from your own top brass.'

It was still daylight when Wilde got back to London. He made his way to Kensington and asked to speak with Vivienne Chalke. The maidservant who answered the door said her ladyship was otherwise engaged but perhaps sir would care to leave a message.

'Tell her Tom Wilde called and I'll be with her at ten tomorrow morning to sit for her.'

'Of course, sir.'

'It seems we have a fight on our hands, Englishman.'

'That couldn't have been predicted.'

'We need to be a little more direct,' Lukin said. 'We cannot let them find Rheinhaus before we do. So we hunt the hunters: no more Wilde, no more Bentall, no more problem.'

CHAPTER 24

Gus Baxter was at Leconfield House when Wilde arrived. 'Care for a coffee, Tom? Or perhaps something a bit stiffer? We could saunter along to my club, which isn't a million miles from here.'

'I have to see Bentall, I'm afraid.' He desperately needed to see her to discuss events at Harwell and the murders of two men who might just be innocent bystanders.

'Oh, forget that. Mother's in a long-winded meeting with Percy and Guy and others at the War Office. Something very hush-hush. She won't be back for hours, if at all.'

Wilde looked at his watch. It was after 5 p.m. He couldn't break into an official meeting. 'All right, Gus,' he said. 'I'll take you up on that.'

'Wonderful.'

'When you say *your club*, that wouldn't by any chance be The Green Bear in Walworth, would it?'

Baxter grinned. 'Not today, Tom, this one's in Pall Mall. Less entertaining perhaps but a lot easier to get to and rather quieter. Good place for a chat. Come on, join me. Let me know how things are going, tell me how I can help.'

The walk might have been ten minutes in better weather, but it took them almost twenty. By some miracle, the radiators were working at full power in his august club and the whole place was delightfully warm, so they left their coats with the doorman and made their way to the drawing room with its secluded corners of leather sofas and armchairs and polished coffee tables. The ticking of the clock, the murmuring of voices and the rustle of newspapers were the only sounds.

Two walls were hung with portraits of former members – all men, of course. A couple of them were prime ministers, there was a renowned empire builder, a great industrialist who had constructed railways across the world and half a dozen men distinguishable only by their complete anonymity, their former fame long forgotten.

Baxter immediately headed for a corner beneath one of the high windows looking out onto Pall Mall and ensconced himself in a leather sofa, lounging back with a contented sigh as though it were a chaise longue. Wilde took the armchair at his side and inhaled the smokey, privileged air of a room where time seemed to stand still. Was this hallowed space ever touched by the harsh realities of war and poverty, he wondered? Did anything disturb its entitled upper-class elegance? They ordered coffee and brandy from an obsequious waiter.

'Tell me about that evening at the Bear, Gus. In particular Len Goodrick – what did you know about him?'

'I thought I was going to be asking the questions. See how things are going for you, help get you up to speed.'

'Well?'

'All right then, have it your own way. Len Goodrick. Tragic chap. His prick led him into grave danger and he paid a terrible price for his indiscretions.'

'But why him? Why did the Soviet Union target him?'

'What makes you think the Soviets had anything to do with it?'

'Well, someone tipped off Number Ten.'

'I don't rush to judgement, Tom. Obviously he was being blackmailed but who's to say it wasn't just some grubby low-life seeing the chance of some easy cash? Plenty of those around the Bear.'

'No, it was Stalin.'

'Have it your own way, Tom. Of course, if it *was* Uncle Joe's lot, I suppose they wanted to control him and he didn't want to be controlled.'

'Quite a coincidence that he was at The Green Bear at the same time as us.'

'Was it a coincidence? Or just happenstance? It certainly wasn't his first time there.'

'How well did you know him?'

'Oh, I think we've been over this ground.'

'Have you heard of Basil Rheinhaus?'

'I beg your pardon?'

'Rheinhaus. Atomic scientist.'

'Where did that name come from?'

'Well?'

'The name means nothing to me.'

'Oh, bollocks.'

'Look, Tom, I don't know how things worked in the OSS, but in MI5 we don't just go about spilling information simply because someone poses a question. Yes, I've heard of Basil Rheinhaus, and that's all you're getting from me.'

'Any idea where I might find him?'

'What on earth could you want him for? And why do you think I might know?'

Wilde simply shrugged and let the question hang.

'That's that then,' Baxter said after a few moments' silence. 'So now, it's my turn to fire the questions. What have you been up to since you got out of hospital?'

Wilde laughed. 'You're very subtle, Gus – and do you know what, we didn't go around spilling information in the OSS either. So let's turn the conversation to lighter matters – such as the delightful Dolly. She's really something, isn't she. Movie star looks, voice like a barrow boy. Sweet girl.'

'Not really my type.'

'Julian was more your type. Goodrick's too.'

'Are you with the morality police? Is this the Spanish Inquisition?' Baxter's sharp tone revealed his displeasure at the way the conversation was going. He clearly hadn't expected a verbal assault from his guest.

The brandy and coffee arrived. Baxter tipped the spirit straight into the coffee and ordered another large one.

'Very well,' Wilde said, 'I'll try to answer your question. What have I been doing with myself? Well, I liked The Green Bear so much I went back there. Met up with Dolly and we had a delightful conversation. Then your chum Terry Adnams turned up and was charm itself. Didn't even threaten me with an ice-axe.'

Baxter drank his piping-hot, brandy-infused coffee while he considered this information. 'I did hear about the events in your college rooms. And yes, I have been looking into Adnams. I knew about his predilection for ice-axes.'

'And?'

'Well, I certainly don't think he killed poor Everett Glasspool. Hardly his territory.'

'But he might have supplied the weapon – to someone who was trying to make a statement.'

'Yes, that's possible.'

'Who was the buyer then, Gus? Find the buyer, find the killer.'

'If I could answer that question, Mother would be the first to know, quickly followed by the boys in blue.'

'Glad to hear it.'

Baxter wasn't smiling now. He gave Wilde a long, hard stare. 'Are you insinuating something?'

'Now why would I do that? We're both on the same side, aren't we?'

'Damn it, Tom. You're really beginning to get my goat. Look, I'm not as dim as I might appear, so it's clear to me that you're up to something, that you're not just swotting up on tradecraft in anticipation of some future reincarnation of the OSS. So, please, what's going on? Perhaps we can help each other.'

Wilde sighed. 'It's the murder of Everett Glasspool, of course. How could I not want to find out who invaded my space in such a brutal fashion?'

'But that doesn't quite explain what Everett was doing there. Why Cambridge? Why *your* set?'

'He asked me to meet him there, that's all I know. I had only met him briefly during the war, but beyond that nothing. Anyway, I agreed to see him at college out of vague interest, but I had my doubts. I thought Freya either wanted to tap me for information or to recruit me, but I'm beyond all that now. I'm a history professor and a family man, nothing more.'

'Are you?'

'Oh, come on. I'm giving lectures, supervising undergraduates, getting involved in the life of the college, looking after my six-year-old son.'

'You can't be surprised that I might wonder about you, though.'

'I'm wondering myself. Everything's changed. How could it not? I have inadvertently found myself in the middle of something but I have no idea what it is. Perhaps you can enlighten me on that score, Gus?'

'If I knew, I'd tell you.'

'Would you? Yes, we could help each other, work together. But in reality you seem to resent my presence and I don't think you're alone in that.'

'Mutual assistance works both ways. Why are you interested in Basil Rheinhaus?'

'I have my reasons.'

'And that's it?'

'He's a friend of a friend, that's all.'

'God damn you, Wilde. I'm off. Find your own way back to the office.'

More than anything else, Wilde needed his wife. Her instinct, her good sense, her ability to see things he hadn't.

He met Lydia at The Old Bell at seven. The pub, convenient for St Ursula's, was already rowdy and full of cheer, the pianist plonking out some old favourites while the customers sang along. Wilde and Lydia settled into a corner away from the piano where they could hear each other talk, but without prying ears.

He gave her a detailed rundown of the days since their last meeting and she listened intently.

'Bloody hell, Tom. Who were the two poor bastards at the old army camp?'

'Most likely a couple of innocents caught up in something ghastly. A Polish pilot and a British squaddie, both demobilised but short of somewhere to live.'

'Well, I'm glad you've got back in touch with Geoff Lancing, but I really thought we'd left all this mad stuff behind, Tom.'

'I thought so too.'

'You want my advice? Here it is. You're involved in this now and you can't just walk away. As I said when we were at Freya's, she needs you and you know very well you're not going to let her down. It's not in your nature.'

'So where do I go from here?'

'Wherever Freya wants you to go. Right now, I'd rather like you to take me to supper and attend to your nuptial duties. Burton's Hotel will do just fine.'

CHAPTER 25

In the morning they took breakfast together and Wilde mentioned his plan to visit Vivienne Chalke in Kensington and sit for his portrait. Lydia was doubtful.

'Do you really have time for such nonsense, Tom?'

'Well, she knows where Basil Rheinhaus is – that's the information I need. I'm more convinced than ever that he's central to this, whatever it is. Anyway, where else do I go?'

'Sounds a bit of a lost cause, but you go your own way. The taxi's here and I've got to get back to St Ursula's for anatomy pretty sharpish. Dr Belmer does not tolerate tardiness.' She leant across the breakfast table and kissed him goodbye.

He rose to escort her out of the hotel.

'Sit down, Tom, finish your coffee. I'm going to try to get back to Cambridge this weekend to see Johnny and find out how Janet's doing. It would be good if you could make it too.'

'I'll do my best,' he said.

He arrived at the Chalkes' large house at ten as he had said he would and was immediately taken by a maid to Vivienne's studio at the rear of the building. It had three tall windows, filling the space with northern light. A palm tree in a vast pot spread its leaves across one side of the room.

Enormous radiators churned out enough heat to keep winter at bay. The whole room was made brighter by the snow on the roofs of the buildings at the far end of the garden.

Canvases, some empty, some half-painted, some seemingly finished were piled against the walls or hung at odd angles on hooks. In the centre of the room, a rather good nude seemed to be close to completion. The smell of oil was strong and pleasing to Wilde, especially as there was also the hint of an aroma of lemons, which was strange in this most untropical of seasons.

He took a seat on a battered old sofa, looked around at the artworks and waited.

She turned up ten minutes later, full of apologies, sweeping in like a gust of wind. This time she was not in flowing robes, but in brown corduroy trousers and a thick blue fisherman's pullover. On her hands she had woollen gloves with the fingers exposed.

'Tom, sweetie, so sorry to have kept you waiting. Coffee is on its way unless you'd prefer something else.'

'Coffee would be perfect.' It would help keep him awake after a second night in a row with little sleep.

'Now then, how are we going to do you? Clothes on or off?'

He laughed out loud. 'No one wants to see my body!'

'Oh, I don't know.'

'I really don't have a great deal of time to spare, so you might like to just concentrate on my face.'

'I agree. You have a simply wonderful face. Anyway, I always start with a little preliminary sketching.'

She removed the nude painting from the easel and replaced it with a drawing book opened at a blank page. Without hesitation, she squinted at Wilde and began with confident strokes. 'Chin up a bit, Tom,' she said.

He obeyed her. The coffee came and was deposited on a table near the sofa. Then the servant departed.

'OK, let's stop a moment and drink our coffee.'

The coffee was good, better than the hotel's offering, which had been a little weak this morning.

'Where do you get this?' Why was it that everyone else – Freya, the hotel, The Green Bear and the Chalkes, had access to commodities usually denied him?

'The black market, of course. Where everyone shops.'

'I thought you had communist sympathies – surely you like to share the discomfort of the working man and woman.'

'Oh, what nonsense. And who told you I was a communist?'

'I heard it somewhere. You know how these things get around.'

'Let me guess: Cecil Eagles. He's about as discreet as a foghorn. And yes, I do have communist sympathies. This is surely the future of the world.'

'Murder, repression, secret police? How do you think you'd fare with your great wealth when the Red masses come calling?'

She smiled with a hint of condescension as though talking to a dim child. 'I care for the world, not my own skin. Stalin is condemned for his purges and for tyranny, but you must take the long view. His actions will inevitably lead to progress, Tom.'

'Not much progress for those he shoots.'

'You can't make an omelette without breaking eggs.'

It was the old excuse for murder from the likes of Lenin, otherwise known as *the end justifying the means*, and he gave the familiar response. 'So where's the omelette?'

She brushed the question aside. 'Enough politics for a February morning. Tell me, Tom, why are you here?'

'You said you wanted to paint me.'

'Yes, but I didn't expect you to actually come.'

'You've stumped me, Vivienne . . . I don't know what to say.'

'Spit it out. You've come across London from God knows where on a bitter morning and here you are.'

He hadn't anticipated such directness. 'Very well,' he said, 'I confess it: I'm intrigued by you. I wanted to see you again.'

'Now that's more like it. That's what I want to hear. So finish your capitalist coffee, shut up and sit still. I don't want you to move a muscle.'

The drawing continued all morning, without conversation. The only sound was a quiet rendition of a Tchaikovsky symphony on a gramophone player in the centre of the room, followed by some Chopin.

At twelve-thirty, she snapped the stub of her charcoal in half and flung the pieces across the room. 'That's enough for today. I'm otherwise engaged this afternoon. Are you staying for lunch?'

'That's very much up to you. This is your home.'

'Well, stay then and I can find out a bit more about you. It'll only be some sort of soup, with fresh bread and maybe a bit of cheese and a glass of something.'

'You promised lobster as I recall, but soup would do very well.'

'We'll get down to the actual painting next time you come. For the moment, let's find somewhere cosier.'

He glanced at her drawing and saw that she had achieved a good likeness. 'Very flattering,' he said.

'It's just you, Tom. I never flatter.'

'But you have made me look rather hard.'

'Perhaps you *are* hard.'

They went through to a small side room with a warm coal fire and a square table laid with white linen, silver and china. One of the servants immediately brought through warmed bowls, newly-baked bread and a tureen of soup.

'What I don't understand, Tom, is what on earth you were doing with Cecil Eagles. You make a very odd couple.'

'We're not a couple.'

'You know what I mean. You don't seem to fit each other's circles.'

'I don't keep to a particular circle. I never have. Cecil amuses me and I enjoy learning about art from him. There is a powerful connection between history and art history, the one often informing the other. They're inseparable. Whether the same will be true this century, now that we have film and photography, I don't know.'

'A very good point. And tell me, did you manage to make contact with our friend Basil Rheinhaus?'

'Not yet. Perhaps you could put in a word for me.'

'Of course. I'll do just that next time we talk.'

'Could you not just tell me where he is?'

'That would be breaking a confidence. So no.'

The white-gloved waiter was at Wilde's elbow with a white cloth across his arm and a bottle of wine ready for pouring. Wilde looked at the bottle with interest.

'It's a 1937 Montrachet, sir.'

'Pour away.'

'Tuck in, Tom,' Vivienne Chalke said. 'We don't stand on ceremony here.'

'Will your husband be joining us?'

'I sincerely hope not. He's only useful for one thing – money. I can't stand the slimy bastard.'

She was speaking in front of the waiter. Did she not realise servants had ears? Or did she simply not care? Wilde suspected the latter.

'Now then, Tom. What are you really? We all know what Cecil is, of course, a bloody spy for the establishment. What about you? Who do you work for when you're not cramming tales of kings and queens into impressionable heads?'

'My work at Cambridge is a full-time job.'

'Yet here you are in London in the middle of the Lent term. They must be missing you.'

'My wife is working down here.'

'Really? Do I know her? What does she do?'

'She's a doctor.'

'Gosh, how very modern – a woman doctor. Hospital or general practice?'

He was getting in too deep with these lies, but he had felt compelled to give a reason for his presence in London. Also, he had something else to do; his reason for being here. 'You know, Vivienne, do you mind if we continue this conversation in a while? I'm desperate for the lavatory.'

'Just along the corridor to the hall, Tom. I'm sure you can find it yourself. A man of your great intellect.'

He rose and nodded, then left the room. Yes, he could find the lavatory all right, but that wasn't what he wanted. It was the address book on the telephone table on the opposite side of the hall. And there it was. Wilde looked around, half-expecting to see one of the servants behind him in the corridor, but he had the place all to himself.

He opened the gold-trimmed leather volume and skimmed through the pages to the 'R' entries. There were forty or fifty names – the Chalkes had a lot of acquaintances – but no Rheinhaus.

Cursing under his breath, he flicked the pages back to the 'B' section. Again, there were dozens of names, addresses and phone numbers, but no Basil. This was impossible.

'Having fun, Tom?'

He turned as if he had been shot. Vivienne Chalke was standing there, cigarette in hand, gazing at him languidly.

'I was hoping to find Basil Rheinhaus's number.'

'I rather thought you might be. Did you find it?'

'You know I didn't. It's not here.'

'Look, Tom, I'm used to having MI5 drudges taking an interest in me and my friends because of my politics. It's been that way for the best part of fifteen years, but you're an American. So don't you think it's time you came clean and told me exactly who you are and why you're here?'

'All right, I was in the OSS and I still do a little security work when called on. And at the moment I would very much like to find Basil Rheinhaus.'

'Are you going to tell me why?'

'I can't. It's too sensitive.'

'Nothing to do with his work as an atomic scientist by any chance?'

He shrugged. 'I can quite understand why you might think that. What I don't understand is why you aren't prepared to help me meet him.'

'Perhaps I'm protecting him.'

'From me?'

'As I said, I'm not really very sure who you are. Neither is Basil.'

'It sounds as if he's hiding from something – or someone.'

'You think what you like, Professor Wilde. For the moment, I rather think lunch is over, don't you? I'm sure your undergraduates would love to see you back in Cambridge. The door is just in front of you . . .'

CHAPTER 26

'What in God's name have you been up to, Tom?' Freya Bentall seemed almost more furious than the last time they confronted each other. 'Gunshots in the night? Bodies in some arctic wasteland near bloody Harwell? Have you taken leave of your senses?'

'What have you heard?'

'What do you think I've heard, for pity's sake? I've heard just about everything. The Harwell police and the local plod were on to London within the hour, then the Yard detectives realised this was way beyond their competence given the crime scene's proximity to the atomic energy establishment and, hey presto, it's all passed over to the Special Branch, followed in short order by MI5 and yours truly. The minister is not happy.'

'The War Office meeting? I should have realised there'd be a reaction. I'm sorry.'

'This friend of yours, Augustin Lancing, can he keep his mouth shut?'

'Yes. And he prefers to be known as Geoff.'

'Well, make it clear to him that I don't want a word of this reaching Fleet Street or anywhere else for that matter. Bodies in a disued army base near Britain's first atomic pile? Not a good look. Not good for confidence. And as for your apology, it simply won't cut it. I want the whole story.'

For the next hour, he told her everything that had happened at Marbourne.

'Go on, Tom, all the rest.'

'That's it.'

'No, I'm thinking 1939, the months before the war. The name Lancing came up then – so did yours. Some horror involving the Cavendish Laboratory in Cambridge.'

'Very well, you can have all that too.'

Dredging the painful memories of that summer, he detailed all the events involving Geoff Lancing and the foiled attempt to wipe out the country's most brilliant scientists. This was in the very laboratory where the atom was first split by John Cockcroft and Ernest Walton as long ago as 1932. John Cockcroft, who now led Harwell. At last Wilde drew breath.

'Yes,' Freya said, 'I confess I knew all about those unfortunate events involving the Cavendish and the Nazis' attack. There was some suggestion that Lancing's sister played some role in events – and then she vanished.'

'That's another matter altogether. As for the attack itself, do you not think it's possible that it's happening again? Substitute Harwell for the Cavendish and Stalin for Hitler?'

'I think Harwell is a great deal better guarded than the Cavendish Laboratory ever was. Many of those in power were very naive in the pre-war years.'

'There's something else I should mention, which may or may not be relevant. I called on Vivienne Chalke again, even sat for her. I did so for one reason alone – to get into her house. I want to find Basil Rheinhaus and she knows where he is. The Harwell scientist I mentioned, Klaus Fuchs, seemed astonished that he might even be in England. But he is – I've seen him. And now I can't locate him. What is he up to – and why is Vivienne Chalke keeping me from him?'

Freya frowned. Somehow he had disturbed her.

'What is it?'

'I'm not sure this is a line you should be pursuing. Get back on to Eagles, Baxter and Stone.'

'Oh, you know very well that's going nowhere. If you ask my opinion of the three men, I will happily list their attributes and deficiencies as I see them, but if you want to know whether any are traitors, I have no idea. They're all too smart for that. And as for Stone, he won't even have anything to do with me. Unless you're suggesting I put on a dirty mac and fedora and follow him like one of your shadows?'

She laughed. 'You're much too visible. We demand very precise qualities in our surveillance men: they must be about five foot eight – not too short, not too tall; neither good-looking nor ugly, simply unremarkable; perfect vision without spectacles and excellent hearing; good reactions to changing circumstances; patient and tough. So you see, you would fail on at least a couple of counts.'

'Am I not tough or patient then?'

'Very funny. Anyway, I'll bring you and Stone together again and then I suggest you invite him to the pub or something – whatever it is you men do when you're trying to mend bridges. Get to know him.'

As she spoke, her door flew open and Cecil Eagles stormed in. His brow was red with fury. He did not bother with small talk or courteous greetings, merely launched a tirade.

'How dare you, Wilde!' He spat the words and for a moment he seemed about to launch a physical attack, but then thought better of it and turned to Freya. 'This man – whatever he is – this man is ruining years of good work. God damn it, Mother, you've brought a half-witted bloody cuckoo into the nest.'

Freya was standing up now and stabbed her finger at the intruder. 'Never step into my office again until you're invited.'

'I've had enough. I'm taking this to the top – Percy Sillitoe will hear of this.'

'You're making a fool of yourself, Cecil. Shut the door, sit down and pull yourself together before I have you thrown out of the building.'

Eagles slammed the door shut but didn't take a seat. His voice lowered but grew even more intense in rage. 'Has this bastard told you what he's been doing?'

'Yes, I believe we're up to speed. Calm down and tell me what's riled you.'

'Mother, I took him to Vivienne's because I thought it was somewhere safe, somewhere he could do no harm, watch me at work, the way I inveigle my way into society – and listen for gossip. Instead he wades in with his big fat American size twelves and does his best to unwind years of work.'

Wilde stood silent, harbouring more than a faint suspicion of what this was all about.

Freya patted rather than slammed her small palm on the desk. 'Get to the point, Cecil. Are you going to tell me what this is about or just skirt around the edges all day?'

'In front of *this moron*? Is he supposed to listen in while I tell you what I've been trying to do and what's now happened?'

'I trust him, Cecil. Speak.'

'You *trust* him?'

'As much as I trust anyone in this office. Now get on with it.'

Eagles built himself up as if unsure whether to explode or turn and walk away. Finally, he said it: 'Everyone thinks she's a committed Bolshevik – but she's on *our* side, damn it. Vivienne's one of us, that's what this is about – and this . . . this man . . . this friend of yours . . . goes spying on her. I've been cultivating darling Vivienne for years. She gives me chapter and verse on every fellow traveller in society and now he's probably blown the whole thing apart. She's livid, feels compromised – and wants nothing more to do with me.'

'I didn't spy on her,' Wilde said. 'I was looking for someone. She knows where he is.'

'Yes, you're looking for Basil Rheinhaus. Mother, can we please put a bullet in this man's head? Even better, two bullets and then bury him ten feet deep in a lead coffin.'

Freya sat down again. For a few moments she said nothing, simply twirled a fountain pen between her fingers, then addressed herself to Eagles. 'I want you to go now, Cecil. We will talk in private when you are a great deal calmer. And I have to say that you should *not* have told me about Vivienne. If she is an important source of information to you, then you should protect her – even from those with whom you work and trust. I would have thought better of you. Tell no one else what you have told Tom and me, or you could place her in grave danger. Now go.'

Cecil's haughty demeanour suddenly crumpled and he looked chastened because he knew that she was right; he had spoken in anger and let too much out. He didn't seem to know what to do, then suddenly nodded to her, glared at Wilde, and shuffled from the room.

'Nor will *you* tell anyone, Tom,' she said when Eagles had closed the door behind him, much more softly this time.

Wilde looked at her with admiration. Bentall the interrogator. Cecil's anger had been his downfall. Freya Bentall must have been a formidable advocate in her legal days and even more danger-ous when questioning suspects for MI5. 'Don't worry about me. I've had enough of these machinations and I'm going back to Cambridge tomorrow to resume my life.'

'Your week's not up.'

'Oh, I think it probably is. And if not, well, I'm breaking my promise.'

She looked at her watch. 'I think today's over. I'm going to take an early cut. You'll at least stay with me tonight, yes? Ethel man-aged to get some neck of mutton so I'm pretty sure she'll have cooked a decent Irish stew. Get Lydia over too if you like.'

'No, I'll see her in Cambridge.'

Wilde and Freya went back to her flat together in her ministry car. The weather was raw but the air was dry and the roads passable. Her mood had mellowed and she apologised for over-reacting. 'But this is tough, Tom. I simply don't know where it's all going.'

'Basil Rheinhaus means something to you, doesn't he? I'm right to be looking for him – he's not just a bit-part player.'

'There are things I can tell you and things I can't. Unlike Cecil Eagles I am not about to break faith simply to keep you happy.'

'You're not talking sense, Freya.'

'And you're in danger of becoming bloody rude.'

'Rheinhaus is the reason I went down to see Geoff Lancing at Harwell. And you know the upshot of that little foray – so don't go telling me he has nothing to do with this, nothing to do with the threat revealed to you by your German intelligence friend. You have been asking me to find a mole at the heart of your organisa-tion but you've kept back half the story.'

'This sort of work is no mystery to you, Tom. You know how things are.'

'And what of Dolly Coster? Why has nothing happened about her? She probably knows the name of the assassin who killed Everett Glasspool in my college rooms. Aren't you going to talk to her at least?'

'We've tried.'

'Really? And what was the upshot?'

'Couldn't find her. She wasn't at The Green Bear and no one there knew where she was, or so they said. They certainly didn't like being questioned by our Special Branch boys.'

Her words chilled him. A visit by Special Branch officers was not a subtle way to make contact with Dolly. Their arrival at The Green Bear would have done Dolly no favours. She could now be in danger.

They were still in the back of the car, a black pre-war Wolseley. 'Let me find her, Freya. Would your driver take me on when he's dropped you off?'

'I think that will be acceptable. Will you be back for supper?'

'Hopefully.'

Wilde got out of the car on Kennington Park Road near the underground station. 'Would you wait a few minutes, driver?'

'At your service, sir.'

There were no street lights, of course. The gloom was relieved only by the Wolseley's headlights, but that was enough for him to see the tobacconist near the entrance to the Tube. It was closed and the lights were out.

The door at the side of the tobacconist was ajar, however, and he pushed it open. He flicked the switch, but no light came on. He had a small torch in his pocket, something he always carried these days, but the batteries were low and it threw out nothing but a dim yellow beam.

Climbing the stone staircase, he came to a single door on the right and knocked at it. There was no answer, no sounds from within.

From the description given him by Dolly Coster, he was sure this must be her home. He knocked again then turned the door handle. It was unlocked and he stepped inside.

The flat was desperately poor. One room with a single metal bed, a wooden table and two chairs, a gas cooker, and a sink which probably doubled as a basin. It was mean and austere but Wilde guessed it was probably looked after well by Dolly and kept clean. Today, however, it had been ransacked. The bed was on its side, the table smashed. Her few belongings – a couple of books (Dickens and du Maurier), clothes, a wireless – had been scattered, torn and upended.

Someone had been here looking for Dolly or looking for something she owned. Wilde said a silent prayer that she had not been found for whoever did this was not about to treat her with kindness.

He looked at all the papers for some clue to where she might have gone, but there was nothing. After ten minutes his torch died and he gave up the search, leaving the flat as he had found it.

The car was still there, its engine purring and its headlights the only illumination on the road apart from a distant bus. The driver's window wound down.

'Got what you came for, Mr Wilde?'

'She wasn't there so I want to talk to her neighbours. I don't suppose you carry a torch?'

'You're in luck, sir. Got one here with new batteries.' He fished in the glove compartment, produced a sturdy instrument and handed it to Wilde.

'I'll be as quick as I can.'

Wilde took the new torch, re-crossed the road and went to the house on the left of Dolly's. This one had a modern bell-push and a boy of about eight came to the door within moments. 'Yes, mister? Mum says she's not buying nothing.'

'I'm not selling anything.'

'And she ain't got no rags, bones or old iron.'

'Can I speak to your mum, please?'

'Mum!' the boy shouted down the corridor. 'There's a bloke here wants to speak to you, says he ain't selling nothing.'

'What's he want?'

'What do you want, mister?'

'Just a few words.'

'Mum! He wants a few words with you.'

'Oh, for God's sake.'

Half a minute later she arrived at the front door, wiping her hands on her apron. She looked about eight months pregnant. 'Yes?' she said warily. 'How can I help?'

'I'm sorry, this is obviously a difficult time.'

'Feeding time at the zoo. Anyway, I'm here now, so speak.'

'I'm looking for your neighbour, Dolly – Amelia – Coster.'

'And who might you be exactly?'

'My name's Wilde, Tom Wilde.'

Her demeanour changed. She looked him up and down, then glanced behind him into the street. 'You'd better come in, Mr Wilde.'

He stepped into the short corridor and followed her through to the kitchen, where three more children – even younger than the boy at the door – were busy eating their tea and squabbling noisily. They took no notice of the newcomer because they were too interested in their toast and jam and their fights.

'This is the zoo, Mr Wilde. Charming bunch of little bleeders, aren't they?'

'I'm sure they all have their individual virtues.'

'Taking a long time to come through though. Anyway, you want Amy for some reason. Well, she lives in the flat above the baccy shop next door.'

'She's not there, but someone has been. The place has been turned upside down.'

'I thought I heard some noise. Bastards. And you say your name's Tom Wilde. Would you have any proof of that? You could be anyone for all I know.'

'I don't have anything on me at the moment – I was robbed.' He turned his head to show her the bruising. 'Took a bit of a kicking and lost my wallet.'

'Yes, Amy mentioned that. What's your favourite drink?'

'Whisky.'

'And you're a light-heavyweight boxer?'

'Middleweight.'

She shrugged. 'Well, in the absence of a passport, ID card or any other sort of identification, that'll have to do for now. Anyway, you give a good impression of an American professor, so I'll take you at your word. Why do you want Amy?'

'I'm worried about her. I think she's in danger. The state of her flat seems to confirm it.'

'All right.' She turned to the dresser and took the lid off a tea caddy, then removed a slip of paper. 'Here you are,' she said, placing it in Wilde's palm. 'Amy asked me to give this to you before she left this morning. She said someone was out to get her and she had to absent herself for a while. Look after her, Mr Wilde. She's a good 'un.'

'Thank you. I intend to do just that. What's your name, by the way?'

'Carol. And I'm sorry but I'm not going to offer you a cup of tea. The boy will see you out.'

Outside in the ice-cold street, as he was walking back to the car, he saw a face in the headlights. Just momentarily, then it was gone.

A face he recognised. Shadox Stone.

CHAPTER 27

Wilde tried to follow the man but he disappeared as suddenly as he appeared. Had he slipped into the park or down the Tube? Wilde scanned the area with the torch, to no avail. And then he began to doubt his eyes; had that really been Shadox Stone, the MI5 man who left him holding a bacon sandwich and a cup of tea at Smithfield?

What possible reason could he have to be here in Kennington, close to Dolly's flat? It made no sense.

Returning to the car, he looked at the scrap of paper the young neighbour had given him and read an address in East London. Nothing more.

'Where now, Mr Wilde?' the driver inquired.

Wilde studied the piece of paper. He was in two minds: East End or West End?

'Miss Bentall's flat.'

'Yes, sir.'

Freya Bentall was relaxing by the fire with her feet up, a glass of brandy at hand, the wireless at her side regaling her with the day's news. Tensions were rising between the US and the Soviet Union and the Voice of America radio station was now broadcasting propaganda into Eastern Europe.

'Help yourself to a drink, Tom, and tell me how you got on.'

'Dolly's fled, her place has been turned over.'

'Now that is unfortunate.'

'She knows too much – the Special Branch visit will have made her a target.'

'Are you blaming me? I didn't tell them how to go about it, just told them to bring her in.'

'Well, she's at risk but I have an address for her. My problem is this: I'm convinced I saw your man Stone outside her flat in Kennington. Now why would he be there?'

'Shadox Stone? Are you sure?'

'No, I'm not. But what if it *was* him?'

'Then I would want to know what he was up to.'

'Was he watching me – or watching for Dolly?'

'A question I can't answer, but I can't for the life of me see what interest he might have in your friend Dolly. That's Gus Baxter's territory and yours. But I'll make inquiries.' She reached out for the phone and dialled a number. 'Is Shadox Stone there? No? Well, as soon as he's home or makes contact, ask him to call Miss Bentall. Thank you.' She replaced the phone. 'He lives in lodgings in Finsbury Park. That was his landlady. Anyway, Dolly . . .'

'I should go to her now. Your driver is outside, waiting for my decision.'

'Go, Tom – and bring her here. Offer her protection but do not, under any circumstances, promise her money.'

'You'll have to bear with me,' the driver said as he consulted a map, 'I haven't been to that part of London before.'

'Take your time. What's your name, by the way? We haven't been introduced.'

'Sims, sir. Ah.' He stabbed the map with his finger. 'Found the bugger. Looks like a little cul-de-sac.'

As they went east of the city, the roads became steadily worse, more icy, more in need of re-surfacing. The housing seemed increasingly poor. Much of it had been bombed during the war as the Luftwaffe did its worst, attacking the docks and those who worked there.

It took them over an hour to reach Bowman Terrace, Poplar, or what was left of it, which wasn't much. Half the houses were gone. Number seventeen, the scrap of paper said. The car eased slowly up the narrow street. No other cars were in evidence because none of the people who lived here would be able to afford one, even if they could somehow access the petrol to fuel it.

'If my navigational skills are correct we're here,' Sims said. 'That house sticking out like a solitary tooth in an old man's mouth must be number seventeen.'

'Will you wait for me?'

'Of course, sir.'

He walked up to the house. There were sounds inside, voices and laughter and dim light of some sort, probably a gas lamp. Wilde waited a few moments to gather his thoughts, then knocked.

Within seconds he was face to face with a thin, unhealthy-looking man.

'Yes?'

'I believe Amy Coster is here.'

'Who?'

'Amy. Amelia Coster. This is seventeen Bowman Terrace, isn't it?'

The man looked past him. 'Is that your car out there?'

'It's the one I'm using.'

'Very fancy. And what would your name be?'

'Tom Wilde.'

'Well, Tom, you'd better come in, hadn't you? My little sister was hoping you might turn up. Reckons you could be the making of her fortune.'

Dolly was in the front room, playing with a small girl of four or five who Wilde took to be her niece. She grinned at Wilde. 'This is Maggie, my bro's girl,' she said, confirming Wilde's assumption.

'Nice to meet you, Maggie.'

The little girl ignored him.

'Carol gave you the paper then? No one saw you there, right?'

That was a tricky question and he hesitated before replying because he had seen a face he took to be Shadox Stone, though the more he thought about it, the less sure he became.

'Because if they did and they put two and two together and worked out that she had told you where I'd gone, they would beat her and threaten her kids to get this address. Terry Adnams has decided I'm a grass, so I'm a dead girl walking.'

Wilde had no option but to confess. 'There was someone outside. I just caught his face in the headlight and then he disappeared.'

'Bleeding Norah, you're having a laugh, right?' She turned her attention to her brother, who was standing in the doorway. 'We're all going to have to move, Bert. And I mean right now.'

'You can come with me, Amy,' Wilde said. 'I've got a safe house – the safest. The car's outside.'

'And what about Carol and her kids? And Bert and Maggie?'

'Have they got anywhere else to go?'

'Oh yeah, they've got their country mansions. Silly me, how could I forget that?'

'The face I saw, I have reason to believe he was following me, not you. I don't for a moment think he has anything to do with Terry Adnams or his gang.'

'Has he got a name then, this face?'

'Shadox Stone.'

'Never heard of him.'

'No reason why you should. He's in the same line of work as Gus Baxter. I'm not entirely sure whose side he's on, but he's not a gangster.'

She looked to her brother. He was less than five and a half feet tall, skin and bone, with insect bites on his neck as though he had been attacked by an infestation. His daughter, however, was the picture of bright-eyed health and shared her Aunt Amy's looks.

'I'll take my chances here, sis.'

'You sure?'

'We'll be all right. You go with the geezer.'

'I promise you she'll be well looked after,' Wilde said.

'She'd better be, mate.'

Dolly shrugged and nodded her acquiescence. 'All right, I'll go with you, Mr Wilde. But leave a quid or two for Bert and Maggie, yes?'

Wilde didn't have much since his wallet was stolen, but Lydia had left him with some money. He took out a big white five-pound note, all folded up, and handed it over to Bert Coster. 'I'd give you more but I got robbed.'

'Well, glory be, that's a five pounder.' He unfolded it and held it up to his daughter. 'What do you think of that, Maggie? We'll eat like kings this week.'

'Can I have sweets, Dad?'

'I think we might find a few ounces on the black.'

At first, the journey west was a great deal speedier than the difficult trip in the other direction. Wilde sat in the back with Dolly.

'Has Adnams threatened you, Amy?'

'For God's sake call me Dolly. I'm used to it now. Can't cope with all these different names.'

'Well?'

'I didn't hang around long enough to be threatened, not once the Special Branch came asking after me. I know Terry too well. He changes on people and then they're done for. I've seen it before. One minute you're cock of the walk, the next you're out in the cold. And if it's something really serious, he doesn't take prisoners. He ain't called Axeman for nothing.'

'Your flat had been turned over.'

'Well, there you are then. He liked you when you turned up with Gus at the Bear, but don't be fooled, Tom, he'll turn on you in an instant, and smile while he's cutting you. Anyway, I'm safe now, you say. Does that mean you've sorted out the monkey for me?'

'I very much doubt you'll get five hundred pounds, but there may be some help if you cooperate.'

The driver turned the car down a side street, then stopped.

'What are you doing, Sims?'

'It might be paranoia, Mr Wilde, but I have a feeling someone's following us.'

CHAPTER 28

They waited for a minute, the engine still running, then Sims executed a U-turn and drove back to the main road. He turned left and stopped again, looking in all directions. There was very little traffic. Nothing obviously out of place. If they were being followed the threat seemed to have evaporated.

The only light came from a few windows, his own headlights and the chill, reflected, light of snowdrifts and ice.

'Must have been my fevered imagination, sir. That's what comes of doing this job: too many threats to consider. Forgive my jitters.'

It was possible he hadn't been mistaken, of course. Wilde understood why anyone should have an attack of nerves. Had Sims been alerted by Freya to the potential hazards of this assignment or was it simply that he always had to be ready for enemy action?

'I don't like this, Tom,' Dolly said. 'I thought I was supposed to be safe with you.'

'We're just being cautious, that's all.'

They were in the City, not far from St Paul's. 'I think I'll turn north and take a slightly different route, Mr Wilde.'

'We're in your hands, Sims. Do what you think is best.'

Dolly was sitting at Wilde's side, shivering. He took off his coat and gave it to her to use as a blanket.

'Crikey, you really are a gentleman, aren't you, prof?'

'Tell me a bit about yourself, Dolly. Were you brought up in the East End or South London?'

'East. Bow Bells girl, me. Can't you tell?'

'I sort of guessed. How did you end up across the river with Terry Adnams and his crew?'

She shrugged. 'It's not much of a story.'

'Tell me anyway.'

'All right, I'll go back to the beginning. Dad was a docker, reserved occupation so he wasn't called up. Might still be alive if he had been. He and Mum died in the Blitz in 1940. They'd sent me to the shelter when the sirens went but couldn't be bothered themselves. "We'll take our chances, love," Mum said. Never saw them again.'

'How old were you?'

'Fifteen. Twenty-two now. Anyway, I went to live with Bert and his slag of a wife. Then Maggie came along so I had to find a place and look after myself, because Brenda really didn't want me around. Got a pub job with a room on the top floor – well, I couldn't stand the thought of a bleeding factory.'

'Where's Bert's wife now?'

'I have no bleeding idea, and nor does Bert and nor do we care. Just upped and left one day. Probably another bloke, but who knows. She liked a drink and she liked the lads.'

'And Terry Adnams, when did you meet him?'

'One day – couple of weeks after the end of the Japanese war it was – Terry comes in mob-handed, throwing his weight around like he wanted to move into the East End. He gives me the eye. The rest is history, as they say. How could I not fall for him, the way he flashed the money and the muscle? Treated me like a queen.' She laughed. 'Course I didn't know then that he just wanted to put me on the game. Like I said, not much of a story.'

'I'm sorry,' Wilde said.

'Sorry about what?'

'That he forced you into prostitution.'

'Well, it pays a lot better than being a barmaid, so I wasn't complaining. Anyway, I need your help not your pity.'

'But you want something else from life, something better. You made that clear.'

'Never had no shoes until I was eight. Anyway, everyone wants something better. The kid with a potato wants a sausage. The kid with a sausage wants steak. That's life.'

When they arrived on the street outside Freya's flat the electric lights seemed to be on, which was a comfort. 'What exactly is this place?' Dolly demanded when the car came to a halt. 'It certainly ain't bleeding Cambridge because that's in the far north, Scotland or somewhere. Is this your home?'

Wilde laughed discreetly. 'No, the flat up there belongs to Miss Freya Bentall, who works for the government. She is extremely important – a sort of senior police officer, if you like.'

'A woman cop? That's ridiculous.'

'Well, they do exist, you know.'

'Wouldn't give tuppence for their chances against a villain like Terry.'

'There are many different ways of upholding the law, Dolly. Anyway, she's a lot tougher than she looks, so come and meet her because she can help you. She'll keep you safe – but you need to answer her questions honestly. She'll always know if you're lying.'

The meeting was not what Wilde was expecting. He had braced himself for a hackles-raised confrontation between two territorial felines who had taken an instant dislike to each other.

Instead, Freya beamed a maternal smile that Wilde didn't know she possessed. The office nickname of Mother was supposed to be ironic, casting aspersions at her supposed lack of the maternal instinct.

With the smile, she put out her hand. 'You must be Dolly. Can I call you Dolly? Is that all right?'

'Yeah, that's all right. What do I call you, missus?'

'I'm Freya Bentall and I'd be very happy to be called Freya. Would you like a cup of tea? Or hot chocolate, perhaps?'

'Hot chocolate.'

'Come on in then and make yourself comfortable.'

At first the evening went well. Freya asked Dolly about herself and got much the same replies as Wilde. She apologised that they really wouldn't be able to give her five hundred pounds for information leading to the conviction of Terry Adnams and others, but that the security service would be able to help her set up a new home with work, perhaps in another town where no one knew her.

Dolly listened and occasionally nodded and threw in a question such as 'what other town?' but Wilde could see that she wasn't convinced.

After supper, Freya turned to Wilde. 'Tom, I'd rather like a little time alone with Dolly for a bit of girl-talk, would you mind terribly leaving us and disappearing into your bedroom. There's a copy of *The Times* with half the crossword unsolved, or help yourself to a book from my shelves.'

'Of course.' In fact he was rather glad to have a little time to himself.

He stretched out on the bed and tried to do the crossword, filling in a few clues. Then turned his attention to a Peter Fleming travel book about his journey across the Soviet Union to China. It was intriguing at first, but his thoughts were elsewhere: the face of Shadox Stone outside Dolly's flat in Kennington; the possibility that they were followed back from Poplar; intruders at the home of his old friend Geoff Lancing followed by the discovery of two corpses at an abandoned barracks near the Harwell atomic research establishment; the disappearance of a scientist named Basil Rheinhaus.

His eyes were growing heavy and he began to realise he needed to get ready for bed when there was a knock at the door.

'Yes?' he said.

'It's me, Freya, we've had our little chat so you can come out now.'

Wilde opened the door. 'Actually, I was just thinking of brushing my teeth and turning in for the night.'

'Oh, a little nightcap won't do you any harm. Come on, Tom, I've made up a bed for Dolly and she's taken herself off. She's a lovely young woman, isn't she?'

'Yes, yes, she is.'

He stepped outside and that was when they both heard the sound of shattering glass. He looked over Freya's shoulder and saw that something hard, the size of a fist, had smashed through the centre of the window that gave on to the road below. It rolled across the floor like a cricket ball, then stopped.

In the same instant, Wilde realised what it was. He grabbed Freya and dragged her into his room, flinging them both to the floor in the process.

The hand grenade exploded.

CHAPTER 29

The shattering blast ripped the silence and splintered the air. Furnishings and glasses and vases and pictures were torn from their places and hurled across the room. First a blinding flash, then utter darkness, smoke and dust as the explosion shot upwards and outwards from the floor into the walls and ceiling, smashing bulbs, killing the lights.

Wilde's ears rang, his nostrils were choked with dust and debris. His skin felt both hot and cold from the shock of the blast. He held Freya down, protecting her, but the instant was over and he knew they were both relatively unharmed and safe.

Unless a second grenade came.

He began to crawl. Slowly, he moved to his knees.

'Dear God,' she said, or at least the limited and muffled sound in his ears suggested to him that that was what she said, for little penetrated through the ringing and the havoc of confusion.

Somewhere in the corner of the sitting room, he saw a flame flickering, then it caught the tattered hem of a curtain and flared bright, scorching its way up towards the ceiling, spreading outwards to the other curtain.

Wilde's hesitation lasted no more than a second. He tore the blankets and sheets from his bed and stumbled towards the sitting room window. He tugged at the flaming curtains, pulling them and the curtain pole to the floor, then he beat at them with the bedclothes, smacking the flames into smoke and ashes.

Breathing deeply, he edged towards the gaping hole where once there had been a window and looked down into the street one storey below, partially lit by lights from other windows. He heard a crack and seemed to feel the wind of a bullet passing his neck and instantly ducked down.

From outside he heard voices. Neighbours coming out to see what had happened? Or the would-be killers? They couldn't hang around for long.

The fire was out, but now once again there was no light. He still had Sims's electric torch in his pocket, so he switched it on, scanned the devastated room and saw the horror on Freya's face and then the stunned bewilderment in the wide eyes of Dolly, who was standing at the doorway from the corridor, her mouth open.

Wilde nodded to her. 'We're OK,' he said. 'Stay out of the room. There's jagged glass and shrapnel everywhere.'

She nodded back.

Tentatively, still in his socks, he made his way to the telephone. Miraculously there was still a tone and he dialled 999, then he gathered up Freya and Dolly and moved them towards the kitchen, as far away from the shattered window as he could manage.

'What happened?' Dolly said.

'A grenade was thrown through the window.'

'Terry bloody Adnams. The bastard.'

'A hand grenade? Is that him?'

'Well, it's not his usual style. Maybe someone's trying to kill *you* or Freya.'

'That's a possibility.' His eyes flicked to Freya. 'What do you think?'

'We were all targets. Whoever did it doesn't care who dies.' Freya was shouting because she couldn't hear her own voice. 'You've got to get out – go to Nowhere Lane.'

Wilde was wondering what to do next. His initial instinct was to go down to the street to see if the assailant was still there. But he wasn't armed and there was a real possibility the would-be killer or killers were waiting for survivors to emerge.

It had to be better to stay here until the police and ambulance arrived. Safer for them all.

Through the ringing in their ears, they could just make out the jangling of cars and fire engines arriving in the street. Now they were safe.

But where, Wilde wondered, was Nowhere Lane? Was it a real place or a metaphor?

After the fire brigade examined the damaged area and declared it fire-free thanks to Wilde's work in beating out the flames, the police and medics took control of the situation. They wanted all three of the occupants to be conveyed to hospital, but they all refused.

'You look well enough, Miss Bentall, but there is a very real possibility that your eardrums could have been damaged.'

'I'll talk to my GP in the morning. I haven't got time for hospital now.'

'I do think, however,' the senior police officer said, almost shouting to be heard, 'that you will have to vacate the premises tonight. We need to go over the place with the proverbial tooth-comb, ma'am.'

'Of course. And you will need to liaise with the Special Branch. Just tell them my name; they know who I am.'

'So where are we going tonight?' Wilde said.

'Oh, I think we probably deserve a night at a good hotel, don't you, Tom? How about you, Dolly?'

'I've never been to a hotel.'

'No better time to start.'

'I think you must now tell me the whole unvarnished truth, Freya,' Tom said. The two of them were sitting in the bar at Burton's, nursing glasses of brandy. Sleep seemed almost impossible, with the fear and excitement still pulsing.

They had left Dolly alone upstairs in the twin room she would be sharing with Freya. She was luxuriating in the richness of her new surroundings, having never encountered such a comfortable bed and furnishings and bathing facilities.

'What do you want to know?'

'I want to know about Basil Rheinhaus and Harwell. There's something you're not telling me.'

They were in a corner of the room. Only the barman was present, no other guests.

'Very well,' she said, 'but you'll have to move closer because I can't judge my own voice and this cannot be overheard, even by the man behind the bar.'

Wilde shuffled up beside her.

'Rheinhaus is offering us information. He says that Harwell has been infiltrated, that there is a Soviet spy there.'

'So you've already had dealings with him?'

She nodded. 'Cecil has been liaising with me. He was deeply shocked when you recognised him at the Chalke Gallery. Only then did he realise that Rheinhaus could be in danger.'

'And you didn't think to tell me?'

'He wasn't your brief. Cecil Eagles is dealing with it.'

'But I was supposed to be investigating Cecil. I thought you didn't trust him.'

'I don't. That's the point.'

'Well, what's Rheinhaus saying about Harwell? How does he know there's a spy there?'

'Because the spy tried to recruit him.'

'Does this Soviet spy have a name?'

'I'm sure he does, but Rheinhaus isn't telling us. He's negotiating.'

'Money?'

'No, immunity and asylum. I can't tell you more.'

'Surely you can find out who he has worked with, then make an educated guess.'

'It's really not that simple. At one time or another, Rheinhaus has worked with everyone from Sir John Cockcroft down, including your friend Geoff Lancing from what you've told me. But the one you met at his place, Klaus Fuchs, is definitely on the list of those who need a close look. What did you make of him?'

'Interesting character. Brain as big as the moon, flirted with Cathy Lancing, gave nothing away. But then nor should he as a senior man at a top-secret establishment.'

'Well, he's on our radar.'

'So where is Basil Rheinhaus now?'

'Vanished. Even Cecil has lost him. I had already interviewed him twice over the phone before the incident at the gallery. But now? He's gone into hiding either because he's scared – or just being plain difficult. Obviously Vivienne Chalke can make contact with him, but beyond that we're a bit stuck because she won't even tell Cecil. I suspect Rheinhaus is trying to up the ante, making sure he gets a better deal from the British government. Our big problem is that we don't even know whether he's telling the truth – whether there *is* a Soviet spy in our atomic programme.'

'Offering something he doesn't have to save his neck?'

'Exactly. That could be it. Or maybe *he's* the Soviet spy – and this is all a Kremlin disruption mission. If we end up not trusting anyone at Harwell the whole project will be compromised and will probably fall apart.'

'This is alarming.'

'It can't be allowed to get out. We can't let it be known that there is even the hint of a chance that Harwell or our security services have been infiltrated. The effect on our already rocky relationship with Washington would be devastating, not to mention the hit to our already low morale here in Britain.'

'I see that.'

'The point is I have never felt this taut. Everett was killed, we've just been bloody bombed, my flat's uninhabitable, and there are two bodies laid out in a mortuary somewhere in Oxford. And someone – probably one of my own men – is not a friend but an enemy.'

'Well, we know Gus Baxter is interested in Rheinhaus. But he just passes it off as office tittle-tattle.'

'Yes, that rather floored me. Shadox Stone is another matter. He has a real connection, a family link. His sister worked for Rheinhaus's family in New York in the late thirties.'

'So they know each other?'

'There's no evidence, but it's possible – perhaps likely.'

'Where does Vivienne Chalke come in?'

'One of Rheinhaus's oldest friends. She was the one who introduced him to Cecil Eagles so that he could begin negotiations.' Freya held up her hand to summon the barman. 'I need another drink, a large one. You, Tom?'

'Why not?'

The barman nodded, took their order and wandered away to fetch the drinks.

'Then we have to find Rheinhaus – and Vivienne Chalke is our only lead. I'll have to go back to her.'

'Not yet. Let me talk to Cecil again. First we need to protect Dolly and see what we can extract from her. She's already told me quite a lot, including a name.'

'Anyone we know?'

She shook her head. 'George Blain. The name means nothing to me. Dolly said he's the one who bought the ice-axe from Adnams, which surely makes him the killer. She also said she had seen this Blain around The Green Bear on other occasions.'

'Description?'

'Young guy, full of himself, carries himself like a fighter. Hoity-toity voice – her words not mine. I imagine the name is false, but we'll have to look into it.'

'How did you persuade her to reveal that?'

'I made it clear she had no option. Poor cow, she's had no sort of life, has she?'

'She told me she didn't want my pity.'

'Maybe not, but she needs our protection. Tonight's attack demonstrates that none of us is safe.'

'So we need a hiding place.'

'I want her as far away from London as possible, Tom. In the morning, you must take her to Nowhere Lane. And I should tell you something else – something I've kept from you: Everett Glasspool had also spoken on the phone to Rheinhaus. We conducted the interviews in tandem.'

CHAPTER 30

They took breakfast together in the hotel dining room. Dolly was astonished by the food on offer, including bacon, fried bread and one fried egg each. She also spoke incredulously of the luxurious bath she had enjoyed.

Wilde noticed that the other guests could not take their eyes off the young woman. She had the aura of a Vivien Leigh or a Merle Oberon. Beauty at a higher level. And yet there was another dimension, an almost imperceptible edge of hardness forged in her tough upbringing.

As she gushed like an excited child, Wilde's thoughts strayed elsewhere. During the night, he had pondered a single question: why make an attempt on the life of Freya Bentall? The simple answer was that the motive must be the same as the one behind the murder of Everett Glasspool.

So what was that?

Perhaps the answer was that Glasspool and Freya were getting too close to some truth – or that her enemies *feared* they were close to it. And the same went for Wilde. That was what had made them all targets.

The train clattered through the snowy landscape, belching out clouds into the grey sky.

'So we're going to Cambridge, Tom?'

'First of all, Dolly, then some branch lines into Norfolk.'

'Bleeding hell, where are these places?'

'Do you know how to read a map?'

'You making fun of me? School taught us reading, writing and arithmetic and that was it.'

He drew a simple map of Britain on the copy of *The Times* he had brought, then placed dots for London and Cambridge and another dot for Whitwell & Reepham Station in Norfolk, and linked them all with lines and explained how many miles were involved and how long each leg of the journey would take.

Snow was falling when they pulled up at the long platform in Cambridge. God, thought Wilde, how many days, how many weeks had it been like this? Would it never end? He couldn't let it get him down, though, there were things – other people – to think about.

'We're going to my house now, Dolly. You can meet my boy Johnny and my wife Lydia.'

'My customers don't usually introduce me to their wives.'

'I can imagine they don't. But then I'm not exactly a customer, am I?'

'You'd like to be, though, wouldn't you, Tom? Haven't met a man yet who wouldn't.'

He laughed. 'I'm sure I've already turned down your offer.'

'That's as maybe but I know your prick wants me – and so do you if you'd only admit it to yourself.'

'You're talking nonsense, Dolly. Come on, there'll be no taxis so we've got a bit of a walk.'

Dolly had been lent a warm woollen coat, hat and gloves which Freya had salvaged from her wardrobe. She shivered as they left the station but pulled the coat about her.

'So this is Cambridge. I've never been out of London.'

'It's what's called a university town where young men and women – but mostly men – come to learn special skills when they've finished school.'

'If they've finished school they should be earning a living.'

They passed the grocer's shop where he had bought the peach. There was nothing in the window this time. He considered going inside just in case, but thought better of it.

Lazar Lukin had watched the train departing. He was irritated with himself. His initial instinct had been to stay in London, because that, surely, was where Rheinhaus was hiding. But now he wasn't sure.

'We have to follow him,' he said. 'Next train to Cambridge.'

He realised he had made a mistake and he was angry. He never made mistakes. Never. That was why he was still alive. This mistake had been born out of frustration. In trying to kill Wilde, he was reducing the chances of finding Rheinhaus. It was not just possible that Wilde knew where he was, it was almost certain.

Wilde would lead them to their prey, then they would kill both of them.

The Englishman wasn't sure. 'What if Rheinhaus is still here?'

'What if he's not? Wilde is the key. If he's leaving London, he's going to their safe house. That's where he's taking the girl. Rheinhaus is already there.'

'I'm not sure.'

'We follow Wilde. If Rheinhaus is still in London, your English friends can find him.'

Johnny answered the door and leapt into his father's arms. Behind him in the hallway stood the new housekeeper, Janet.

'I'd like you both to meet my friend Dolly from London. Dolly, this is Johnny and this is Janet, who has been looking after him while his mother and I are away.'

The two young women looked at each other suspiciously, but they all moved indoors and went to the kitchen because it was the warmest room in the house.

'Is Mrs Wilde here?'

'She called to say she couldn't make it after all because of work and she said she'd call you later,' Janet replied.

He was sorry to hear it, but not surprised. Her studies at St Ursula's were more demanding than she had ever imagined. 'Well, I'll explain why I'm here and what we're all about to do, but perhaps you'd do the honours and make us all a cup of tea, Janet. There was no restaurant car on the train.'

Dolly gazed around the room. Her tension was palpable. She was obviously struggling to understand the events of the past twenty-four hours and was unclear why she was here in this strange house in this strange town with these strange middle-class people who seemed to speak a different language to those in Poplar and Walworth.

'Johnny, why don't you show Dolly around the house. Show her your bedroom and your toys, yes?'

'But I want to be with you, Daddy. I haven't seen you in ages.'

'Oh come on, just for five minutes while I have a little chat with Janet.'

'All right, Daddy.' He held out his hand to Dolly and she took it self-consciously and allowed herself to be guided out of the room. Wilde shut the door after they had gone.

'What do you want to chat about, Professor Wilde?' Janet said as she spooned tea into the pot.

'Something has come up, something rather alarming. There was an attack on me in London last night.'

'Oh no, are you all right? Is that the cut on your head?'

'I'm fine. But someone means me harm.'

Her eyes opened wide. 'Is this something to do with the murder at your college?'

'Possibly. The thing is that Dolly is also in danger. I'm not at liberty to tell you the full details, but she needs protection.'

'And you want her to stay here?'

'No, I'm taking her on to a place in Norfolk, miles away from any hint of danger. My concern is that those who wish me harm are likely to know about this house – which implies that you and Johnny might also be in jeopardy.'

'I don't like the sound of that.'

'No, nor do I. Which is why I want you and Johnny to come to Norfolk with us.'

'I have no problem with that, but what about Johnny's school?'

'I'll call them.'

As he spoke the telephone rang.

'Shall I get that call, professor?'

'No, it might be Lydia. I'll be back in a minute to explain more.'

He went out into the hall and picked up the receiver. 'Hello, Wilde here.'

'Ah, Tom, so glad I made contact. It's Philip – Philip Eaton.'

The last voice that Wilde wanted to hear. 'Hello, Philip, how can I help?' He was aware that his voice was stiff and unwelcoming, but it was how he felt.

'Oh, I was just ringing to see if you were in. Thought we might get together for a chat. You recall that little event at Magdalene with the Soviet delegation?'

'How could I forget?'

'Now, now, it wasn't all that bad. Anyway, our Red chum Lazar Lukin is coming back to Cambridge and he's very keen that you should meet up. He rather thought you were the sort of chap who would actually get things done rather than just talking. Are you around this evening? We could meet at The Eagle or somewhere else suitably pleasant. What do you say?'

What could he say? He was very interested in meeting Comrade Lukin again. But that wasn't in his plans just at the moment; he was supposed to be moving onward to Norfolk this afternoon. 'I'm busy today,' he said. He had no intention of telling Eaton or anyone else what his actual plans were. 'How about tomorrow?'

'He may not be here.'

'I'll have to take my chances then.'

'All right, my rooms at 2 p.m. tomorrow while there's still daylight. Call to confirm in the morning if you would.'

Wilde immediately put the proposed meeting out of mind. He would be long gone before then.

No one else disembarked from the train at Whitwell Station. Why would they, when it was in the middle of Norfolk, at least a mile from the nearest settlement, the tiny Georgian market town of Reepham?

They stayed in the waiting room while the stationmaster called through to the house. Fifteen minutes later, he returned and told them that their transport had arrived.

The trip from Cambridge had taken three hours and involved two changes and it would soon be dark.

A murder of crows, hundreds of them, shrieked and burst forth from the skeletal trees as Wilde, Janet, Dolly and Johnny stepped from the station door and gazed upon the white expanse.

Standing in front of them, steam pluming from their nostrils, were three grey horses, harnessed as a sort of Russian troika pulling an ornate sleigh with steel runners. The coachman hopped down from his perch and introduced himself to his four passengers.

'I'm Reeves, ladies and gentlemen, at your service. Jump in. It'll be a bit of a squeeze but there are blankets and the ride won't be long.'

The four passengers didn't move straightaway. They were all staring at the carriage and its three horses with astonishment.

'Is this how people normally get about in Norfolk?' Wilde asked.

Reeves laughed. 'It's an antique. Miss Bentall's grandfather was a merchant in Russia long before the revolution and had this beauty shipped home from Moscow. She spends most of her time in a barn – the sleigh that is, not Miss Bentall – but she's proving her worth this winter.'

They all piled aboard, and it was a squash, but with the blankets and their bodies so close together it was remarkably comfortable and warm. Reeves regained his place and urged the horses forwards.

They went down the icy road beneath the railway bridge, through a tunnel of winter trees until Reeves turned his horses right onto a road that seemed little more than a farm track. 'We're now in the famous Nowhere Lane,' the coachman announced with what Wilde took to be some pride.

'And why is it called that?' Janet asked.

'No one knows, miss. Maybe because it's in the middle of nowhere – or perhaps because it goes nowhere, as some folk say. For me there's a third option – it means you're now here.'

They took another un-signposted path on the right of Nowhere Lane. 'And this is the driveway to Blackwater Grange, ancestral home of the Bentalls.'

Perfect, thought Wilde. This really was in the middle of nowhere and, without any indication that this rather ordinary-looking track even led to a house, let alone this one. It would be nigh on impossible to locate without detailed knowledge of the area. Not the sort of place one would be able to find easily even if one had a map reference. No wonder Freya had thought this might be a good place for Dolly to hide out.

Half a mile down the drive, a large house came into view. It wasn't a mansion, more in the manner of a large rectory, probably late Queen Anne or early Georgian. Magnificent but delightfully unassuming, it looked like a home rather than a symbol of status.

Snow was banked up in drifts – fifteen feet high in places. The circular forecourt and what would almost certainly be lawns were thick with snow, as was the roof of the house. A large cedar tree was weighed down and white. Woodland stretched out to the southern side. Farmland and associated buildings held the north. Smoke rose slowly from two of the main house's great chimneys.

'Here we are, ladies and gentlemen.' Reeves stepped down and began helping his passengers out. He was in his late twenties, not tall, but powerfully built. He didn't wear gloves and he wore just a shirt and pullover, no jacket or coat and didn't seem to feel or notice the cold. 'Miss Barnes has asked me to show you indoors. She is presently in the stables, mucking out. Joanna will see to your needs.'

'Joanna?' Wilde said.

'The housekeeper, sir. For many years when Miss Barnes was a child and Miss Bentall was away, Joanna was nanny. She will make you some tea and show you to your rooms. Miss Bentall has said you are all to have the run of the house and we are to assist in any way we can.'

'Thank you, Reeves.'

'I hope your stay with us meets your expectations. Food is scarce, of course, but we do have stores from the cottage garden and game from our guns. Most of the farmland that you can see belongs to the house, but Miss Bentall rents it out to a neighbouring farmer.'

'I don't suppose you could carry my bag, could you?' Janet said to Reeves.

'Of course, miss.'

'Oh please, call me Janet. And you, surely, must have a Christian name.'

'Reeves will do just fine, miss. That's what everyone calls me.'

Wilde walked towards the house hand-in-hand with Johnny. The two women were on either side of them and not for the first time Wilde suspected that there would be no love lost between them. Janet had made conversation with him on the train journey, but Dolly had remained sullen and taciturn.

Did they see themselves as rivals for some reason? Hopefully Freya's niece Emily Barnes would help ease the tension.

A boxer dog bounded around the corner and approached them with its docked tail wagging furiously. Suddenly Dolly smiled and patted the animal, then put down her bag and wrapped her arms around the animal's head, which made it wag the remains of its tail even more.

'You're beautiful, what's your name?'

'That's Hamond, miss,' Reeves said.

'I always wanted a dog.'

'Well, that one loves attention so I'm sure you'll be best of friends.'

Seventy-five miles away in Cambridge, the Englishman consulted a large map of East Anglia. He had a fountain pen in his hand and he peered closely at the area of Norfolk a few miles to the west of Norwich. 'Got it,' he said, then scratched circles around a little-known town called Reepham and a railway station called Whitwell.

It had been easy enough. The ticket office at Cambridge Station was most obliging. All the Englishman had to do was adopt his cut-glass accent and ask the fellow if he could trouble him for some information. A man, two women and a child – all friends of his – would have bought tickets; he was supposed to join them by taking the next train but had somehow mislaid the card with the details of their destination. He didn't suppose the ticket man recalled seeing them and where they were going. Of course, sir, the railman said, that's no trouble at all. How could he possibly forget issuing tickets to Whitwell in Norfolk? Until today, he hadn't sold any to little Whitwell in goodness knew how long.

'What sort of place is that?' Lukin asked the Englishman.

'Oh, it's probably a pleasant little town, surrounded by farms and churches. I doubt anything ever happens there. Big news would be the birth of a calf.'

Lukin smiled. 'Oh, I think we can improve on that.'

CHAPTER 31

They all settled into their rooms. Wilde shared a spacious twin-bed room with Johnny at the rear of the house, with views across bare fields and woodland in what felt like the rural heart of the county.

'This is a nice house and I like Hamond,' Johnny said as he unpacked his small bag. 'But why are we here, Daddy?'

'It's a winter holiday. You'll have a lot of fun here. Reeves told me they've got a sledge you can play on, and you can learn to ice skate on the pond.'

'But won't I miss school?'

'Don't worry, I've told your teacher you'll be away for a few days and I've brought some books for you to read. She's quite happy.'

He took the boy downstairs and wandered out into the grounds. They found the stables, which were extensive with boxes for at least a dozen horses. A woman whom he took to be Emily Barnes was shovelling horse dung into a steaming pile.

'Miss Barnes?'

She turned and smiled. 'And you must be Tom Wilde. Welcome. And who is this?' she demanded, bending down to look Johnny in the eye.

'My name is Johnny.'

'Of course it is. Aunt Freya said you would be coming. Do you like horses, Johnny?'

'I think so. They look nice but I've never ridden one.'

'Well, we'll have to see what we can do about that, won't we?' She stood up again and smiled at Wilde. 'I trust Reeves and Joanna have been taking care of you.'

'They have and I must apologise for intruding like this, but it was Freya's idea.'

'And a very fine idea it is, too. It's my pleasure to have guests in this otherwise bleak, quiet season. We can have some jolly times together. Games of cards, Mahjong, perhaps. And I'll crank up the gramophone and play Freya's old thirties records. She loves a lot of obscure blues music.'

'So do I.'

'Then you'll be in heaven. And you must treat the whole house and estate as your home. There are no forbidden places here. Reeves is a dear and will do anything for you, as will Joanna. She'll be cooking roast pheasant for supper. One of the last ones, unfortunately – shooting season's finished!'

Wilde put Emily's age at thirty. She was rosy-cheeked, her hair tangled, no makeup. A real countrywoman. She had a strong familial likeness to her aunt, but was a great deal less guarded and serious than Freya.

'Pheasant will be excellent, thank you.'

'You know Professor Wilde, Aunt Freya always tells me that she's a civil servant but she never mentions quite what it is she's supposed to be doing, so I just assume that she's somehow involved in the world of secrets.'

'Not my place to comment, I'm afraid.'

'She's much too discreet to give anything away, but I'm sure she did her bit to defeat Hitler and his hideous crew.'

'Again, what can I say except that I know she works tirelessly on behalf of her country and is a remarkable human being.'

'Anyway, with that in mind, I am assuming that you or your friends might be in some sort of danger.'

'That is a remote possibility, yes, were anyone to find us here. But no one will.'

'Freya hinted that it would be best if we didn't shout about your presence. Not that I'm in the slightest bit worried, but just so you know, we do have firearms, both shotguns and rifles.'

'I'm sure they won't be needed.'

'The gun room is next to the boot room at the back of the kitchens. Help yourself if you want to try for some rabbits. There are also a couple of airguns if Johnny wants to try his hand.'

'Thank you.'

'What is he, six? That's when I had my first airgun. I once lined up my dolls and shot them to pieces. Best fun I ever had.' She laughed out loud. 'To be honest I didn't really like the dolls, but people insisted on giving them to me. God knows why.'

In the evening, they clustered in the warmest part of the house, the sitting room, with an open log fire, and sat at a table brought in by Reeves to eat supper together.

Joanna, the housekeeper, had cooked and served the food and then joined everyone else at the table to eat, as did Reeves. There was no standing on ceremony here, no division between master or mistress and servant. Emily, Joanna and Reeves were more like a little family, so close that they barely needed to communicate.

There was a contentment to them that Wilde liked but couldn't quite explain. Emily was easy-mannered, warm, of average height, good-looking but unmade-up, and with obvious intelligence. Joanna had to be about sixty, grey-haired but still strong and full of energy and welcoming despite the extra work the visitors would be causing her. Reeves was also strong, a solid working man with a face that had seen lots of weather. It occurred to Wilde that if ever a film was to be made of *Far from the Madding Crowd*, he would make an excellent Gabriel Oak.

What was most interesting was the relationship between Reeves and Emily. To an outsider coming here for the first time, such as himself, the first reaction might be to wonder whether they were lovers or engaged to be married. But intuition told him that that was not the case. Perhaps there had been something between them in the past, but it wasn't there now. Just friendship and affection.

Afterwards they listened to records, including some Bessie Smith – much to Wilde's delight – and played gin rummy at Johnny's request or read in front of the fire. Hamond the boxer laid himself out as close to the heat as he could get, snoring peacefully and farting at will.

When the card game palled, Dolly and Janet kept apart from each other, Dolly letting Johnny read to her while Janet spent most of the time latching on to Reeves.

At the end of the evening, long after Johnny had gone to bed, Wilde took Emily aside. 'You know I've got to go first thing in the morning, but the others will be staying?'

'So I understand. Reeves will take you to the station. I think there are trains at five past nine and five past eleven, but I wouldn't pay much heed to the timetable in these conditions.'

'I'll try to get the earlier one.'

'Fine. Oh, and your friends, Dolly and Janet, they're a bit of an odd couple, aren't they?'

'They hadn't met before yesterday. Rather different backgrounds. Dolly comes from the East End of London and has never before left the city.'

'And Janet?'

'Clearly clever. Went to Girton college, Cambridge. I believe she has been rather unlucky in love.'

'So when's it due?'

Wilde frowned. 'I'm sorry, when's what due?'

'The baby, of course. When's Janet's baby due?'

'What makes you ask that? She's not pregnant.'

'Of course she is. I've lived among animals all my life so I always know when the female of the species is with child or cub. I can tell when a mare or a ewe is pregnant without the help of a vet. We're not much different to the animals, you know. In fact, we are animals, Tom. Even you.'

'So Janet Spring is pregnant? Well, I think she might have told us.'

'Three months at least, I'd say, perhaps four. I take it there's no father in evidence?'

'No.'

'That might explain her reluctance to tell you. Even in the modern post-war world, there is still a great stigma about such things. Also it might explain her interest in Reeves. She wouldn't be the first girl to see him as ideal husband and father material. Good with his hands, cheerful nature. Hey-ho, what a fine merry-go-round.'

What a fine merry-go-round indeed, thought Wilde. Janet Spring was clearly a little lost. A single mother with no man in sight would be an outcast in modern society.

'Is Reeves married?'

'Not yet, but there are plenty of local girls who have tried to snare him. He's a great deal too canny for all of them and I rather think that Janet will be no match for his altar-dodging skills.'

Wilde slept well until Johnny jumped on him at 6 a.m. The room was ferociously cold and icicles hung outside the window, so they both got dressed as quickly as they could and made their way down for breakfast, which was porridge or toast and Marmite.

Before leaving, he found time to talk with Dolly. 'I realise this is a very different place for you. They do things at a slower pace here. Listen and learn from Emily, your host.'

'I don't need lectures, Tom.'

'Forgive me, of course you don't. I'm just stating the obvious. But it's important to me that you remain safe and stay as happy as possible here. I'll be back as soon as I can, but I have a few matters to attend to. One thing, though: Freya Bentall told me you had given her a description of the man who bought the ice-axe from Adnams. You said his name was George Blain.'

'That's right. What of it?'

'Perhaps you can tell me some more about him.'

She shrugged. 'He was young, good-looking. Not exactly my type, but he definitely had the looks. Yeah, very handsome, very full of himself. Talked posh, too – even posher than you or Freya or Gus Baxter.'

'Was he with Baxter? Did you see them together?'

'No. Why do you ask?'

'Because I need to find the man – and if Baxter knows him, that would be a lead.'

'Well, I can tell you one thing I didn't mention to Freya. This Blain bloke is a dead ringer for that film star with the posh voice. You must have seen him – he was in that film that came out in the war, the rich fellow with the big house whose wife died and the horrible woman who runs the house. What's his name, something Oliver?'

'Laurence Olivier? And the film's called *Rebecca*.'

'That's the one. I've got the book. But it wasn't him, I can tell you that. So not quite a dead ringer. Anyway, this George Blain doesn't have a moustache. I love the flicks.'

Wilde nodded. 'Me too.' The description meant something to him but for the life of him he couldn't work out what. A merest unfocused glimpse of something or someone, deep in the recesses of his brain. 'What more can you tell me about this George Blain?'

'He fancies himself. I had to service him once on Terry's orders.'

'Service him?'

'You know what I mean. Anyway, it was all over within half a minute, so it didn't make much of an impression, and there was no small talk like some customers want.'

'Any distinguishing features? Moles or other marks?'

'No. He's a handsome fellow, but there's a darkness to him.'

'Thank you, Dolly.'

The train arrived at Whitwell Station on time, but the journey thereafter was dogged by stops and delays and dragged on incessantly. He didn't reach Cambridge until one o'clock. He had changed his mind; he'd go and meet the Russian after all. He just had time to go to college and put a call through to Eaton confirming that he would be at his rooms in Trinity at two.

After devouring a taste-free lunch from the buttery and checking his mail, he talked to the porters about his ailing college servant, Bobby. There hadn't been much change, he was told.

Wilde asked to be remembered to him before strolling along Trumpington Street, then through the centre of town, arriving at Trinity College where he was well known by the porters, who pointed him in the direction of Philip Eaton's set of rooms.

The door was open but he knocked anyway and Eaton shuffled towards him, limping heavily and holding his stick with the hand of his remaining arm.

'Tom, old boy, so delighted you could make it.'

'Is Comrade Lukin here?'

'Any moment.'

Eaton was now leaning against the wall beside the door, supporting his damaged left leg. Awkwardly, he reached out his right arm and the two men shook hands.

'Do. come in, Tom. My gyp's off with the flu today, so perhaps you'd help me put the coffee on or, if you prefer something stronger, I'm sure I've got something drinkable somewhere.'

'Coffee would do just fine.'

'Me too.'

Ten minutes later they settled down in front of a meagre coal fire and waited. And waited. Chatting about inconsequentials, the weather and varsity politics.

'He's not coming, is he?' Wilde said at last.

'It's not looking good.'

'God damn it, Philip, exactly who is this Lazar Lukin? If he's part of an education delegation, then I'm Mickey Mouse.'

'What are you suggesting?'

'You know bloody well what I'm suggesting. You didn't serve in the SIS all those years without being able to spot a hostile agent.'

Eaton sipped the last of the coffee. 'This is disgusting. Damned acorn dust or some such.'

'Well?'

'Well what?'

'Who is he – and why are you consorting with him? Are you doing a bit of freelance work now you've left the service?'

'Whether he has a dual role is not my concern. But in a world of atomic weapons, we need to do all we can to maintain peace. So if our young future leaders can learn to like and respect each other through exchange visits, I'm all for it. And if Comrade Lukin has other motives for his visit I don't give two hoots.'

Wilde got to his feet. 'You disgust me, Eaton,' he said.

Without another word, he walked out, closed the door behind him and stalked back across Trinity's great court. He had to get away from the snake-like Eaton. He had to get back to London.

It was dark, of course, by the time he turned up at Leconfield House. Freya Bentall was sitting at her desk staring at the telephone by the light of a hurricane lamp. After a few moments she looked up and signalled him to come in.

'Sorry, my ears are still ringing and I was lost in thought.'

Wilde's hearing had returned to normal quite quickly, so he was surprised. 'You'd better get your ears checked,' he said.

'Already have. The doctor wondered if I had a burst eardrum, but thankfully not. Best advice seems to be that it will sort itself out in due course.'

She indicated the chair opposite her and Wilde sat down.

'As for being lost in thought, I know the feeling,' he said. 'I've spent most of the last two days on trains with little to do but think.'

'So, all delivered safely? All well at Nowhere Lane?'

'It's Dolly's first time out of the big smoke but she'll be fine there. Your niece is a very warm and generous hostess.'

'And how is my darling Emily?'

'Up to her knees in horse manure.'

That made Freya smile. 'Nowhere she prefers to be. She's a country girl through and through.'

'I take it she's your brother or sister's daughter?'

'My late sister's little girl. Died soon after giving birth. Emily's father died when she was two, so I took her in. Best thing I ever did, though of course I've had to have a lot of help from nanny and boarding schools along the way. I only wish I could see more of her but she's simply not interested in coming to London. The exact opposite of our friend Dolly. Anyway, I take it everything's all right at the house?'

Wilde leant back in the chair. He hadn't realised how exhausted he was. 'Yes, everything's in order. Good food, plenty of wood to burn.'

'We always were a bit spoilt there. A lot of game, plenty of local farm produce and no shortage of fallen branches or coppiced trees. That said, we've always allowed our less-well-off neighbours to come and help themselves. The Grange has been in my family a hundred and fifty years. But back to the present: what now?'

'I have to find Basil Rheinhaus. I'm certain he's at the heart of this – and I'm pretty sure you feel the same way.'

'I feel such a fool. We should have insisted he come to us rather than relying on damned telephone calls.'

'I'll get him. To which end, I'm going to seek out Cecil Eagles and try to make amends. He's closest to Vivienne Chalke and he has to persuade her that it is her duty to give us access to Rheinhaus.'

'Easier said than done.'

'Why?'

'I've no idea where he is. Try his home. Unfortunately the phone lines are all down.'

'And your flat? What's happening about that?'

'The forensics boys have been crawling all over the place, hoping to find a bit of shrapnel with a print on it. But they won't succeed. So far all they can work out is that the grenade was standard British army issue. And I have to thank you properly for dragging me to the floor so promptly. I'm told it saved me from potentially devastating injuries.'

'It was just reaction.'

'Shame we couldn't save my beautiful flat, though. It will take forever to repair. I'm going to have to stay at Burton's until I can find a temporary place to rent.'

'I'll probably need to join you at Burton's for a night or two. By the way, I don't suppose you managed to have words with Shadox Stone? Was that really his face I saw in the headlights outside Dolly's flat in Kennington, or an apparition?'

'That's just another of my problems, Tom. I'm afraid Shadox hasn't checked in and his landlady says she hasn't seen him recently. I sent Sims around to see if he's ill or something, but there was no one in his room. Things really are falling apart.'

Two agents missing. Almost as if it was planned, Wilde thought grimly.

CHAPTER 32

Wilde wondered what was known about Shadox Stone. He had already discovered that he was difficult, of course, went his own way, came from the north of England.

That didn't amount to much in the maze of spies and espionage. Loners were ten a penny, so were awkward customers. Freya filled in Wilde on some of the rest. Stone had no wife, no known lover of either sex, though there was gossip around the service that he used prostitutes.

'Something of a cold fish,' Freya had said. 'But he feeds us useful information from the left of British politics.'

'How do you know it's accurate?'

'We've had no problems so far, but you make a good point, Tom. And that might be why I have the occasional doubt.'

On the plus side, she said, he played sax with a little jazz band from time to time and he had enjoyed a good war catching and turning a couple of Nazi agents.

His speciality these days was the Communist Party of Great Britain and the trade unions, along with the multiple points at which they intersected. It had always been clear that both the unions and the Labour Party included covert Bolsheviks in their numbers.

The question in Freya's mind was whether Shadox Stone had gone native, switched his allegiance from commie-hunter to commie. It was always a possibility. Not quite the same as with Philip Eaton, whom Wilde suspected of having *always* been a Kremlin stooge rather than a recent convert.

The son of a mill worker and a maid from Lancashire, Stone had been a scholarship boy, the first from his family and school to go to university. He had excelled at his studies, gaining a first from Cambridge, then joined the army as an officer in the early days of the war, very quickly being moved over to military intelligence. Apart from that, little was known about his motivation or his private life.

It occurred to Wilde that the recruiters of MI5 might have sought a little more detail when vetting him.

First things first, however. For the moment he was focused on Cecil Eagles and finding a route to Basil Rheinhaus.

He rapped at the door of Eagles's flat in Soho.

After a minute's pause and a muffled call of 'hang on', Eagles finally opened the door. He was garbed in dinner jacket, bow tie and high-sheen patent shoes. 'Well, well, you're still alive, Tom. How unfortunate.'

'I've caught you on your way out, haven't I?'

'Well done, Sherlock, there's hope for you yet.'

'May I come in for a minute or two?'

'If you insist. Is this at Mother's behest?'

'She knows I'm here. She was worried that you might have gone missing.'

'Well, you can set her mind at rest, can't you?'

'And you could answer her calls.'

'Fuck you, Wilde.'

He followed Eagles into his artwork-rich flat. The great paintings glowered down at him from the walls as though he was an unwelcome intruder in their sanctuary.

'I'm not going to offer you a drink.'

'I'm not here for a drink, Cecil. I'm here to make amends for any perceived harm I might have caused your relationship with Vivienne Chalke. But more than that to discuss how we can persuade her that we're not the enemy and that we really need to talk to Basil Rheinhaus.'

'And ask him what exactly?'

'What he knows about the Atomic Energy Research Establishment and the people who work there.'

'To what end?'

'Oh, I think you know very well. Is Rheinhaus a danger to us – or does he know who is? Because it's one of those two things. He's trying to bargain with the government, which should mean he has something solid to offer. We need to prise it out of him sooner rather than later, before any more damage is done.'

Cecil Eagles sighed heavily, then reached down to an occasional table and opened a silver box of cigarettes. He took one out and lit it. 'The curious thing is, Tom,' he said as he let out a stream of smoke, 'you somehow successfully identified that Rheinhaus was important to us, but then you scared him off. All was going swimmingly but now he's got it in his head that you're a threat – in fact that we're *all* a threat – and he's gone into hiding, with his friend Vivienne's assistance. Then, to compound the problem you've created, you go sniffing around Vivienne's house and her address book. I guess Mother was right all along – you really do need some tutoring in tradecraft.'

'I had vague memories of him from before the war, in a lab in Cambridge, that's all. Nothing sinister. I was just surprised to see him in such an unfamiliar environment. It was all quite innocent. I said nothing threatening.'

'But you can surely understand why he's jittery. If he has the information we think he does, then he could be in grave danger. He doesn't know if he can trust any of us.'

'But you know the truth, Cecil – and you're close to Vivienne Chalke. Can't you get her to cooperate?'

'I'll see what I can do. Can't promise anything. For the moment, though, I simply must dash.'

'Thank you.'

'I won't say it's my pleasure.' He tipped ash from his cigarette onto the carpet, then nodded past Wilde. 'The door's over there.'

On his way out he noticed a photograph in a silver frame and did a double take. The picture showed Eagles with his arm around another man's shoulders. Both men were smiling. Wilde hadn't noticed the picture when he came here before.

He looked closer and saw that the other man wasn't just anyone. It was a young Olivier. Except it wasn't, was it?

'Who's this, Cecil?'

'That's Willie. You sort of met him when you were last here, didn't you?'

'Well, I didn't actually meet him. He dashed past clutching his clothes as I recall. What is he to you?'

'Mind your own bloody business, Tom Wilde. Just sod off.'

What was he to do with this new piece of information? Cecil Eagles's friend Willie had to be George Blain, the man Dolly said had acquired an ice-axe from Terry Adnams. The man she said looked uncannily like the actor Laurence Olivier, as did the man in Cecil's picture.

It couldn't be just a coincidence. No wonder her description struck such a chord.

The information was jangling in Wilde's brain. Was Cecil's boyfriend the man who took an ice-axe to Cambridge and drove it into the head of the MI5 officer Everett Glasspool?

And if he was, where did that put Cecil Eagles?

An hour later, Wilde arrived at Burton's Hotel and called up to Freya's room. 'Can we meet downstairs in the bar. I think I might just have the information you've been looking for.'

'I'm on my way.'

After he told her everything he had discovered, she kept silent for a minute, rolling her brandy glass, allowing the fumes to ascend to her nostrils.

She looked up from her contemplation. 'Couldn't you find a surname for him?'

'Willie the Olivier lookalike? Unfortunately not. Unless you believe the name he used at The Green Bear – George Blain.'

'I'll have Cecil's flat watched. Chances are he'll be back there.'

'This must put Cecil Eagles in the frame. I've found your man,' he said. 'Cecil is your mole.'

'I'm not sure.'

Nor was Wilde. There were inconsistencies. But he had to be investigated. 'What happens next? I take it you'll bring him in and interrogate him formally?'

'That's a decision for the director general. What we need is to compile all the evidence we can. I'll ask the shadow boys to enter his flat and get a copy of that photograph. Then we'll show it to Dolly Coster and secure a watertight statement from her. Finally,

I want to arrest the whole bloody crew from The Green Bear. The DG will love that – big gangbuster in his police days.'

'So my work is done.'

'Not quite, Tom. We still need to find Basil Rheinhaus.'

'But if Cecil Eagles *is* the traitor, he's the one keeping Rheinhaus from us. For all we know he might have done away with him.'

'Vivienne Chalke has the answer. Go to her, arrest her if she doesn't agree to help us. I'll have a warrant ready for you.'

She looked at him coldly. Colder than the snow that was falling yet again. 'You've got a bloody nerve coming here.'

'I mean you no harm, Vivienne, but I'm afraid this is official. We have to get in touch with Basil Rheinhaus and you're our only conduit.'

She was wearing a thin robe, her arms crossed around her torso for a semblance of warmth. 'Oh, come bloody in, sod you, I can't stand on the doorstep arguing the point in this weather.' She led him through to the sitting room. 'Believe it or not, I'm having a quiet night to myself. My life is taken up with entertaining and being entertained and sometimes I just want to curl up with a good book.'

'What are you reading?'

'*The Grapes of Wrath*. Again. Third time actually. Have you read it?'

'Yes, but only the once.'

'It's an antidote to London society. Snobs and counter-snobs. The preposterous upper-classes with their noses in the air, the equally ridiculous fellow travellers with their holier-than-thou disdain for the middle classes – i.e. themselves.'

'I thought you were a communist.'

She laughed and went over to the fire to scoop in some more coal. 'I don't believe you were fooled for a moment. It's always been an affectation because it amuses me.' She went to the sideboard, fixed two neat drinks and handed one to him uninvited.

He took the drink and sniffed it. Scotch. Well, well, not such a wasted journey. 'Thank you,' he said, 'but to get to the point of my presence here, we have to talk about Rheinhaus.'

'We used to be lovers, you know. He might be younger than me but he's my best friend in the world. I would do anything for him and protect him with my life.'

'Like a mother with a child.'

'What are you, some sort of trick cyclist? It's nothing like a mother with a child, it's a meeting of minds and bodies. We thought he was safe while he negotiated with the government, then you started sniffing around and we realised that there were people on all sides who would actually rather like to see him dead. Too many secrets.'

'What sort of secrets?'

'Atomic secrets. More precisely, atomic scientist secrets. A certain name. But I'm not telling you anything that you don't already know, am I?'

'I know some of it. But I swear that I wish him no harm, nor you. That said, we badly need your cooperation because we must bring him in. We can probably offer him better protection than you can.'

'We?'

'The security service. Didn't Cecil Eagles tell you?'

'Cecil tells me as little as possible. He's good at his job.'

Perhaps not as good or as trustworthy as she imagined, Wilde thought.

'Will you at least put me through to Basil Rheinhaus on the phone? His life *is* in danger, but not from me. My superiors are prepared to talk seriously about offering him a deal. Asylum and immunity – though I have no idea why he needs it or what he is alleged to have done in America.'

'I don't quite know what it is about you, Tom Wilde, but do you know what? I do trust you.'

'I won't let you down.'

'All right, I'll call him.' She went out to the telephone in the hall. A sharp wind was blowing through the gap at the bottom of the front door. She dialled a number and said just four words: 'Tom Wilde is here.'

Then she put the phone down.

'What now?'

'We wait.'

CHAPTER 33

They ambled back to the warmth of the sitting room and their drinks. No conversation passed between them. Wilde listened for the phone to ring back, but there was no call. Three or four minutes later the door to the room opened slowly.

Basil Rheinhaus stood there. He was wearing corduroys like the ones Vivienne wore when she was drawing Wilde. Perhaps the same ones for they were not dissimilar in size and shape. He also wore an open-neck cotton shirt with frayed collar and a heavy woollen pullover. On his feet he had threadbare moccasin slippers as if he had just come down from his bedroom. Beneath his tousled hair, his tanned face still had the healthy glow he had acquired in the tropical seas in the vicinity of Bikini Atoll. His expression was grim and unsmiling.

Was it possible he had been in the house all along? It was big enough to get lost in. Perhaps Vivienne had a separate phone with a different number somewhere.

'You wanted me, Wilde?'

'Freya Bentall would like you to come in to discuss matters with her. You have unfinished business.'

'Well, we were getting nowhere. What is she offering?'

'Protection. Possible asylum and immunity from prosecution in British territories. A sympathetic ear for your other requirements.'

'No guarantees?'

'I'm afraid not.'

He shrugged. 'If you had offered guarantees I would have known you were lying. So I guess you're telling the truth. OK, I'll come with you.'

'I think you have made a good choice. Thank you.'

His slippered feet shuffled further into the room. 'You're from across the pond like me, I take it?'

'My father was American, my mother Irish. She now lives in Boston.'

'I did my math doctorate at MIT. Did you study in that part of the world?'

'No, I was schooled in England, then Chicago University.'

'So what now? Do you have a car?'

'I can get an official car here within the hour. I think the chances of a taxi in this weather are slim at best.'

An hour and a half later, they were at Leconfield House. The night watch let them in and within a couple of minutes Freya Bentall arrived from her hotel.

Wilde made the introductions then the three of them went to her office, where they all took seats still in their overcoats because there was no heating at that time of night.

'Are you prepared to talk now, Dr Rheinhaus?'

'Mr Wilde said you would protect me. I take it that includes protection from extradition.'

'That will depend on what you give us,' she replied, 'but yes, that should be possible. I've talked it over with my superiors who, in turn, have talked to the Ministry of Supply and the War Office. All are agreed that if there really is a traitor at Harwell, then he – we assume it's a man – has to be weeded out. So that's where we are.'

'Fair enough, I suppose. And Mr Wilde here, what role is he playing in all this – and how much does he know? You can understand why his slight American accent spooked me.'

'He is working for me and this is a wholly British operation.'

'So you have no link to the Internal Revenue Service, buddy?'

'None at all,' Wilde said. 'Why, is that what this is all about?'

Freya leant forwards. 'Do you want to tell him, Dr Rheinhaus?'

'OK, why not? We've come this far. Let's put it this way, I have a bit of a tax problem. Actually, it's not a bit of a problem – it's a real son-of-a-bitch catastrophe. I'm being done for tax evasion of a similar magnitude to the amount that put Al Capone inside. And when the IRS are on your tail, you're in the jaws of a bull terrier.'

Wilde was stunned. How had a nuclear physicist ended up in such a hole? Rheinhaus read his mind and addressed the unasked question.

'Gambling,' he said. 'I've tried to stop. I can't. And I don't even want to.'

'And you can't do a deal with the IRS?'

'It'll never happen. If they could get their claws into me, they would do their best to lock me up forever. I wasn't safe from their dirty clutches even when I was with the atomic task force in the Marshall Islands. The IRS sent a message to the captain of the warship I was on, ordering me to be hauled home to face the music. But I wasn't under lock and key and fortunately for me, the vessel had to make a detour to Manila, where I jumped ship and hitched a ride on a British freighter to Singapore. I stayed there for four months, trying to work out my options. But the old habit did for me. I fell foul of some local gambling joints, so I skedaddled. Caught a series of flights to London and here I am. That's the unvarnished truth – I have no illusions about myself. Nor about the IRS. They won't let me slip away a second time.'

'How are you feeding your habit in England?'

'Oh, there are games here and there. No questions asked. Anonymous. All cash no credit.'

'The Green Bear, for instance?'

'Someone mentioned it, but no. Not yet.' He shook his head, his brow creased. 'You know if I could stop, I would. But I can't. Betting to me – on anything, horses, cards, roulette – is like air. It's more important than breathing. I lost my marriage to it. I once had a lot of money, but it's all gone – and my problem with the IRS goes back more years than I care to recall. Only my above-average grasp of particle physics and the modest pay I receive has kept me going. I accepted the chance to go on the Bikini mission as an observer thinking I would be removing myself from the temptation to gamble. But I was fooling myself. I can find a card game anywhere and ships are easy. Lot of bored sailors below decks.'

'That all explains your motivation for wanting asylum and protection here. But you have something to offer in return?'

'I sure do. I know the name of the biggest traitor you'll ever come across.'

'And how do you know this person is a traitor?'

'Because he tried to recruit me for the Soviets. He knew I was desperate for loot and he offered me thousands of dollars to help him get the secrets out of Los Alamos to his contact.'

'Did you accept his offer?'

'I told him to get lost.'

'Why didn't you report him immediately?'

'Because I had him over a barrel. I knew his secret so I could tap him like a rubber tree, which I'm afraid I did.'

'I think it's time you told us his name.'

'Yup, you're right. But remember one thing. You will have no physical evidence and no corroboration, just my word – so you'll still need me.'

Freya smiled. 'Of course. Don't worry. Now then, his name?'

'Klaus Fuchs. The cleverest son-of-a-bitch scientist I ever met. He can out-think Oppenheimer, Fermi and Teller any day of the week, whatever the subject. He knows the whole Manhattan Project inside-out. And by my reckoning, he's given it all to Uncle Joe Stalin.'

That name. A sliver of cold ran down Wilde's back as if an icicle had broken from an overhanging eave and found its way beneath his collar onto his skin.

Klaus Fuchs. The youthful, rather charming, chain-smoking, womanising physicist who turned up at Geoff Lancing's home in a sports car and began flirting with his wife.

He recalled that he had noted a shift in the man's demeanour when the name Basil Rheinhaus was mentioned.

Now he knew why.

'I tell you what, though,' Rheinhaus continued. 'Fly me back to one of your colonies near the Equator. The two explosions I witnessed at Bikini a few months back were hotter than hell, but I'd take the climate there any time over this goddamned miserable arctic excuse for a country.'

'No one asked you to come,' Freya said, clearly irritated. 'We like our seasons. Anyway, it looks as if you're rather stuck here, whatever the weather.' She turned her attention to Wilde. 'So now

I want you to get Dr Rheinhaus somewhere very safe, and I think we know the place.'

'I'm OK with Vivienne Chalke,' Rheinhaus insisted.

'No, Dr Rheinhaus, you really aren't. When you came to England a few weeks ago all your fear was of being sent to America. It never occurred to you that there might be a threat to your life from the other side. Well, that has all changed.'

'You're scaring me.'

'You have every reason to be scared. From now on, you will be in the care of Professor Wilde, who has a great deal of experience in intelligence and security matters. Tonight, you will accompany both of us to a hotel and in the morning Tom will take you to a safe place.'

'I suppose I have no option.'

'Your only other choice is a prison cell.'

'I need to think about this.'

'There's really nothing to think about.'

They looked at each other as though neither would concede. Wilde broke the moment.

'What was it like, Dr Rheinhaus?'

'What was what like?'

'The nuclear explosion at Bikini Atoll.'

Rheinhaus smiled, grimly. 'I witnessed two of them. One in the air, one under water. I turned away at the blasts, but then looked at the clouds and felt the air sucked from the world. There was darkness in the day and crazy colours and things I can't even talk about. Utter madness, life and death in a vanishing moment of time. Nothing made sense.' He breathed deeply. 'Say, is there a bathroom here? I need to pee.'

'The security man outside the door will escort you.'

Nothing made sense in the Pacific, nothing made sense here in England. There were too many unanswered questions. While they waited for him to return, Wilde posed the obvious one: 'What happens with Klaus Fuchs now?'

'We have to proceed with the utmost caution. We can't afford to spook Washington and I don't want to alert the Kremlin. So I think an informal, friendly little chat might be in order. One of the more charming Special Branch officers.'

'You won't just arrest him?'

'Fuchs has already crossed our radar. Everyone at Harwell has, but Fuchs more than most. He was at the Cavendish with Alan Nunn May, who as you must know was arrested for spying last year and then there is his background as a German exile and the suggestion he was once associated with the German Communist Party, and so these matters have been taken into account. Our investigations boys in B Branch over in the St James hovel have arranged with the Harwell security officer to keep a note of his movements.'

'Softly, softly . . .'

'Exactly.'

'Would it not be wiser to simply remove him from Harwell while investigations continue?'

'Fuchs isn't someone you can just dispense with. He was vital to the work at Los Alamos and he is vital to the work at Harwell. If he's spying for the Soviets, then he's also been doing a lot of excellent work for the Allies. And at the moment we have just one man's word against his – and we know that Rheinhaus has motives of his own. Who knows, perhaps Rheinhaus is the Soviet spy. Perhaps Stalin is providing the money to feed his habit. Perhaps his mission is to wreck Harwell by having us turn on our best man. Watch Rheinhaus carefully, Tom. Oh, and I'll organise a pistol for you. Do you have a preference?'

'Not too heavy, easily concealed.'

Terry Adnams eased his thick, muscular arms into the sleeves of his sheepskin coat, then shook out his shoulders like the prize-fighter he was. Finally, he pulled his cap down tight onto his brawny head.

'Time to call on your friend Lady Chalke, Mr Eagles. Never met a real-life lady before. Do I bow or curtsey?' He picked up an ice-axe and swung it loosely from side to side, enjoying the feel of its heft. 'But you stay here and wait for us, eh?'

His sidekick, Fletcher, moved towards the door.

Adnams put his face up close to Cecil Eagles, so that they could smell each other's breath. 'You sure about this, though, yeah? You sure she'll know where to find Rheinhaus?'

'Yes, she's hiding him.'

'Good man, well done.' He patted Eagles's cheeks.

'Please, don't hurt her.'

'Now why would I do that? Just want the information, don't I? I'm sure she'll tell me everything I need to know, because I can be very persuasive.'

Cecil Eagles was trembling uncontrollably, his body was soaked in sweat beneath his dinner jacket. His shiny shoes were wet with blood, so was his bow tie.

'Please . . .'

'Don't you worry about a thing, Mr Eagles. You just stay here and make yourself comfortable. Make yourself at home while Fletcher and I deal with this. All will be well.'

'Please . . .'

'Oh, and Willie says goodbye.'

Adnams swung the ice-axe back further, like a tennis racket, and brought it forwards with the force of a forehand drive. The adze edge of the tool smashed into Eagles' face, throwing back his head as it drove his teeth, nose and cheeks deep into his brain. Eagles fell backwards and slightly sideways from the chair and his head cracked into the stone floor.

Adnams stooped over him and wrenched out the ice-axe. 'Bit of gore on your Sunday best, Mr Eagles. Looks like you're going to have to take it to the dry cleaners. What a shame.' Then he swung again, from the side and shattered his victim's temple.

Cecil Eagles hadn't even cried out. His slaughter was too sudden. He lay on the ground, his feet and fingers twitching, to all intents and purposes dead although the further reaches of his body had not yet received the message.

His killer pulled the ice-axe back again. This time he wiped the blood and brain on Eagles's smart evening wear, then secreted the tool in a deep pocket on the inside of his coat.

'Get someone to clean up this mess, Fletcher. I want it spotless by the time we get back.'

'Yes, chief.'

'What a fucking ponce, eh? This is going to be a good night.'

CHAPTER 34

Emily watched the scene with a weary eye. The rather humour-less woman named Janet was all over Reeves like a spider's web. Touching his arm, laughing girlishly – though Emily was not fooled for a moment that she was actually amused – running her fingers through her hair, batting her eyelashes behind her specta-cles. It was both odd and a little sickening to watch.

The day had been exhausting and she wondered what had pos-sessed Aunt Freya to think that sending these people here was a good idea. At one stage she feared that Janet and Dolly might come to blows over some pathetic disagreement over who sat where at the lunch table. It was obvious what it was about, of course; Janet wanted to sit next to Reeves and Dolly had got there first simply to annoy her.

'I think they're going to kill each other,' Joanna said softly in Emily's ear.

'It's rather looking that way. Quite funny though, isn't it? I rather like the Cockney one, though, don't you? At least she doesn't have any airs and graces.'

Now it was evening and they had got through supper without a major incident. The boy, Johnny, was keeping everyone amused by singing songs he had learnt at school: 'Boney Was a Warrior', 'Girls and Boys Come Out to Play' and 'What Shall We Do with the Drunken Sailor?'

Everyone joined in except Dolly, who had never heard them before. At the end she suggested they might sing 'Roll Out the Barrel', which she knew from the East End pubs, but by then Johnny had moved on to his repertoire of hackneyed comic-book jokes before yawning and asking if he could leave the table and play with Hamond. Janet said he could if it was all right with Emily.

Without a word, Reeves got up, too, and went to replenish his beer mug from the keg in the kitchen. He returned to the sitting room and stood by the hearth, sipping his well-earned pint. That was when Janet joined him and began doing her best to catch his interest.

The thing was he couldn't resist flirting back; it was his nature. The upshot, Emily knew, would be the young woman's heartbreak.

A few feet away, Johnny was kneeling down beside the dog, stroking him and cuddling his head. Then, unprompted, he jumped to his feet and went over to Janet and clutched her hand.

'I think I want to go to bed now, Janet.'

'I'm just talking at the moment, Johnny. In a little while, yes?'

'But I'm sleepy and I'd like a story, please.'

'Wouldn't you like a new reader for a change? How about Emily or Joanna? I'm sure they'd love to read to you? Or even Dolly . . . if she can read.'

Lazar Lukin and the Englishman watched the house until the lights went out.

The Englishman. The man the Lubyanka knew as Virgin, the man those at The Green Bear knew as George Blain, the man Cecil Eagles and Lazar Lukin knew as Willie Tristram, which happened to be his real name.

Lukin and Tristram waited another hour.

The man from the East was used to such cold, but Tristram wasn't and he shivered in his thick jacket, gloves, long johns and covering of horse blankets that they had found in a tack room on the way across the icy fields.

They were in a byre full of cows, which gave a good deal of animal warmth and associated aromas, but they had already been cold when they arrived here after a confusing series of cross-country treks from the station. It had been awkward because the stationmaster had looked at them and their ski bags with suspicion when they said they were joining the party that had arrived recently.

He said he didn't know who they were talking about and suggested they walk the mile to Reepham and ask there in the pub. Someone might know.

'These country people, they don't like outsiders,' Tristram said.

Lukin laughed. 'Same where I come from. Same all over the world.'

The two men had met in Potsdam in late July 1945, when both had been with their respective delegations to the leaders' conference. Lukin knew of Virgin, of course, and had sought him out on Beria's orders. He had been recruited several years earlier and had already done some fine work. He seemed to enjoy killing to order, but perhaps lacked the skill and professionalism of Lukin.

He was seen as a valuable asset. Beria had hoped that Virgin would eventually manage to weasel his way into one of the British security services, but so far he had failed. He had, however, found his way into the War Office and into the life of Cecil Eagles and in some ways that was even more useful, for Eagles was not as discreet as he should have been and Tristram did not come under so much scrutiny.

Which is how they came to know what has happening.

Cecil's eager lips, whispering across the scented pillow into Willie's ear.

Whispering of his coup. A scientist named Basil Rheinhaus had arrived in London with a remarkable tale of treachery. For a price, he would name the traitor at the heart of the British atomic programme, and Cecil Eagles would take the credit. Why, he might yet end up director general of the service.

Whispering to Willie, he might as well have been broadcasting directly to Josef Stalin.

The trek through the wilds of Norfolk had not gone well. They had had no option but to stay the first night at the pub. No one helped when they asked questions about some people who had arrived from Cambridge – two young women, a man and a boy. One man looked at their skis and made a joke about there not being many alps in Norfolk, but mostly they just either turned away in silence or shook their heads. Incomers were not to be trusted, especially when they asked questions. Their money was readily accepted, however.

All day they had explored. The only person who gave them the time of day was the local vicar. 'Ah, yes, I think I know who that sounds like,' he said cheerfully and then gave them directions. 'Two or three miles from here, though, so you'll have quite a trek and it won't be easy to find. No sign on the gatepost. Good luck.'

They arrived at the byre after dark, early evening, and waited. Lukin asked Tristram about his life. 'When did you discover the Party, comrade?'

'I think I was always aware. My parents were Quakers, peace-lovers. But their way did nothing to help the working man. The light went on when I arrived at Cambridge as an undergraduate and began to read Marx.'

'And you were never squeamish?'

He laughed. 'I was brought up on a farm.'

'You have not joined the Party?'

'My initial contact told me to avoid doing so at all costs. I was never to attend meetings, never to reveal my true politics to anyone, not even friends. If anything, it was suggested I might camouflage myself in the cloak of fascism.'

'Very smart.'

'But I couldn't do it, not that. And you, Comrade, when did you join the Party?'

'At the very beginning. But no more questions or I will begin to think you might be a double-agent.'

'Likewise you.'

Their eyes met knowingly. Both were aware of the paradox of their trade. How could you ever tell whether you were being fed information or disinformation? Who would trust spies when their whole life was about deceit?

Instead they talked of family, home, inconsequentials and Cecil Eagles.

'You have no idea how much I loathed the man. The stench of his perfume, the creepy softness of his body. Every time I buggered him I thought of Berkeley Castle and wanted to use a hot poker instead of a prick.'

Lukin laughed. 'I had no idea, English boy. This all really means something to you. And your friend Terry Adnams, I should meet him.'

'No, comrade, I really don't think you should.'

'But why not?'

'Because he's a fascist and you're a foreigner. And Axeman Adnams doesn't like foreigners except maybe Americans. He doesn't like many people.'

'But he likes you?'

'We have an understanding. But he doesn't really know me.'

At last, Lukin picked up his Sten gun and slung it across his chest. 'Ready, Willie?'

'Ready.'

'This will be easy. They will never know what has happened to them.'

'For the cause.'

Lukin nodded. To him, black work was just that – work. Work for the furtherance of the revolution. To Willie Tristram it was a way to cleanse the world.

The house stood gaunt against the dark sky. The two men slid their boots into the toe-irons of their skis and secured the toe-straps. These were skis for cross-country, so no heel pieces. Courtesy of the Soviet Embassy.

Tristram's toes were so cold he wondered whether he might lose some to frostbite, but Lukin snorted with derision. 'How did you soft people ever win an empire?'

'It was mostly in warmer climates than this.'

The two men had already strapped electric torches to their upper left arms. Lukin switched his on – they only needed one for the moment – and it threw out a light that would at least reveal hazards along the way. Cradling his sub-machine gun across his chest, he held up one of his poles to signal the move and they set off across the snow-thick field.

Their skis were silent through the deep, powdery snow. They stayed parallel to each other but three yards apart, poling their way forwards on the up stretches, letting gravity take its course on the down parts. They were in no hurry. Silence, calmness was the thing.

Somewhere ahead of them a dog barked.

'Fuck,' Lukin said. He hated dogs.

'Don't worry, it means nothing. Dogs bark in the night. They smell a fox or a badger and they bark. No one will take any notice.'

'If it comes near me, I cut the bastard's throat.'

Wilde was against the idea of going back to Kensington. It had never been a safe house for Basil Rheinhaus and it was not a good move to return there. But Rheinhaus was insistent. He had things to collect.

'We can have them sent on, or collect them when this is all over.'

'No, Wilde, you do this one thing my way. My notebook is there. Photographs of my family. I have put myself in your care and I have given you the name of the traitor, the Soviet spy. So you can allow me this one thing.'

Wilde couldn't object. Somehow he hadn't imagined Rheinhaus having a family; he seemed such a loner, like so many gamblers. Sitting at a table playing poker or standing on a racecourse terrace with binoculars pinned to his eyes negated the necessity to actually engage with living, breathing, human beings.

The car arrived outside the Chalkes' large house. Sims stayed at the wheel and left the engine running while Wilde and Rheinhaus went to the front door. They had told the driver this would be a quick visit; in and out in no more than a few minutes.

No one answered the door. And yet the lights were on inside.

'Get back in the car and lock yourself in,' Wilde ordered Rheinhaus. 'Tell Sims to watch the road fore and aft, be prepared to go at a moment's notice. With or without me.'

He tried the front door one more time, then made his way around to the back of the house, where he found a back door open, leading into some sort of laundry room.

'Hello, anyone home?'

There was no reply, but he heard muted scratching sounds from deeper in the house. Cautiously, he moved further into the heart of the building, calling out every few steps but becoming increasingly certain that his calls would not be answered.

He tried each door as he came to it. Turning the handles, switching on the lights, peering inside. It felt empty, a ghost house, and yet he had a powerful feeling that he could hear something, sense some life or movement.

In the kitchen, he saw a line of knives and took one, though he wasn't quite sure why. He already had the pistol Freya had given him. Still, two weapons had to be better than one. The knife was a curved-blade carver, razor-sharp and pointed.

Looking in the high-ceilinged studio he saw his portrait on the ground, as though thrown aside. The last room he opened on the ground floor was the sitting room. The lights were on, the fire was alight though down to embers, but no one was in evidence. He looked behind the sofas, under tables, behind curtains.

He had no option but to go upstairs, which felt like an unacceptable intrusion into the privacy of the Chalkes, but unavoidable. Vaguely he found himself wondering whether Sir Vernon Chalke was ever home; from the dismissive way Vivienne referred to him it occurred to Wilde that her husband might spend most of his time with his mistresses.

The staircase was dramatic and winding and carpeted, so his tread was silent.

At the far end of the landing he heard the noise again, this time more distinctly, yet still muffled. It was real, though, coming from a room on the right-hand side, its door shut.

Wilde turned the handle, but it was locked and there was no key. He called out again: 'Hello, it's Tom Wilde here. Is anyone in there?'

A scraping noise, the sound of laboured breathing, or his imagination. He pushed at the door with his shoulder but it didn't give. He stood back, raised his right leg and kicked in the centre of the wood, near the handle. It was shut solid, a heavy door secured by a serious lock and the kick sent a bolt of pain up through his thigh.

There was no choice now; he had to get in there. He removed the revolver from his pocket. It was a Colt .38 Special with four-inch barrel and six rounds in the chamber. He aimed it sideways an inch from the lock and fired a shot. In the confined space, the air was rent by a harsh boom. He turned the handle again and the door opened to darkness.

He flicked the switch and the light of a single ceiling bulb revealed four bodies scattered around the floor – two men and two women – their arms bound tight behind their backs, their mouths gagged, their ankles tied together, hog-tied so they could not even crawl. One of the men had a lot of blood on his forehead and cheeks and his jacket was ripped.

Instantly, he knew that none of them was Vivienne Chalke.

CHAPTER 35

He saw movement, first one of the women, then two more of them, squirming helplessly against their agonising bindings. Only the man with the bloody face did not move.

With the knife from the kitchen, Wilde set about slashing through the cords, gently removing the suffocating gags from their mouths. He didn't say a word at first, let them stagger to their knees and then their feet, all gasping for air.

He turned his attention to the lifeless man. Wilde recognised him as the waiter who had served lunch to him and Vivienne. Feeling for a pulse at the man's throat he was relieved to find one, but he was unconscious and in grave danger.

Looking at the other three, he realised that one of the women, the younger of the two, seemed to be recovering more quickly than the others. 'Get to the nearest phone. Dial 999. Ambulance and police and stress the urgency. This man needs help without delay.'

'What of Lady Chalke?'

'Where is she?'

'We don't know, they took her away.' The woman's voice was breathless, the words tumbling out. 'Their faces were covered by balaclavas. Two of them. One of them had this double-headed axe like the ones climbers use. He hit poor Mr Smythe when he refused to do what they ordered.'

'Just call the ambulance. Go!' As the woman scuttled away, he looked at the other woman and man, who were beginning to recover their composure. 'Do either of you have any first aid training?'

The woman held up her hand.

'Then help me with our friend here.'

A hundred and twenty miles north-west of Kensington, Lazar Lukin and Willie Tristram moved in for the kill.

Their targets were clear: Basil Rheinhaus, the prostitute Dolly Coster and the interfering American Tom Wilde. There were others in the house and they would die, too. Collateral damage. Deaths of no particular benefit or political consequence, but adding to the cause: testing the cracks in a vulnerable establishment; causing chaos as Uncle Joe Stalin demanded; perhaps even nudging the capitalist West towards its inevitable collapse. Not today perhaps, nor tomorrow, but surely the day after.

The dog was barking incessantly now. As they approached the back of the building, behind a group of outhouses, they could see the animal in the torchlight. It was chained to a hook at the side of a door into the main house.

'It's no threat,' Lukin whispered. 'Cutting its throat would silence it, but that very silence might act as an alarm. I think we leave it to bark.'

No lights had gone on in the house so it was reasonable to surmise that the animal sounded off like this every night, that the residents indoors were used to the infernal noise and simply put up with it.

They slipped out of their skis. With purpose, they entered the house through a back door, which was unlocked. Lazar Lukin was experienced in the art of assassination; he knew how to move silently at a steady pace, eyes and ears alert for threats. Willie Tristram was less experienced but he had been to an English public school founded by a Quaker, had served in the Officer Training Corps at Cambridge and had seen bloody action in the war.

On orders from Moscow he had assassinated an officer in the Counter-Intelligence Corps in the American sector of Berlin. He was told that the officer was getting too close to discovering the identity of another Soviet agent. Tristram had not asked questions. Orders were orders. He had watched the man emerge from a bar late at night and had shot him in the head.

Then he had taken his wallet knowing that the killing would be written off as a straightforward robbery. Not unusual in the dark, hungry days of Berlin 1945. The action made him feel clean. God had not intervened and had not struck him with lightning.

Tristram understood danger and he knew how to kill.

The house was silent indoors. The lights were off so everyone must be in bed. This had to be done with cool precision.

Lukin pointed forwards to the staircase, then raised his finger. The house was asleep so there would be nothing on the ground floor. They tested each step for loose boards, gradually making their way upstairs. Lukin pointed at Tristram, then along towards a closed door and mouthed the words, 'That one.'

They split to either side of the landing. Lukin twisted the handle of what he reasonably assumed to be a bedchamber door. Each of them now had their torches switched on and their Sten guns pointing straight ahead.

The weight and brutal cold metal of the weapons was somehow comforting, built with a singular purpose: to penetrate human flesh, shatter human bone, destroy human organs.

Lukin gazed into the bedroom, his finger light but steady on the trigger. The room was large and had a double bed, all made up, but no sleeper. It smelt of must as though no one had been here in months or years, as though waiting for a weekend visitor who never appeared. He turned back to the landing. Tristram was coming out of the room on the far side. They both shook their heads. No one there.

But this house was the main dwelling in a large farm and would have at least six bedrooms, very likely more. They took them one by one until they came to the last. This time they heard something from within, the deep drone of snoring.

They entered together. Lukin hit the switch. The room was bathed in a yellow glow from low-wattage bulbs in four wall sconces. The window was curtained in heavy red damask and the bed was very grand. It was definitely the main bedroom and there was someone in here.

An old man, his mouth wide open, lay on his back against a bank of pillows, his long neat beard splayed on the sheets that covered his chest. He was fast asleep, snoring.

Lukin and Tristram looked at each other with astonishment. There was only one explanation.

They were in the wrong house.

Lukin's first instinct was to let the man sleep and simply leave the house in silence and melt away into the night. After all the man clearly lived alone with his dog and could cause them no harm.

His second thought was better. The man must have local knowledge, so wake him, question him about which house in the vicinity was hosting a group of strangers.

He touched the man's face with the muzzle of the Sten. The man grunted and snorted, then turned on his side. Lukin slapped him, hard, across his pink cheek and he shot up in bed with a startled look on his bearded face, looking without seeing, blinking in the unwelcome light. His wrinkled, deeply-veined, right hand emerged from the bed and fumbled for his spectacles on the bedside table. Lukin removed them from his claw-like fingers, snapped them in half and crunched them underfoot.

'What's your name?' Lukin said.

The man was shaking and blinking, unable to see his assailants properly. 'What? Who are you?'

'Never mind who we are. What's your name?'

'Coleman. Please, why are you here? I've nothing of value.'

'Are you alone?'

'I have a pound or two, that's all. There's nothing hidden. Just a bit of silver downstairs in the dining room. Take that. Please, take it and leave me.'

'I repeat, are you alone? Is anyone else in the house?'

'No, why would there be?'

'Get up, Coleman. We want to talk to you.'

'You can't do this, entering a man's house.'

Lukin pulled back the sheets and blankets, grabbed him roughly by the beard and wrenched his head sideways, then took a grip on his arms and flung him to the floor. 'On your feet or I'll put a bullet in you.'

'I can't see, I can't see.'

Lukin smacked the stock of the sub-machine gun into his head. 'Help me, here, Willie, let's get this dirty kulak up.'

Together they dragged him from the floor and dumped him unceremoniously on a high-backed wooden chair by the curtains.

Coleman was in blue pyjamas, his thinning hair splayed in all directions, his eyes unfocused and constantly blinking as though that would somehow enable him to see properly. There was blood on his lip, either from the sharp edge of the Sten gun or the fall to the floor.

'We have some questions for you. If you don't answer or if you lie, you will experience great pain. Do you understand?'

'No. I don't know who you are or what you are doing here in my house.' Blood came from his mouth in a fine pink spray as he spoke.

'You know all the houses around here?'

'Yes, of course. I have lived here all my life.'

'You know their business, you hear who comes and who goes?'

'Not always. I don't get out so much.'

Tristram had been silent during this exchange. Now he spoke. Perhaps an English accent, a familiar sort of voice, would work better. 'You are not helping yourself, Mr Coleman. We know that a house in this vicinity has a group of visitors – two women, a man – most likely two men – and a boy. Which house would that be?'

Coleman screwed up his eyes and seemed reluctant to reply. Tears began to run down his cheeks.

'You know something, don't you?'

He shook his head, his bloody mouth clenched.

Lukin pointed his Sten gun at the man's bare feet. 'Left or right? Left.' He loosed off a single shot and his victim's scream almost drowned out the gunshot as the bullet splintered bone and flesh in his left foot and smashed through into the floorboards.

'I will ask you one more time, that's all,' Lukin said. 'What do you know?'

His mouth was open in agony, his hands clenched with the intolerable pain. He couldn't speak.

'Last chance.'

'Please, this is nothing to do with me.'

'It's everything to do with you.'

'Do you mean Blackwater Grange?'

'Who lives there?'

'Emily Barnes, of course.'

'And she has visitors?'

His breathing was fast and shallow, his eyes clenched tight so that he couldn't bear to see even the blurs of these hellish men. 'I don't know,' he gasped. 'It's possible.'

'Tell me about Emily Barnes. Who is she?'

'Everyone knows her. She's always lived here. She's Miss Bentall's niece?'

'Miss Bentall?'

'Freya Bentall. Everyone knows her.'

Lukin and Tristram looked at each other and smiled. 'I think we're getting somewhere. So, Mr Coleman, perhaps you'd tell us exactly how to find Blackwater Grange and then we'll get out of your hair.'

CHAPTER 36

It was half an hour before Wilde found Vivienne Chalke. The police and ambulance had arrived at the house in Kensington, the unconscious serving man had been removed to the hospital and the other three captives were being questioned. Rheinhaus and the driver, meanwhile, had been brought inside.

What was known was that two men had burst in wearing balaclavas. The leader had an axe, the other had a knife. Mr Smythe had tried to resist and had suffered heavily for his brave effort.

Each of the three servants told their stories. They were all shattered by the experience and terrified for their mistress who had been dragged away.

They were on the first floor, but this was a three-storey house with dormers on the upper floor.

Wilde took himself away from the rest of the group and climbed the stairs to the top floor, and that was where he found her. She was hanging by her wrists from a hook, her toes just touching the floor, her mouth gagged, her eyes wide open and imploring. Her dress had been torn down the front and her legs were bare.

The room was bitterly cold and Vivienne Chalke was shivering.

But she was alive.

Wilde eased her down and then cut her bindings. 'Are you all right, Vivienne?'

'No,' she said, her voice suffused with both fear and anger. 'No, I'm really not all right. I was scared witless. My arms and back are killing me. I've never known such pain. I really thought I was going to suffocate.'

'Sit down on the bed, try to breathe easily. We'll get you to hospital.'

'I just want to kill them. They threatened me with torture – terrible, hideous torture.'

'They were looking for Basil Rheinhaus, I suppose?'

'Yes. I'm not a heroine. I told them he had gone with you. I'm sorry but the things they said, the threats . . .'

'You did the right thing.'

'Who *were* they, Tom? What on earth has Basil got himself into?'

'You can ask him yourself. He's downstairs. We just came to pick up a few of his things. Clearly, he is not making himself very popular with certain people.'

'It never occurred to me that there might be danger – that we all might be threatened. I would never have allowed him to come to the gallery if I had known. Who did this, Tom?'

Wilde had his own opinion of who might be behind it; Terry Adnams, obviously, but who was he working for? Why would a South London villain be involved with Moscow?

Once again, the intersection of crime and espionage, feeding off each other, devouring the innocent. Maybe there really was no difference. Maybe Stalin and Hitler and Mussolini and all the other totalitarians were simply gangsters who got lucky. Maybe Capone and Dillinger and Bonnie and Clyde just hadn't got around to subjugating a nation before the IRS and the G-men cut short their bloody careers.

Lukin and Tristram were much further from their target than they had imagined, perhaps four miles across country. It seemed that this Blackwater Grange was off a road called Nowhere Lane. They had ended up north of the little town of Reepham when in fact they should have gone south from the station.

It would be dawn soon and they did not want to travel in daylight; they had already been seen too much in these parts. Any more sightings of two strangers skiing cross-country could spark the interest of the local police who might, in turn, alert the military. And so they would stay low in this old farmhouse until dusk at least. Special tasks were a thing of the dark.

Most of the way, Wilde and Rheinhaus travelled in silence, soothed by the rhythmical, mechanical clattering of the train. Rheinhaus had his papers and his books and buried himself in them.

Vivienne Chalke had gone to hospital for a check-up which showed no serious injury and Smythe had regained consciousness but his cognitive powers seemed uncertain and there was still concern that he might have suffered some damage to his brain.

The regular police had handed over the inquiry to the Special Branch and Freya Bentall had been fetched from her bed at the hotel by Sims. She took control of the situation and listened in silence as Wilde briefed her on the evening's events.

'You did well, Tom. Thank God we got Rheinhaus out before the attack. There is still the question gnawing at the back of my mind. Your initial reaction was that the link to Cecil Eagles's friend or lover or whatever he calls him must put Cecil firmly in the frame. But I'm still not sure – and now he's vanished again. Nor can we find Shadox Stone. What's going on?'

'Any thoughts?'

'There are only two options: either they're dead or they've decamped to the other side. Whatever else you might think about Eagles or Stone, neither of them would ever fail to check in.'

'I understand your fears. What about Gus Baxter?'

'He's around and he's actually been out there trying to find some leads to Shadox Stone's whereabouts. Making unannounced calls on various members of the CPGB. Not a word. My priority at the moment is the safety of Basil Rheinhaus. You have to get him to Nowhere Lane. Wait there until you hear otherwise from me personally.'

That suited Wilde fine because he wanted to be near his son. He was also concerned about Lydia and managed to talk to her by phone before his departure.

'I'm fine, Tom,' she said. 'I'm really fine and I'm staying put. I have too much work to do. Exams are not that far off.'

He also told her about the suggestion that Janet Spring might be pregnant, which Lydia thought was hilarious. 'That will explain the bouts of sickness, of course. What sort of doctor will I make if I can't spot an obvious symptom like that?'

'Aren't you worried?'

'About what? Woman has baby shock horror! Crikey, that'll make the front page of the *News Chronicle*, won't it?'

Wilde couldn't find an answer. He wasn't quite sure what his concern was. 'Just be careful, darling,' he said.

'It sounds rather as if you might be the one who needs to take care, Tom. I'll be fine. As for a pregnant single woman and the self-righteous crew who would cast her into eternal damnation for the sin of having sex, I think the world needs to calm down.'

She was right, of course. Shame created havoc in too many lives. Len Goodrick had killed himself because he could not bear the shame of the world seeing him engaged in homosexual acts, young women went to great lengths to cover up the shame of having made love without a wedding ring on their finger.

On the second part of the journey, from Cambridge onwards, Rheinhaus looked up from his studies, yawned and began to talk, addressing Wilde as though he had asked him a question. 'It all began with my belief that there had to be a system to beat the odds. I could apply maths to poker and to the horses. All I needed was a small margin in my favour and I couldn't lose.'

'Your initiation into gambling?'

He nodded. 'It was OK at first. My mathematical system really did work – certainly with the horses, particularly in the high stakes races where there was less doping and sharp practice among the trainers and jockeys. The card games were not so good. But I made quite a few dollars and we bought a fancy car.'

'Something obviously went wrong. I take it the system wasn't as foolproof as you calculated.'

'No, the system was perfect. The problem was me. I began to enjoy the kick, the thrill of winning, the disappointment of losing. That became more important than the money or the science. It was the sheer joy of gambling that got me, and so I left the system behind and began punting on whims rather than science. Your Newmarket racecourse has a lot to answer for. Spent every day I could there when I was at the Cavendish. More fool me, huh?'

'Are you still married?'

'I suppose so. Never signed divorce papers, anyway. Got a daughter and a son somewhere in America. They'll be eleven and twelve now, but we've lost touch.'

'I'm sorry.'

'My own fault, buddy, I let them down.'

They had the train carriage to themselves so they could talk openly. 'Tell me more about Klaus Fuchs,' Wilde said.

'Have you met him?'

'Why do you ask?'

'Because you're somehow involved in all this.'

'Well, yes, I have met him – but only briefly and purely in a social setting. He's a friend of a friend.'

'You mean Geoff Lancing, of course. And what did you think of Fuchs?'

'He didn't come across as a traitor. What about you, though – were you surprised when he tried to recruit you?'

'I suppose I was. I certainly never suspected him, nobody did. But he sees into your soul, he could tell what I was, he knew I was broke. He took me to a bar in Santa Fe and came out with it, offered me money if I would do some little tasks for him, carry some packets – just envelopes – to friends. That's when I knew.'

'Did you play him along or did you say no straight away?'

'I suppose I played him along, just to see how high the money would go. Got it up to fifteen hundred before I suggested he go fuck his mother. He may see into your soul, but that doesn't mean he always reads you right. At that time I would do almost any-thing for money. The word *almost* is important, because there are things I wouldn't do. I may cheat my taxes but I'd rather shoot myself in the head than betray America.'

'Why didn't you tell the FBI or the security people at Los Alamos?'

'What proof did I have?'

'Still, they'd have wanted to know so they could keep an eye on him.'

'You're right, of course, but to be honest I always liked hav-ing that hold over him. I smiled at him every time our paths crossed. Yeah, he might know about me, but I knew worse about him.'

'You've put yourself in danger.'

'But you'll look after me, won't you, Professor Wilde?'

'I'll do what I can.'

'You keep bringing me more people,' Emily said. 'You're like a tour guide, Tom.'

'If you say so.'

'Don't you have work to do? Giving lectures, supervising undergraduates, that sort of thing?'

'They'll survive.' In fact he felt bad about abandoning his university responsibilities. It was never meant to be like this.

'So tell me, are we in danger?'

'I hope not.'

'I mean should we be sitting at the windows with rifles at the ready? Should we organise ourselves in round-the-clock watches?'

He had arrived with Rheinhaus an hour earlier. The onward journey following the change of train at Cambridge had been much the same as before.

Rheinhaus was allotted a small bedroom that might once have been servants' quarters and he was there now, sleeping off the long, exhausting hours since the events in Kensington.

Emily's question and her glee at the very thought of a threat made Wilde wonder: should he be worried? Was there danger here? Perhaps he had placed too much confidence in Freya's assurances that this place would never be found.

'These people we are avoiding, they are not nice.'

'And nor would I be if it came to a fight.'

'You have a lot of your Aunt Freya in you, Emily.'

'You mean pig-headed stubbornness, I suppose.'

'Something like that, but it was meant as a compliment. The word I was probably looking for is *toughness*. Your aunt is tough.'

'I suppose I should have gone into a similar line of work as her, defence of the realm and all that, but as I think I mentioned,

I really can't stand to be anywhere but the country. Anyway, you're dodging my question.'

'All I can say is that we should be cautious. Freya has assigned your home the status of safe house, a term which always suggests a slight element of risk simply because the people brought to such a place are there because someone means them harm.'

'So we *are* in danger?'

'I really can't see how our enemies could find us here.'

'Perhaps there are enemies among the people you have brought to my house.'

'No, that's not possible.'

'Aunt Freya always told me that *anything* was possible, that your dearest friend might betray you. But that's the world she inhabits, isn't it?'

'I can't comment on that.'

Emily was in her jodhpurs, her face gleaming with perspiration, having just returned from a hack across the snow. They were standing in her stables and her horse was back in its box, steam rising from its swelling flanks. The smell of the place was intoxicating. Hay, dung, sweat and leather polish.

'Do you ride, Tom?'

'A bit when I was young and on holiday in Ireland, not much since.'

'Do you shoot?'

'I have done, but not as a matter of course. Quite honestly, I rather enjoy seeing birds alive and in flight. And singing in the spring.'

'But you carry a gun, a little revolver. I couldn't help but notice the shape of it in your pocket. And if I'm not mistaken it's been fired quite recently because I have a remarkable, some say animal, sense of smell and I could almost swear that I detect a hint of powder about you.'

'That's very careless of me. The thing is that there are people who wish to kill Dolly Coster and Basil Rheinhaus. They are both important witnesses.'

'I rather thought they were the ones. What about you, are *you* in danger?'

He laughed. 'Oh, don't worry about me.'

'I'm not. Just interested, that's all. It's nice to have a vague idea what might be in store for us.'

'I still don't understand why you chose our way, Willie,' Lukin said. 'You had an easy life, yet you took the hard road.'

'Are you doubting me?'

'I doubt everyone until proven wrong. Well?'

'Injustice, I suppose. I was surrounded by injustice. Wherever you look in this country and its colonies, you see it. The poor get poorer, the colonised are treated like dirt and the moneyed classes spit on them all.'

'But your parents are farmers ... landowners. Peace-loving Quakers. You come from a privileged bourgeois family.'

'So did Lenin. The haves owe an unpayable debt to the have-nots. I think Comrade Lenin understood that.'

'Ah, you have an answer for everything.'

'Because it's the truth. And I will add this for those who denounce the Soviet Union: there is no birth without blood, though I confess I am not the first to say it.'

Lukin laughed. 'You are a poet!'

'No, a mathematician. I like its purity. There is no argument about maths. It is not a matter of opinion. It is clean.'

Cleanness. Lukin had noticed that about the young man. He liked purity. He would stab his mother's eyes if he could be convinced that it was in a good cause.

The dark was almost upon them. They were standing at the back door of the Coleman farmhouse, preparing themselves, checking everything, ensuring their weapons were in perfect order; this winter ice could jam the best of guns.

Coleman's corpse was still in his bedroom. It would stay there, decaying, until some neighbour or relative wondered enough about him to check that he was well. The dog, too, was dead. The temperature was dropping by the minute.

Lukin strained his eyes across the fields of white. 'You know, Willie, I do believe we have company.'

CHAPTER 37

Emily's words had unnerved Wilde. Surely there was no threat here in this beautiful but empty place? Freya had been certain they would be safe and so had Wilde when he first arrived here. But now that Emily had brought up the subject – and with such gleeful excitement as though it were all some game – he could not get the possibility of danger out of his mind.

There were eight souls in the house: Wilde, his son Johnny, Emily, Joanna, Reeves, Janet, Dolly and Rheinhaus. Of those, three were clear targets.

No, that simply wasn't true. The fact was that if just one of them was under threat, they all were. These people would not hesitate to kill a six-year-old boy or a sixty-year-old housekeeper merely for being in the way. Bloodshed was in their nature. Compassion was an alien concept.

As for defenders, there were certainly three of them: himself, Emily, Reeves. All three of them could handle themselves in a gunfight and there were enough firearms in the house. If necessary, he and Reeves would also give a decent account of themselves in hand-to-hand combat.

The rest were more doubtful, though it was possible that Rheinhaus was tougher than he looked. Dolly, too, she wouldn't go down without a fight.

'Supper!' the welcome call went up from Joanna and pushed lethal thoughts to the back of Wilde's mind.

They were all hungry and dived for the table. Johnny sat next to Wilde. Janet beat Dolly to the seat next to Reeves and a steaming casserole of mashed potato was plonked in the centre of the crowded table.

'This is the last of the spuds so make the most of them,' Joanna said. 'And don't take more than your fair share.'

She brought another large serving dish. 'And here we have game stew. Rabbit, hare, late-season pheasant and partridge, carrots, parsnips and herbs. Reeves had to use a pickaxe to get the parsnips up because the ground's rock-hard. Anyway, it's my own recipe. If you don't like it, you can lump it because it was all we had left in the larder. Someone's going to have to go shooting rabbit or squirrel tomorrow if you want meat again. Oh, and rice pudding and our very own honey to follow.'

Reeves stood up, pint of beer in his hand. He hammered the table with his fist. 'As Emily and Joanna well know, I'm not given to many words, but I just wanted to say what a pleasure it is having all these fine friends of Miss Bentall to stay. You've warmed up the house – and turned the coldest winter known to man into spring. So cheers – and very good health to you all.'

He took a deep draught of his beer and they all stood up and joined him in the toast.

Then Wilde heard a noise from outside. His eyes caught Emily's and she understood.

'I've just got to dash for a pee,' he said, getting to his feet. 'Please tuck in, don't wait for me.'

As he left the room, he automatically removed the Colt from inside his jacket. He went to the back door and stared out at the dark expanse of Norfolk countryside and listened. Somewhere in the distance he heard a fox cry. Apart from that, nothing.

He stayed there for a couple of minutes, then went back inside, locked and bolted the door, then flushed the downstairs lavatory in passing and rejoined the supper party, sitting between Johnny and Rheinhaus.

'You look as though you have seen a ghost, Mr Wilde.'

'Oh, don't mind me, Dr Rheinhaus.'

'We are safe here, yes?'

'I'm sure we are. No one other than Freya Bentall knows of this place.'

'Shall we play cards later?'

That made Wilde laugh and relax slightly. 'Not for money.'

'Not even farthings? That's like a quarter of a cent, right?'

'Not even farthings. I think it's about time you broke your habit, don't you? Now's as good an opportunity to start as any.'

'You're a hard man, Mr Wilde.'

The evening wore on in good spirits. It really was beginning to feel like a party. Emily put some music on the gramophone and found some old rhubarb wine in the back of the larder.

Wilde drank in sips. His instinct told him this was not a good night to imbibe. At nine, he took Johnny up to bed, told him a made-up story until the boy's eyelids grew heavy, then kissed his forehead and switched out the light.

Downstairs in the sitting room, Janet had paired off with Reeves, and Dolly had somehow made a connection with Rheinhaus. Wilde couldn't help wondering what they might have in common to talk about, but he guessed that it was a skill of her profession to be able to converse with all sorts of men, perhaps flattering them in the process.

'An interesting evening.' Emily had come up behind him.

'Shall we go to the gun room?'

'I think we should.'

Wilde gazed around the surprisingly sizeable room. He spotted a hunting rifle, three shotguns and the two air-guns that Emily had mentioned. He picked up one of the shotguns and frowned. It didn't look or feel quite right. 'What is this thing?'

'Elephant gun. Double rifle for big game made by William Evans. My father's pride and joy. He took it on safari to East Africa in the twenties. Heavy, solid bullets will bring down any of the big beasts. They'll go through bone like other bullets go through flesh. There wouldn't be much left of a human head if one of the bullets from that thing hit it. So not really a shotgun though it breaks like one.'

'Do you have the ammunition?'

'Half a dozen rounds that Father brought back with him and about thirty for the rifle. Just what's left from before the war. I've never used the elephant gun and we use the sporting rifle very sparingly, just to supplement our rations and help the neighbours.'

'And shotgun cartridges?'

'Plenty, probably a dozen boxes.'

Wilde took down the rifle and recognised it as an old Mannlicher-Schönauer. It was dusty and clearly had not been used for a long time.

'Don't worry, Tom. It still works.'

'It could do with a clean, though.'

'That should keep you busy.'

He put the gun back.

'Look, how are we going to play this?' she said. 'I can tell that you think something is going to happen. You jumped up like a hare when you heard a sound.'

'Just being cautious. Tell me, how near is the local police station?'

'There's a police house in Reepham, of course, but only one constable. Whether he has a firearms cabinet I don't know, but to be honest, I doubt it. The constable doesn't even have a car, only a rusty old bike with a basket.'

'Any army camps nearby?'

'There were, but not anymore.'

He should call Freya, see if there might be any way of bringing in extra armed protection, but he really didn't want to use a telephone line. Too insecure. It would defeat the object of being in the middle of nowhere.

'Do you ever keep your dog outside at night? Will he bark if he hears something?'

'Hamond's not a guard dog, he's a pet. We've never had any need of a guard dog. No one around here even locks their door. Why would they?'

'But boxers can be used as guard dogs – they have a powerful bite. It might make sense to give it a go.'

'Except it's as cold as Hitler's heart out there. Poor Hamond will freeze.'

Wilde raised a quizzical eyebrow.

'All right, have it your own way, Tom. I'll tie Hamond up in the stable yard so he has a bit of cover.'

'Thank you. And Emily, you know this house better than any-one. If you were going to attack it, what are its weak points?'

'The doors and the windows, of course. I don't really know what you mean.'

'Let me put it another way. How would you place your guns if you were trying to defend the place?'

'Upstairs windows, all sides.'

'I think we need to get Reeves into this conversation.'

Emily raised an eyebrow. 'Good luck trying to drag your preg-nant friend Janet off him.'

'I'll wait here. You go, say you need him to do a quick job – dripping tap or something. Bring the dog, too. I think we'll all sleep better if the three of us take it in turns to keep watch.'

The attack came halfway through Wilde's guard stint at 2 a.m.

Dolly was in bed with Rheinhaus in his room. He had offered her two pounds for sex and she had accepted the offer. Everyone else was still in the sitting room with them at the time and so they slipped out separately, then made their way upstairs together.

He had taken her hand as though they were lovers, which suited her fine, and guided her to his little room where once a servant had lived. There was no heating, so he threw off his clothes and climbed under the bedclothes. 'Come on, Doll, what are you waiting for?'

'It's bloody cold, that's what.'

'Hey, I'll warm you up.'

'Where's the money?'

'In the States you get the money afterwards.'

'Well, we're not in America, are we. Where's your wallet?'

'God damn it, it's in my jacket pocket. Hand it over here.'

'I'll do it myself.' She found the money and took out three notes.

'Hey, we agreed two pounds.'

'Plus tip.'

'You're a hard little bitch.'

'If you say so, Dr Rheinhaus.' Actually, she thought he wasn't so bad, didn't smell, not overweight, a bit soft, but that was fine. 'And you're about to have the best night of your life, so shut up and make room for me in there.'

Two and a half hours later, she said, 'Happy?'

'You told the truth, Doll. Best night ever. Even better than that night in the speakeasy casino in New York when I won more than two thousand dollars playing blackjack.'

Reeves was in his room, in bed with Janet. Emily had mentioned to him that she was undoubtedly pregnant so he reasoned that there was no risk involved, no unwanted children for him to worry about, no withdrawal necessary. His watch would begin at 3 a.m., so he would have a perfect excuse for asking her to leave. The elephant gun was under the bed, both barrels loaded.

'Why do you live here, Reeves?' she said as they laid back in each other's arms after making love.

'It's a nice house and I like Emily and Joanna. Anyway, I've got no money saved, so what could I afford? Renting a two-up, two-down dilapidated farm cottage somewhere? This place is a lot better.'

'Do they even pay you?'

'Of course. I need money for beer.'

He was stroking her breasts and her belly. She had a good body and was generous with her love-making.

'But you've got skills, Reeves – you could make something of yourself. There's going to be a lot of reconstruction work in the cities in the coming years. You're worth more than handyman for Emily and her aunt. Whatever they pay you, I doubt it's enough.'

'I don't want anything else. This suits me fine. We're like family and we get on. I live in a big, comfortable house in the best countryside in the world, so I reckon I'm rich.'

'It seems a waste, that's all. You know you're a very beautiful man.'

He laughed. 'No one's ever called me that before.'

'Well, they should have.'

He was pleased to feel her hand sliding over onto his belly. 'Oh, that's good,' he said.

'Do it to me, Reeves, with your fingers.'

'You're a very bad girl, Janet.'

'Am I? How bad?'

'Very, very bad. But you knew that, didn't you?' He turned on his side, fully erect now, and gently pushed her legs apart, and brought her up and over him, and he entered her and they both gasped. 'What would your husband say if he could see you now?'

'Don't worry, I'm not married.'

'But the baby . . .' He gasped again, pushing deep into her.

Her body froze. 'What?'

'Ssh, relax.'

'What did you just say?'

'I said relax. Move your body with mine. Slowly this time.'

'You said the baby.'

He stopped, raised himself on his elbows and looked up into her eyes, shining in the candlelight. 'Yes, your baby. Emily told me.'

'Told you what?'

'She told me you're pregnant, of course. But now you say you're not married. Does that mean you *are* pregnant or you're not?'

'Why did she say that to you?'

He shrugged. 'We tell each other pretty well everything. If you must know, she said this was safe – that you were already in the family way so you couldn't get pregnant.'

Janet pushed herself away from him. 'How dare she? How dare *you*? Is she your procuress? Get out.'

He was puzzled, but he tried to make light of it and laughed gently. 'But this is my room, Janet. What's the matter? If you're pregnant and unmarried I don't care. I'm a farm boy, these things happen. It's natural, it's life – that's all.'

She was out of the bed now, scrabbling around to collect her clothes, shivering as she struggled into her skirt and blouse and pulled on her sweater, not bothering with her bra or stockings, simply gathering them up with her shoes.

*

Emily was in bed alone in her room, but she wasn't asleep. She had spent the last half hour cleaning the Mannlicher-Schönauer and now she simply wasn't tired. Too much was going on. Sleep wouldn't come, not tonight.

Johnny was in the room next to Joanna's. Both were asleep.

Wilde was downstairs, close to a small window at the back of the house in complete darkness, his pistol cold in his hand. The double-barrelled shotguns were leaning against the wall close by, both loaded. He was straining his ears and eyes for sounds and movement.

The dog whimpered. No barking, just a whimper, then a long, low growl. It was enough.

That was when Wilde knew. The attack was under way.

CHAPTER 38

Silently, with intense but controlled speed, he made his way upstairs. Without knocking, he entered Emily's room and saw her sitting on the edge of the bed with the rifle. He pointed urgently down in the direction of the rear of the house. She nodded, fully aware of what he was indicating, and got up from the bed.

'Should we wake the others?' she said.

'Wake Joanna. She knows the safest places. Tell her to hide with Johnny.'

Next he pulled Reeves from his tangled bed, vaguely surprised not to find Janet with him. Reeves was almost asleep but became alert in a second.

'We've got visitors,' Wilde said.

'I'm with you.'

'Stay up here, at the window. Keep the lights out.'

All three knew their designated roles. The others would wake soon enough.

They had planned for this: Emily and Reeves would take the upstairs windows at front and back with their rifles, only firing when they were certain they had a target. Each round had to count.

Downstairs there was a splintering of glass. A window in the formal dining room at the north-western corner of the building. Wilde was there within moments. He saw a vague shape, dark against darker, outlined by the random movements of a torch lighting the backyard, swaying side to side with the jinking of the man carrying it.

The shape vanished momentarily just as Wilde fired the Colt, just the one round. A wasted shot, perhaps, but even if he didn't hit anyone it was good to let them know that the people inside the house were awake and armed. Just to be clear that they could not just enter this place without suffering death or injury, that murder would not come easy.

He had brought a box of twenty-four rounds from Leconfield. Before starting his watch he had emptied them into his pockets.

They weighed heavily on him but it meant that they were with him at all times and easily accessible for reloading.

His shot at the window met a shattering response: a burst of fire from a sub-machine gun, cratering the wall just above his head. He leant back against the door jamb, turning away towards the deep interior of the house, minimising the target.

Dear God, this was bad. He hadn't anticipated that sort of firepower.

A cold blast of wind followed the gunshots through the jagged-glass frame.

From upstairs he heard two shots, one from the front, one louder from the back. Good, that was giving the attackers more to think about. Another two-second burst came from the sub-machine gun. Not in his direction; the attackers had turned their attention towards the upstairs windows.

Lukin was surprised. He had worked on the assumption that they would find a house full of sleeping people. A silent entry, then pop-pop-pop, room to room, no need to disturb them before dying. Clean kills.

And yet this was happening. How could those inside the house have been aware that they would come? How did they know they had arrived? The dog hadn't barked.

They must surely have thought that this place in the wilderness of rural England would never be found. Was it possible that he and Tristram had been seen against the skyline on their skis and somehow word had got to Wilde? He assumed it was Wilde.

The man was a more dangerous enemy than he had imagined. At that college in Cambridge with the useful idiot Eaton, Wilde had seemed little more than a college professor with a wartime interest in intelligence matters. There were many such people, dragged into the war effort from Cambridge and Harvard, Oxford and Princeton. Bourgeois amateurs every one, the sort to be dismissed with a shrug and a neck-shot in the Lubyanka cellars.

And who else was in this house? The hooker, the small boy and the other woman, Rheinhaus and whoever else.

Only one thing mattered: the death of Rheinhaus. The others were of no consequence to his masters in the Kremlin.

Rheinhaus had to die for one reason – and one reason alone – to protect Klaus Fuchs.

He was the only witness against the man who had supplied the Soviet Union with every detail of the design and construction of the bombs that America had detonated at Hiroshima and Nagasaki and Bikini Atoll – and he was still valuable for he was there for them, his eagle brain taking in every detail of the technical advances on both sides of the Atlantic.

The Kremlin and its scientists had no more valuable source than Klaus Fuchs.

Rheinhaus threatened to bring him down so he had to be removed. No Rheinhaus, no witness, no threat to Fuchs. This was the Special Task, Uncle Joe's great expectation. This was what that little meeting in Stalin's office was all about. Everything else was just collateral, a little chaos to amuse Joe and confound their enemies.

But how to do it now that it had become clear the house was defended?

Options slalomed through his brain in fractions of seconds:

They could storm the building, but they were up against an unknown number of guns. The chances were that one or more of those going in would go down.

Or they could besiege the place, toss in the two grenades they had. That would work for a while because they had cut the telephone cables. But a siege would have to be short-lived, because there were other houses in the vicinity and the sound of explosions would travel, and help would be called out sooner rather than later.

No, they couldn't wait. This had to be executed now, whatever the cost.

Uncle Joe didn't accept failure.

'Go to the front, Willie, tell Terry they have to smash their way in. I'm going in here.'

Terry. Terry Adnams, the black marketeer with a taste for putting axes into people's heads. He had somehow made it up here with his sidekick, Fletcher.

Tristram didn't reply. An obedient soldier, he ducked low and loped at speed around the side of his house, his skis long since discarded.

Lukin waited until he heard hammering and gunfire from the far side of the building. He pulled the pin from a grenade and rolled it through the destroyed window to the far side of the room, near the door where he had seen the flash from a revolver.

He fell to the ground, shielding his ears with his hands. The grenade exploded with brutal force. Debris flew past him. Without hesitation, he picked himself up, curled in through the low window, loosing off a one-second burst from the Sten. A dozen pieces of lead smacking into walls and furniture at body height. A circular spray of destruction.

Emily was on the first floor in her bedroom at the front of the house. They were firing at her with automatic pistols. Two of them – she had seen them both, illuminated by their torches. Now a third man appeared. One of the original men backed away down the path as if to get a better angle for a shot at her window. She had a clear target and took him down with a single shot to the centre of the head.

The man fell without a sound.

Her nerve had held, she hadn't trembled. But now her heart was pounding like a steam piston.

'What the fuck!'

They weren't her words, but an exclamation from a few feet below her. She looked out and down and saw a weapon pointing at her. She threw herself back and bullets splattered the ceiling above her head.

Damn it. That was heavy. And close.

The window below had already been turned to scattered shards. Now the front door was being beaten with something that might be a sledgehammer or axe, and within seconds it cracked open.

Oh my God, they were in the house.

Terry Adnams had found the axe at the farm where they had left the dead man, the place he and Fletcher had rendezvoused with

Tristram and the foreigner. It was a good axe, designed for splitting logs.

This was way out of his territory. In the war, he had managed to dodge the call-up so anything vaguely like a military manoeuvre was not in his repertoire. But when he got the call from George Blain – or Willie Tristram as he now knew him – he had decided to come out to this desolate place because he couldn't abide unfinished business.

He had never ducked a fight in his life and it wasn't going to happen here. No one was going to come out of this bloody house alive, not now they'd blown Fletcher away. He was a useful lad, Fletch, he'd been with him since the early days when they first took over Walworth and set up shop in The Green Bear. He'd be difficult to replace.

Adnams swung the long-handled axe back and brought it in a great arc at the door. Wood cracked and splintered and the sundered remains of the door flew inwards. Adnams stepped into the house and peered into the darkness. The batteries had long since died in his torch.

A dull light appeared in front of him and he pulled back his axe to strike again.

'It's me,' Lukin said. He flicked a switch and suddenly the hallway was bathed in electric light. 'They're all upstairs.'

'Well, we'd better go up there and kill the fuckers.'

Wilde was watching from behind the sitting room door. He crouched and raised his pistol just as a burst of gunfire sprayed across the wall behind him. The air was thick with dust, fine particles of snow and the stench of gunpowder.

Damn, he hadn't seen Tristram with his Sten gun. Wilde rolled away and scrambled to the far reaches of the room, but Tristram was advancing.

Wilde was quicker. He fired his last two shots and from the sound of the scream, one hit its target. Tristram went down, but his finger held tight to the trigger and the Sten splattered bullets across a wide range. Then stopped. The 32-round magazine was empty.

Next came Adnams, standing tall, broad chest puffed out, swinging the axe from side to side.

'So now it's just you and me, Tom. Would have preferred it in the ring, but this'll do. How many bits of lead you got left in that little pea-shooter? Let's find out, shall we?'

Wilde was reloading, one hand fishing rounds from his pocket, the other operating the opening gate of the chamber to receive them. But the process was too slow because Adnams was already on him and the axe plunged down as though he was intending to split an oak log in two.

The intended target was Wilde's head, not a log.

He jinked sideways and the axe crunched past him into the beautiful old, polished flooring, throwing up a shower of wood-chips. Adnams tugged at the axe-handle to pull it out and try again, but it didn't come easy and the Colt was loaded now, the chamber clicked closed, the hammer cocked.

Adnams roared like a bear, finally wrenching the axe free and brandishing it as though he would fell a tree with one blow. Wilde fired. One shot, two, three.

The axe was over Adnams' bald head. He stood there, still puffed out like a beast at bay, then he glanced down to see three crimson blooms neatly grouped and growing on the chest of his tan leather jerkin. For a moment he looked puzzled, then the axe fell from his grip and he seemed to smile as he began to wobble.

'Points decision to you, Tom,' he said.

His legs gave way and he fell to the floor, dead.

Wilde stepped over him and edged his way towards the door. This wasn't done yet. Lukin was in the house somewhere. Maybe others, he had no idea how many there were.

He looked into the hallway. Lukin was nowhere to be seen. He heard a sound behind him and turned.

Tristram was on his side, injured but operational, slotting a full magazine into the Sten.

Wilde had forgotten about him, assumed he had been neutral-ised. His bemusement lasted a half-second. He was raising the pistol, but Tristram was quicker and Wilde had a premonition of impending death.

He shrugged and looked into the Sten muzzle, knowing it would spit a dozen bullets into his body and head and there was nothing he could do about it.

But he didn't die, the bullets didn't come.

Instead he heard a thunderous boom like an exploding shell and watched awestruck as a gaping hole appeared where once Tristram had had an abdomen. His dying – or already dead – body was still moving backwards, knocked several feet across the floor into the hearth.

Wilde turned. There, halfway down the stairs, stood Reeves, gripping the smoking elephant gun.

He nodded to the man who had saved him and breathed again and listened to the blessed silence.

But the silence was a sham. This was a long way from over.

CHAPTER 39

Together, Wilde and Reeves combed the wreckage of the ground floor. There was no evidence of Lukin or anyone else. He tried the phone but it was dead.

'Stay down here, Reeves, I'm going upstairs to set their minds at rest.'

He found Emily in her room, still watching from the window, rifle held like a sniper. At the sound of his step, she swerved around and levelled the muzzle at him, then lowered it as he switched on her light.

'I got one of them, Tom, outside. Clear shot, went down like a hare. Is it over?'

'Possibly. We've got two more but at least one other is unaccounted for, a man named Lazar Lukin, a Russian. Reeves is downstairs, keeping watch. Time to round up the others and make sure they're all right.'

They found Dolly in her room, hiding under her bed. Rheinhaus was there, too, under the sheets and blankets, clutching them as though that would somehow save him from the ministrations of an assassin.

'You can relax,' Wilde said. 'But stay here. I'm pretty sure we've got the better of them. There's a lot of damage downstairs and blood has been shed, but thankfully none of ours.'

'Well done, prof,' Dolly said. 'Sounded like a bleeding cowboy film.'

'Terry Adnams was here. He won't be troubling you anymore.'

'What happened to him?'

'I'm afraid I had to shoot him to save my own life.'

'That's fair enough then. He'd have done for you and me if he could. Just like he's done to others, dirty bastard.'

Janet Spring was in the next room, pacing around, clutching her gently swollen belly, her eyes wide in panic. 'What's happened, Mr Wilde?'

He explained a bit of the background, the threat to Dolly and Rheinhaus. 'I thought this place was completely safe. It was unforgivable of me to bring you along and place you in such danger.'

'And Reeves? Is he all right?'

'Yes, he's safe and sound. He showed tremendous courage.'

'I must go to him.'

'All in good time. First we have to be sure we're secure, so stay in your room until we've got the all-clear. Hopefully the police will be here soon. The phone line's cut but there are neighbours a mile away and they must have heard something.'

'What about Johnny?'

'I'm going to him now. He'll be with Joanna.'

He went to her room, but she wasn't there, nor was Johnny. He searched the cupboards and he looked in his own room. No sign anywhere. He called out their names, but in vain.

Ten minutes later, after an increasingly frantic search of the whole house, from top to bottom, the terrible truth dawned on Wilde.

His son was missing, and so was Joanna.

'I'm going out there after them.'

'I'll come with you, Tom,' Reeves said. 'You can't go alone.'

'You have to stay here with the others. The bastards could come back at any time. Work it out between you and Emily. Keep everyone in their rooms until the police arrive. Keep your ears open for Hamond. He alerted me before.'

He went out from the back door, feeling certain that that was the way they had come. Strapped to his back, he carried the Sten gun he had retrieved from the body of Tristram, complete with a full magazine of thirty-two rounds. He had quickly pulled on some old boots which weren't a bad fit and a thick hunting jacket which he found in the boot room at the back of the house.

His son was out there somewhere, in the hands of a man who didn't know the meaning of the word mercy. How had Lukin got to Johnny and Joanna? What in God's name had gone wrong?

He blamed himself and he felt crushed and more terrified than he had ever felt in his life.

Carrying two electric torches he kept one lit to trace the steps and ski tracks in the snow. He was aware that the batteries were low and would fade and die quickly, so he used them sparingly. As he moved away, three sets of footprints diverged and one set was much smaller. It had to be Johnny.

For pity's sake, what was his son wearing? Please, let him have had time to at least put something around his shoulders and shoes on his feet. The cold out here bit to the bone.

He was thinking hard, working out all the scenarios. He was sure now that Lazar Lukin was alone because there was only one set of footprints that resembled a man's. The thought he came back to was that Lazar Lukin had no reason to kill Johnny or Joanna. Their only use was as hostages. He had no reason to kill them unless threatened.

And in return, what would he want? The corpses of Rheinhaus and Dolly and Wilde himself. That was why he and the others were at Blackwater Grange. Everyone else was incidental.

It was clear that of the targets only one really mattered: Basil Rheinhaus. The Kremlin wanted him dead because he threatened their asset.

In which case, how would he negotiate? How would he go about swapping the lives of two innocents for the man he really wanted?

Lukin had to be in trouble out here, couldn't really have much idea of where he was or where he was going. He couldn't know this area, he couldn't make contact with reinforcements or transport.

In which case, perhaps there was another motive for the abduction of the old woman and the boy: as protective shields to save Lukin's skin.

Wilde dragged himself on through the night. He didn't feel the cold, was unaffected by exhaustion. His mind went to Lydia. She would never forgive him for this. He had brought Johnny here because he feared their home in Cambridge was vulnerable and that he and Janet would be safer, but that was no excuse. He had placed their beautiful boy in danger.

And now he was caught in a nightmare.

The tracks changed. Now there were only two sets of footprints. Johnny must have been picked up. He was being carried, almost certainly by Joanna.

They could not be moving fast. Lukin could drive them on as hard as he liked, but a woman of sixty and a child of six could not match an adult man's progress, certainly not in these conditions.

Was that a speck of light up ahead across the field near the woods? There was some sort of building there, a hay barn perhaps. The light, such as it was – no more than a pinprick – appeared to be moving. That had to be them, surely.

He increased his pace. Trudging onwards, breaking into a run. Despite the cold, he was dripping with sweat from the exertion.

The speck of light vanished.

Wilde didn't stop, only increased his pace. He knew the general direction they had been going and he still had their footprints to follow. No snow was falling, so the tracks remained and there was nothing Lukin could do about it.

The building was an old hay barn, isolated and not large. Wilde stopped momentarily for the tracks seemed to go straight to the gaping doorway. They had gone inside, but why?

Did Lukin know he was being followed? Surely he must have assumed Wilde would come after him and if he had looked backwards – as he must have done – he would have seen the dim torch beam.

The Russian was waiting in the barn, waiting to obliterate him before moving on.

This had to be done with extreme caution. There could be no gunfight, not with Johnny and Joanna in the crossfire.

CHAPTER 40

Joanna Douglass held the boy tight, hugged him to keep him warm and whispered into his ear to reassure him that this was just a big adventure and he would be fine, that there was nothing to fear.

She had come to Blackwater Grange almost thirty years earlier, back in the last months of the First World War when Freya was working as a secretary at some government department in London. The house then was home to Freya's father and the toddler Emily and a woman was needed to run the place and care for the child.

Joanna had come from Walsall in the West Midlands, the only child of a schoolteacher father and a mother who stayed at home and wrote endlessly, dreaming of one day becoming the new George Eliot. It was all in vain. In the last months of her life, dying of breast cancer, the poor woman had taken her box full of writing out to the garden and burnt every last sheet.

When she heard what had happened, Joanna was heartbroken. She would have loved to have read the words her mother wrote.

Without prospects, Joanna felt she had few options. Try to be a teacher like her father, get training as a shorthand typist and seek work as a secretary, or become a nanny. There were so few marriageable men at the end of the war – and no man had ever taken much interest in her anyway – so that did not seem the way her life would go.

So she chose the third option because it was the one that presented itself first in a personal advertisement on the front of *The Times*.

She had several jobs for various families but none of them lasted long until she came to Blackwater Grange at the age of thirty. While Freya Bentall was away she needed someone to look after her niece and also to be housekeeper to her widower father, who had retired to the life of a country gentleman and game-hunting traveller.

It had been a good fit from the start, much better than her previous posts. She loved the child unreservedly and got on well with Freya's father, who was a kind man. In particular, she felt an immediate kinship with Freya.

She understood early on that Emily was Freya's baby, not her niece. But nothing was ever said and nor would it be. And if Emily herself ever suspected the truth she never said anything. To her, she was always Aunt Freya, not Mummy.

Joanna didn't mind that she had never married. That was simply the way things were and she was not alone in that regard. A million young men had died in the trenches so there was always going to be a surfeit of women. If she had one regret, it was that she had never had a child of her own. But Emily was her child in all but name and they would always be together.

Now she had a new and unexpected responsibility to a child, this little boy Johnny, snug in her arms, but in grave danger from a man with a sub-machine gun. He had marched them here to the old hay barn with threats and curses.

'Please, don't hurt the boy. He can't harm you.'

The man simply gestured to the hay pile at the far end of the barn.

'Go over there. Don't make me kill you by doing something stupid.'

Wilde stood outside the barn to the side of the open double-height entrance, his back to the wall. It was of wooden construction and he was aware that bullets from Lukin's sub-machine gun would simply tear through and kill him. To improve his chances, he lowered himself on to his belly.

'Lukin, send them out. Send them to me and you can just walk away. I won't try to stop you.'

'You know what I want. Bring him to me. Just you and him. No guns.'

'I know exactly what this is about, but you must understand that I can't do that. You know I can't.'

'This is your son, yes? You want him back? Just bring me Rheinhaus. A fair swap.'

Wilde was silent a few moments, unsure where this could go. It was non-negotiable. Perhaps in the Soviet Union such a deal might be done, but not here, even when your own child's life was at stake. One could not just hand over a man to be murdered.

'You can still get out of this, Lukin. Free the boy and the woman and I swear I will ensure that you walk away from here unharmed. I believe you have a diplomatic passport and the immunity that goes with it, so you can get back to Moscow in one piece.'

Lazar Lukin actually laughed at that and Wilde guessed why. The very notion that an agent of the Soviet Union could return home with his mission unaccomplished and still remain in one piece was inconceivable.

'Come on, Lukin,' Wilde continued. 'You were there at the dawn of the revolution, yes? And you were fighting for a better world. Well, that better world did not include harming six-year-olds, did it?'

'The end justifies the means.'

'That old excuse for murder. You don't believe it for a moment.'

'Don't tell me what I believe.'

'Send them out to me and I will walk away with them and you can walk in the other direction and no one will follow you. You will live to fight another day.'

Once again, silence. They all waited, and continued to wait, and the sweat on Wilde's neck began to turn to ice. Finally, Lukin spoke.

'Come inside, Comrade Wilde. Let me look at you.'

'Very well.'

'Leave your weapons outside.'

'You know that isn't going to happen.'

Wilde eased himself up, switched on a torch then stepped into the barn. They were all at the far end. Joanna was holding his son close to her breast, stroking his hair as though she were his mother.

Lukin was standing right by them, his Sten gun pointing at the boy's head from no more than two feet.

Johnny looked up and saw his father. 'Daddy!'

He heard Joanna whisper. 'Ssh, Johnny, Daddy's come to join our exciting game, but you have to stay with me for the moment – and we all have to speak softly.'

'This is over, comrade,' Wilde said. Lukin held the sub-machine gun loosely, its muzzle pointing down at a forty-five degree angle. 'You're a professional soldier, you know when it's time to retreat.'

'I have work to do. My mission is not complete.'

'Nor will it be. There's a house full of guns waiting for you back there.'

'But I have your son. A man will do anything to protect his child.'

He raised the muzzle a fraction. 'Professional soldiers do not target children. You harm him and you die with an indelible stain on your memory and your cause. Any support Comrade Stalin has in the West will evaporate.'

Lukin was not moving. His killer eyes shifted from Wilde to the woman to the boy.

Wilde knew that this was not the first time Lukin had been sent out by Stalin to kill. It was written in the hard, unblinking gaze. This was routine for him.

'Let them walk over to me, Lukin, and we leave you without turning back, then you go your own way and I'll ensure you are not found. That way we all live.'

'Put down your weapon, then they can go.'

'No.'

'So how can I trust you?'

'You can't and nor can I trust you, so we both keep our guns.'

A smile crossed Lukin's lips. 'I was told you were soft.'

'And who would have told you that?'

Lukin shrugged. 'Never mind.'

But Wilde knew. It had been Philip Eaton who said it. But when he said *soft*, he had not meant lacking in grit or courage, he had meant that he had a conscience and would not put a bullet in the head of an unarmed man.

'Which shows how little faith you should put in a man like Eaton, comrade. Such friends of the Soviet Union are no friends at all. They will let you down every time.'

The Russian was nodding, the smile now fixed. 'Maybe you are not so stupid. Maybe you are right.'

'You know I am.'

Lukin reached out and placed his hand on Joanna's back, then pushed her forwards, Johnny still in her arms. 'Go, woman. Go before I change my mind.'

CHAPTER 41

By the time the army arrived and sealed off Blackwater Grange, Lazar Lukin was long gone.

He didn't have the woman and the boy to slow him down and even without skis he knew how to move at speed in these conditions.

He had lost one battle, but this was not over. He could not return to Moscow while Rheinhaus still lived.

The British police and security services would expect him to head south, so he travelled north and west, walking through streams where they weren't iced over so that his footprints would be lost. Just before dawn he arrived at a sleeping town called Fakenham and made his way to the railway station. Eventually a train arrived and he slumped back into his seat in a carriage on his own, then slept.

'No, we're staying here,' Emily said when Wilde suggested that she and Joanna and Reeves would have to move out of the house because of the extensive damage. 'We'll board up the windows until we can get them glazed and we'll fill in the bullet holes and redecorate as and when. A jolly good project for Reeves.'

'I suppose I should have expected nothing less from you.'

'We'll manage. We're very self-sufficient. And you know Aunt Freya isn't short of a bob or two for new furniture and paint.'

He stayed with Johnny the whole morning, wouldn't let the boy out of his sight. He offered his profuse gratitude to Joanna for looking after him.

She explained that they had been captured by Lukin because she had taken Johnny down the back stairs, hoping to get out and find shelter in the stables, well away from the gunfire and grenade explosions.

On their way, Lukin saw them and forced them to go with him.

The army and police were now swarming around the place. They managed to repair the phone line and Wilde placed a call to

Freya, who had already received an initial report of the attack and had instructed the local police that this was a matter of national security and they were to await orders.

Some of the soldiers had traced the trail of the attackers back to a house to the north of Reepham, where they had found the bodies of an elderly man named Coleman and his dog. From there the trail was lost because there had been snowfall early the previous evening.

What now, though? That was the big question Wilde and Freya had to deal with. They didn't dwell on the security breach that had caused it because the most pressing issue was what to do with Basil Rheinhaus and how to keep him safe.

It was assumed that the threat to Dolly Coster had evaporated with the death of Terry Adnams, but it was still very real in the case of Rheinhaus.

'I think you should bring him back to London, Tom. The service might be better equipped to deal with him here. We'll keep him a virtual prisoner. He can accept it – or take his chances. I suspect he'll be happy enough. And I need to proceed with my interrogations, face to face this time.'

'Does that mean you now trust those around you – Eagles, Stone and Baxter?'

'It means nothing of the sort, I'm afraid. But I trust the Special Branch, and they'll be doing the protection work.'

'What is Eagles saying about his lover, Willie Tristram?'

'He's saying nothing at all because I have no idea where he is.'

'Have you found Stone yet?'

'I haven't and I am concerned.'

'So two of your officers are still missing?'

'Yes. Alarming, isn't it?'

It was and Wilde had to fear the worst, particularly in the case of Eagles. His link to Tristram placed him right at the heart of a conspiracy. He had either defected or he had outlived his usefulness to Tristram and Lukin and had suffered the consequences.

'And Fuchs? Will you bring him in?'

'No, I can't. I need rock-solid evidence before I can proceed against him. The people in power at Harwell and even the

government consider him too important to the atomic programme and they'll do anything to keep him on. When I spoke
to the minister he simply parroted the standard line: "Well,
Rheinhaus would say that, wouldn't he? He's simply trying to
save his own skin. You need proof, Miss Bentall." And we don't
have that, do we? We have the word of one compromised man.
But let's see what we can find. I'm certainly not giving up.'

If anyone could nail down some hard evidence from Rheinhaus, it was Freya Bentall. Wilde had no doubts about that.

Nor did he have any doubts about the guilt of Klaus Fuchs. He
had sold secrets to the Soviets and was probably still doing so.

Janet Spring was reluctant to leave Blackwater Grange. Her argument with the new love of her life, Reeves, had been forgotten in
the emotional aftermath of the attack and she had melted into his
arms, thanking him with all her heart for saving them all from the
terror. The fact that Emily and Wilde had also played a vital role
in the defence of the house was either forgotten or ignored.

'Johnny needs to get back to school, I'm afraid,' Wilde said.
'There is no longer any threat to our home in Cambridge.' Also,
he was not too happy about the thought of his son living in this
grenade- and bullet-shattered house. A bit of normality, the company of schoolfriends and the comfort of his own bed and books
was needed to get the boy back on track. For the moment it was
impossible to calculate what psychological damage he had suffered during the night.

'Perhaps I could stay here?' Janet suggested.

'That would be up to Emily, of course.' And we would have to
find a new nanny for Johnny, thought Wilde.

CHAPTER 42

The progress of the weather was worse than Wilde or anyone else could have feared. By early March, temperatures of more than twenty degrees below zero were recorded, howling blizzards swept snow into drifts as high as a two-storey house, unemployment reached an unprecedented level, power cuts became the norm.

Many small and vulnerable birds – among them goldcrests and wrens – died in such numbers that it was feared they might become extinct.

And then, in the middle of March, the cold spell broke. After seven of the longest, hardest weeks that anyone could remember, warmer air edged in from the south-west of England.

But that wasn't the end of the misery. Beneath the snow the compacted ice and frozen soil prevented the meltwater from draining away, which resulted in massive flooding all over the south of the country. Nor was meltwater the only problem, because the warm air was accompanied by heavy rainfall.

In Cambridge, Tom Wilde had resumed his duties as a professor of history and his biggest concern was the shortage of paper for his undergraduates to write their essays. Janet had accompanied him and Johnny home because Emily had been firm: she was afraid Miss Spring could not stay at Blackwater Grange. It was not a hotel.

With the thaw and the rain, the River Cam broke its banks and flooded the town.

Further north in the Fens and to the east in Norfolk, the situation was even more dire, floods turned fields into lakes and roads into rivers.

Throughout the country, German prisoners of war were drafted in to help the British army in its efforts to contain the worst of the damage with strategically placed sandbags, but for many people, homes and businesses were awash and would take months to dry out and repair. Any hope that the crippled economy might start to mend this year evaporated.

Wilde hadn't realised that fine snow had found its way into the attic over the preceding weeks and now it was melting and water was dripping through the ceiling. He was well aware, though, that many were worse off and at least the house was not flooded from below.

'It's like a third world war, professor,' Scobie the head porter said, looking across the drenched court as Wilde arrived at college. 'And we haven't even got the bloody worst of it here. Excuse my language, sir.'

'No bloody apology needed, Scobie.'

'But there is some good news. Bobby's on the mend, insists he'll be back at work next week.'

'Is he really up for it?'

'You can't keep a man like Bobby down, professor. I called in on him today and he was very chipper.'

'Well, that *is* good news.' The best he'd heard in a long time. He had feared the worst for his serving man, not that this meant he was out of the woods, of course.

'Oh, and could you call Miss Freya Bentall. She says you have her number.'

They hadn't communicated for more than two weeks and Wilde was glad of it. Despite the shocking weather, some sort of normality was returning to his life. Johnny was back at school and Janet was trying to write her novel and get over her heartbreak. 'At least I've got a story now, Professor Wilde,' she said. 'I'm going to call it *Nowhere Lane*.'

'Good title. I'll look forward to reading it.'

The swelling of the young woman's belly was becoming noticeable and she seemed to be accepting the prospect of single motherhood. The lack of criticism from the Wildes seemed to help. 'We'll be here for you, Janet,' Lydia said, putting an arm around the younger woman's shoulders. 'Anyone who doesn't welcome a child into the world isn't worth knowing.'

Lydia had been remarkably sanguine when she heard of the events in Nowhere Lane. Bullets, bodies, even the abduction of her own boy were accepted with equanimity. 'The important thing is you're all alive, Tom.'

Wilde put her calmness down to the toughening-up process of medical school. Doctors had to maintain their composure in the most trying of circumstances.

He dialled Freya's number at Leconfield House and was put through without delay.

'Tom, hello stranger,' she said. 'How is Cambridge coping with the change of weather?'

'Not well.'

'Flooding, I suppose?'

'A great deal of it. But I'm sure that's not why you asked me to call.'

'Indeed not. I thought you might be interested to know that we've found Cecil Eagles.'

'Where was he?'

'In the Thames Estuary near Tilbury Docks. Very dead, with wounds to the head similar to those suffered by poor Everett Glasspool. Almost certainly an ice-axe, poor dear.'

'Well, it can't have been Terry Adnams.'

'Oh, Cecil has been dead quite a while, probably killed about the time of the unpleasant events in Kensington and Nowhere Lane. So I would suggest either Adnams or Tristram probably did the deed. The body was in a bad way but there was evidence he had been tortured.'

'They thought he knew where Rheinhaus was hiding.'

'Indeed.'

'Damn shame. He might have been loose-tongued, but he didn't deserve that. Thanks for letting me know, Freya.'

He was about to hang up.

'Tom?'

Oh God, the tone of her voice told him a demand was about to be made, an unearned favour about to be called in. 'Yes, Freya?'

'This isn't over yet, you know.'

'My part certainly is.'

'I was hoping you might take a little journey down to Harwell to talk to your friend, Dr Lancing. I'd very much like his opinion on Klaus Fuchs. Off the record, of course, but I want to know whether he has ever had any doubts, any cause to believe that Fuchs might be giving away secrets. Anything at all, slightest thing out of place. It could make all the difference to our case.'

'So no more from Rheinhaus?'

'Nothing.'

'Didn't the events at Blackwater Grange convince anyone?'

'Not enough to persuade the ministry and Sir John Cockcroft. Please, won't you see what you can get from Dr Lancing?'

'If Geoff had any evidence against Fuchs he would have handed it over already.'

'I understand that. But he might be able to give us a more rounded picture of the man, point us in the direction of his other friends, the people he consorts with both inside and outside the premises. It's a long shot, I know.'

'What of Rheinhaus, where is he now?'

'In London, under round-the-clock protection from Special Branch. I've interrogated him myself twice more and I'm not going to get any more out of him. It's simply his word, nothing more, nothing that would hold up in a court of law. We're under pressure from America, too. They want him extradited to face trial for tax evasion – and the government here is minded to agree as a sop to Washington.'

'And the Russian, Lukin?'

'No sighting. He might very well be back in Moscow by now. But tell me, Tom, do you trust Geoff Lancing one hundred per cent?'

'Ninety-nine per cent.'

'Good. No one is completely trustworthy. So will you do this for me?'

'How do I get there? The roads are impassable. Are any trains running?'

'I believe the main line to London is working. Sims will get you to Harwell.'

'Very well, Freya. But no more.'

'No more.'

'Can you get me access to the Harwell facility itself? I'd really rather like to know what I'm dealing with.'

'I'll try.'

Dear God, why was he letting himself be sucked back into this intelligence maelstrom?

CHAPTER 43

Cathy Lancing seemed delighted to see him. 'I don't know how you got here through the swamp that used to be called England, but thank heaven you did.'

It hadn't been easy. Sims, who was now settling in at a nearby guesthouse, had to take diversions on several occasions when he arrived at impassable floods.

'And still we wait for some good news,' Wilde said.

'Actually there is good news, or at least there will be.' Cathy was clutching her docile baby Peggy in one arm. 'One day, hopefully in the not-too-distant future, the country won't be paralysed when the weather prevents us from getting coal from the pits to the power stations, because the power stations will be fuelled by atomic piles – and they will work whatever the weather. The lights won't go out.'

'And that's what Geoff is doing.'

'Exactly.'

He wasn't going to mention the possibility that Geoff might also be developing an atomic weapon for Britain, because that could never be discussed, let alone confirmed.

He handed over a bottle of champagne which had been provided by Freya. 'A little something for having me to stay again. Hopefully it won't be as dramatic as last time.'

A little later, as he and Cathy shared a pot of tea in the kitchen, Geoff arrived home.

'Tom, you made it.'

'O ye of little faith.'

'And he's brought champagne,' Cathy said.

'Then we'd better crack it open.'

Wilde shook his head. 'No, it's just for you two, not to be wasted on me.'

'Bollocks.'

Later, while Cathy was upstairs settling Peggy, Wilde and Lancing sat and exchanged small talk, nursing glasses of brandy.

'Well, Tom?' Lancing said at last. 'Why are you here?'

'I'd love to say it's a purely social call, Geoff, but you wouldn't believe that for a moment.'

'Dead right I wouldn't.'

'It's about your boss, Klaus Fuchs, the chap you introduced me to on my last visit.'

'What about him?'

'Well, how much do you know about him?'

'I told you, he's brilliant. Finest brain I've ever encountered and I've worked with some of the very best. I doubt whether anyone at Los Alamos had a more complete understanding of the various elements that went into the atomic bomb, and I include Oppenheimer and Niels Bohr in that estimation. He'd almost certainly be director at Harwell if he was British by birth.'

'And?'

'What do you mean, *and*?'

'And what else? Outside work. Who does he consort with? Does he have hobbies? Where does he go on his days off? Who are his friends?'

'You sound like a spy.'

Wilde shrugged. 'What I really want to know is this: do you trust him?'

Lancing was silent for a few moments and took a long sip of his brandy. 'Yes,' he said finally, 'I suppose I do.'

'Why?'

'Because he did a remarkable job in Los Alamos and he's doing great work for us. Why wouldn't I trust him?'

'No doubts at all then? No qualms?'

'None. Yes, he fancies Cathy and needs slapping down when he starts pawing her, but that's just who he is. It certainly doesn't make him a traitor.' There was an edge to Lancing's voice now, an edge of intense irritation. 'And I have to say, Tom, this almost sounds like an accusation against me.'

'That's certainly not my intention.'

'Because if I had ever had the slightest suspicion that anyone I worked with might be a foreign agent, I would have reported it without a moment's hesitation.'

'Fair enough. I take your point. The thing is, I value your opinion.'

Lancing managed a smile. 'I'm sorry, I know you have probably been asked to do this, Tom, but this isn't the first time the scientific community has not seen eye-to-eye with those in intelligence. We realise that we're under constant surveillance – and not just by the Harwell security police but also MI5. It's a real source of friction.'

'Like atoms colliding?'

Lancing relaxed and laughed. 'But far more explosive.'

'Look, Geoff, when I come with you to Harwell tomorrow, I'd like to meet him again.'

'You're not going to interrogate the poor man, are you?'

'No, that's not my job. I just want to meet socially and see how I feel about him.'

'Why this sudden interest? Last time you were here you hadn't even heard of the man until Cathy mentioned that he must know Basil Rheinhaus.'

This needed to be said. He lowered his voice. 'I want to tell you something, but this really is just between you and me. You don't tell Cathy and you don't tell anyone at work.'

'You have my word.'

'Rheinhaus is accusing Fuchs of working for the Soviets. He insists he was doing so in Los Alamos and that he tried to recruit him. There are those who are certain Rheinhaus is telling the truth, but there are others – including John Cockcroft – who won't hear a word against Fuchs.'

'Well clearly not, he recruited Fuchs, sent for him while he was still at Los Aalamos.'

'So it's difficult.'

'Bloody right it is. Of all the people at Harwell, Klaus is the last man I would have suspected. He worked his guts out in America and now he's doing the same for Britain.'

Which was the whole problem for Wilde and for MI5. The actions of Lukin and the Kremlin in trying to kill Rheinhaus suggested strongly that he was telling the truth. Yet everyone who knew Fuchs well could not believe he was an enemy spy.

'There was something though.' Lancing mumbled the words as though reluctant to say them at all.

Wilde was taken by surprise. 'Something about Fuchs?'

Lancing nodded. 'It may mean nothing but I should mention it: there is a terrible darkness in Klaus's background, something you'd never suspect when socialising with him.'

'Go on, Geoff.'

'He has suffered tragedy in his life. His sister Elisabeth jumped in front of a train in Prague a few years ago – just before the war, I think.'

'How awful.'

'That's not all. A few years earlier his mother also committed suicide, by drinking acid. Simply the worst way to die. Klaus must have been about twenty, I think.'

'That is deeply, deeply shocking.'

'There is a suggestion, too, that his grandmother took her own life. You wouldn't know it to meet him, but I think he comes from a very troubled family. His other sister also had mental problems. These are things he never talks about, but others who have known him for a few years pass on in hushed tones.'

'You're right, this is all very dark.'

'The strange thing is that knowledge of these things makes him very attractive to certain women who believe he is vulnerable and in need of motherly comfort. But of course none of this means there is any relevance to your inquiries.'

'But it does speak of a traumatised man, someone whose judgement might be askew.'

'If you insist.'

'I want you to watch him for me, Geoff.'

'Spy on my own boss?'

'Yes.'

*

Wilde's first thought on entering the Atomic Energy Research Establishment at Harwell was that it looked like a building site which had ground to a halt half-finished. There were building materials everywhere, old aircraft hangars from the days when it was an RAF base, prefab houses lining the perimeter inside the barbed wire, men in uniform patrolling.

And yet work continued at a furious rate and, according to Lancing, had done so even in the depths of the blizzards. In a few months it had gone from a run-of-the-mill bomber base to an energised modern factory, designed to forge mighty power from the humble atom.

'The prefabs are going up at a rate of knots. Cathy won't hear of moving in here, but it would be easier for all of us. By the end of the year there will be a kindergarten, a school, a couple of shops, even a beauty parlour.'

'Are the prefabs that bad?'

'We looked at one. She said just three words. "*There's no kitchen.*" And that was that.'

'On the plus side you could live here your whole life without venturing out.'

Lancing looked askance. 'Now you *are* joking.'

He was. If Wilde was supposed to be impressed by the living quarters at Harwell, he wasn't. There was something bleak and utilitarian about the place. They were asking the most brilliant men and women in the country to come and work here, so surely they could do better than this?

'If you want to see the labs or Gleep, you'll have to wear a white coat and gloves and remember to touch nothing.'

'Remind me about Gleep.' Cathy had told him but the meaning of the acronym now escaped him.

'Graphite low-energy experimental pile. Controlled fission – unlike the bomb, which is uncontrolled. You won't be able to do much more than heat a bath with it, but we will learn the way ahead.'

'So you're not building a bomb?'

'Don't even mention that word here or the security police will haul you away. No, we are not building one of those things you just mentioned. Come on, where first?'

'Can't we just casually run into Klaus Fuchs in the bar or some-thing?'

'He's not stupid, you know. He'll have wondered about you first time around, second time his hackles will be up because he's had to go through masses of security checks already, both here and in North America.'

'Then he won't be surprised by another one.'

'All right, I'll give you a brief tour, the sort of thing we do for ministers of the crown, then I'll take you to Ridgeway House. It used to be the officers' mess when this was an airbase, now it's rather like a hotel with rooms for the senior men and women and visiting scientists. I stayed there for a few weeks when I first arrived until I found our lovely house in Marbourne. So did Klaus until he moved out to Abingdon.'

For the next two hours, they wandered around the grounds and into the vast hangars which, on the inside, had become remarkably modern in a short space of time with doors which automatically opened when people approached and closed after them.

'The idea being, of course, that you don't have to touch them – and contaminate them.'

'This is rather like a science fiction film.'

'Except it's real, Tom.'

They ducked in and out of laboratories but Lancing refrained from introducing Wilde to the technicians who mostly didn't bother looking up from their workbenches. All around him, he heard the low hum of voices with a multitude of accents, mostly English but also European and many Australian and Canadian. Everyone seemed extraordinarily young and fresh-faced.

Lancing showed him the area where Gleep was being built. He looked up at the array of uranium rods and fuel channels – like an enormous trellis – and felt a little nauseous.

This really was another world, a world that boasted of its peace-ful intent but was born out of the horror of hundreds of thou-sands of lost and maimed lives at Hiroshima and Nagasaki.

'I think I need a drink, Geoff.'

'That we can do. Come on, Ridgeway House beckons – or Staff Club A as some still call it.'

They went to the building which was rather more impressive than the prefabs that were shooting up and they made their way to the bar, where Lancing ordered two Scotches and booked a table for lunch.

'This is the only civilised place on the site,' he said. 'We have dances and jazz nights. This is where affairs start and relationships end, and Klaus is more than happy to play a central role in all that. He's fissile material. Apparently Oppenheimer said he had become the destroyer of worlds. Well, Klaus is very much the destroyer of marriages. And right on cue, here he is.'

Wilde turned and saw Klaus Fuchs entering the bar. He was taller, more languid than he recalled from their first meeting at the house in Marbourne.

Lancing waved to him and gestured him to come over.

'Klaus, you remember Tom Wilde, don't you? History professor from Cambridge, one of my oldest friends.'

Fuchs met his eyes and thrust out his hand. 'Of course I do, Tom. What a pleasure to see you again.'

The clipped German accent was slightly muffled by the attentions of a Gestapo fist to his jaw back in the early thirties when Fuchs's flirtation with the Communist Party had forced him to leave his homeland and find shelter in Britain. Freya had told Wilde all about it. The authorities in Britain and America had been content that he had left his youthful politics way behind him.

'The pleasure is all mine, Klaus. Geoff has very kindly been giving me the grand tour and to say I am overwhelmed by what is happening here would be a gross understatement.'

'Have you learnt anything?'

'I have learnt how little I know.'

'And that is the same with all of us. Einstein, Born, Bohr, Fermi, Peierls, Oppenheimer of course and my brilliant friend Geoff here. The more we learn, the more we realise how ignorant we still are. The universe has given up only a minuscule fraction of her secrets. But what I do know is the delight of a pint of beer and a smoke before luncheon. Can I buy you two gentlemen a drink?'

'We're on whisky.'

Fuchs held up his hand and summoned the barman. In his other hand he held a half-burnt cigarette.

'Tell me,' Fuchs said, 'I believe you were looking for my old friend and colleague Basil Rheinhaus for some mysterious and unexplained reason – did you ever find him?'

'I did actually.'

'At a casino or racecourse, I imagine. Well, do send him my very best regards and tell him he is very welcome to visit me whenever he wishes. I'd love to talk about old times. Lucky old Rheinhaus, wafted in from Bikini on a warm tropical breeze.'

'I think he misses the weather.'

Fuchs picked up his beer and drank half of it in one go, then wiped his mouth with his sleeve. He met Lancing's eyes and grinned. 'You know what, Geoff, I really think we could find a position here in the Theoretical Division for Basil, couldn't we?'

'The more the merrier.'

'He's got a good brain – a very good brain. He does himself no favours with his obsessive attempts to beat the odds, but we can live with that.'

Fuchs dropped his cigarette on the floor and squashed it with his heel. Behind his round metal-rimmed glasses his eyes shone.

And Wilde knew without a doubt that he was a spy. More than that he knew that there was no way that he would be able to pick up any evidence against him, either in casual conversation over drinks and lunch here or in hard interrogation in a cold cell at Scotland Yard.

Fuchs was too clever for all of them.

'Satisfied, Tom?'

'He's very self-controlled, but yes, I'm as satisfied as I can be.'

Lancing shook his hand. Wilde was about to get in the car with Sims for the drive back to London. 'But perhaps not in the same way as me, eh? Well, if he is a spy, he's very good at it because he's got me fooled.'

'He's very gentle, isn't he? How does he carry his authority?'

'All who work for him have nothing but admiration for his mind. None of us would even think of questioning his judgement when it comes to physics.'

'Well, thank you for everything, Geoff.'

'It's been wonderful to see you. And no, I won't spy on my boss. But yes, if anything does occur to me, then of course I will report it.'

CHAPTER 44

The Empire Hotel in Paddington had seen good days. Built in the 1880s of London brick, it had exuded an air of grandeur with red velvet drapes, gold-plated fittings and an expensive piano in the lounge bar. In 1947 the decor merely looked faded and sad, the piano hadn't been tuned in fifteen years and the place survived by renting rooms by the hour to whores and their customers.

Dolly Coster and Basil Rheinhaus met here three times every week – Mondays, Wednesdays and Fridays. It might not have been the last word in luxury but it was a great deal more comfortable than the rooms she used for her professional services in Walworth. And there didn't seem to be any bedbugs here.

She treated Rheinhaus with utter contempt, which was just what he wanted. Dolly had never played the dominatrix before, but she learnt fast and within half an hour was able to make him beg for mercy.

Outside the closed door of the room, his two Special Branch protectors grinned at each other, for the walls were thin and they could hear everything. Later, at the end of their shift, they would laugh about it over a pint or two. This was a cushy little number, keeping a close watch on the American scientist with the German name.

'How long you stuck with the Keystone Cops, Baz?' Dolly said as she rolled on her newly acquired nylon stockings.

'I wish I knew, Doll. I'm dying to stake a few dollars in a game but they're funny about it.'

'I'm sure we can fix something for you.'

'Green Bear? Is it still there now Axeman's dead?'

'Still there, under new management. Leave it with me, yeah?' She snapped her suspender clips on the top of the stockings. 'Same again Friday, Baz?'

'Don't suppose you'd marry me, eh? Make an honest man out of me?'

She slapped his cheeks gently with both palms. 'You just want it free with cooking and cleaning thrown in. I see through you, Basil Rheinhaus. Naughty boy, you're going to need more punishment.'

Wilde made his way to Kensington and was ushered in by Smythe. 'Lady Chalke will receive you in the studio, Professor Wilde.'

'Thank you, Smythe. But tell me, how are you now? I heard you were recovering well from your injuries.'

'To be honest, sir, I don't think I'm quite one hundred per cent. I get a little forgetful and tired sometimes. But the doctors assure me these things will continue to improve. The good news is that I am back at work and the wound to my head has healed well. Lady Chalke has been most generous in allowing me extra time off.'

Wilde found his own way through to the studio at the back of the house. She was in her painting clothes, oversized corduroys tied at the waist with string and legs turned up at the ankle, man's shirt ballooning around her slender torso.

'Tom, so good of you to come.' She took him in her arms and kissed him on the cheeks in the French manner.

'I should have come earlier.'

'Are you back in Cambridge now? In your other life?'

'I am, and very happy about it too.'

'So what can you tell me about dear Basil? He sent me a letter, you know, but without a return address. He apologised for inadvertently bringing terror into my home, but of course it wasn't his fault, was it?'

'No.'

'Am I allowed to know where he is?'

'I'm afraid he is still in danger but I can get a message to him for you.'

'Would you do that? You are a sweet man, Tom Wilde.'

He raised his eyebrows. 'There are many who would disagree with that sentiment, probably including my wife, but yes, I would be happy to be your postman. I suppose you heard about Cecil Eagles.'

'Oh God, how awful. The poor man. Who could do such a thing?'

'I'm afraid it was the same people who came here. Probably the same ice-axe which felled Smythe.'

'Can't these hideous men be found and brought to trial? They're like bloody Nazis. Surely they'll be hanged?'

'No, they won't be brought to trial and they won't be hanged. It's too late for that. It seems they have already met their maker.'

'And did *you* have anything to do with that by any chance?'

'I won't answer that.'

'Well, I offer my gratitude and congratulations to whoever meted out justice.'

Wilde looked at the picture she was painting. Her style had changed. Everything in the studio when he was here before had been figurative: life studies, portraits, still lifes. But the large canvas she was now working on involved swirls and whorls like some sort of vortex with a point of light at the centre.

'What do you think?'

'It's a bit different.'

'It's an experiment, therapy. I'm trying to heal myself. You can't imagine what it was like being strung up and utterly at their mercy for those hours. And then the sounds of everyone downstairs and no one thinking to come up and save me. It was horrible, Tom, and I don't really know if I'll ever recover.'

Tears were streaming down her face. She blinked and took a deep breath.

'You're one of the strongest people I've ever met, Vivienne.'

'Am I? I don't feel it when I'm lying in bed at night hearing every sound, wondering who's in the house. And then when I eventually get to sleep it's even worse . . . the nightmares.'

He didn't know what to say. Should he hug her? It felt wrong. Any words of reassurance would seem cheap and futile.

She blinked again and formed her mouth into a smile. 'Anyway, enough of that. Can we continue with your portrait? If you could come up for a few days at Easter I really would love to paint you.'

'I would be honoured.'

He took his leave of Vivienne Chalke, carrying a letter from her to Rheinhaus. Freya Bentall was his next stop and she would be able to pass it on.

Freya was in her office at Leconfield House. She seemed distracted.

'What is it, Freya?'

'Oh, you know, I just can't get a solid case together against Fuchs.'

'Any word on the Russian?'

'The Soviet ambassador, Georgy Zarubin, was summoned to the Foreign Office. A furious Ernest Bevin told him that Lukin's actions were intolerable and that he must be repatriated to Moscow without delay.'

'And?'

'And Zarubin said he had no idea where Comrade Lukin was, that as far as they were concerned he had been on a legitimate educational tour and had gone missing, and they were worried about his welfare. So no, they weren't in a position to send him home. Of course if Comrade Lukin was found to be guilty of any crime on foreign soil, he would face the full force of the law in Moscow. Comrade Stalin was not in the business of allowing Soviet citizens to sully his country's good name abroad.'

'Very funny.'

'You might very well think so. Bevin and Attlee are not so amused. They want the bastard found and slung out.'

'And how long can you keep Rheinhaus locked away from the world?'

'As long as we have to. It feels a bit like stalemate at the moment. We have his testimony about Klaus Fuchs but those in power insist it's nowhere near enough and that you couldn't convict a shoplifter on such flimsy evidence.'

'Rheinhaus must be getting awfully fed up.'

'Too right. We are trying to keep him happy by feeding him at least one of his many vices. Actually your good friend Dolly Coster is doing the feeding. What a girl, Tom!'

What a girl indeed. Wilde hadn't seen her since Blackwater Grange but it sounded as if she was back in harness practising her profession. Adnams might be in his grave, but she was still at

The Green Bear and had got a message to him that she would love to see him again.

As he would be staying in London overnight and taking Lydia out to dinner, he had time to kill. So, yes, he would be delighted to pay a call on young Dolly.

CHAPTER 45

The first and most obvious difference was the change of name. A workman was up on his ladder screwing a new signboard into place. No longer was it The Green Bear.

It was now called Dolly's.

Which was a most unexpected metamorphosis. Wilde pushed open the door and stepped into the front bar, which hadn't altered one bit. It was still packed out with the din of conversation and the air thick with smoke and alcohol fumes.

He looked around, hoping to catch sight of her and wondering why the place was now named after her. Maybe there was no connection with Dolly Coster at all, just an interesting change of emphasis to signify that the days of Terry Adnams were over. But that didn't make a lot of sense – of course it was named after her.

Fighting his way to the bar he saw a familiar face – Gus Baxter. That was no surprise because Freya had suggested they meet here.

'Tom Wilde, I heard you were coming. What pleasure.'

'Hello Baxter. Just paying my respects to Dolly.'

'You can't keep away, can you. So Mother allowed you out to play?'

'Don't talk about her like that.'

Baxter pulled back his shoulders as if offended. 'What's got *your* goat?'

'She's your senior officer, show some respect. What is it, can't stand to take orders from a woman?'

'Well, it's not the natural order, is it? Anyway, I know Dolly will be thrilled to see you.'

'I suppose you heard something about our unpleasantness in the wilds of Norfolk.'

'Oh indeed, big news in the security service. Not quite such big news in the national press, which seems to have kept it to a manageable three-paragraph story on page two. Mother's doing again, one supposes. By the sound of it you did well to come out of it intact.'

'Yes, I was lucky. Others not so fortunate. You knew Adnams, of course – but what about his man Fletcher and Willie Tristram?'

Baxter stroked his chin as though deep in thought; Wilde wasn't fooled for a moment.

'I suppose I must have encountered Fletcher. Terry had a few heavies on the payroll and I imagine he was one of them. But Willie Tristram? Name doesn't ring a bell, I'm afraid.'

'He was close to Cecil Eagles.'

'Really? That does surprise me. Dreadful news about poor Cecil.'

'Almost certainly killed by your former pal Terry. Interesting circle of connections. You knew Cecil, Cecil was Willie's lover, Willie joined Terry on an attack in Norfolk – and Terry knew you.'

'And there the circle breaks because I didn't know Willie.' Baxter was no longer smiling. 'Is this an interrogation? You're bloody impertinent, you know.'

'My apologies. I didn't know you were such a sensitive soul and so easily offended. Anyway, let's talk about other things. I was surprised to see the name change here. I thought The Green Bear was part of the South London landscape.'

'As it is and will be, probably more so, because Dolly has big plans for the place. She's taken over the lease.'

Wilde was having trouble computing this news. 'Dolly doesn't have any money. She came from nothing and she still had nothing when I last saw her two or three weeks ago. How could she have taken on a place like this?'

'Backers, Tom. She's a smart one, our Dolly, knows whose arm to twist and whose prick to fondle.'

'But why her? There must have been a queue to take the place on. The Green Bear is a gangsters' dive and undoubtedly very profitable. Surely Adnams had lieutenants, so why would they have given up control?'

'Money. She raised the money. Money talks in these parts. Money and knuckle-dusters. Come on, you're thinking too much. Let's get you a drink and when Dolly's free, you can ask her your- self. I know she's looking forward to seeing you.'

This was strangely disturbing. But, yes, he needed a drink. They elbowed their way to the bar.

'This one's on me, Wilde – let's see if I can remember. Scotch, right?'

'Thank you.'

The barman was with them almost immediately. 'How can I help, Mr Baxter?'

'Two large Scotches, your finest.' He turned to Wilde. 'How about a peaty single malt?'

'I think that would slip down very nicely.' So Dolly had backers. One of her clients, perhaps. He supposed she must have done favours for various wealthy men during her career in vice, so perhaps it wasn't so unlikely that she had found a way to raise investment loans. Yes, she was a smart one, and he had underestimated her.

Baxter paid for the drinks then had a quiet word with the barman, who nodded and went off towards the back, where he spoke to another man. A minute later he was back.

'Miss Coster is a bit tied up at the moment. She'll be about twenty minutes, maybe half an hour.'

'Can you wait, Wilde?' Baxter said.

He checked his watch. There was plenty of time before he was due to meet Lydia. 'Yes, I'll wait.'

He settled down with Baxter and his whisky and took in the heaving, lively scene around him. This was all very unlike the slow, discreet world of the scholar, but he found himself curiously attracted to it. The sheer exuberant life of the place. The seedy glamour. Everyone seemed to exude energy – the sort of money-making energy that was needed if this country was ever to get back on its feet after the devastation of the war.

The conversation came around to the missing MI5 man, Shadox Stone. 'Still no sign of him, Baxter?'

'Still no sign. I'm beginning to fear he might have met the same fate as Cecil.'

'Maybe someone here knows. Did Stone ever frequent this place?'

'Good Lord no, much too busy with the communist brethren and the dreary trade union boys.'

'Would any of them have cause to do him harm?'

'All of them probably. He knows which Labour Cabinet ministers are commies and he knows how the money gets from Moscow to the CPGB. He watches them every step of the way. Anyway, what about you, Wilde, have you gained anything from your brief association with Five? Are you champing at the bit to set up a new American service?'

'I've learnt a few things.'

'Well, I think everyone in Five and Six hopes Harry Truman hurries up and gets the OSS back together in some form or other.'

'Oh, I'm sure it will happen.'

He kept looking at his watch. It was over half an hour. He couldn't stay too long because he didn't want to be late for his dinner date with Lydia. They had a lot to talk about, in particular what to do about Janet Spring.

How would she be able to cope as housekeeper nanny if she had her own baby to look after? He knew Lydia well enough to realise that she would never turf out a woman in need. In particular, she would go out of her way to assist someone who was likely to face ostracism for the supposed sin of bringing new life into the world. That support had been made clear to Janet. She was safe at Cornflowers.

He was brought back to the present by Baxter's broad grin.

'Well, well, look who's arrived.' He nodded towards the door that gave way to the gambling den at the back. 'Here she is, Queen Dolly of Walworth.'

Indeed, there she was, making her grand entrance, surrounded by men who towered over her and seemed to be hanging on her every word. She looked more gorgeous than ever and was dressed a great deal more expensively. Baxter held up a hand to hail her and she smiled at him, then noticed Wilde at his side.

Within moments she had ditched her acolytes and the crowd parted to let her through to the bar. She brushed past Baxter and made straight for Wilde.

'My hero,' she said, tilting her face for a kiss.

Wilde obliged her by pecking her cheek. 'Well, this is a turn-up, Dolly.'

'The girl done good, yeah?'

'How did you manage it?'

She tapped her nose. 'Mum's the word but it's all above board and almost legal. I own the lease.'

'But this came out of nowhere.'

'Oh, I always had plans, Tom. I think you knew I was going places. And as you wouldn't get me the five hundred I had to get it somewhere else, didn't I? But you know what, I owe an awful lot to you. You showed me how life could be – that night in the hotel with you and Miss Bentall. I'd never been in a place like that before. Then the big house in Norfolk with its huge rooms and stables and everything. I didn't understand that people could live like that. And you know what makes the difference? Money. Huge amounts of lovely money, and then even more money. So I'm going to make something of this place – and make something of my life.'

'I suppose I have to congratulate you.'

'Not too soon, darling. I've got to pay back the loans or I'll be dog-meat, know what I mean? Also got to pay off the likes of Billy Hill and Frankie Fraser on a weekly basis when they come calling for a percentage. Terry always told them to get lost but I don't have his muscles, do I? So I need to make a lot of money and this place has to be the best. Anyway, Tom, it's wonderful to see you again. How you been?'

'Fine. Back at work, teaching. But I was in London and thought I'd like to see how you were doing. You had a tough time up in Norfolk.'

She snorted. 'Best result of my life. The slimy bastard wanted to kill me. Had plans to kill you, too, didn't he? Got his just deserts though, the filthy swine.'

His just deserts. Three bullets to the heart and he was out for the count. She was right, of course, it was kill or be killed that night. Why *should* she feel anything but exultation at the removal of the threat to her life? And why shouldn't Dolly make the most of an opportunity that presented itself? She probably had the brain and the toughness to make a go of it. She might not have the muscle in her own slender arms, but by the look of the men surrounding her, she had plenty to call on. Whoever Billy Hill and Frankie Fraser were, they might just meet their match in Dolly Coster.

He finished the drink and she ordered more.

'It's all on the house, Tom.'

'Thank you.'

'Let me show you my office. It's not finished yet but I'm adding a few feminine touches.'

More drinks arrived and they carried them through to the gambling room, which was as riotous as he recalled from his first visit. Baxter came with him, as did one of Dolly's men. He had the carriage of a fighter and the watchful eyes of a bodyguard.

Wilde drank half the whisky and then realised he should go easy, recalling the beating he took on the Walworth Road when he was half-cut before. But he was feeling strange and it occurred to him that the alcohol might already be taking an effect.

He put the half-empty glass on a table and continued across the hall. A caller at the board was shouting the odds, the balls on the snooker table clicked incessantly and he realised his shoes were clicking too.

Dolly placed her small, perfect hand in his and an electric current ran up his arm and his eyes opened wide.

'You look different, Dolly.'

'Oh, I have Max Factor to thank for that.'

'Not just that.'

It was the colour of her hair and the sheen of her skin. They were brighter, painted with golds and scarlets.

'And here we are, prof. My little headquarters. I'm going to have the best radiogram going and some flock wallpaper. What do you think?'

'It already looks fine.' There were two sofas, a desk, a full-length mirror, a painting or print on the wall. A country scene.

'Like the picture? That's to remind me of Nowhere Lane. Fields and woods, cows and horses.'

'How can you afford all this? You still haven't told me who's lent you the money?'

'That's for me to know and you to mind your own bloody business. But look how it's changing. The feminine touch. No ice-axes in my office. I'm subtle, you see. Sit yourself down, prof, relax on the big leather sofa. You look tired.'

'No, I'm not tired but I will sit down.' He couldn't take his eyes off the painting. He didn't recognise the artist and at first he didn't think it was very good, but then the colours changed before his eyes. The greens and yellows were exquisite, flashing like neon signs. And the cattle in the field were alive and moving. 'Dolly, where did you get this incredible picture?'

'You like it?'

No, he wasn't sure now that he did like it because it was all enveloping and he was in the field with the cows, sitting on the damp green grass, staring up at the scudding clouds in a crystal blue sky.

Baxter came and sat beside him. His face loomed large and his pores became caverns from which tiny daggers protruded. Wilde shuddered and backed away from him.

'What is it, Wilde?'

Baxter's voice wasn't human, it was the growl of a wolf. He didn't speak wolf, but he understood the words and knew that they were threatening. He knew Baxter's heart and knew he was a predator.

'Keep away from me.' He couldn't look at the man, so he looked over at Dolly behind the desk. But it wasn't Dolly, it was Lydia and she was floating and smiling and he knew that she had never looked so beautiful before and never would again. He wished he had a camera so that he could capture her forever.

'Lydia, you're here. Have you come to save me?'

'It's working,' Lydia said.

'Yes, it's all working.' She was made of glass so he could see everything, more naked than he had ever seen her. He could see her heart pumping, contracting and expanding, pushing oxygen-rich blood through translucent arteries. He could even see the oxygen, pure and succulent, and he wanted to breathe it in.

He had felt her heart with his hand between her breasts but he had never seen it before, pumping in all its red beauty. Why had he not looked? Simply look and it's there before your eyes and the colours are all exquisite. He would never look at colours the same way again.

The colours were alive all around him, not just in the picture. A face appeared out of nowhere, a face in the headlights, eyes black without soul.

Doors were opening everywhere. The walls were doors and they were opening and the stars were shining, each star a different colour. Colours he had never known existed. As the doors opened, Lazar Lukin came in and smiled at him and ruffled his hair.

'This is good, Dolly,' Lukin said.

Wilde wanted to cry out that no, it wasn't Dolly, it was Lydia, his wife and they shouldn't look at her, but he wasn't sure that he could speak now. Surely Lukin would be able to read his thoughts. They would pass through the ether like waves and the Russian would know everything because he, Wilde, now knew everything.

The whole universe was laid out before him in the sun-bright light and he saw it all, from its birth from the Godhead's loins to its death and the utter emptiness of everything.

He could no longer see. His eyes were open but all he could see was darkness, nothingness. He had heard the symphony of the spheres but now there was only silence.

Deep arctic silence, white light forever.

The visions ebbed and flowed for hours. He would never know how long he was there, stretched out on the sofa all by himself with his dreams, sometimes thrilling and unbearably beautiful, at other times cold and terrifying. At times he was the centre of it all, of everything, a dazzling pinprick of light, and then he was above the cosmos, on the very far edges, billions of light years away, looking on eternity.

Gradually the visions faded. He didn't just wake from the dream, it happened over an hour or more until at last there was a realisation that something had happened to him, that this wasn't right, that Lydia wasn't there after all.

He had been fed some hallucinatory concoction. One of those strange mushrooms, perhaps, or that curious acid that some Swiss scientist had synthesised that was said to warp reality and reveal hidden worlds. He had read about it in some newspaper or magazine. Was that what it was? Or mescaline, maybe?

That single malt had a powerful flavour. Camouflage for a drug.

One thing was certain: something had got into his system and it wasn't just whisky. He knew inebriation and this wasn't it.

As reality gradually returned he looked around and was shocked to realise he was somewhere else. He had thought he was still in Dolly's lair, her private room at the back of The Green Bear – or Dolly's as it was now to be called. To hell with that, it was still The Green Bear to him.

But he wasn't there anyway, because everything was unfamiliar. There was no light and there was no noise from beyond. No shouting of the odds.

He was alone. His head was throbbing with a hangover like no other and his hands were slightly sticky. Why were they sticky? And what was that smell? He knew that smell, the stink of blood.

Panicking now, he had no idea where he was or why. He seemed to be flat on his back on something like a divan or bed, but he could see very little, just the light grey of dawn through the curtains. He rolled over and fell to the floor and found his way to the wall and a light switch.

He was in a room with two single beds. It had the feel of a hotel room, but how could he be in a hotel? The bed he had been laying on was rumpled. The other bed had someone in it, fast asleep, head on pillow, body tucked beneath sheets and blankets.

Who was he here with? Was that Dolly? Had she brought him here? God, what had he done? He had never been unfaithful to Lydia, never would be, whatever the temptation. At least he was fully clothed, that had to tell him something.

The pain was all-consuming, pounding inside his head, but he had enough cognisance to know that something was very wrong about this situation. He went to the other bed and touched the shoulder and knew instantly that this was not Dolly, nor was it alive.

He pulled back the bedclothes and saw the body in its coat of blood. The eyes were open, so was the mouth as though it would gulp for air. Death was certain; no need to take a pulse.

Blood soaked the clothes and the sheets, but the throat and the chest were worse – much worse. The throat had been cut and the chest had been stabbed. Blood had gushed like a fountain but was now dried and coagulated or still sticky, like his hands.

Basil Rheinhaus was dead. They had got to him.

CHAPTER 46

After his initial touch of the shoulder, he made no more contact with the body. The room had a basin so he washed the blood from his hands and inspected himself in the mirror. He looked dreadful. He combed his hair with his fingers, gulped down two mugfuls of cold water, splashed more water over his face, then went back to the bed on which he had lain in a stupor and sat on the edge.

He had to think hard and with great care, work out what had happened here. The obvious conclusion was that he was being set up. But where was the murder weapon? Quickly, he searched the room, looked in the wardrobe and beneath the beds, behind the curtains and in the drawers of the little table.

If there was a weapon in the room, he couldn't see it.

He had to get out of the place and contact Freya. Without her assistance, this could become very bad. His watch told him it was five-thirty and the silence told him it was morning. He opened the door and looked out into the corridor.

No one was about. The only sound was a light snoring from one of the other rooms. He shunned the lift and crept down the stairs. He was in luck; there was no desk clerk, no night porter and he was able to slip out of the front door unseen, into the rain.

Without any idea what part of London he was in, he looked back at the hotel and saw that it was called *The Grand*. If ever there was a misnomer. This place had never been grand and the name told him nothing. Nor was the street recognisable. A rain-swept thoroughfare with deep puddles. It could be anywhere in the country.

He found a street sign which told him he was in Horsegate Road. Again, it meant nothing to him but on balance he surmised he probably hadn't been brought far from the Walworth Road.

Fifty yards away, he saw the dim light of a phone box. Fishing in his pocket he discovered that he had a few coins. Just enough to feed the meter for a quick local call.

It took Freya an age to answer. She sounded groggy.

'Freya, it's me, Wilde.'

'It's not quite the crack of dawn, Tom.'

'I'm in deep trouble – and there's worse. I don't even know where I am, some street called Horsegate Road near a seedy hotel called The Grand. Do buses or tubes run at this time of day? Could Sims pick me up?'

'Of course buses and tubes run. But you said there's worse.'

'Rheinhaus is dead. Murdered.'

'Stay where you are.'

An hour later, he was at Freya's flat. It turned out Horsegate Road was in Peckham, South London, less than two miles from The Green Bear.

'What now?'

'The Special Branch are already on their way. Room on the first floor, number six, yes?'

'That's right.'

'They'll deal with it. You'll have to be officially interviewed, of course, but you need to be very circumspect because national security is involved – as well as your own neck. I'll sit in with you. I was a criminal barrister between the wars, so I will guide you in your answers.'

'I would appreciate that. You do believe me, Freya, that I had nothing to do with this?'

'Of course I do, but that doesn't mean you don't have questions to answer. And you're sure this is Dolly's work?'

'Yes. But, dear God, I was blindsided. I thought she was a friend.'

'And Baxter?'

'He's involved, I'm sure of it. I was hallucinating a lot of the time but I have no doubt that he was part of it.'

'Which he'll deny.'

'In my delirium, I thought I saw Shadox Stone, too. But that could be nothing because I also thought I saw Lydia and she certainly wasn't there. Have you heard of that strange Swiss concoction – I can't remember its name?'

'Lysergic acid. Curiously enough our lab boys have been looking into that, wondering whether it might have properties as a truth drug.'

'It was powerful. I was there at the birth and death of the universe.'

'You mentioned Shadox Stone. You really think you saw him?'

'Lukin, too. But I really don't know if any of it was real.'

Half an hour later, the phone rang. The Special Branch officers had found a blood-stained knife in the room and it seemed highly likely it was the murder weapon.

'My fingerprints will be on it,' Wilde said.

'Almost certainly. They went to great lengths to get you into a hotel room with a corpse, so they weren't going to balk at planting the knife in your hand. There's more, Tom. Your names are on the register – you and Rheinhaus. Apparently you both signed in last night at about eight o'clock.'

'Forgeries.'

'The deskman says he remembers you both. It seems he even describes you both accurately. He says he was unhappy because he was worried you might be there for immoral and illegal purposes.'

That made Wilde laugh. 'As if The Grand would care about such matters.'

'That's not the point. Juries care.'

'I need to contact Lydia. I was supposed to meet her yesterday evening.'

'Yes, she called me when you didn't turn up at the restaurant. I tried to put her mind at ease, said you must have been caught up in something and couldn't make contact.'

'I won't be popular.'

'Your wife is a very understanding woman. As for me, I have two problems – getting you off a murder rap and trying to work out what to do about Klaus Fuchs now that the only witness against him is dead. The man who gave Stalin the plutonium bomb has got away with it and can carry on handing over secrets. But we'll be watching him.'

'What are you going to do about Lukin and Dolly and Baxter?'

'Well, as far as Miss Coster is concerned, I'm going to raid her bar, rip it apart to find evidence of murder, then close it down. Lukin will be kicked out of the country as soon as we can find him and Baxter ... well, I badly want to have him done for murder too. But we'll need some sort of smoking gun.'

'And Shadox Stone?'

'I think he's already dead, don't you?'

By 11 a.m., Wilde had made contact with Lydia and apologised profusely and said he would explain everything in due course.

An hour later he was at Scotland Yard with Freya Bentall. He had made a statement and was now in an interview room with a detective inspector named McLevan.

'Your fingerprints were on the knife, Professor Wilde.'

'I have explained what happened in my statement and referred to the likelihood that those who have attempted to frame me would have planted my prints on the murder weapon.'

'And your name is in the register.'

'Obviously written by someone else. I must have been carried in. So if the desk jockey is saying otherwise, I suggest you investigate him.'

'You do realise the background to this, don't you, detective inspector?' Freya said.

'Of course. But procedures must be adhered to.'

'One thing that interests me is how your Special Branch colleagues managed to lose Basil Rheinhaus. Their brief was to keep him under surveillance at all times.'

The officer looked distinctly abashed. 'I agree that is shocking, Miss Bentall. The two duty officers have been suspended and are mortified.'

'What happened?'

'Yesterday afternoon, Dr Rheinhaus told them he was going out for some fresh air and he wished to go alone. They objected, but he insisted that Britain was a free country, he was here legally and he was not under arrest or charged with any crime.'

'Didn't they just follow him anyway?'

'They would have done but a black car was waiting for Rhein-haus at the corner. He jumped in – and it shot off. The officers had no vehicle of their own and no way of giving chase. They had no way to stop him going.'

'Didn't they take the registration number?'

'Of course they did, but it was a fake. The officers suspect the involvement of a certain young lady of the night who was permitted access to Dr Rheinhaus.'

'Dolly.'

'Indeed, that was her name.'

'What about the driver? Do they have a description?'

'Nothing of any use. Look, Miss Bentall, this is difficult for me. I don't believe Professor Wilde is guilty, but there is a clear prima facie case against him.'

'He's being framed.'

'I'm sorry but he has to be held on a charge of murder. The fingerprints . . . his presence in the room . . . blood on his clothes . . . his name in the register. There's more than enough to proceed.'

'Inspector McLevan, you and I have worked together over many years. I trust you and I think you trust me.'

'Impeccably, ma'am.'

'So give me one day and you have my word that Professor Wilde will be delivered back to you if this isn't sorted within twenty-four hours. Can you do that?'

'I don't know how I could explain such a course of action to the commissioner.'

'I'll talk to him. Harold Scott is a practical man and he'll understand.'

'Do you agree to this, Professor Wilde? Do I have your word that you will return here tomorrow?'

'Yes.'

The detective inspector turned his attention back to Freya. 'Let's call the commissioner then.'

They returned to Leconfield House two hours later. Wilde was rather hoping to see Gus Baxter but he wasn't there.

'I'll get him in,' Freya said. 'In the meantime, I think you know what to do.'

'Do I?'

'You're going to disappear, Tom. Vanish. And don't come back until your name has been cleared.'

'But you've given the commissioner your word.'

'To hell with my word. If you're banged up in Wandsworth, you're no use to anyone. The way things are, Lukin's got everything he wanted: Rheinhaus is dead and you're taking the rap. He returns to Moscow with clean hands and Stalin will pat him on the back.'

'Where do I go?'

'You're a clever man, Tom. You work it out.'

'Before I go, there's one thing I have to know. When Baxter took me to The Green Bear that first time, back in the deep freeze, that wasn't pure chance, was it? You told him to take me there and it wasn't just about ice-axes. You were interested in the place before Everett Glasspool was killed, weren't you?'

She looked uncomfortable. 'I might have had my reasons.'

'It was something to do with Len Goodrick. You knew he went there and you knew he was vulnerable?'

She shrugged.

'But you didn't think to tell me.'

'Need to know, Tom. Need to know.'

'Damn it, Freya, I *did* need to know.'

'I wanted you to go there with an open mind.'

'And Vivienne Chalke? You told Cecil Eagles to introduce me to her?'

'He didn't like the idea, but yes, I did.'

'Because of Basil Rheinhaus?'

'Of course. I thought Cecil was keeping him from us. I knew Vivienne's link to the man.'

'And there was me thinking these things were crazy coincidences.'

'No such thing in our game, Tom. There are occurrences and there's enemy action. Coincidence is for the birds. Now make tracks.'

CHAPTER 47

He knew now where Dolly Coster had got the money to secure the lease on The Green Bear. From Lazar Lukin and the Soviet Union. And in return, she had handed them Basil Rheinhaus for the slaughter and Tom Wilde to go down.

Dolly, née Amelia Coster, had the face and body of a Hollywood movie star. A face to turn heads and whet desire wherever she went. A manner that bespoke innocence. But behind the sweet, open-eyed visage, she was eaten up by ambition. Her heart crawled with worms.

He knew, too, the truth about Gus Baxter. He was the traitor Freya had been looking for. Wilde initially suspected Cecil Eagles. No more. He, too, had been a victim – of his lover Willie Tristram and his colleague Gus Baxter.

Wilde walked on in the rain, thoughts swirling. He had twenty-four hours of leeway, then every policeman in the city – and possibly the land – would have his name, a description of him and his photograph. So he had a day to find shelter and work out a strategy.

He badly wanted to talk to Lydia but he knew that she would be hard at work at St Ursula's. She was unaware of last night's events, probably intensely irritated at having been stood up. He'd call her this evening and once she had calmed down she would certainly have ideas. But it was still only midday and he couldn't simply wait for hours and do nothing.

He walked eastwards along Piccadilly, then down to Pall Mall. The rain was unceasing. In Trafalgar Square he ducked into the National Gallery simply to escape the downpour for a while and to think.

The paintings had been brought back from their wartime hiding place in a slate mine in North Wales less than two years earlier, and they were a comfort, for they had survived. He was drawn inexorably to Holbein's *The Ambassadors*. All life was there: music, literature, globes of the heavens and the earth, the luxury of furs, war in the form of a sword, and lastly death as if seen through a corner of the eye. Death, waiting at the toe of the picture – but actually in the very foreground – as a reminder of its inevitability.

He thought back to the hallucinations of the night before, or at least those elements he could recall: the sense of looking down on the universe from the very edge of existence, like an impotent god, watching but powerless to intervene. The colours that couldn't exist. The surrealism. This painting, grounded in the real world, offered so much more than the dream.

It took him back to the Tudors, his own period of history, and the normality of his college life.

Apart from which it was an extraordinary painting. Clever, devious men transported vividly through the ages by the hand of a remarkable artist. Ambassadors? That had always been a genteel euphemism for spies and nothing had changed.

'It's quite something, isn't it, sir?'

He turned. One of the gallery attendants, a man with military bearing, was standing beside him, eyes fixed on the picture.

'Yes,' Wilde said, 'yes, it is.'

'Only I couldn't help noticing that you have been looking at it for at least ten minutes. Almost as if you were lost in it.'

'I suppose I was.'

'I look at it a lot, too, and I think of all the comrades I lost in the trenches. It's the skull at the bottom, you see. Sometimes I want to weep, but I never do, for that would not be appropriate.'

'I think it's appropriate to weep for lost friends.'

'Do you, sir? Thank you. That makes me feel a lot better.' The old soldier turned his face to Wilde's and smiled, then walked back to his place by the door.

The paintings. The art. He was surrounded by it and it was speaking to him. No one would look there, would they? There was no reason to. Vivienne Chalke, artist and art lover, wasn't a friend, barely an acquaintance and yet they must have a common interest in bringing the killer of Basil Rheinhaus to justice.

Good God, the chances were she didn't even know yet. Why should she? The body was only discovered a few hours ago so the morning newspapers wouldn't have had an opportunity to print the story.

It's never easy getting a cab in the rain, but Wilde struck lucky and he had an easy ride to Kensington. He expected Smythe or one of the other servants to answer the door. But it was someone else, a man in his mid-fifties with oiled hair and grey sideburns. He stood a few inches shorter than Wilde and had the look of someone who was very wealthy and very pleased with himself.

'Whatever it is, we're not buying.'

'And I'm not selling. I was hoping that Lady Chalke would be in.'

'Really? Why? Who are you?'

He was thinking fast. 'I'm here for my portrait. I commissioned Lady Chalke to paint me.'

'More fool you. She's a bloody dauber and she certainly doesn't need the money. Still, it keeps her out of my hair. What's your name?'

'Tom . . . Thomas. Richard Thomas.'

'Well, Mr Thomas, you'd better come in, hadn't you.' He held out his hand. 'I'm Vernon Chalke, Sir Vernon to the servants and lower orders.'

'Delighted to meet you.'

He shouted out. 'Viv, where are you? Are you in? There's some fellow to see you, name of Thomas.'

One of the servants appeared in the hallway behind the master of the house. Wilde's hopes shrank. He was about to be addressed by name. He badly didn't want Vivienne's husband to know he had been here, the covering of tracks began here and now.

'Lady Chalke is in the studio, Sir Vernon.'

'Well, you'd better escort chummy here through.' He nodded to Wilde. 'Good luck, Mr Thomas, rather you than me, old man.'

'Tom, I wasn't expecting to see you back so soon. What a thrill.'

'It's not such a thrill, I'm afraid. I come with terrible news.'

She had already moved on from her abstract whirls and light and was painting a curious still life, a bunch of daffodils in an old black leather army boot. A sign of spring regeneration after a winter of destruction, perhaps.

'You've got me worried.'

'Can we sit down somewhere?'

'Let's go to the sitting room unless my bloody husband's there.'

'He's just gone out.'

'Did you meet him?'

'I did and I told him my name was Richard Thomas and I had commissioned you to do my portrait. I'll explain more about that in due course.'

'Hideous man, isn't he?'

They made their way to the sitting room with Vivienne ordering coffee on the way.

'Now then,' she said as they settled on a wide and deep sofa. 'Tell me the worst.'

'Basil Rheinhaus is dead.'

She did not respond at first, not really taking the news in.

'I found him myself. He had been stabbed to death.'

'No, I can't bear it.'

'I'm sorry.'

'But you told me those people who came here in balaclavas and attacked us were dead.'

'The Soviets got to him. They were behind the threat all along. He knew too much. I expect it'll be in the evening papers.'

'Are you sure about this, Tom? Please tell me it's a tasteless joke.'

'Basil's dead.'

'I can't believe it. I won't.' She slumped, her head down. Her breathing was short and panic-stricken. She looked up, blinking. 'Basil dead?'

'I'm sorry.'

'He was terribly flawed but he was brilliant too and could be so very funny, often at his own expense.'

'I found his body myself in a hotel room in South London. And there is something else. I am in the frame for the murder. I was drugged and left in the same room. My prints are on the murder weapon, my name is in the hotel register. By this time tomorrow I will be a wanted man. That's why I gave a false name to your husband.'

'Oh, Tom, I can't bear it. I thought the coldness was over. The daffodils . . .'

'I need your help, Vivienne.'

'Did I ever tell you about Basil? How we met?'

'You told me you were lovers.'

'It was more than that. We were in love. I met him in New York in the thirties. He was twenty-five, just out of the Massachusetts Institute of Technology masters programme and I was twenty-eight and had been married two years.'

'Were you on holiday or working?'

'Following my husband. He was over there for three months exploring business ideas for his bank and I had nothing to do all day except take in all the galleries. I was beginning to realise that I had made a terrible mistake marrying him, but we are both Catholics and divorce is not an option. In New York, Vernon made me dress up to the nines to show me off every evening and then we'd go to the swankiest restaurants in town to entertain his potential clients and business partners. God, those people were dull. Have you ever met City types, Tom?'

'None that come to mind, but probably.'

'Avoid at all costs. Basil was nothing like those people. His brain was a beacon summoning me. He wasn't good-looking, didn't have the body of an Adonis, but he loved life and understood everything – even his own shortcomings.'

Wilde wanted her to continue talking. She had to get this out of her system so that she could grieve, for she probably had no one else to talk to, certainly not her husband. 'So where did you meet Rheinhaus?'

'At a party. Basil's mother and father were not wealthy and were still in Switzerland, but his uncle Henry – Heinrich, actually – was a stockbroker in New York and he was taking an interest in Vernon because he wanted to know where the bank was investing. Anyway, Basil was staying with Uncle Henry for the summer while he contemplated whether to come to Cambridge, where he had been offered a post by Rutherford. In fact he spent most of his time at the racetrack – Aqueduct, Belmont Park, wherever – or in gambling dens. He was good, too, he won money with his system. But I suppose you know the rest of the story.'

'And when your time in New York ended?'

'He stayed for a while, I came home, but we always kept in touch and then later when he took up the Cavendish post we met frequently.'

'Have you ever heard of a man called Shadox Stone?'

'Not that I recall.'

'He's MI5. His sister worked for Rheinhaus's family in New York before the war. Perhaps it was Uncle Henry, I don't know.'

'Well, you know there *was* an English girl there, I think she was working as a nanny for Henry's young children. He was on his second marriage and the house was full of screaming brats. But I don't recall the nanny's name and I certainly never met anyone called Shadox Stone.'

That didn't mean that Stone hadn't heard of Rheinhaus or Vivienne Chalke, of course.

'I can't believe he's dead, Tom.'

'I'm sorry to bring the news.'

'He gambled, he loved women, he smoked dope and he built atom bombs. I suppose he was never going to survive.' Tears were running down her cheeks but now she smiled. 'But he lived a life and at least the IRS can't get their hands on him now.'

'That's true enough.'

'I'm sorry, you said you needed my help.'

'I have to clear my name and I have to bring his killers to justice. I need somewhere to stay.'

'You want to stay here?'

'No. But I know you're well off. It occurred to me you might have other properties. It's a long shot, but I'm all out of ideas at the moment and time isn't on my side.'

'Well, of course, we have our country estate, but that's in Northamptonshire.'

'I need to be in London.'

The maid arrived with coffee and laid the tray on the table. 'Leave it, Maud, I'll pour.'

'Yes, ma'am.'

The maid curtsied, then left the room.

Vivienne rose from the sofa, tears still streaming and began to pour the coffee. 'Cream?'

'Black, please.'

'You know, Tom, I think I might have an idea.'

CHAPTER 48

'Take this,' she said, handing him a velvet pouch containing a rectangular object of roughly pistol weight, but not a pistol. She had left the room for five minutes before returning with the pouch and one or two other things.

'What is it?' Wilde demanded, accepting the velvet bag.

'The best thing to come out of Germany since Beethoven's ninth.'

He pulled open the drawstrings, looked inside and laughed. A little Leica 35mm stared back at him. 'Thank you.'

'Well, you're looking for evidence. You never know. The camera never lies, they say.'

'Is it loaded?'

'Fully loaded. And put these on.' She handed him a pair of tortoiseshell spectacles.

'Glasses? I only wear them for reading small text or ancient documents.'

'These are plain glass. I used to run a little amateur dramatics group and accumulated quite a lot of props and costumes. They wouldn't disguise you to someone who knew you but they'll remove the instant hit of recognition to an officer on the beat with only a description and perhaps a blurry photo to go on. So let's hope you don't run into acquaintances.'

'Fair enough.'

'And how are you with accents?'

'What are you thinking – German, French?'

'English. Your accent isn't strong after all these years in England, but if you could just lose the hint of American you have retained. The cops will be looking for an American. The newspapers will probably call you American.'

He smiled at her. 'You're good at this, Vivienne.'

'I rather think I am. Now, you're going to hide in plain sight in the place you'll be least expected – The Savoy Hotel.'

'That's insane.'

'No, you're wrong. No one will notice you. Heads turn at The Savoy when Coco Chanel or Humphrey Bogart stroll in or when Churchill arrives for lunch. You'll be nothing more than a bespectacled face in the crowds. If anything, they'll look at me, not you.'

'What are you talking about? How will they look at you?'

'Because I'm part of the disguise – I'm coming with you. The police won't be looking for a couple; they're hunting a single man. Meanwhile, Smythe will have told my husband that I've gone to Paris so I won't be missed here.'

'You're serious about this, aren't you?'

'Damned right I am. I'll remain Lady Chalke because they know me too well at The Savoy, and you are my cousin Richard Thomas, up from the West Country. I've already been on the phone and our separate but adjoining rooms are booked. Supper, too.'

'This is remarkable, but why would you do this?'

'Oh, that's simple. I want to bring down Basil's killers as much as you do.'

Their taxi-ride to The Savoy and the checking-in went without a hitch. Vivienne had packed a large suitcase and she had found a smaller valise and a change of clothes for Wilde – from her husband's expansive wardrobes.

It was early evening and the rain had stopped. Wilde already had the seeds of a plan. They ate at six-thirty with only a single glass of wine apiece, took a long time assessing various costumes for Vivienne so that she wouldn't look absurdly out of place in the less wealthy parts of London, and then managed to persuade a taxi driver to take them south and west to a rundown street in Battersea, near Clapham Junction.

The driver seemed a little nonplussed. 'I've heard of slumming, but I ain't never had a fare from The Savoy to this part of the world before, guv'nor.'

'Just drive, don't think,' Vivienne said.

'Sorry for being alive, missus.'

'Pull up here.' Wilde paid the driver and watched him depart, then he and Vivienne walked up the steps to a decent Victorian house in a street full of similar properties which had somehow escaped the bombing.

The door was answered almost immediately by a man in a vest and trousers who looked nothing like his younger brother.

'Mr Smythe?' Vivienne asked.

'And you must be Lady Chalke. Very pleased to meet you, m'lady. Come in.'

The man was the elder brother of Vivienne's servant Smythe, the survivor of the blow to the head when Adnams came calling. He was a plumber and he had something that Wilde and Vivienne wanted – an anonymous van with a tank full of petrol.

Smythe the younger had called his brother on their behalf. At first Smythe senior was unhappy. He was busy, busier than he had ever been because so many pipes had burst in the big freeze and so many homes were flooded with the onslaught of rain.

But he was offered five pounds in cash and, anyway, he would do anything for his brother.

'We won't come in,' Vivienne said. 'We're in a bit of a hurry.'

'Quite understand, m'lady.'

'We're extremely grateful to you and sorry if we're disrupting your work.'

'Don't worry about that. As the wife pointed out, I've got plenty of work on within walking distance, so I've taken all my tools indoors. Keep it as long as you need it. All I ask is that you return it in one piece.'

'You're a fine man, Mr Smythe. And your brother tells me you're good at keeping your mouth shut.'

'I won't tell a soul about our little arrangement. Come on, let me show you the vehicle.'

Wilde drove the van to the inappropriately-named Grand Hotel in Peckham and then parked across the road from the entrance. Vivienne went in to the reception area and looked around. There were no police officers in evidence so she supposed they had garnered all the information they needed.

The man on the desk was tall and thin with a swan neck and dark hair combed forwards across his brow. She approached him with a smile, notebook and pencil in hand.

'Are you the concierge?'

'Con-see what?'

'You man the desk?'

'Well, you can see I do, can't you? One pound twelve and six for a single room for the night, darling. Or I can do you a deal by the hour.'

'I don't want a room. I'm a reporter from the *News Chronicle*.'

'You don't look like no reporter to me.'

'Well, I am. Anyway, what does a reporter look like?'

'They're blokes.'

'Well, just take my word for it, I'm a reporter and I'm doing a story about the terrible murder here last night. Were you on duty at the time?'

'Of course I was.'

'Can I see the register?'

'No, the cops have taken it.'

'And what time did the two American gentlemen arrive? Mr Rheinhaus and Mr Wilde, I believe.'

'I don't know. Quite late, I suppose. Eight, maybe nine. Why you asking all this stuff? I don't have to answer, do I?'

'I'm afraid you do. What was their demeanour?'

'De-what?'

'Their mood. Were they friendly? Did it look as though they'd been drinking?'

He shrugged. 'Just two blokes. I dunno.'

'So neither of them needed helping up the stairs to their room?'

'No. They both walked up normal-like.'

'I want to see the room.'

'Well, you can't. Cops say it's not to be used at the moment. Crime scene, they call it.'

'I didn't get your name.'

'That's because I haven't told you it. And I ain't going to neither.'

She was scratching away in her notebook, like a real reporter. 'Describe the two men. First, Wilde – he's the killer, yes – what did he look like?'

'I dunno. Quite tall. Just an ordinary bloke.'

'Hair colour?'

'What is this? I've told the cops everything I know.'

'Did I mention the money?'

'What money?'

'The money my newspaper will be paying for your story.'

'You pay for stories?'

'Of course. Two quid, perhaps more if you've got good details.'

He held out his hand. 'Go on then, hand it over.'

'First I need your name.'

'Randle. Dave Randle.'

She handed him a one-pound note, which he examined with suspicion then shoved in his trouser pocket. 'That's just for starters, Mr Randle. Now I need your address.'

'I ain't giving you my address. Don't want that in the papers. Too many nutters in the world.'

'All right. When did you discover the body?'

'When the cops turned up. Somebody called them. I had no idea there was a body. Gave me a proper turn, it did. Murder in The Grand? Never had one of them before. Plenty of illicit nookie and other goings-on, even a heart attack once, but not murder.'

'Did you see the body?'

'Yeah, I had to open up the room for the cops. Bloody mess it was. And who's supposed to clean it up and wash the sheets? That's what I want to know.'

'Did you hear anything in the night?'

'Not much, just night noises.'

'Nothing suspicious?'

'Not really. There's always something going on though, isn't there? Wives screaming and shouting when their men walk in drunk and start laying into them. Occasionally a bang, someone letting off a pop gun or firework. That's life in Peckham.'

'All right, Mr Randle, thank you for your time.'

'Oy, two quid you said. You've only given me one.'

'And you haven't given me much in the way of detail, have you?'

'What's *your* name, darling?'

'Well, it certainly isn't darling.'

'Fuck you, sweetheart.'

'His name's Dave Randle.'

'We just sit and wait.'

'I riled him. We won't have to wait too long.'

They were sitting in the van. The street lights had come on in much of London, but not here and so they were shaded in darkness about thirty yards from the dimly-lit entrance to The Grand Hotel. Wilde was in the driver's seat.

She had definitely got to Dave Randle. Within five minutes, he left his post at the front desk and hurried through the cool evening air northwards. He didn't even think to look about him to see if he was observed.

They tracked him at a distance, crawling along, stopping, crawling a bit more. When he skipped over the fence into a park, they couldn't follow him but Wilde knew exactly where he was going, so he turned left and picked up speed until he reached the Camberwell Road and drove northwards until it became the Walworth Road. He slowed down and waited. In the rear-view mirror he saw a tall, thin figure striding along.

Vivienne turned around. 'That's him.'

'Well, we now know for certain how they organised last night's events. And we know who put the knife in the room after I'd gone.'

They parked the van close to the entrance to the establishment now known as Dolly's. Wilde had the little Leica 35mm out now, but he was concerned. 'Without flash, I don't think this is going to work. Not in this light.'

'It was just an idea.'

'But let's see. I'll wait until he comes out. He's already panicking, we can panic him even more.'

*

Dolly Coster didn't hesitate. The man had been useful fixing the scene at the hotel for a few quid and he could be a convenient witness against Wilde, but now he had become a liability.

The bleeding halfwit had come to The Green Bear.

She might have said something to him such as, 'You really thought it was a good idea to come here, Randle? Are you stupid?'

But she already knew the answer to that question, so it didn't need to be posed. And it took her no more than a couple of seconds to compute that it didn't really matter if Wilde was convicted or not so they could do without Randle as a witness. Wilde in jail waiting for the noose? That had always been little more than a smart way to tie up loose ends.

But in the scheme of things, with Rheinhaus and the others all dead, Tom Wilde was just a bit of an irrelevance. The danger was this fool Randle. The only link between The Grand Hotel and The Green Bear.

'Sit down,' she said. 'I'll be back with you in a minute. Help yourself to a drink to steady yourself.'

'I'm sorry about this.'

'Don't worry, Dave, these things happen. No one's blaming you.'

Out in the noise of the gambling den, she touched Gus Baxter on the shoulder.

'Well, Dolly?'

'Hotel boy has lost his nerve. He's a danger to us.'

'Did he arrive alone?'

'No sign of anyone else. He said a reporter turned up and began asking questions and that spooked him.'

'You're sure he wasn't followed?'

She shrugged. 'All I know is that he's a hazard.'

'OK, I'll do it. Give him a couple of drinks, loosen him up. Makes it easier. I'll be with you in five.'

She returned to her office. Randle had fixed himself a large gin and she smiled at him. 'So tell me more about this reporter, Dave. What sort of questions did he ask?'

'It was a woman. She wanted to know everything about them. Asked me my name, where I lived. Even offered me dough, though I wouldn't take any.'

'And did you tell her your name?'

'No, I'm not stupid.'

'But she worried you, which is why you came here.'

'Well, it's big, ain't it? Saw the *Evening Standard* late edition – front-page news. I'm for the rope as an accessory if things go wrong. Same as you. Yes, Dolly, I'm well worried.'

'Of course you are, Dave. But there's nothing to worry about, I promise. The Yard have already got the killer thanks to your testimony. You'll pick him out in the line-up easy. They're not going to look any further, are they? Lazy bastards, cops, don't do any more than they have to. Here, let me fill you up.'

The gin wasn't going to make any difference, of course. You couldn't get tight in ten minutes flat. But a condemned man deserved a last drink. And a smoke. She pushed the cigarette box towards him. He took one and she gave him a light.

'You're a good-looking fellow, Dave Randle. Did anyone ever tell you that? I'd like to show you a good time one night, thank you for all you've done for us.'

'You've paid well enough, Dolly, but I wouldn't say no to a little extra.'

She smiled again. No one ever said no to her. Well, only one.

Randle was standing with his back to the door, which was opening. Gus Baxter was stepping in, his shoeless feet silent. Dolly was pouring Randle's drink, smiling all the while, touching his face with the back of her hand, then tracing a line with her small fingers, down his long neck and body to his prick. She cupped his balls and he gasped, the cigarette dropping from his mouth.

It was his last gasp.

The garotte was around his swan-like neck in one smooth and brutal motion. Baxter turned the stick like the expert assassin he was, tightening the ligature at astonishing speed.

Randle's hands were like talons, reaching up to his throat, desperate to loosen the wire, but completely helpless. Dolly kissed him on his dying lips, then gave his testicles one last hard and painful squeeze.

CHAPTER 49

'This is taking longer than I thought,' Wilde said. 'It has to be possible that he realised he was being followed and has escaped by a back door.'

'So what do we do, Tom?'

'I'm inclined to go in.'

'Alone? Unarmed?'

'Who said I was unarmed?'

'And what would the point be if Randle has already got away? We needed a photograph of him with the backdrop of the bar, something to identify the place to prove his connection to Dolly Coster.'

'God damn it. I thought we had the bastards.'

A couple of customers entered the bar. Two men with their hands in their pockets. They were laughing without a care in the world, eager to get a pint or two down their throats and stake a couple of bets. Wilde watched them disappear and thought how easy life was for them. All he wanted was to be back in Cambridge with his wife, his son and his undergraduates. He wanted to study, to teach, to write and to live in peace with his fellow human beings.

Another customer approached. He was wearing a raincoat and a flat cap. A working man at the end of his day. But then Wilde tensed. There was something familiar about the way he walked, the way he held himself. Everyone's gait was different, almost as unique as a fingerprint, and he had seen this one before.

He had walked alongside the man, had entered Smithfield meat market with him and had ordered a hot bacon sandwich from a little kiosk in the cold hours before dawn.

Shadox Stone. The face in the headlights. The face in his hallucination. Maybe he really had seen it among the swirling colours and the eternal songs of the stars.

This was Stone all right, and he wasn't a drug-fuelled figment of his imagination.

'What is it, Tom? You look as if you've seen a ghost.'

'Not a ghost, someone far more elusive. You remember I told you about a man called Stone, whose sister worked as a nanny for the Rheinhaus family in New York?'

'Vaguely, yes, but I didn't know him. Nor did I know his sister's name. I just remember that the nanny was English and that Rheinhaus's rich Uncle Henry had a house full of squalling, squabbling children.'

'That doesn't matter. It's just that a thought has come to me. What if Stone's sister casually told him about the people she worked for, maybe in a letter, or maybe when she came home for Christmas? She might have mentioned the poor young nephew who was an atomic scientist and was always talking about gambling.'

'That's not impossible.'

'What if Shadox Stone's first instinct was to think such a man might be pliable, that he could one day be recruited for the Soviet Union?' He realised he was thinking aloud, telling her too much. Dear God, suddenly there was no doubt in his mind. Back in the days of Los Alamos, Stone had persuaded Klaus Fuchs that Rheinhaus could be used as a courier.

Shadox Stone with his flat cap and raincoat was the traitor. And his supposed spying on the Communist Party of Great Britain? A nearly perfect double bluff.

'You're losing me a bit, Tom.'

'It doesn't matter. It's all clear to me now. I have to go in there. We've been looking for that man for weeks – I can't let him get away.'

'And your pistol – are you sure it's loaded?'

'Oh, I'm certain.'

'Do you want me to come with you?'

No, he didn't. He shook his head.

'You can't leave me out here, you really can't.'

'It could be nasty in there.' But then again, he needed a witness. 'It's risky.'

'I understand that and I'm scared. God knows I'm scared – but I don't even know what I'm scared of. What is this hellhole?'

'It's a bar and a gambling den and it's run by gangsters – the people who killed Basil.'

'Give me the Leica.'

'Are you sure, Vivienne? This is a lot to ask.'

She kissed his cheek. 'This is for Basil. The lion's den beckons.'

As they entered, faces turned and the din abated, first to a murmur and then to silence. The crowd began to move apart, looking at him strangely. Was it anger, fear or pity – or a mixture of all three? Their faces told him they remembered him, knew who he was and what he was said to have done to Axeman Adnams.

Vivienne was supposed to be hanging back by the door, but she stayed with him in lockstep, looking about her into the crowd of drinkers, gamblers, thieves and hedonists. This was a new world for her but she concealed her fear and held her head high.

They continued through the bar area to the door at the rear and entered the secret universe of the gamblers. The clicking of the snooker balls subsided and ceased, as did the shouting of the odds. Even the soft flicking of playing cards and the tinkle of dice stopped.

Wilde gazed about him, looking for any sign of Stone or Dolly. He saw a group of heavies bristling and a couple of them moved towards him, muscles rippling against over-tight shirts and jackets. He shook his head slowly; *don't come near me if you value your life.* Remarkably, the two men halted in their tracks and allowed him to pass.

Even the thick cloud of smoke seemed to part.

They arrived at the closed door to Dolly's office and paused briefly. Wilde had his hand in his pocket, resting lightly on the butt of the Colt .38, a round in the spout, the safety off. He turned to Vivienne. 'Just stand aside a little. If there are bullets, hit the ground.'

He didn't knock at the door, merely turned the handle and pushed it open in one quick movement.

His eyes opened wide in horror and astonishment. Whatever he had expected, it wasn't this.

CHAPTER 50

Dolly had taken at least one bullet to the face, right between the eyes. There may have been a second shot, but it was impossible to tell with the blood still oozing. She was on the sofa, head thrown back, arms wide

Gus Baxter had taken one to the temple and one to the chest. His right hand held a stick attached to a wire which, in turn, was wrapped around the corpse in front of him – a body which Wilde immediately recognised as Randle, the desk man they had followed from The Grand.

Randle's eyes were bulging from their sockets. His claw-like fingers were at his own throat, even in death scraping at the piano wire.

All three of them were dead, there could be no doubt.

And the killer? No doubt about that either. Shadox Stone with a handgun, fitted with a silencer. But he was no longer there.

The question of *why* he had killed them was another matter that would have to be addressed later.

Wilde turned back and addressed the nearest heavy, who had come up close to him and was also peering into the scene of carnage. 'I know it will go against the grain,' Wilde said. 'But I really think you should call the police.'

'Fuck me,' the heavy said, his jaw dropping. 'How the fuck . . .'

Vivienne had moved towards the door. 'Oh my God,' she said.

Wilde went into the room and felt for pulses on the three bodies. They were all dead, killed very recently. No more than two or three minutes.

This crime scene had to be handed over to the police and MI5 with utmost urgency.

The sequence of events would take a great deal of working out. Two people shot, one strangled with wire. Not easy to follow the logistics. Why was Baxter shoeless?

Vivienne had started taking pictures of the scene. She was also taking pictures of the gambling hall, which was emptying rapidly with the likelihood that the police would soon be here in force.

Wilde's eyes strayed to the back door; that must be the way that Stone had made his exit. He stepped over the bodies of Baxter and Randle and opened the door. A gust of cool air blew in as he looked out into the darkness. The ground he trod on was paved, so there were no footprints. It was impossible to know which way Stone had gone. He strained to hear any noise which might give him a clue, but there was nothing save the normal sounds of the city.

'What do we do now, Tom?'

'First I call Freya Bentall, then we wait until the police arrive.'

He used the phone on Dolly's desk and felt a pang of sadness among the horror. The girl who started with nothing and tried to fly without wings. Yes, she had betrayed him, sold her soul to the Soviets in her hunger for riches, but the bitter gall of her fate was nonetheless unfair for all that.

Life had dealt her a bad hand, so she tried to fix the pack. But it never works. The house always wins.

Freya picked up at the second ring.

'It's Tom. You'd better come to The Green Bear on Walworth Road, and bring some back-up. Gus Baxter and Dolly Coster are dead and they were killed by Shadox Stone. But it looks a lot more complicated than that.'

As it turned out, it was now all much simpler. At least as far as Tom Wilde was concerned, for the evidence was clear that he was innocent and would no longer be a wanted man.

A couple of the legitimate workers at The Green Bear had remained behind, as had the heavy who called the police. All three of them confirmed that Wilde and Vivienne Chalke had walked in on the murder scene and that neither of them was responsible.

Vivienne, too, was able to give details of her conversation with Randle and his clear link to The Green Bear and Dolly Coster.

'The Yard accepts our version,' Freya said. 'You were set up for the killing of Rheinhaus. Randle was part of it. He must have either assisted or facilitated the depositing of Rheinhaus's body in the hotel room and probably helped get you up there in your drugged state.'

'And Gus Baxter's role?'

'Less clear, but I think we can state with certainty that he was not on our side. Whether he was working for the Kremlin or the gangsters will have to be sorted out in due course. As for Shadox Stone, I just don't know. But if I can find him, I'll throw the bloody book at him. For the moment, Tom, have a drink and get some sleep.'

Lydia joined him at The Savoy Hotel for the night. The room had been booked so it seemed a waste not to use it. He introduced her to Vivienne Chalke with some trepidation and was astonished that they hit it off instantly

A shared love of art and loathing of convention was enough to seal their friendship.

He had worried that Lydia would think there was something more than a mutual desire for justice between him and Vivienne, but he couldn't have been more wrong. Now that he came to think of it, of course, they would get on; there was a bit of the Bohemian about both of them.

Nor was Lydia very interested in hearing what they had been through together. They met in the bar late at night, ate sandwiches and drank nightcaps and spoke of Velázquez and Goya and Michelangelo and Picasso.

Wilde might have felt a little left out but in truth he was happy to sit and swirl his drink and listen to the two women discuss their shared enthusiasms.

Back in their room as they prepared for bed, Lydia said, 'I'm sure you think that whatever you've been up to has been incredibly tough, Tom Wilde.'

'Hang on, I haven't said anything.'

'But let me tell you something – it can't compare to the sheer physical endurance test and mental exhaustion of a medical degree. The food is awful, I never get more than six hours sleep, no one does.'

'I'm sorry to hear that.'

'So before you start complaining about being lured into Freya Bentall's web of secrets, think on this: do you have any idea how many illnesses there are? How many cancers? How many bones and veins there are in the human body? Each with its own name, often obscurely Latin. And that's just for starters. So don't go looking to me for sympathy.'

'I won't.'

'Anyway, I'll be back for Easter in a week or two. I'll talk to Janet Spring and see what she wants to do and whether she'll be able to manage with Johnny and her own baby when it arrives. We can't just kick her out, Tom.'

'Of course not.'

'The world is not kind to unmarried mothers, nor their children. You could help, too, of course. Your work hardly takes up every hour of the day, does it.'

'I suppose it doesn't, but I do have a book to write.'

'And I'm sure Doris will help with the children. She loves babies – I remember she was marvellous when Johnny was born. Everything will be fine. Summer will soon be upon us, we'll sort out some holidays . . .'

'Geoff Lancing has asked us down for a few days.'

'Well, there you are then. Life is already burgeoning. The flowers are blooming, there'll be more food on the table.'

'You are talking quite a lot, Lydia. We have a beautiful luxurious Savoy bed. Don't you think we should try it out?'

She was standing there, naked, beautiful. She put her hands on her hips and gave him one of her looks. 'Is that really your best line, Professor Wilde?'

He just laughed, delighted for a bit of normality after the long, bleak winter of blood and snow. Summer, that was something to look forward to: a time of fruit, of strawberries, raspberries . . . and perhaps even a peach or two.

In Moscow, Leonid Eitingon was received with great warmth by Stalin. It was generally agreed that his Special Task under the name Lazar Lukin had been a triumph.

'Comrade Beria tells me the threat to our asset is removed.'

'That is so, Comrade General Secretary.'

'I am led to believe that you also spread a little chaos and confusion. You are a good man. Lenin would be proud. When the warmer weather comes you will spend a few days with me at my dacha and tell me every detail and we shall laugh uproariously.'

'Thank you.'

'A little black work, too?'

'Yes, a little.' He had lost count of the corpses left in England, but in the great scheme of things, the figure was small enough.

'And their MI5, they still don't know who to trust?'

'They all suspect each other. There is great confusion in their ranks.'

Stalin slapped the table with his hand, scattering cigar ash over a wide area. 'But none of this will come back to Moscow?'

'Not directly, comrade, no. There will be suspicion, of course, but no proof.'

'All clean then? No more diplomatic complaints from our British allies? No more concerns for Ambassador Zarubin?'

Eitingon could hardly deny that there had been some communication with the embassy. Indeed, that the British Foreign Office had demanded his removal from the country. 'There will always be complaints, Comrade General Secretary.'

'But no proof?'

'No proof. My clean-up man has seen to everything.' His clean-up man. Shadox Stone. Removed from the game early on, saved for the endgame. All neat. As clean as – what was the word? – a whistle. Why a whistle? Why was that clean? These English with their curious idiom.

Baxter, however, *had* been compromised, the whore had been expensive. They had left a trail that could be followed. Bad tradecraft. Even as Eitingon was flying home to Moscow, Shadox Stone was clearing up.

Stalin cradled his dead pipe and lit it, blowing scented clouds into Eitingon's breathing space. 'But there is one more thing. Are you certain that no hint of suspicion fell upon Comrade Fuchs?'

How could he answer that honestly? Of course MI5 had Fuchs marked down as a Soviet agent. Rheinhaus had told them all he knew.

'All I can say, Comrade General Secretary, is that the British security service has no direct evidence against Fuchs and he has been neither arrested nor interrogated. He is still in his position of importance at their atomic base.'

'You couch your words carefully, Eitingon.'

'I could not swear on the Communist Manifesto that our asset is not watched by MI5.'

'So he has no value? Did you not think that it might have been time to bid him farewell?'

'He will be building the British atom bomb. He is right at the heart of the project, a man of great seniority. Head of the Theoretical Division at their atomic research establishment. His colleagues know they need him and will not hear a word said against him. And yet he is still one of us.'

'Then one day, we must reward him.'

CHAPTER 51

At the end of March, with the Lent term newly finished and the undergraduates departed, Wilde took a call from Freya Bentall. She said she had a request and he immediately stiffened, preparing himself mentally for a flat refusal.

'Would you perform a rather unpleasant duty for me – go and see the family of the MP Len Goodrick? They have been told you were the last person to see him alive and they would very much like to meet you and talk to you.'

'Who do they think I am – history professor or spy?'

'Both. And they believe you were a friend of their son.'

'So I'll have to lie?'

'I'm sure you'll find a way of phrasing things to everyone's satisfaction.'

'And this is his mother and father you want me to see?'

'Yes, his parents and sister, not the estranged wife.'

'All right. But nothing more.'

'Nothing more.'

He took the train to Nottingham and caught a taxi from the station to the Goodrick family home in West Bridgford, not far from Trent Bridge.

It was a modest but decent house. Wilde had already found out as much as he could about the family. Arthur Goodrick was retired but had worked as a bank clerk, rising during the war to the position of acting assistant manager. The mother, Dorothy, had spent her adult life as a housewife, bringing up the children and looking after the home. She had earned extra money as a seamstress, taking in clothes for alteration and mending.

They were known as a quiet family, immensely proud of their son's achievements in the world of Labour politics, but then devastated by the collapse of his marriage and, even worse, his resignation from the government and suicide.

'I never agreed with our Len's politics, you know,' his father said as they settled into the sitting room around a pot of tea and four cups. 'Always been a Liberal myself, but I respected his right to differ and he argued well.'

'I know he was well-respected in Parliament, by members on all sides of the House,' Wilde said.

'He was a good man. A very fine man. He is greatly missed by this family and we thank you, Professor Wilde, for coming to see us. We are led to believe you were the last to see him before . . . before . . .'

Arthur Goodrick had seemed so taut until that moment, then he could not continue. He shook his head, unable to speak. His wife, sitting at his side on the sofa, put her arm around him and they both dissolved into tears, their ageing bodies racked with grief.

Their daughter, Bella Thwaite, was in one of two armchairs, the other occupied by Wilde. He understood that she was a married woman with two children, but she had come here to the family home alone. She smiled at him. 'We believe you were one of his many friends, professor.'

He nodded. 'I would like to have known him better, of course. I just wish I had had some inkling of what he would do – perhaps I might have prevented it. But he was distraught at the collapse of his career in government.'

'You see, that's the thing, professor. We don't really understand what happened. The letter from Mr Attlee spoke highly of Len but gave no background to the rift that came between them. Was it a political disagreement or something of a more personal nature? Did they fall out?'

'Perhaps a bit of both. No one is totally sure because his resignation came out of the blue. But these things do happen all the time in government. It is in the nature of politics, I'm afraid. You're up one minute, down the next. And no two people will ever agree on everything. Something about the direction of the Party or the government must have got to him. But the distress it caused him was clearly of a different order. None of those who knew him would have anticipated what happened.'

'He was always a sensitive man, perhaps too sensitive for the rough-and-tumble of politics.'

'You may be right, Mrs Thwaite.'

'You can see what it has done to Mum and Dad. If only we could understand a bit more, perhaps we could find some peace.'

Wilde dearly wished that he could offer some words of comfort, but there were none.

'We would like to show you something,' Goodrick's sister continued. She stood up and went to the sideboard and came back with an exercise book. 'Mum found this in his bedroom, in the bedside table drawer. He must have left it here when he was last up here, a week before he died. He had made a special effort to come up through the worst of the snow. It was the last time we saw him and he clearly wasn't himself.'

She handed the book to Wilde. It was typical of a classroom exercise book. There were no words on the front or back. 'Can I look inside?'

'Of course. It's in some sort of code. We can't make head nor tail of it.'

Wilde opened the book, then flicked through the pages. There were numbers and letters, none of which added up to a complete word. So, yes, it was written in cipher and was about a quarter full, the rest of the pages left blank.

'Had he written in code before? Did he keep a diary?'

'I think he did as a child, but everyone does, don't they?'

'And do you have them?'

'Mum? Do you have any of Len's old diaries?'

She looked up, wiping her tears with a large handkerchief. 'No, dear, no, I've never seen anything like that.'

'Would you like me to take this away to be deciphered?' Wilde asked.

'Yes,' Arthur Goodrick said, having recovered some of his composure. 'That's exactly what we were hoping for.'

'We were told you had some connection to the security services, so we thought you must know how to do it,' Bella said. 'Could you try for us?'

'I'll do my best. Just one word of warning, though. It's possible the reason he used a code was to protect state secrets. I'm sure you know that in the Ministry of Supply, he was involved in the work currently underway at the Harwell Atomic Establishment. The establishment itself isn't secret, but what goes on inside the wire is highly classified.'

'You mean you might not be able to tell us what the book says?'

'I'm afraid I mean exactly that. But of course it's also possible that it's more personal and might explain a few things to you. Would you like me to try?'

The three family members looked at each other and then they all nodded. 'That would be most kind of you, Professor Wilde.'

A week later, just before Easter, with the days becoming longer and warmer, he accepted a lunch invitation from Freya. The train journey from Cambridge was a great deal faster and more reliable than it had been in the midst of the harshest winter ever known – seven weeks in which the temperature never rose above freezing, where it snowed somewhere in Britain every day, where the sun wasn't seen and birds froze to death in the trees.

'I wanted to thank you, Tom. It's only fair to deem your work for me an extraordinary success.'

'Basil Rheinhaus was murdered. I don't see that as a success.'

'My brief to you was to discover the mole in our midst, that was all. As it turned out, you discovered two – Baxter and Stone. Three if you include the ghastly Willie Tristram. Though he wasn't in MI5, he had access to our work through his relationship with Cecil Eagles and he had contacts at the highest level of the establishment in the War Office. It seems our garden was a veritable maze of mole hills and tunnels and you have cleared it up.'

'That's a bit of a strangulated metaphor, Freya.'

'Perhaps, but you get the point. The infiltration of our security services is greater than we could ever have imagined. It has left us all looking over our shoulders, watching our backs.'

He understood. And yet he couldn't feel good about the operation given that Klaus Fuchs remained in place at Harwell and so many had suffered, including poor Len Goodrick, the unfortunate man from the Ministry of Supply, a man who would rather die than live with shame. And the others who were slaughtered simply because they were in the wrong place at the wrong time; an old farmer, living his peaceful life alone with his dog until death came calling; two veterans of the war murdered at an old army base near Harwell.

And then there was the trauma suffered by Vivienne Chalke's household in Kensington, and all those at Blackwater Grange in Norfolk. Innocents caught up in a filthy war of murder and secrets. Even his own son, God damn it. Johnny did not seem to be suffering any lasting effects of his abduction by Lukin, no nightmares – but who was to know what the long-term effects might be?

He sipped his wine. They were at Simpson's-in-the-Strand. The place was packed and the whole world seemed to be out making the most of the fresh, warm air.

'Any word from your codebreakers?'

She nodded. 'Oh yes, easy-peasy cracking Len Goodrick's rather obvious code.'

'And?'

'It confirms everything we now know about Gus Baxter, with quite a lot more added on for good measure. It is a cry from the depths of poor Goodrick's soul, a howl of despair like your namesake's *De Profundis*. The emotional pain he was under was terrible, even before the threat to expose him. It seems he had been seduced by Gus Baxter over a year ago and he had been held in his power ever since. He was at the heart of government and Baxter was demanding more and more from him. Then the Russian turned up with photographs and it was all too much. His marriage had been destroyed and, most of all, he was terrified that his family would discover his true nature.'

'I rather suspected as much. What do I tell them?'

'I think you probably know, Tom.'

Of course he did. He had already laid the groundwork. The code had been broken and it did, indeed, contain state secrets, so the book could not be returned and nor could they be allowed to see the full transcript. But there were some words at the end which might bring the family some comfort. Something like his conflicted feelings about working with atomic power in the wake of Hiroshima and Nagasaki and perhaps a little about his distress at the end of his marriage. And then, at last, his reassurance that he loved his family with all his heart and his certainty that he was going to a better place.

Not exactly those words, perhaps, but something of that order. Typed up so that it looked official and genuine.

'I'll work on it, Freya.'

'Thank you, Tom. You have been an absolute marvel. Lydia's a lucky girl.'

'She doesn't always think so. Anyway, how are your living arrangements these days? Your flat? The house in Norfolk?'

'They're getting there. Probably both needed a bit of renovation and refurbishment, truth be told. Fortunately I have the money and there are plenty of demobbed servicemen who need work. By the way, Emily sends you her love.'

'She's rather special, your niece.'

'Indeed she is.'

Wilde noted the catch in her throat. For a moment he wondered whether she might shed a tear. The tough-as-nails MI5 officer had a softness at her core when it came to Emily.

A few tables away, a group of three men were enjoying lunch and Wilde had a strange feeling that their eyes kept drifting towards him and Freya.

'You know, Tom, I meant it when I said Lydia was lucky to have you. There have been times in my life when I wished I had a husband. Not often, but now and then. I get scared too, you know.'

'Only psychopaths don't feel fear.'

'I hate it when they call me Mother.'

'I noticed and I sympathise.'

She sighed with a wan, faraway smile. 'There *was* a man once. People see a dried-up spinster when they see me, but there was a man I thought I loved.' She shook her head. 'That's enough. Nostalgia's pretty awful, but what-might-have-beens are beyond the pale.'

He smiled too. He had wondered, of course, but to have asked would have been horribly ill-mannered. Hurriedly he changed the subject. 'What of Shadox Stone?'

'Ah, that's the remarkable news. He came into Leconfield House on Monday, as though he had never been away. Cool as you like.'

'Are you serious?'

'Full of apologies. Said he had had a nervous breakdown. The effects of the war. He told me he had been away in the West Country, alone in a little cottage, drinking and weeping. Dreadfully sorry, Miss Bentall, can you ever forgive me?'

'I take it he's now in Wandsworth Prison?'

'No, I said I was desperately sad to hear he'd had such a rotten time and that he had been sorely missed.'

'But he killed Baxter and Dolly in cold blood.'

'Indeed he did. And the only evidence we have is your testimony that you saw him entering The Green Bear.'

'What did he say to that?'

'Nothing, because I didn't put it to him and nor will I. We have no evidence from anyone else at the Bear, not a single witness who saw or heard anything. A court case would let loose far too many worms from the can and he'd be acquitted anyway. Worst of all, it would tell the Americans how badly we've been compromised, and we can't allow that; they already think we're bloody amateurs. The case of Alan Nunn May's spying has done us untold harm.'

'So what now?'

'I'm keeping Shadox Stone in place – and he will unwittingly become one of my greatest assets. We can feed disinformation to Moscow through him. I have looked again at his background and his recruitment into the service and it is clear that from his schooldays he was always a committed revolutionary. He originally told us his father was a Lancashire mill worker who was killed in the First World War. Not quite true, as I now know. In fact his father went to Moscow in 1918 to fight alongside Lenin and was killed in 1920 in the Soviet civil war. In retrospect, Stone's uncompromising dedication to the cause is self-evident and should never have been missed.'

'How *was* it missed?'

'Our appalling recruitment process. Stone went to Cambridge so that was enough. Must be one of us, old boy. You know the sort of thing. Same with Philip Eaton at SIS. In fact I believe Six is a great deal worse than us. Anyway, I now know all I need to know about Shadox Stone. He will lead me to other traitors and to other enemies. Never again will we assume that the intelligence services are clean. Inadvertently, he has done us a favour – he has opened our eyes.'

A roar of laughter came from the table with the three men. Once again it seemed they were looking in his direction. Freya caught his gaze.

'Office workers out for a jolly, I suppose,' Wilde said. 'Probably lawyers or journalists in this neck of the woods.'

'Actually, Tom, those three are in the same business as you and me.'

'Really? Do you know them?'

'The one with the soft face is Kim Philby. I used to work with him for a while before I was moved to Five. Charming fellow – on the surface. Good war apparently, but I could never quite make him out. The one with the horse face is Major Blunt, who was in Five until the end of the war. Anthony Blunt, now Surveyor of the King's Pictures and a very big name in the art world.'

'And the other one?'

'Guy Burgess. Foreign Office but with links to Six, never washes and smells like a polecat. Three old friends from college, I suppose, meeting up to talk over old days lazing by the Cam with a picnic.'

'Cambridge men then?'

'Indeed. All three of them Trinity actually.'

Wilde nodded, surprised that he had never seen nor heard of them before. 'Trinity, eh? Just like Philip Eaton.'

'What are you suggesting, Tom?'

'Oh nothing. Nothing at all.'

POSTSCRIPT

It is historical fact that Klaus Fuchs came under the suspicious eye of MI5 in 1946, but he was not arrested until 24th January, 1950, when a confession was extracted from him by MI5 operative and former Special Branch officer Jim Skardon in Room 055 at the War Office in Whitehall.

In five closely-written pages, Fuchs admitted handing secrets to Soviet agents, both in America and Britain. From 1941 onwards, he had given them all the secrets of the atomic bomb and its construction.

He did not seem to realise that in confessing he was liable to prosecution. His only regret seemed to be that he was worried that his friends at Harwell might suffer in some way because of his actions.

Fuchs's betrayal had, in fact, enabled the Soviet Union to build and detonate an atomic bomb two years earlier than might otherwise have been expected – in August 1949. This was five months before his arrest.

At his trial, the point was made that when Fuchs was at Los Alamos during the war, he was not handing secrets to an enemy – but to an ally. For the Soviet Union at that time was on the same side as the British and the Americans.

Lord Chief Justice Goddard was not impressed and sentenced him to the maximum of fourteen years in jail for breaking the Official Secrets Act. Had he been charged with treason, he could have faced the death penalty.

His absence from Harwell was a huge loss for the British atomic programme because at the time of his arrest he was one of the top four physicists working in the country.

He was released from prison early, in June 1959. He might have liked to have stayed in Britain, but the British nationality that he had been granted when he sought asylum was removed and he had no option but to go to East Germany.

As an enthusiastic communist he was treated well and he was given a car, a house and an important job as director of the Atomic Research Institute in Dresden.

But having confessed to the British, he was never fully trusted by the Russians and was excluded from the main Soviet atomic programme. Nor did they admit ever having used him as a spy, saying that his trial was merely anti-Soviet propaganda.

He was given no awards or medals. And despite being one of the most brilliant physicists of all time, he wasn't even granted membership of the Soviet Academy of Sciences.

All these years later, Klaus Fuchs is remembered for being perhaps the most important spy who ever lived. Yet in a parallel universe he might have been one of the greatest scientists of all time. The man who built the American, British and Russian atomic bombs.

He never considered himself a traitor. He simply believed that the world would be a safer place if both sides – East and West – had the bomb so that it would, hopefully, never be used again.

* If you want to know more about the events of summer 1939 involving the Cavendish laboratory, Geoff Lancing and his sister Clarissa, you'll find them in *Nucleus*, the second book in the Tom Wilde series.

ACKNOWLEDGEMENTS

My heartfelt thanks to my fine friend Geoff Compton for the wonderful conversations we enjoyed discussing the old-time criminal gangs who ruled the London underworld back in the middle of the 20th century. He encountered many villains in his time as a young journalist on an East End news agency and garnered a wealth of knowledge of their characters and methods. As always, I am delighted to acknowledge the contributions of my brother Brian, my agent Teresa Chris, my editor Ben Willis and all the staff at Bonnier Zaffre. But most of all, I give thanks to my wife Naomi for her invaluable help and support.

If you enjoyed *A Cold Wind From Moscow*,
why not join the
RORY CLEMENTS READERS' CLUB

When you sign up you'll receive a free copy of
an exclusive short story, plus news about upcoming books,
sneak previews, and exclusive behind-the-scenes material.
To join, simply visit:
bit.ly/RoryClementsClub
Keep reading for a letter from the author . . .

Hello!

In these days of climate change and rising temperatures it's difficult to imagine the winter of 1947 when Great Britain suffered under the most bitter weather anyone could recall.

The country was already in dire straits from the lingering effects of the war. Shortages of food and fuel were commonplace. Bread was rationed for the first time (something that had never happened even during the Blitz) and by the winter everything was in short supply. As I mention in this book, even whisky production was halted so that the grain on which it was based could be used for food.

For seven long weeks, roads vanished under snow, coal could not be transported from the pits to the power stations and there were power cuts every day. Hunger was the norm and morale—so upbeat two years earlier with the end of the fighting—was at rock bottom.

For the Labour Government, the timing couldn't have been worse. The Minister of Fuel and Power, Emmanuel 'Manny' Shinwell, bore the brunt of people's anger. He had not made things easy for himself by declaring 'There will be no fuel crisis.' His reward? Death threats and the sack.

Great Britain was impoverished and vulnerable, the euphoria of victory long gone.

And then there would be another concern: a threat from the East.

The warm feelings that many Westerners had for their erstwhile allies in the Soviet Union would soon disappear when it became clear that Stalin was no friend of the British or the Americans and that his spy network had infiltrated our intelligence services and, more alarmingly, our nuclear programme.

With the United Kingdom at its lowest ebb, there would be no better time for Stalin to strike - and this is the setting of *A Cold Wind From Moscow*.

And there is, I think, a moral here. Call me a deluded optimist, but if a country can survive the Blitz of 1940 and the Winter of 1947 – and go on to thrive – then however bad things seem, there must always be hope of better times.

The sun *will* shine again.

If you would like to hear more about my books, you can visit my website www.roryclements.co.uk where you can join the Rory Clements Readers' Club (www.bit.ly/RoryClementsClub). It only takes a few moments to sign up, there are no catches or costs.

Bonnier Zaffre will keep your data private and confidential and it will never be passed on to a third party. We won't spam you with loads of emails, just get in touch now and again with news about my books, and you can unsubscribe any time you want.

And if you would like to get involved in a wider conversation about my books, please do review *A Cold Wind From Moscow* on Amazon, on Goodreads, on any other e-store, on your own blog and social media accounts, or talk about it with friends, family or reader groups. Sharing your thoughts helps other readers, and I always enjoy hearing about what people experience from my writing.

Thank you again for reading *A Cold Wind From Moscow*.

With best wishes,

Rory Clements